The Nature

of

Water and Air

a novel

REGINA MCBRIDE

SCRIBNER PAPERBACK FICTION

Published by Simon & Schuster

New York   London   Toronto   Sydney   Singapore

SCRIBNER PAPERBACK FICTION
Simon & Schuster, Inc.
Rockefeller Center
1230 Avenue of the Americas
New York, NY 10020

SCRIBNER PAPERBACK FICTION and design are trademarks of
Macmillan Library Reference USA, Inc., used under license by
Simon & Schuster, the publisher of this work.

Designed by Kyoko Watanabe

Manufactured in the United States of America

1 3 5 7 9 10 8 6 4 2

Library of Congress Cataloging-in-Publication Data
McBride, Regina, 1956–
The nature of water and air : a novel / Regina McBride.
p. cm.
1. Mothers and daughters—Fiction.
2. Women—Ireland—Fiction. 3. Ireland—Fiction. I. Title.
PS3563.C333628 N38 2001
813'.54—dc21   00-061888

ISBN 0-7432-0323-2

For my husband, Neil, whose spirit of loving generosity is a constant wonder in my life,

*and for my little daughter, Miranda.
My peach. My angel.*

Acknowledgments

Gratitude and love to my editor, Doris Cooper, and to my agent, Regula Noetzli. Love and thanks to my best friend, Sarah Fleming, for encouragement, feedback, and ever-enduring friendship.

I am indebted also to Naomi Trubowitz for her intuitive insights, and to Tom Quinn for his generosity, Michael Roberts for musical advice, Nancy Graham for early enthusiastic feedback, Ciaran O'Reilly for generosity and friendship, and to Jason Price for copies!

Deepest, deepest love and thanks to my husband and daughter for incredible patience and support.

Much gratitude to the National Endowment for the Arts.

Wilt Thou forgive that sin where I begun,
Which is my sin, though it were done before?
Wilt Thou forgive that sin through which I run,
And do run still, though still I do deplore?
When Thou hast done, Thou hast not done,
For I have more.

—John Donne

The Nature

of

Water and Air

PART I

Agatha

WICKLOW, IRELAND
1960–79

Wait
for the dawn to make us clear to one another.

—*Eavan Boland*

Is fada cuimhne sean leanbh
(An old child has a long memory).

—*Irish Proverb*

My MOTHER WAS NEVER EASY IN THE WORLD OF HOUSES. SHE was a tinker, a traveler girl who had married a wealthy man. Her name was Agatha Sheehy. I don't know her maiden name. There are silences all around my mother's story.

People stared at her when we walked on the old road to Dublin or in the nearby fields on our way into town. She was an anachronism, like a vagabond who'd walked off with a wealthy woman's traveling case.

A pretty, red-faced girl with long white-blond hair, she had about her a wild, unrefined grace, and a penchant for sequins and beads and things that glimmered. In the bright of morning, on her way into town to shop for eggs and rashers, she navigated the often sopping fields in opulence, dragging the hems of long silk dresses, raking her black boots in mud. Even the old women wore their practical woolen skirts near the knee.

She watched the eyes of the townspeople, choosing to read their silent stares as approbation or envy; but some days when her mood was more suspicious, a suppressed smile could send her scudding back across the field and into the house in a breathy tirade about the ugliness of the little ramshackle beach town of Bray, calling the Wicklow hills "lumps," insulting the land as if it were inseparable from the people. She laughed at the Irish Sea, which we could see from the parlor window, and said that even at their most tumultuous, the waves were "demure" in comparison with the waves of the great Atlantic in the rocky west of Ireland, beating and spuming at the Galway crags.

We lived in an old estate house on Mercymount Strand, isolated between fields gone out of cultivation. Mrs. O'Dare, the woman who lived with us and did the cooking and cleaning, called it a "decrepit castle." It had no central heating, just the "fires," as the old woman called them: plug-in heaters too puny to heat the vast, high-ceilinged rooms.

Most of the house we left empty and unlived in, while my mother, twin sister, and I slept all together in the parlor and Mrs. O'Dare in a smaller, connecting room. In a pillowcase under her bed, my mother kept all the things my father had given her during their courtship, objects I took out secretly sometimes to wonder over. A glass sea horse with pearls for eyes. A porcelain Dutch girl holding a tulip. A pair of linen gloves with a mysterious blue stain on one finger.

In the one picture we had of my father, he was standing near a tree, squinting his eyes, his hair ruffled by the wind. The air around him was blasted with daylight so his face looked milky and blurred and I stared hard at him, struggling to read his expression.

Though I had never known him, I felt as if I knew more about him than I knew about my mother. With him I associated the area known as Dunshee in the west, straight across on the other side of Ireland; and I could imagine the great mansion in which he'd grown up, and where he'd brought my mother to live.

But my mother seemed to have come from nowhere.

The one story I knew about my mother's life before I was born was how she and my father had met in the west. He had been thirty years old and suffering from heart disease. My mother had been fifteen.

He'd first seen her, standing on Ailwee Head, facing the noisy Atlantic. He'd just come through a week confined to his bed having experienced serious palpitations. She had not heard the engine of the car, deafened as she was by the booming surf on the rocks below. Frank Sheehy had the driver stop. He got out and stood awhile watching her push the hair from her eyes in the wind, her rough skirt stirring wildly at her shins.

He'd later tell his unmarried sisters with whom he lived that when he saw her he felt his heart steady in his chest, and a surge of strength come into his body. Overcome by a desire to take care of her, the world seemed a different place. The sun lit the backs of the waves and in the depths of him something vital stirred. He had a dream that same night that she came to live in his house, and he took this as a sign from God that he should find her. Every day after that he went along the beaches and headlands looking for her but a year passed before he saw her, to his surprise, from an upstairs window, driving three cows up a rocky road on the outskirts of his property.

Careful not to frighten my mother off, my father had his sister Kitty overtake her on the road and invite her to tea. Surprised and a little suspicious, she agreed, and Kitty Sheehy followed her as she returned the cows to the farmer who'd hired her to drive them upfield.

When she'd first come into the house her skin was windburned and her feet hard and black, callous. "More like hooves than feet," Kitty Sheehy had whispered to her sister, Lily.

Before tea Kitty directed my mother to the lavatory to wash her hands. When she did not come back to the dining room, Kitty found her at the other side of the house having lost her way through the corridors.

My father was fascinated. At tea he stared at her unabashedly with a cocked half-smile on his face. If she expressed interest in any little object on the table he gave it to her. A porcelain salt shaker shaped like a windmill. A cluster of crystal grapes. A pink and gilt cup with a rose painted in the bowl of it. He offered her everything she touched, no matter that the things belonged to his sisters. Kitty and Lily held their breath tolerantly, seeing how she animated him, but behind the kitchen door they moaned about the smell of her, how her hair must be crawling with bugs.

Much to their distress my father insisted she stay in one of the guest rooms. They agreed so long as she let one of the servants bathe her and give her something clean to wear. My mother'd been horrified about the bath, particularly when the servant washed and pumiced her feet. And then she expressed uneasiness with staying on one of the upper floors so Mrs. O'Dare, who'd been working for the Sheehys at the time, offered her own room that was behind the kitchen.

Right away my mother took to Mrs. O'Dare. "I was the only one among them that treated her kindly. None thought they should be serving her."

She hated using the toilet in the lavatory and crept from her room at night to do her water in the cold grass. The servants whispered about her odd ways. A rumor spread among them that she had been living in one of the caves in the sea cliff. A fisherman had reported seeing a dim fire flickering among the rocks each night until the tinker girl met my father.

My mother liked Frank Sheehy right away, gazing at him with the same gentle inquisitiveness with which he gazed at her. She was touched by his attention, and though it had never been revealed to her that he was responsible for her invitation to the house, she knew, and her warmth to him increased his affection for her.

Soon enough she realized the advantage he afforded her; that it was his word that was most important in a house full of women and servants. She sidled up to that and as she grew more comfortable, sneered at the reluctant servants and pushed her weight with them. Once, she deliberately spilled a bowl of oatmeal and demanded that a certain haughty kitchen servant clean it up.

Frank Sheehy asked questions. Where was her mother, her people? Why was a fifteen-year-old girl on her own so? She met his inquisitiveness with dismay and silence, and he did not persist, afraid of driving her away. She was not interested in talking much, except to ask about little glimmering objects. They went for walks together in the house the way most couples go for walks outside. They toured the house, him speaking with a gentle formality, pointing out paintings, statues. Decorative novelties. Her eyes shined. She touched his arm.

"The man's besotted with the creature," the servants whispered.

"Whatever's wrong with his heart has made its way into his brain."

One particularly stormy night she urinated in the water pitcher in her room rather than face the rain or the toilet. The servants complained to my aunts and my aunts approached Frank, wanting to know when she was going to leave.

Mrs. O'Dare remembered an argument behind closed doors. She

saw my father storm from the room breathing fast. He stopped as he ascended the stairs and shouted to his sisters, "She's keeping me alive." In the middle of the night he had a mild heart attack. The week he was in hospital my mother kept near Mrs. O'Dare. My aunts went out of their way to be kind to my mother, promising Frank that she'd be there, well treated and comfortable, when he returned.

My father married my mother in a service in the conservatory in Drumcoyne House. She'd been put through a trial by the priest and had proven she was a Catholic to his satisfaction by reciting the Angelus, the Act of Contrition, and the Hail Mary. He'd asked her, "Who is God the Father?" and she'd answered, "The maker of Heaven and earth."

Rumor ámong the servants was that Frank Sheehy had schooled her, but others cited the fervent Catholicism of many of the tinkers who loitered in the backs of churches on Sundays, earnest for the word of God.

My father died the following spring, almost a year after they'd married, and a few weeks before my mother discovered she was pregnant.

After his death, Drumcoyne House was a lonely place to my mother. She walked on the beach for hours. A few nights she stayed outside on the windy shore, sallying into the house after dawn, trailing damp sand and weather after her. The brocade and velvet skirts that had been made for her were torn or ruined from walking in the salty tides.

And she took things. Cups and saucers. Figurines. She took a small, very expensive bottle of perfume and a pair of sapphire earrings that belonged to Kitty Sheehy, the older, more nervous of Frank's sisters.

"Your mother didn't like Kitty Sheehy," Mrs. O'Dare once told me. "She knew the woman had little patience for her."

Kitty Sheehy said that she couldn't take it, that her nerves were too frayed by Agatha's presence. What would they do with the creature, pregnant as she was with their brother's child?

Kitty floated the idea about sending Agatha east across Ireland to live at the family's empty house on Mercymount Strand. Lily said they should wait until the birth but Kitty insisted that would be worse; that she ought to start a new life elsewhere; that they could provide her with everything, but elsewhere.

And so my aunts shipped my mother across Ireland, discharging the old woman to take care of her in the deserted house.

2

V AST AND COLD, MOST OF THE ROOMS IN THE HOUSE WERE empty. The walls were pocked and riddled blue with broken paint, wallpapered areas stained and swollen. In one room, cornices ran along the ceilings replete with stuccowork herons and angels. A piano, draped haphazardly with sheets, sat in a far corner. Before it, a dining table chair with a collapsed seat.

When we were barely three years old, our mother brought us to the threshold of the hallway that led into the uninhabited area of our house. Squatting down between us she whispered fervently, "You children stay out of those terrible rooms!"

The walls issued a damp, forlorn odor.

"What's wrong with the rooms?" my sister asked her.

"They're sad rooms," she said, staring into the gloom with the same fear and curiosity that filled us.

When we were four years old, in an attempt to dispell our uneasiness, Mrs. O'Dare took my sister and me up that hall, the two of us squeezing the hem of her flannel skirt in our hands.

"They're just empty rooms, for cripe's sake!" the old woman insisted.

One night during a rain we heard a crash from somewhere down the hallway and Mrs. O'Dare went to investigate. Darkness swallowed the light from her battered torch. We could hear the echoes of her footsteps and a snapping like twigs underfoot.

She came out complaining, saying that it was ridiculous that the rooms were left in such a condition. An old gas lamp had fallen from its fixture on a waterlogged wall.

Mrs. O'Dare was always on my mother about getting men in to wire and paint. It was a sore point between them, as was the fact that my mother had "lost" the only keys to the door on the second-floor landing that led to the upper house. Once Mrs. O'Dare had snuck in a locksmith who discovered that not only had nails been driven from the door into the walls, but something heavy also blocked it from behind. It was not his area of work to dismantle the door so he left.

Mrs. O'Dare said she was tired of the madness and threatened to telephone our aunts in the west to complain about the terrible conditions and ask them to arrange for repairs.

My mother's argument never changed: she could only manage to live there as it was; in just the area needed and the rest shut off. It was just too big a house for her.

But Mrs. O'Dare came back, saying that it was perfectly fine for my mother to live only out of the kitchen and the parlor, but that the rest of the house should be cleaned and wired for electricity. It wasn't safe otherwise. She had two daughters who should not be raised like animals.

"The rooms are full of echoes," my mother pleaded.

"Echoes can be driven out with fresh air and good rugs and curtains."

"No, Missus! You can't do that," my mother cried. "You have to leave the dead a place to themselves."

"What, love?" the old woman asked, looking inscrutable into her face.

"The dead, Missus," my mother said softly.

"Agatha, stop! The dead are in your mind and not in those rooms."

"If you open and light the rooms you'll drive them into the rest of the house and we'll have no peace from them. You'll drive me out into the fields to sleep!"

Only in the kitchen with its low, off-kilter ceiling did my mother feel truly comfortable. It was a misplaced, aboriginal room that contained a hearth, a turf fire burning in the grate. She'd told the old woman that she did not trust the little plug-in ranges, the steady orange light glowing through the grills. She did not trust a fire that did not tremble as it burned.

Before my sister and I were born, our mother had Mrs. O'Dare move a bed in so that she could be near the hearth. The old woman called it the "buried bedroom," dark as it was with only one small window high up on the east wall, but level with the earth at the back of the house.

My sister and I were born in the buried bedroom within half an hour of each other on February first, the feast of Saint Brigid, the night that ends the darkness of the Irish year. "Like peas in a pod, the two of you," Mrs. O'Dare said with emotion, remembering the night, points of sweat appearing on her great red brow. "Everything the same down to the veins in your tiny temples! And isn't your sister still your thinner, sadder replica?"

My mother had refused to go to hospital when she started her labor and Mrs. O'Dare had been unable to find a doctor or a midwife so she'd sent for her sister, a Kildare nun who had, during her novitiate many years before, worked as a nurse's assistant.

I was born first, drawing in a great gust of air and clamoring loudly. The moment the blood had been wiped from my eyes Mrs. O'Dare was sure to God that I was waiting for my sister to follow.

Mare was born with no instinct to breathe, and only after gentle tormenting from the nun did she open her eyes and attempt to pull at the air.

"Like a tiny wheezing banshee, the sound of her," Mrs. O'Dare said, pressing a hand to her bosom. "Never had I heard so godforsaken a sound as that wee creature trying to breathe."

Even when I was alone running in the field fronting the sea, it was as if my sister were breathing into my ear. The misbegotten noise was recorded in my own cells. "And you, dear Clodagh," Mrs. O'Dare had said to me time and again, smoothing my hair, "you're so hearty. In that way the two of you are as different as night and day."

But her words were of little comfort to me. I felt faintly ashamed of my heartiness and thought of Mare's frailty as a kind of saintliness.

Mare had been alive nearly an hour when, after a sudden riotous fit of breathing, she exhaled and went quiet. Sister Veronica prodded and pressed at her until she drew again uneasily at the air.

And each time Mare seemed to stop breathing altogether my mother wept aloud, demented with the panic. Once she cried out: "She's not ready for the world yet, Missus. Put her back in me, for the love of God!"

Sister Veronica, the only one managing to keep her head, pressed an ear to my sister's chest and said to my mother, "She is breathing, but ever so quietly. Her lungs may be confused, dear, but her heart is as sound as a bell! Just listen to it when you're afraid she's disappearing."

It was on that first night of our lives that, with all the weeping and invoking of the Holy Mother, my sister was named Mary. In the days that followed, the name Margaret was added to it. "Whatever might strengthen the petition to God to keep the wee creature alive," Mrs. O'Dare had said. "Mary Margaret. The Holy Mother and a great Virgin martyr standing together."

When we first began to speak, I could not manage the four syllables of my sister's name so I called her "Mare." For me it would always be her name.

"A mare is a horse," my mother would complain.

But that was a delight for Mare, constrained as she always would be from physical exertion, and she'd imagine herself freely galloping the fields.

Air would always confound and imprison Mare. It struggled to separate her from me. And the fear was ever present in our house that one day air would be all she'd be composed of, eluding and containing her.

For the first five years of my life my mother woke repeatedly every night to check on my sister. I must have tuned myself early on to the rhythms of her fitful sleeping because I remember lying anxiously in wait for her, feeling her stir and seeing her shadow loom. Until I was two we were still in the buried bedroom, the dying turf light flickering on her face as she peered at my sister. And then she'd bow over me so I could feel the sweep of her hair on my skin, and hear the gentle bumping of her heart as she pressed an ear to Mare's chest.

3

THE RAIN WAS INCESSANT EARLY IN OUR SIXTH SPRING. EVEN when it broke for an afternoon, the air was dismal and misty and the sun shown only faintly on the horizon like lamplight through curtains.

We were five, trapped inside too much of the time, the grounds of our crumbling house gone to muck and saturation, the limestone walkways lichened. My mother stood at the parlor window, arms crossed at her chest. The sea and sky were gray and diffused, inseparable. Through the screen of the open window we could hear the nervousness of the water and smell the iodine-rich kelp stranded on the shore.

"I've seen this weather before," my mother said to Mrs. O'Dare. "A spring that refuses to flower."

"Spring will come in its own time, Agatha," Mrs. O'Dare said.

"It feels like it never will, Missus. It'll be dark again this day by four." She looked uneasily at Mare, who dozed in the soft little chair my mother had fashioned for her out of bed pillows and bits of tired silk from old slips and blouses.

For days Mare'd been lethargic and our mother blamed it on the dismal weather. At night she'd loom over Mare, looking at her as if the turning of the world depended upon her. Some nights she'd carry her, sleeping, into the kitchen where she'd light a turf fire in the hearth, then sit before it rocking my sister in her arms, the smell of damp, burning earth wafting through the darkness of the house.

"Come sit down, Agatha," Mrs. O'Dare said.

Mare stirred, drawing a noisy, labored breath, and my mother clenched as if it caused her physical pain.

"She's off again in one of her dreams, poor Mary Margaret," Mrs. O'Dare said softly.

My mother knelt before my sister's chair, smoothing her hair. Through her sleep Mare grew earnest about the eyes, as if she were dreaming that like the spring, she was about to disappoint our mother.

"The rainy weather can't hurt her, love," Mrs. O'Dare said, leaning forward in her chair. "There's nothing at all about fresh rain that's bad for weak lungs."

"But if she gets too cold in all the dampness . . ."

"She'd be on fire in an icestorm with all the cardigans and shawls you keep the poor creature wrapped in!"

My mother shot her a pained look. "You don't understand how the dismal light is driving her to the end of herself. Bloody sun, holding out on her so."

"Come and sit down now and have a smoke, love," the old woman said soothingly, and my mother obeyed. Mrs. O'Dare lit a cigarette and blew out the match. A little black ghost from the flame escaped, wriggling upward on the air.

She passed the cigarette to my mother, wincing as she straightened her legs. "I'm crucified with the arthritis," she said, leaning back in the chair. She was not a large woman, but soft and lumpy like pillows. What would she fix for tea? she wanted to know. There was a bit of bacon left. Would she boil that with cabbage and potatoes? She didn't want to be driving out to the shops in this dismal weather to fetch anything like chops. She watched my mother's eyes, which were set on the bleak sky outside. Graceful nets of smoke climbed the air.

I went to my sleeping sister, lacing my fingers through hers. I knew Mare could feel me through her sleep. I could feel her softness coming back at me.

Her forehead was round and hotter than the rest of her face, her eyelashes gold at the roots and feathery brown at the ends. She slept with her mouth open, her head leaning to the side, her body faintly humming. Her eyes opened ever so slightly as I touched her, a little damp light glistening at me from a distance.

"Leave her be, Clodagh!" my mother said.

I stiffened, but with soft defiance continued to stroke my sister.

"She's hurting nothing, Agatha," Mrs. O'Dare protested.

My mother was quiet for a little while but I could feel her watching me.

"Leave her be, Clodagh! Give the poor creature a bit of privacy!" she cried out with a fierceness in her voice, as if I were the source of Mare's suffering.

"Agatha . . ." the old woman began in my defense.

"Stay out of it, Mrs. O'Dare!" my mother cried. "Stay out of what's between my daughters and myself!"

When we woke the next morning, rivulets of rainwater dripped down the walls of the vestibule, forming puddles in the uneven dips in the floor. One of the walls was soft to the touch and issued an ancient smell. As my mother and I huddled in the parlor doorway looking at the mess, a chandelier crashed to the floor, bringing with it chunks of waterlogged plaster.

"Sweet Mother of Jesus!" my mother cried.

Mrs. O'Dare came running out at the noise. When she saw the disaster, an angry, self-satisfied flush burned her cheeks. She telephoned workmen, looking imperiously at my mother as she did.

When they arrived they had to break down the door to the upper house. A dank smell descended the stairs, filling my mother with dread. Each time there was a boom of footsteps above us or a banging of hammers, she cried out to the Mother of God.

Mare's breathing grew more dissonant and drawn, and her cry strange, like the bleat of a weakling lamb. As my mother loomed over Mare, I touched her arm and she stiffened. She made Mrs. O'Dare take me, saying that she had enough on her over my poor sister.

That first day with the workmen upstairs, Mrs. O'Dare took an oil lamp and a broom into the dark hall. With my mother and Mare locked behind the parlor door, I helped the old woman sweep, her lamp casting an ambery church radiance over the broken walls.

"Your mother can fight me if she likes but I'm opening the house.

The men will replaster and do the wiring in here once the leaks are taken care of."

After she cleaned she left the oil lamp still lit on the floor in the usually dim hallway, and my mother, on her way to the kitchen, stopped in her tracks when she saw it. Mrs. O'Dare was standing nearby, ready for a fight, but my mother did not give her one, just stayed awhile where she was, staring.

The next day was Saturday and the men did not come. Mare and I played quietly with dolls in the morning and when she drifted off to sleep I went into the kitchen looking for my mother but did not find her there.

Mrs. O'Dare had relit the lamp and left it burning in the dreaded hallway in a determined attempt to get my mother used to the idea of renovation. I stood at the threshold, drawn in by the lamplight, which emanated a warm fragrance of burned minerals.

From a place where the corridor turned I saw the smear of a shadow and every muscle in my body tensed, but released again slowly when I saw that it issued from my mother, who stood looking into a room, one hand touching the frame of the door. Her face was lifted as if with expectation, and I had the distinct sense that she was looking for someone.

As I moved closer to her, the floorboard stressed under my foot. She froze but did not turn. Her terror and expectation flooded the air between us so I thought I would swoon, and it was as if I felt her heart bumping under my own in the soft of my stomach.

She turned slowly, and her face, beatified by terror, darkened when she saw me. "Jesus," she cried. "Christ on earth! Can you not leave me a moment of my own, Clodagh?"

My throat constricted and tears heated in my eyes.

She turned from me, and moving up the hall, looked around even more earnestly. Who was she searching for? Was it my dead father? Once I'd heard her say to Mrs. O'Dare that ghosts listened and watched, remembering for you the things you let yourself forget.

While retracing her steps, her body grew heavy. She stopped a moment and stared at the floor, then walked from the hallway, the flame in the lamp stirring the shadows on the blue, decrepit walls as she passed.

Breathing in the cold dankness of the air, I remained in the shadows where she'd left me, listening to the din in the silence.

・ 4 ・

BEFORE BED I WALKED UP TO MY MOTHER, FOLDING MY HANDS
as if praying, and looked into her face. "Forgive us our trespasses," I
said.

She blinked, taken off guard. Color rushed into her face. I reached
for her and hesitantly she put an arm around me before withdrawing it,
and saying in a low voice, "Off to bed with you now."

In the throes of that agony, I went in the car with Mrs. O'Dare to
the shops the next afternoon. Driving south we passed a group of
northbound tinkers going to settle in a field, their caravans moving
slowly toward us, some people walking with their horses.

Two wild, freckled girls ran alongside a slow-moving car with their
hands open.

"Please, a few pence," one cried in a shrill voice.

The driver threw some coins into the grass on the roadside and
they ran to gather them, laughing. Having found them they turned
together in a circle, dancing a reel. I watched, envious of the way they
fell laughing together and rolled in the grass, fascinated to think they
slept at night in a caravan that creaked in the wind.

My own mother had been such a creature. A sun-speckled girl
with dirty ankles and wild hair, bleached with weather. People who
moved along roads and fields. My mother's people. Uneasy with
houses.

"They run in herds," Mrs. O'Dare said thoughtfully, puffing on her
cigarette as she drove. "Like horses."

"The rain must have thrown them off course, poor desperate creatures," Mrs. O'Dare said. "Tinkers don't usually arrive to this field until
summer."

A tall thin girl passed us with damp staring eyes and I thought of
the dark-eyed seals that came in the summer riding the surf.

"These are not the same tinkers that usually come through here. I've never seen any of these before," Mrs. O'Dare remarked.

A woman with an infant at her breast walked toward us at a steady pace, holding out her hand.

"Where's that poor woman's shame?" she asked softly. "Suckling an infant in the light of day. Walkin' along the road as if 'twere nothing. There could be men in this car and do you think she'd hide her naked breast?"

The tinker woman held the infant in one arm, her long freckled hand wrapped gracefully around its bald head as if it had been made for only that purpose. As we came up close to her I pressed my face to the glass of the window. "Give her something, Missus!" I cried.

"Why, Clodagh! I've nothing extra to give her," Mrs. O'Dare said.

"Give her something, please!"

"I have nothing, love."

When we passed her I knelt on the seat, looking out the back window. The woman turned and met my eyes. My heart drummed hard. She had the same pink speckled skin as my mother, though her hair was a coarse dark rope flopping at one shoulder. The infant trembled and shifted as the woman twisted further round to look at me. Staring after the woman, I was filled with an urgency for her. "Missus," I whispered. In a moment she was lost among the gathering on the roadside.

I opened the car window for a better smell of the fire in the field. The same smell that was carried toward the sea every summer when the other tinkers arrived in that same field. The smell that agitated my mother.

Mrs. O'Dare had slowed the car and was watching me, a crease forming between her eyes as she looked into mine. "What are ye thinking, lass?" she asked.

Silence filled the car. I was confused by my longing for the dark-haired young mother. My face heated with shame.

After we made our purchases in the shops, Mrs. O'Dare took me to a tea shop for biscuits and a lemonade. The place was mostly vacant, it being an off hour. We sat at a table near a big window that looked out on an ascending street of houses with rough, gray walls, three or four bicycles leaning against one of them.

Our table was covered with a cracked, plastic cloth, a bright pink plastic flower in a bud vase in the center. After we ordered and the woman disappeared into the kitchen, Mrs. O'Dare sighed and sat back on her chair. "It's nice to sit so in the quiet and have another bring you tea." She smiled, the lines softening on her forehead as she looked out at the houses on the damp road.

"Why don't tinkers live in houses?" I asked.

"On still about the tinkers, are you?" she said, rolling her eyes.

"Do you know why, Missus?"

"I suppose they're suspicious of houses," she said, sighing. "That they have strange ideas about houses, like your own mother not having the rooms properly wired and cleaned." She ran a hand through the coarse gray of her hair, smoothing it in place.

From the inland-facing windows at the back of our house we could see the distant field where the tinkers camped in summer. Sometimes my mother stood outside watching the light and smoke from their fires.

"But how are they so different from the rest of us?"

"They're rough people," she said, lowering her voice. "Impoverished." A mysterious, wild-sounding word. "Impoverished," I whispered. Like the noise the wind made in the hawthorn tree.

"Your mother's an odd one, though. She was all alone when your father saw her in the west. Too young to be on her own. She's a mystery, lass."

"Did my mother beg on roadsides?" I asked.

"I don't know, lass. And don't you dare ask her such a question."

"Why not?"

"Your mother's ashamed of what she comes from."

"Why?"

At that moment the woman returned from the kitchen with my biscuits and lemonade, and when she left I had to ask my question again.

"It's nothing to be proud of, Clodagh, being a tinker. There's hardship in that life."

"Where is her own mother?" I asked.

"She'll not breathe a word on that subject. Not a peep about her life before she met your father. And you mustn't dare mention anything I've told you."

"She'll get angry?" I asked. I felt a pang in my stomach when I thought of how easily, how unwittingly I could upset my mother.

I took a bite of a biscuit but it was stale tasting, a simple water biscuit. I'd forgotten to ask for chocolate or jam-filled biscuits.

I put it down, thinking of the tinker woman. "Did my mother once hold me to her breast the way the tinker woman held her baby?"

"Yes, lass. That woman was feeding her child. Suckling it."

Before tea that night I took some coins from my mother's purse, snuck quietly from the house, and crossed the field and the old Dublin Road in a light rain. I walked to the tinker camp to find the woman with the infant. I looked into each face peering out of open caravan doors or from under the tarp where the fire was lit. They were all quiet, their eyes on me. But I could not see the woman. The women I did see had fierce faces and none had an infant at her breast.

As I ran home across the field and the road I saw my mother standing behind the house, her hand shielding her eyes from the rain.

"What in God's name were you doing?" she cried out.

I stopped a few feet from her, my heart pounding.

"I was looking for a lady."

"What lady?" she cried.

"There was a lady with a baby that I saw when I was in the car with the Missus."

"And what did you want of that lady?"

"To give her something."

"Give her what, in the name of God?"

I opened my hand and revealed the coins.

"Where did you get those?"

"From your own bag," I said.

"Little thief!" she cried. "Give them here."

I gave them to her and she stood quiet, her mouth tight. "I want to know what you wanted with that woman!"

"I wanted to talk to her."

"Why?"

"I wanted to ask her something."

"Ask her what?"

I did not know how to answer her. I wasn't sure what I wanted to ask the woman.

I shrugged and she let go a soft, involuntary laugh. But the gravity returned to her eyes. She looked away from me, uncertain of herself.

"Come in out of this weather," she said, and I followed her inside.

In the middle of the meal my mother looked up from her food and said that tinkers were a dejected lot. Her face flushed so the ginger-colored hairs of her eyebrows grew indiscernible. She watched the quiet that passed between me and Mrs. O'Dare. Her breaths came quickly through her nose.

"What have you been telling her about me, you old cow?"

Lying in bed, I tried to imagine the night of my nativity. Maybe there was a clue in the buried bedroom that might lead me to remember how it had happened; how I had made the passage so intact; how Mare had never fully left the water of our mother; how she breathed in air like she was drowning.

I did not understand that my sister and I had come of a slow process within our mother's womb. Mrs. O'Dare had told me once that identical twins like Mare and me had begun as one baby that split into two. I imagined that Mare had been the original, that I had come from her body the way the priest described Eve coming from a bone in Adam's body. Perhaps, coming from her as I had, I'd taken too much of her heartiness and left her with none for herself.

I went to Mrs. O'Dare's room and woke her up. She startled and put her arm around me, shaking faintly. "What's the matter, lass?" she asked.

"Why is Mare so sick?" I asked.

It never occurred to Mrs. O'Dare that Mare's affliction was my fault. "God makes mistakes sometimes as if he were as human as the rest of us," she whispered, and made the sign of the cross.

5

My SISTER AND I GREW USED TO THE COMINGS AND GOINGS OF the workmen, their tools and tarps and ladders left out, but our mother never did. She was nervous and fidgety over the bumping in the walls.

Once they'd finished upstairs, they replaced the demolished door. My mother took charge of the keys and once again the upper house was inaccessible.

Then they began work on the first floor, uncovering the windows so that the dark, once forbidden hallway was now flooded with soft gray daylight. They ripped down moldings and door frames, replacing water-damaged support beams and replastering, careful not to damage the existing stuccowork designs. Once they wired they put in electric fixtures and bulbs so that the rooms looked vast and unearthly.

They'd grown used to Mare and me, our timid, peering presences. At first they spoke to us, asking our names and such, but we never answered and then they were quiet when we appeared, hammering, turning a screwdriver, swishing a paintbrush. Two men with brown beards and one with a red one.

Most of their labor was concentrated in the rooms farthest to the back and we were free to visit the piano room, to sit side by side on the bench and explore the sounds of the keys.

Mrs. O'Dare knew a few songs. "Mary and Her Little Lamb," and a fragment of one she called "Clair de Lune." Mare leaned into the old woman, studying the movement of her stiff hands, demanding to see the pieces played again and again, understanding just by looking at the relationship of the keys on the piano that they ran in scales, that she could mimic the melody in a lower or higher register. The two simple pieces rolled from Mare's hand within half an hour and she was frustrated for something more complex.

Mrs. O'Dare said she might be able to produce fragments of a piece that required both hands, something she called "The Turning Sea," or "Sea Turns." She couldn't remember.

Mare picked it up quickly, revising the old woman's mistakes, elaborating new sounds. Mrs. O'Dare left us to ourselves. I sat to Mare's left and she labored with me, teaching me the lower notes to the piece, her hands so restlessly adept, so in tune with the gradations of sound.

I breathed the humid warmth Mare issued, everything she learned flowing to me. Like thoughts that were nonexistent one moment and there the next.

The lower notes, the ones I played, evoked the boom, the underrush of the sea, and she played the melody, the higher pitch of the waves, the mood and the yearning, the sparkle of the spume. We held hands, my right and her left, the two resting between us on the piano bench.

Over many rainy days waiting for spring to come, the music grew into a kind of breathing, her hand moving in a graceful side crawl, her fingers strangely independent of each other, quickening, flexing and slowing. She was the force that sent out and drew back the tides of my playing. Her left hand sweat in my right. She squeezed my fingers. We had grown accustomed to finishing the piece by softening our pressure on the keys until we barely grazed them, and found ourselves in silence, the vast heights of the room remembering the brilliance of the music, vibrant and awash above us.

I pressed the side of my face to hers. My original. My beloved, knowing in the heat from her hand and shoulder that she was about to draw me after into "Sea Turns" again.

One day in the middle of May, with still no sign of spring, the men were working in the piano room. Mare was restless and fidgety, wanting to play a hiding game. To keep her from exerting herself, my mother suggested that instead we defy the weather and take her out in a wheelchair, rigged up with umbrellas and an oilcloth tarp. But the wheels sank in the blackened ruts of the road and we had a terrible time pulling it loose.

Inside Mare asked again to play the hiding game, begging until our mother agreed. Mrs. O'Dare and my mother went to the kitchen and counted to twenty-five.

In the vestibule were two closet doors, one of them a "dummy." In various places throughout the house niches and closets had mates: one useful, one dead-ended, put there apparently to give the appearance of symmetry in the architecture. Mare was fascinated by these oddities. She stood before the dummy door, opening and closing it. "This is the tiniest room in the house," she whispered, "but we can fit inside it and they'll never know to look for us here."

We could barely close the door. I thought they'd find us right away with the noise of Mare's uneven breathing, amplified by the tight space. But again and again we heard our mother's bewildered footsteps passing our hiding place, and her calling out, "Where are you? Where are my lambs?"

Long after I was ready to come out, Mare held me back, lips tight, suppressing her laughter. "She can't find us!" Mare whispered. "She can't find us!" Even when we heard anguish in our mother's voice and the urgent echoes of Mrs. O'Dare's nailed shoes as she searched, too, Mare was giddy over the deception.

"I hate her," Mare whispered, looking elated.

"You don't," I said, stunned.

She snorted. "I don't, but I *do!*" I had to pry her hand loose of the knob to open the door and once I did she seemed relieved, disoriented as she stepped out.

"We're here!" I called out, and our mother, followed by Mrs. O'Dare, rushed in to us from the parlor. Our mother took Mare in her arms. "You'll keep to your little chair the rest of the day, love. Promise me that," she said.

Mare rolled her eyes.

"Promise me!"

"Yes!" Mare said.

*   *   *

But all that day my sister was restless to play. In the afternoon when the men had gone, our mother walked across the damp field into town and Mare and I visited the piano room.

They'd finished painting now and the walls were a clean apricot color, the moldings and cornices bleached: fat, snow-white infants peering through vines.

While Mare stood before the piano moving her hands softly over the high keys, I asked her, wasn't it an odd thing that our mother had once lived in a cave in the wall of a cliff in the west and that our father had brought her into his house; that she was a tinker and never wore shoes so she'd had dark, leathery feet that had to be scrubbed, and bugs that had to be washed from her hair?

Mare listened thoughtfully, tilting her head, her fingers running a quiet scale. I reminded her about the two tinker girls who had begged on the roadside and the freedom they'd had to play. I asked her, wouldn't it be a wild, free life, sleeping outside at night? I described the way they'd rolled about in the grass, and saw my own exhilaration reflected back at me in her face.

She lay down on the floor and rolled from one end of the room to the other while I jumped over her, both of us giddy. Breathlessly I described the reel the tinker girls had danced together and we held hands spinning until the air swirled around us like water. We had both fallen to the floor joyful, the earth shifting wildly beneath us, when we heard Mrs. O'Dare's nailed shoes echoing in the hallway. Finding Mare lying on the floor without cardigans and shawls, face flushed and eyes damp with exhilaration, Mrs. O'Dare lowered herself painfully to her knees. "Ah, lass, you'll not let your mother see you so. Quickly now, let's fix ye up before she's back."

She settled Mare in her chair in the parlor, admonishing us softly the entire time.

That night at tea Mare reached for my hand under the table, squeezing it with the pleasure of our secret. She leaned into me and whispered, "We are wild tinker girls."

But for that afternoon of joy, my sister paid with a night of labored breathing, and me awake beside her feeling helpless, the air moving effortlessly in and out of my lungs.

The next morning my mother sent me from the room when Mare had a breathing fit. I sat in a chair in the vestibule listening to the chaotic gasping behind the closed parlor door. Whenever Mare suffered I held myself very still, closing my eyes, my mouth filling with a brackish taste, a pain concentrating itself at the soft point under the arc of my ribs. When I heard her quiet I got up and ran dizzily into the room. Mare's face was sweat soaked, and though my mother hovered over her, Mare kept her focus on me. I reached with my right hand for her left and heard my part in the "Sea Turns," and soon felt Mare accompany me.

Afterward when she slept I lay with my face beside hers on the pillow, and smoothed her hair. Watching nervously from the doorway, my mother told me to leave her, but I wouldn't get up. I told her I was tired too, and closed my eyes. There was in me, that day, a wildness to be near Mare; an unquenchable loneliness for her. With "Sea Turns" between us we were almost one; and on the verge of sleep we remembered who we once were: something singular and faceless. Drenched in light.

The doctor came and examined Mare that afternoon. Afterward when he sat down in the foyer, Mrs. O'Dare gave him a cup of tea. He sighed, holding his cup in one hand, his saucer on the palm of the other, gazing distantly at the wall as if he were staring out the window.

My mother waited for him to say something and when he didn't she pleaded, "Will she be all right?"

He turned his head, and the daylight coming through the vestibule window pooled on his glasses, obscuring his eyes. "She's weak. Keep her comfortable, Mrs. Sheehy."

When he left my mother fretted and sighed, guilty over having let her play the hiding game.

*   *   *

After helping Mrs. O'Dare do the washing from breakfast, I stood before the parlor door. Mare sat on the bed while my mother knelt at the foot of it, ransacking the drawers of her small oak chest, usually forbidden to us.

When she'd first come to Mercymount Strand my aunts in the west had, over the telephone, set in place for my mother an account at Rafferty's Antiques and Acquisition Shop in Bray so that she might furnish the mostly empty house. But instead of buying furniture she had bought knickknacks and crockery and jewelry; little charms and novelties of all kinds, and hoarded them in chests and presses.

From the doorway I could see a selection of her precious keepsakes laid out before my sister, my mother leaning with her elbows on the perennially unmade bed, examining something in her hand, speaking in a whisper as if she were in church.

"Clodagh! Come in here," Mare cried. A shadow crossed my mother's face when she saw me, but she looked back at the object in her hand.

The window was open a crack, the air mineral-smelling from dim blasts of lightning breaking over the sea. I came in slowly and stood near the bed.

The object in my mother's hand was a watch with a cracked crystal and a little garnet like a bead of blood over the twelve. The metal that encased it had turned green.

"It doesn't tick," Mare said when my mother offered it to her.

"It doesn't matter, Mary Margaret," my mother said. "Look at the beauty of the thing."

"Yes," Mare said and passed it to me.

I did not see the beauty of it. I must have made a face because my mother took it from me and said, "You have to develop a taste for beauty."

She held it again, seeming to cradle it in her hand. Everything about her slowed down. It seemed to be the stillness, the steadfastness of the thing, that captivated her. And I thought then that if it had ticked she might have liked it less.

Her mood and the soft noise of Mrs. O'Dare sweeping in the hallway made me feel sleepy.

"A beautiful thing like this will outlive us all," she said, holding it to the globe of the lamp. "Such little things are slow to change."

I wanted to understand her reverence for things kept in the locked chest, taken out into light only on occasion, fawned over and returned to airlessness.

In Mare's lap I saw a hair comb with a satin ribbon attached to it, and the porcelain Dutch girl my father had given to my mother. My heart constricted in my chest. I knew somehow that my mother had given these things to my sister. But I told myself that Mare deserved special treatment. Her tie to the world was so tenuous and mine so strong. She deserved the tenderness of our mother. And I told myself that whatever our mother gave to Mare she also gave to me because the cords that once connected us in the womb still kept their phantoms in our sides. In spite of all these thoughts, my face burned.

I ran my fingers roughly over the tangle of necklaces and jewels on the bed and my mother stiffened.

"Stop that now!" she admonished in a harsh, quiet voice.

I looked angrily at her, holding back tears, stirring the necklaces again roughly before withdrawing my hand.

The rain deepened outside and the light from the sea seemed bright and dark at once, the shadows of the rain moving over the bed where everything lay, and making the little novelties on my sister's lap appear to shiver.

That night while Mare slept I went into the kitchen where my mother and Mrs. O'Dare sat at the table smoking.

"Clodagh!" the old woman said when I appeared in the doorway in my nightgown.

The back of my mother's chair was against the wall. She leaned one arm on the table and her legs were crossed. I approached her quietly, watching her face. "Can I have one of the presents my father gave you?" I asked.

"What?" she asked impatiently.

"You gave Mare the Dutch girl."

"You're rough with things, Clodagh," she said, looking away from me and puffing on her cigarette.

"I'm not," I said.

She would not look at me.

"I'm sorry if I was rough with the necklaces," I said.

"Go to bed now, Clodagh," she said.

But I did not move, hungry, uncertain.

"Agatha, love!" the old woman said. "Give the poor creature a kiss!"

My mother stiffened. "Go to bed, Clodagh!" she said in a soft, angry voice.

I walked from the room and stood in the darkness of the hall listening to them.

"Why must you always intervene between myself and that one?" my mother cried.

"For the love of God! Don't you see how much that child needs you?"

"Yes, I see it! I bloody well see it. She watches me like a cinder that won't go out."

"Why can't you offer her any comfort?"

My mother let out an exasperated sigh and the certainty left her voice, replaced by something faintly desperate, regretful sounding. "I don't have enough in me for the two of them, Missus."

A moment of silence passed before the old woman said, "You do, love."

"Things'll be better when we have a bit of sunlight again, Missus. Mare will get better and I'll be better in myself."

I crept up the hall and got into bed.

A few minutes later I heard the door creak open. "Clodagh," my mother whispered and I sat up. She put her arms around me and I felt her heart beating against my throat.

"Good lass," she said in a light, high-pitched voice, tender with guilt. She kissed the top of my head. I lay down and she pulled the blanket up around me and moved away in the dark to her own bed.

Mrs. O'Dare drove to the shops in the morning for fresh bread and sausages. She stopped at Bourke's, the newsagent's for the *Irish Press*, and after breakfast she read it at the table, muttering, making little interested sounds as she turned the pages.

"Bless us, Holy Mother! It says here that the weather is about to turn!" she announced.

"I'll not believe it until I see it," my mother said, her voice still softened by confusion as if the old woman's words from the previous night had not left her. She looked plaintively at me, then away.

"The seasons always change, Agatha," Mrs. O'Dare said.

"No, Missus," she said and gazed into her teacup. "There was a spring once in the west of Ireland . . . that did not flower."

"Maybe there were no flowers in the very rocky places . . ."

"Even in the rocky places the maidenhair ferns and the little purple flowers come up between the stones," she said slowly. "But one year I was there they never came up at all."

"I don't remember that," Mrs. O'Dare said.

"'Twas before I met you, Missus," my mother said softly.

The old woman lowered the newspaper from her face and gazed at my mother.

"That particular year the rain destroyed the Brigid's Beds," my mother said.

"Brigid's Beds?" the old woman asked.

"Have ye not heard of such things?" my mother asked.

"No, love," the old woman breathed.

"A grave for an unbaptized child. The rain was terrible that year, exposing the infants in their awful privacy, sending them adrift in the washes."

Mare fidgeted in her chair.

"Tell us, love," Mrs. O'Dare said. "Was it before you were alone in the cliffs?"

My mother held her breath. For a moment she looked so much like my sister that I could have believed Mare was her own twin and not mine. She seemed to be considering how she might answer and if the old woman's voice had not suddenly rushed with insistence, maybe she would have.

"Tell us, love," the old woman piped, leaning toward her. My mother's forehead tightened and the graceful vein that ran there appeared and imposed itself, casting a shadow.

"You're full of tricks, you old cow!"

"What could be wrong with wanting to know something of your girlhood?"

"I had no bloody girlhood," my mother cried, her anguish now turned to anger.

"Your language, Agatha!"

"Let me ask you a bleedin' question, Missus! If you never had children o' your own why are your legs swollen and spidery with the veins?"

The old woman drew a breath. "God give me patience," she said.

"Is there a child ye left somewhere in the ditches of Ireland?" She was boisterous now, her voice growing hoarse as it climbed in pitch. "Or was it more than one child?"

There was nothing to be said to her in this state. She was like the force that drives the waves. Deaf and stubborn as the spring that would not come. I retreated to Mrs. O'Dare's skirts, which smelled of potatoes and baking flour. My mother's eyes darted at me as if she thought I was in some conspiracy with the old woman. My head began to drum. She hated me as much in that moment as she hated Mrs. O'Dare.

"I need the patience of a saint," the old woman muttered.

Mare's breaths quickened and grew loud. She scratched the silk skin of the chair with her nails. My mother took her gingerly in her arms and out of the room, Mare disheveled against my mother's shoulder.

"What'll we do, Missus," I asked, squeezing the folds of the old woman's skirt in my fists, "if the spring doesn't come?"

* * *

The next morning a piercing ribbon of sunlight entered the room through the side of the curtain. I slipped from bed and went into the hall, my temples aching with the strain of the light. Without shadows, the architecture of the high rooms felt unfamiliar. The walls blasted with brightness looked pillaged, cindery. Dust motes floated like plankton in clear water.

I opened the front door and was rushed with a clean cold smell of sea air, my nightgown blooming like a sail. The field was flooded with sun, the crests of incoming waves lit a blinding white.

6

THE SUNLIGHT DID BRING A CHANGE. MARE'S LUNGS BEGAN working so quietly, so efficiently, the doctor was stunned and hopeful. "It's as if something has opened," he said.

Mare wanted to hear stories about banshees and phoukas. She ran in circles imitating a banshee's agonized posture and cry, the high-pitched shrieking, the grimacing face and relentlessness of her game designed to torment our mother.

My mother looked startled, pained by Mare's wildness. The silent, intimate dialogue between them changed. She stared at the floor, bemused. Where was her complacent, beloved girl? The earnest little creature?

In the middle of one of those dry, still nights when we could hear crickets outside in the new clumps of mint, Mare woke me and we snuck into the piano room, switching on the bright overhead light. Riding on her urgency we settled at our appointed places on the piano bench. She began "Sea Turns" and I struggled to follow, the music grazing my still-groggy nerves. Mare did not watch her hand on the piano keys. She gazed up at the wall, staring through it, emanating heat. Her pace quickened until it was almost frenetic. I closed my eyes, washed in the swell, the music lifting and dropping me. We reached the pinnacle of tension in the song, the edge of the crescendo, but she would not allow the piece to resolve, backtracking on one phrase again and again, the music tinkling and begging, repeating its bewilderment at the high registers.

And then she stopped. Extricating her left hand from my right, damp and hot, she got up.

"Come on, Clodagh," she said, and I followed her to the kitchen where she found an empty jar, then to the front porch where she switched on the light, waiting for the frail insects we called fairy moths to come. Soon, surrounded by insects, Mare dropped the jar and ran back and forth breathlessly grabbing them out of the air, fiercely clenching her teeth, her arms shaking as she squeezed them to death in the palms of her hands.

When our mother arrived at the threshold, crying out for Mare to stop, she kept going, her hands clotted with the smashed moth bodies and broken wings. For a moment my mother turned off the porchlight, thinking that might stop her, but Mare kept moving as if she did not know how to break the momentum that propelled her.

My mother switched on the light again and grabbed her, kneeling down to hold her still. "Stop it now, Mary Margaret. Stop!"

Mare stilled a moment, fixing our mother with her eyes, before fidgeting to get free. Our mother tightened her hold on Mare's upper arms and it must have hurt because my sister winced and let out a little cry before spitting in our mother's face.

They both froze. Our mother let go of her, wiped her face with her forearm, then dropped her arm to her side. Mare breathed heavily. "Mother," she said weakly and touched her arm, but our mother's face was hard and quiet, the porchlight hitting it as if it were made of crockery or glass.

Our mother got up from her knees and Mare grabbed the hem of her nightgown. "Mother," she said again, but our mother pulled the fabric loose of my sister's hand and uttered, "Don't touch me, you devil." She turned and went inside, a few flurrying insects in her wake throwing themselves at the lightbulb.

My mother went out and was gone all the next day, something she'd never done before. In the afternoon Mare and I sat next to each other at the piano pressing the sides of our faces together. We held hands and she led me in "Sea Turns," our hearts beating out of tune with each other's. The edginess of the previous night was still with her. She had difficulty concentrating. She'd begin a phrase and would lose it halfway through. She huffed and brought her fist down on the keys in exasperation. She was set on the task and overcome with it at once, fast shallow breaths coming through her nose. Perspiring, she focused hard on the keys, and clenched her mouth like our mother did when she was tense.

Our mother came home in the evening with an old-fashioned chiffon gown she'd bought at Rafferty's. She put it on and looked at herself for a long time in the big parlor mirror. The numbness that had come into her face the night before was still there. She didn't join us for tea.

She got out of bed in the dark that night and put on the dress. She stood before the mirror circling a votive candle around her waist, the clear and silver beads glimmering in the flame's light.

At the evening meal my mother would not meet Mare's eyes.

"Mother," Mare said once. My mother's lips tensed and she asked Mrs. O'Dare had she put butter or cream into the potatoes. She was quiet, ate only a little, and left the room. I reached for Mare's hand under the table but she pulled it away. I felt her bafflement like a pain in my side. She'd never fallen from grace with our mother before. She'd never known my mother to be as cold as stone.

After the meal Mare isolated herself in the piano room. Through the closed door I could hear her humming and playing random notes. I wanted to sit next to her, to press the side of my face to the side of hers, to hum with her. When I walked in she stopped and I could feel the terrible drumming of her heart in my side.

She told me to go but I wouldn't, staring at her across a mute field come up between us. I didn't understand then that she was trying to break from me. That it was only me now holding her like a weight to the earth.

The whole right side of me, the side of me that was partly her, felt bereft.

That night she left the bed and went back to the piano room. She chose one note high on the keyboard that she played again and again. When she played it a last time and the sound faded, its tension remained on the air like a question that had been inadequately answered.

* * *

Mare complained of being tired early the next evening. My mother asked Mrs. O'Dare to put her to bed and Mare hung her head as the old woman led her out.

"Good night," my mother said to her hesitantly.

I started to follow but my mother said, "Stay with me, lamb." There was a nervousness about her, an urgency as she held her hand out to me. I could not move, polarized between her and my sister.

"Would you like to see a lovely trinket I bought, Clodagh?" she asked.

"Yes," I said.

"Then come here." Her tone was soft but insistent. She drew something out of a box in one of the cupboards near the sink, then opened her hand, showing me a little black dog made of glass. She let me touch it with the tip of my finger.

"'Tis so lovely a creature, Clodagh," she said in a low voice, strange with sweetness. "'Twouldn't it blind you?" She looked into my face with a kind of appeal.

"Yes," I whispered.

We sat down and she put the dog on the table between us, light gleaming in its dips and curves. It emitted a tranquil din. I lay my head on the table and gazed at the dog, shifting my eyes from it now and again to my mother's face, which was soft with contemplation.

That night my mother slept heavily. She did not get up to check Mare's heart.

Once I opened my eyes and saw Mare's face close and gazing into mine, and once or twice that night through my sleep I thought I heard "Sea Turns"; felt the melody pulling at me, backtracking, refusing to resolve.

In the morning I awoke to a soft commotion.

"She's dead," my mother said quietly. "She's dead."

"Holy Mother of God," the old woman whispered, holding Mare's forearm in her hand. The light hit the curves of Mare's face. It was all surface and weight, with no fret and agitation. Her half-open eyes were brilliant.

"She's dead," my mother said again quietly.

But I heard the noise of Mare's disembodied breathing as if she were resting her head on my shoulder, and as I got up and backed away from the bed it stayed with me, soft and steady.

7

THE SMALL CASKET WAS PLACED ON THE PIANO BENCH IN THE vacant music room, the windows open because the day was so still. But a wind came up later and set the long gauze curtains luffing and stirring and blew out the two candles at the casket's head. Mrs. O'Dare relit them and closed the windows.

She had just set up chairs for the people who would soon come, when my mother appeared in the hallway in her antique dress. The old woman pleaded with her to change into the black woolen one she'd laid out for her on the bed. But my mother would not be persuaded and seemed to take satisfaction from the old woman's distress. Her face was flushed as if with fever.

The room stank of lilies. I turned quickly away when I saw Mrs. O'Dare manipulate Mare's fingers around a white Sunday hymnal. When a few people came from town my mother disappeared. I hid as well, walking restless circles in other rooms. I could not bear their horror and intrigue. Once when I came to peer in at them from the doorway I heard a townswoman say to a woman accompanying her that the poor innocent had been too young to make a perfect Act of Contrition. But to Mrs. O'Dare's weeping face, she spoke of the happy deaths of children called home to the breast of God.

"She's the Holy Mother's little girl now," the woman said to me, clutching my hand in her two damp ones. "You shall meet her again, dear girl, if you stay the right side of God."

When the priest arrived to bless the body, everyone assembled in the chairs. My mother looked like a bride as she walked in, all ice and light with sprigs of lily of the valley in her hair. Even the priest looked up from his book and hesitated. She stood suspended on the hush that rose around her, a soft look of elation on her face.

Mrs. O'Dare took her arm and led her to a chair. Throughout the Mass people looked at her stunned, embarrassed.

I sat heavily in my chair trying to keep my eyes open, all the while seduced by the hypnotic steadiness of my sister's breathing.

Once when no one was talking to her I saw my mother let go of a shallow sigh. She hunched forward and looked into her hands.

Near the end of the day when we thought no one else would come, two women from the Marion Society knocked at the door holding a loaf of soda bread and a small pot of stew. Mrs. O'Dare took the provisions and thanked them, trying to explain that my mother was not up to taking visitors, when she appeared in the doorway in her incandescent dress. She looked rapt, her skin bright.

"We're praying for you, Mrs. Sheehy," one of them cried out.

"God is good to the wee ones He takes unto His breast," said the shorter, younger one, who wore a blue serge hat.

"What a lovely blue hat, Miss," my mother said.

"Oh, thank you," the short woman said, touching it nervously. "It's the color of Our Lady's mantle."

My mother nodded faintly, and as everyone seemed afraid to breathe, she withdrew.

"She's beside herself," Mrs. O'Dare apologized, red to the roots of her hair.

"Of course she is," said the taller woman. "Of course."

"God bless her," said the other.

At the burial service a priest read from a little white book, something about Resurrection and the cycles of suffering coming to an end. Three old women in black stood just outside our small circle. As the gravedigger shoveled earth in over the coffin the women began to keen, a wild, grief-driven shriek that chilled me and brought poor Mrs. O'Dare to her knees with the tears.

My mother stared off at the Wicklow hills, transfixed, and when the keening stopped she watched the women depart.

A flash of anger broke in me and I shook, holding back the urge to rush at her, to hit her with my fists. She must have felt something because she switched her focus to me. There was lethargy and strangeness in her face and when I looked at her, my anger dimmed. I ached for her, and when she looked away from me I was bereft.

As we walked from the cemetery to Mrs. O'Dare's little car, I felt as if I were floating. "I'm dreaming," I told myself. "I'm having a dream."

When we got home I complained to Mrs. O'Dare. "She doesn't cry for Mare at all."

"I don't know where she goes in herself, Clodagh," the old woman said, shaking her head.

But a few minutes later I walked into the parlor and found her sitting on the bed gazing out the window. She did not seem to hear me. Her mouth hung open like the wind had been knocked out of her.

For a few days I let Mare bring me with her into quiet, often dreamless sleep. We drifted above the town, carried along on currents of air. Below we could see the tides moving in and away on the strand. It seemed we moved aimlessly together a long time until I found myself flooded by the smell of the trees coming from a bit of forest in the Wicklow hills and had a sudden, terrible hunger to be located again, to be weighted. I was shepherded back to the ground in a storm of leaves while Mare remained above me, rising and drifting.

I awakened from dreams in which Mare was alive again, shivering and barefooted, smelling of evergreens. Death had been a kind of journey for her. It had exhausted her, left her frail and full of terrible knowledge.

I stopped sleeping at night. I lay in the dark thinking of the night just a week or so ago with the moths when our mother had gone cold to Mare. I let myself feel the anger that had flared up like lightning for a few moments at the burial. I let myself feel it cautiously, looking at my mother's sleeping figure.

While placing Mare's death certificate in a folder of papers and family records, Mrs. O'Dare found a never-before-seen photograph of my father in an envelope: a sad-faced man gazing placidly into the camera like someone looking through a window, the background complicated with shadows.

I wondered if he would recognize Mare if there was a place where the dead walked among other dead. I prayed to him with the same reverent, pleading tone of voice that Mrs. O'Dare used to pray to Christ, to find Mare, to console her. But like Christ, my father was elusive. Reticent. I could not feel him there. My sister remained with me, my system flooded now and then by her excruciating sadness; her bafflement at our mother's withdrawal.

"Sssshhh," I'd say, when I heard Mare stirring uneasily. I curled up, rocking myself, imagining our mother touching her face. "Ssssh, girleen."

I asked the old woman to tell me all the tender things that had been there between my mother and Mare, and then I'd work hard to imagine them, to reconjure them. Mare did not have the energy to remember. I had to help her.

For a while, a few weeks or a month, Mare stayed with me; sleeping much of the time so I could hear her hoarse, steady breathing. Once the shock had settled, I imagined her drifting, traveling out into death. Days passed where she was fully gone from me. I could not sense a pulse or an intake of air or an uneasy thought that was not my own. Sometimes I could not remember her face, strange as that was since her face was so much like my own. I could not quite fix her in my mind.

It was at such times, when the loss of her had grown easier, her memory diffused, that she would return to me with a sudden, visceral power. A pressure in my chest. An aching in my fingers that caused them to shake. I struggled to soothe her, concentrating on our mother's love for her.

I was afraid to approach the piano. Mare had consecrated it; and now like the music that came from it, Mare traveled on air. She swelled and ignited, then dimmed and faded. She was weightless, infiltrating.

I stood at the door of the piano room watching the stiff linen cur-

tain move, afraid and in awe of air that could move things and separate the dead from the living.

If I gazed a long time at the piano so that I was seeing past it and
through it, I could almost see Mare there at the sides of it, and the fear
that filled me in those moments felt like a betrayal.

In the visible world my mother and I were left to each other. I found
myself possessed by a hunger for some pure, original memory of who
we were to each other. A wild notion came into my mind that now my
mother might fall in love with me. I left the little bed I'd shared with
Mare and got in beside my mother. I longed for her to press her ear to
my chest and listen with faint desperation for my heartbeat. Or to gaze
into my face, appealing to me as if my existence might sustain the
world.

I fashioned early memory for myself out of the details Mrs. O'Dare had
already supplied. My mother hovering over me in the reddish light of
the turf fire, fiercely tender. The reedy high-pitched noise of her voice
as she sang to me. The bumping of her heart as I suckled her breast.

My greed for her coursed through me each time I closed my eyes
and conjured that moment. The sweetness of her filled my mouth. A
taste I now associate with impermanence.

And if I made the moment real enough in my mind, if I searched the
air of the memory strenuously enough, I could feel her greed for me.

8

More than six weeks had passed since Mare's death.

Mrs. O'Dare said my mother was tired. For five years she'd hardly slept, senses kept awake for Mare. Now with Mare gone she could sleep.

And she did. Long meandering sleeps that frightened me, so heavy and dead did they sometimes seem. I'd press my ear to her back and listen for her heart. With Mare gone, what would keep her here?

We were awakened one morning by wild barking from the sea. I followed my mother out across the field and stood on the grass at the edge of the sand, a strong wind tormenting our hair and nightgowns. She pointed at a group of seals appearing and disappearing like black dots on the crests of waves.

I followed her north along the strand where she'd spotted a few seals basking on a jutting rock. They perked their heads up, watching us approach.

"Sweet girls," my mother said, slowing her pace and stopping a few yards from the rock, my heart quickening at the tender familiarity in her voice. Their faces were earnest, darkly human. Their nostrils moved as they breathed.

Leaning forward from the waist and extending her arm, my mother cried out to them again in a soft, high-pitched voice, "Lovely girls."

One seal twitched, a shiver running the length of its body as if in response. It blinked its eyes.

The wind grew suddenly stronger as a tall wave came in, hitting the rock, a curve of spume rising on the air and spattering down on the seals. They undulated and barked, pulling themselves to the rock's edge. The one that had twitched looked again at my mother before it slid into the sea.

We stayed where we were, watching them ride the swells.

"The seals make me yearn after the west," my mother said.

"The beach at Dunshee?"

"Yes." The word escaped on a breath.

Seabirds keened over the noise of the surf. She let go a sigh and stared off at the horizon, complacent, heavy from so much sleep.

I reached for her hand and she took mine, the mild sunlight causing us both to squint as we moved slowly back to the house.

The next morning she was not in bed when I woke. I went outside and saw her in the distance standing near the jutting rock. As I ran along the sand toward her, she turned and held her hand up as if in warning. That's when I spotted the seal near her on the rock, becoming uneasy at my approach. Before it slipped on its side back into the sea my mother grazed its pelt with her hand.

"You frightened her!" she cried out to me over the noise of the surf.

I moved slowly toward her. "I'm sorry," I said, afraid she'd remain angry with me, but she just shook her head and gazed after the seal on the waves.

I sat at the kitchen table drawing pictures of seals, showing them to my mother who sat near me drinking a cup of tea. Mrs. O'Dare stood at the sink doing the washing up from breakfast.

"Are seals as smart as people?" I asked.

"Some in the west say they are," Mrs. O'Dare said. "There's a tale about seals."

"Tell me," I said.

"What are those creatures called, Agatha?"

"Selkies," my mother said quietly.

"Tell me the tale," I said.

"Something, I think, about a woman who became a seal . . ." Mrs. O'Dare said.

"No," my mother said. "Wait." She got up and went to the parlor, then returned with a small book I'd never seen before, in glossy, pale blue binding.

"Read this to us, Missus," she said to the old woman.

Mrs. O'Dare dried her hands on a tea towel, then sat down with us. My mother leaned back in her chair, crossing her arms, a soft seriousness on her face as she listened to the old woman read:

" 'I am the Irish selkie who emerged full grown from my sealskin, licking a gluey membrane from my own body, and drying myself on the rocky crag, my skin folded carefully beside me like a glossy dress. It was the cries of a fisherman that lured me ashore, lowing like a bull seal, floating in a boat over my bedroom in the night sea. He took my sealskin from me and made me his, then brought me to his home. He married me and we had a child together.

" 'My life was marked by my departure from the sea. I saw the seam between worlds and I thought I'd always be able to pass there. But that kind of grace comes along rarely in a lifetime.' "

As the old woman read, my mother watched her eyes.

" 'I could no longer bear the deception of my life, the dry vacancy of air, the sun lighting everything in my path. When the day came that I found my old sealskin in the floorboards where my husband had hidden it, I left my life ashore and my child, and walked back to the sea. It was, after so many years, strangely easy. I'd grown tired of being human and dreamed of a second chance at grace; pushing the seam between worlds, looking for the glimmer of an underwater room.' "

I waited for something more but Mrs. O'Dare was quiet and closed the book. A soft panic made my heart quicken. "I don't remember it being so dark a story," the old woman said.

"Why did the selkie leave her child?" I asked.

"She was a seal," my mother said softly. "She belonged in the sea."

"Why didn't she take her child with her?"

My mother peered at me but did not answer.

"Why did she go away?"

"Oh, Clodagh, love," Mrs. O'Dare said. "It's just an old folktale!"

My mother lit a cigarette, drew at it and watched the smoke travel on her exhalation.

My heart was in my throat. "Mother," I said and touched her arm. "Tell me why the selkie went back to the sea."

My mother looked fully at me so I felt bright, transparent.

"Don't you remember what it said in the story? She was tired of being human."

My pulses clamored. I searched her eyes. "Did someone make her tired of being human?"

She thought hard before she said, "It was her nature, Clodagh. You can not change a creature's nature."

I picked up the little book from the table where Mrs. O'Dare had put it. Inside were three simple illustrations. The first was of a seal lying on a rock. The second of a blond woman climbing out of the seal-skin. The third of the same woman standing naked beside the sealskin.

I thought of my mother sitting alone at night in the kitchen with the sods burning and the little window open to the cold. She had once made a dim, buried cave of this room to suckle my sister and me.

I was filled with an amorphous yearning for my mother and an uneasy curiosity that would grow in me like an affliction.

It was summer and warm air blew in from the sea. Mrs. O'Dare moved out of the house and in with her sister in Bray, who had sprained an ankle, but she came every morning to see to things, and left each night after the washing up.

One evening near dark Mrs. O'Dare was baking a meat pie in the kitchen by the light of a paraffin lamp. The aroma of the food and the dim light traveled up the hall and to the vestibule where I stood watching my mother through the parlor door. She had opened the top drawer of her dresser and was stirring things about until she withdrew a jeweled comb that she pressed into her hair before the mirror. The top buttons of her dress were open and she ran her hand over her breastbone, then toyed with a bit of loosened ribbon. She leaned into the mirror, a strange excitement on her face as she whispered to herself so softly she barely moved her lips.

The main door was open and on a gust of wind I smelled the summer fires of the tinkers newly camped in the north field.

That night after the meal my mother did not come to bed but sat on the porch humming. She'd opened all the windows in the house and every few minutes the curtains would stir and once they flew almost horizontally into the room and somewhere from the back hall I heard a door slam.

I was afraid to sleep with my mother so wistful. So easily could she have slipped like a shadow into the waves of the night sea.

The next morning she got up in the early dark. I followed her to the kitchen where she lit the kettle. I opened the little smoke window for her as she lay rashers in the pan, stirring them with the fork as they cooked, the smell of bacon passing across the expanse of rooms in the cross ventilation. After she removed the bacon she left the grease to sizzle, cracking three eggs into it where they bubbled and popped and fried up with ruffled edges.

She seemed that morning full of a confused, well-meaning urgency, and she watched me eat as if she were trying to remember something, encouraging me to sop bits of bread into the dripping yolks.

When Mrs. O'Dare came in she ate with her fingers until the old woman was on her to use cutlery. It was the first time since Mare had died I saw her looking to incite Mrs. O'Dare's remonstrances. Everything that was left she ate with her fingers, including an egg gone cold in the pan, the fat around it whitened like pond ice.

But later in the day when the tinker fires began again her mind was elsewhere. She dressed herself and went out for a long walk toward the Wicklow Mountains.

She came home late that night and made a show of undressing and coming to bed. Rain was hitting the window hard when I fell asleep.

In the wee hours her place beside me was empty. I got up to go to the lavatory and noticed that she had a bit of a fire burning in the kitchen hearth, and set up before it was the old folding bed that she used sometimes if one of us was ill and needed the warmth of the turf fire.

Returning to bed I felt a cold rush of air, a barge of shadow moving past me just outside the door to the parlor. I slipped behind the door, my heart pounding. I waited a few moments until I heard the faint sound of my mother's laughter from the kitchen.

The smell left in the wake of the shadow was somehow familiar to me. Dampness and horses and peat. It had come and gone before, I thought, though I could not have said when. A soft barrage of impressions that had the feel of dream residue.

I had a sudden clear flash of memory: I must have been very small because I was in my mother's arms, with just a bit of flickering red light illuminating her. I remembered her heart quickening at the approach of the smell and the shadow.

My mother laughed softly again in the kitchen. Concealed in darkness I walked into the hallway. I saw the large shadow merge with hers. I heard my mother take in her breath.

There was muffled laughter. "Stop," she said softly "Stop." The bedsprings complained as if under a great weight.

"Sssshhh," my mother said as if she were talking to the bed. The deep animal timbre of the other voice sounded muffled as if he were speaking into her neck or hair and the bedsprings began lapping like water at the wall as if the room had somehow been flooded.

And then the soft cries began. The cries I could not understand, the two voices growing indistinguishable. It sounded as if they were caught in some mutual struggle, a sadness building between them. I felt then that what they were doing was terribly dangerous and I wanted to scream out and tell them to stop. But I was polarized, afraid that if I startled her my mother might slip away with him into his animal darkness and never return.

And when I thought I could no longer bear it and that the world itself might end, everything stopped.

The lowing animal voice said, "Bless us, Mother of God."

I peered into the room, and in the turf light saw a big man lying on his back in disheveled clothing, his shirt open. My mother lay with one side of her face pressed to his bare chest, one naked arm and leg draped across his body.

For a brief moment he turned his face away from her so that his forehead and eyes were faintly illuminated, and from his expression it seemed the sadness of the world was upon him.

The next morning while she stood over the stove poking at the bacon as it fried, I said to her, "I saw the man."

"What, Clodagh?" she asked.

"I saw the man who was here."

She stood without breathing a moment then crouched before me, holding my shoulders, her face shining with cooking. "The one you saw was the ghost of your father. Ghosts of men are noisy, clumsy things and they come and go in death the way they do in life."

I was moved by the proximity of her face to mine, and by her earnestness.

"Just the ghost of your dead father, love." Her voice warbled and she touched my temple with her fingertips. "Ye should not tell the old Missus. Ah, there's a good girl. An old ghost gets lonely again for the world. Do ye hear me, love? It's our secret about the ghost."

"What were you doing with the ghost?" I asked.

She paused. "Comforting the poor creature," she said.

"He was very sad," I said.

"Yes, he was," she said, taking me in her arms.

At the threshold of tears, I asked her, "Are you going to go away with the ghost?"

She held me at arm's length and cried, "No, lass!"

"The ghost left muddy footprints in the vestibule," Mrs. O'Dare said, having suddenly appeared from the hallway. She crossed her arms and looked indignantly at my mother, who faced her a moment before storming past.

"What's wrong, Missus?" I asked.

"Nothing, lass. I'm just sorry to hear that your mother is consorting with the dead."

It was that same day, with things uneasy between my mother and Mrs. O'Dare, that the old woman received a telephone call from Lily

Sheehy in the west. We'd heard from the aunts once before Mare had died and after they'd gotten the first bill for the repairs on the house. Mrs. O'Dare had defended the expenses, describing the collapsing walls and unlivable conditions. "You told me, Miss Sheehy, to oversee things here. The conditions were dire. Dire!" Mrs. O'Dare had cried.

Lily Sheehy had said then that they would come to see the house; that it had been too long anyway, and in a more apologetic tone said that they'd been meaning now for a very long time to meet Frank's daughters.

"I told them you were both the image of their dead brother, just to stick the knife in!" Mrs. O'Dare had told Mare and me at the time. "They don't behave like family at all." But the aunts never came.

Now, Lily Sheehy called to let us know that their plans were definite, and they'd be here in two days.

Later I heard my mother arguing with Mrs. O'Dare in the kitchen. "This is my bleedin' house, Missus, and it's thanks to me alone that you have a roof o' your own and praities enough to keep you fat."

"You'll give up your bucking if you want to keep this great edifice over you," Mrs. O'Dare said with gravity. "You better take care to keep your place here."

"Leave off on me, Missus."

"Don't get careless, Agatha, now that your wee lass is gone. You've still got another to think about."

My mother stormed up the hall and slammed the parlor door behind her. A little while later she left the house with her jacket on and a basket on her arm.

"Don't be seen in the tinker camps!" Mrs. O'Dare cried.

"I'm not going to the bleedin' tinkers!" she cried out. "I'm goin' to Mrs. Rafferty's shop."

She came home later that day from Mrs. Rafferty's with a blue platter, which she placed standing up against the shelfback in the linen closet.

I heard her that night rearranging the cabinet. I got up once for a glass of water and saw her in candlelight, holding the blue platter in her hands, admiring it.

When my aunts came to Mercymount Strand, they were stunned by the lack of furniture, and my mother feebly explained that the house was too big for her. Mrs. O'Dare and I had moved the great couch from the parlor into the piano room, and dressed it in the nicest bedding we had, some green and beige striped Irish linens.

When they asked for the key to the upper floors, my mother was resistant about giving it to them. She said that the repairs done up there were bare bones, only things absolutely necessary to save the main living area. There was nothing much to see but empty rooms in need of paint.

But they insisted and Mrs. O'Dare took them up. I stood at the foot of the stairs, stale, forlorn air descending from the open door.

The first afternoon with the aunts there was awkward. I'd run into them in the hallway or the foyer, their expressions serious, appalled. The impression of them was everywhere, fierce shadowy archangels whose strain and disapproval wafted through the rooms of the house like sea air.

I was afraid, in awe of my aunts, yet I wanted them to like me. Lily Sheehy, heavyset with light hair swept carefully over her ears like the feathers of a dead bird, seemed sterner than her nervous sister. Yet she treated me with a reserved kindness. I went up to her once and touched the gold crucifix she wore around her neck. I turned it in the light, a tender feeling passing between us.

Kitty Sheehy, thin and with iron-gray pincurls framing her face, was overanimated around me. She'd brought me a puppet, a red velvety queen with a papier-mâché head, which she worked with her hand, opening and closing its arms with her fingers, speaking in a high-pitched, squeaky voice: "Isn't Clodagh Sheehy a pretty girl?" "Little Clodagh Sheehy" this and that. Her face grew red with the exertion of her game. She'd stop suddenly to recover her breath, extricating the puppet from her hand.

"That Kitty Sheehy," Mrs. O'Dare had said to me in private. "A voice of violets and a heart of briars."

Still I tried to make her like me, feeling my mother's disapproval once when she walked into the parlor and found me on Kitty's lap, my arms around her neck.

The aunts stood together in the kitchen going through the cabinets and cupboards, commenting to each other under their breath. Upon opening my mother's china closet and examining the great cache of chipped, discolored and unmatching crockery, and a few broken ones that my mother'd left there with the intention of repairing, Aunt Lily shook her head and said to Aunt Kitty, "It's what she comes from." I thought of the wild girl living in the cove. The girl who preferred to urinate in the grass. Did my aunts know if she was a selkie?

They sent Mrs. O'Dare to the shops for mutton and vegetables and ingredients for a gravy and a fruit compote. They oversaw her cooking all afternoon, Kitty Sheehy giving nervous instructions, undertaking the chopping of the apples into cubes, getting exasperated from time to time with the poor overwhelmed Mrs. O'Dare, who had grown unused to such demands.

A table was set with a cloth. Two forks and two glasses at each place. Candles were lit and Mrs. O'Dare was instructed to refill the water glasses whenever they were down to half. Aunt Kitty served a wobbling blancmange with silver implements that none of us had seen before and decided later that she must have brought with her.

I felt ashamed of my curiosity. But I could not stifle it. I approached my aunts while they sat alone in the foyer chairs drinking tea.

"Where did my mother live when she was a little girl?" I addressed the question to Aunt Lily. She fixed my eyes as I spoke to her, her nostrils flaring slightly as if I were asking something distasteful.

They exchanged looks and during their silence I felt my face going warm.

Aunt Kitty's eyes darted back and forth.

"Is Dunshee the place she's from?" I asked.

"Yes!" Aunt Kitty said, smiling. "And that's where our dear brother, your father, met her." Her head bobbed slightly when she spoke. She seemed anxious that our interaction be lighthearted. "Dunshee is a beautiful place. A rocky landscape and a crashing sea." She waved her arm dramatically.

I peered at her and held my breath.

"It's a legendary place," she went on, sensing my anticipation. "Not far from Drumcoyne House. They say it's enchanted, the meeting place between the dead and the living."

I wanted to ask what she meant by the "meeting place between the dead and the living," but Mrs. O'Dare came in with the teapot to refill their cups and the three of them became engaged in a conversation about a particular beech tree that looked diseased and what should be done about it. The conversation went on and on. Who might be called. Mrs. O'Dare mentioned the brother of a friend, Mr. O'Halloran, who had experience with trees. She'd ring her friend and ask.

I sat there waiting for them to finish, but as the tea things were cleared away they were taken up with other questions regarding the yards and the plumbing and some talk about the door being removed from the second-floor landing.

"How late does the girl stay up?" Kitty Sheehy asked Mrs. O'Dare in a soft voice as if I could not hear her. She eyed me over her glasses that she'd put on to make notations.

"Clodagh, love," Mrs. O'Dare said, "It's ten o'clock. Off to bed with you."

I was ready to challenge her but the aunts were off ahead of us, disappearing around the turn in the hallway.

When I awoke the next morning they had gone back to the west.

9

MARE HAD, AFTER THE FIRST YEAR OF HER DEATH, TAKEN REFUGE
in me less and less often. When she had come in the second and third
years it was in a flash of sadness or a metallic taste in my mouth;
flashes that felt sometimes like kisses, sometimes like assaults.

By the time I was eight years old I rarely sensed her near except
once in Mass when a woman visiting from Dublin played the usually
silent pipe organ. The eerie joyousness of the music aroused rapture
in me, the light and temperature of the air seeming to change, carrying
an atmospheric smell like damp shoregrass.

Areas of that particular music became caught in my memory,
returning for months. I heard them as if someone was playing a piano
in a room inside me, thinking and feeling her way through the notes
and pauses, moving up to crescendos and lingering there, drawing out
the tension as long as the integrity of the melody would allow, before
descending and ebbing away.

The music remained with me, ribboning out sometimes into mysterious variations of itself, so I'd sit unmoving, hardly breathing, feeling little stabs of joy and surprise.

The September I was eight years old I began school at Immaculate
Conception, a rambling, decrepit brick building run by an order of
strict, intensely devout nuns.

I was terrified of the idea of being so many hours away from my
mother each day; nervous that if I did not maintain my vigilance over
her, I'd come home one day and find her gone.

She came with me the first day of school, wearing a large hat with
a satin ribbon that she'd spent the morning arranging and pinning in
place.

When we got out of the bus near the school, a tormenting wind pulled the hat partly loose and she'd had to hold it in place, introducing herself to Sister Lawrence, our teacher, and bending before the knuckles of the principal, who pulled her hand awkwardly away when my mother attempted to kiss it. Three girls who'd been walking by whispered and exchanged a laugh and my mother froze and looked at the ground. A feeling of shame rushed through me as she shuffled off with the great thing tipping to the side, but too elaborately pinned to her hair to remove. The three girls who'd laughed had stopped to watch her departure, whispering as I moved past them into the school.

Our classroom was in the eastern wing and through the windows we could see the ocean. That first season the weather was always inclement, the windows mizzled with rain, the fog so oppressive I could not see the waves or the petrels, though I could hear them, and the occasional whistle of a steamer moving north to Dun Laoghaire Harbor.

At Immaculate Conception I would study the map of Ireland, follow the blue lines of its rivers and learn of the wonders of the land: the Giant's Causeway and the Cliffs of Moher. The Two Paps of Danaan. Dun Aengus. And concentrated sites of megalithic tombs and primeval ruins. I searched for Dunshee along the western coast but could not find it.

The nuns pointed out beaches and bays where terrible slaughters had taken place at the hands of the English. Glorious near-victories that always, in the end, were lost by weakness or exhaustion or treachery. As if it were destiny; the very nature of the Irish to fall. This feeling of sad inevitability resonated for me in a painful way.

The hours of our days were carefully divided among classes and prayers and chapel. Our afternoon meal was even monitored by the nuns and though many of the girls were resentful of the constant overseeing, I found myself relieved by it. I was intimidated by the boisterous behavior of the girls after school. They ran and gesticulated wildly as they were released through the gates. Some of them kicked and chased each other, screeching roughly like banshees.

At the end of the school day, my anxiety to see my mother made me breathless. I sat alone on the school bus pretending to focus on my books, relieved as the bus slowly emptied and moved progressively north, leaving me, the last to be dropped off on the old Dublin Road.

The nun taught us that one could bear anything if one loved Christ; if we understood that our own wounds were nothing in comparison with those He had suffered to redeem us.

I learned to venerate His Body, memorizing His wounds. The nun said we must imagine them as deeply as we could in order to appreciate what He suffered. I gazed at the pictures on the classroom walls of Christ on the road to Calvary, the fourteen Stations of the Cross.

I stood before the statue of the tired crucified figure in the reception hall, His head resting on His shoulder, and found myself shamefully drawn, for didn't He look like my own father, the man I'd seen my mother with in the dark turf-lit kitchen. I averted my eyes from His near nudity until I was certain no one could see my face and then I'd stare at the long, muscular limbs with legs demurely crossed at the shin, both feet impaled with one nail. Bits of paint peeled from His thighs and knees.

At the hour of the school day when my anxiety was at a peak, I'd sigh and put down my pencil and whisper into my hands, "Dear Christ, please keep her here." Sometimes I repeated His name in a low voice, waiting for Him to appear to me in His resurrected form wearing a glowing robe. And once, after rubbing my eyes a long time, I saw Him a moment in the corner of the school room before He dissolved.

On a warm, brilliant March day, a month after my ninth birthday, my mother and I rushed together across the fields in the uncanny weather to Rafferty's to sort through boxes of baubles. She'd promised that I could pick something out for myself.

I had my eye on a hair comb decorated with green glass shapes.

"Look, Clodagh," she said, showing me a rhinestone pin in the shape of a butterfly. "Look closely at this. There's the body of a tiny spider stuck inside the amber head. Isn't that an odd thing?"

But as I took it from her I noticed out of the corner of my eye a rough-looking snuffbox with the painting of a man's bearded head on it. I was captivated by the masculine face. I opened it, pleased by the cool, woodsy-smelling air that it exhaled.

"I want this," I said.

My mother looked startled by the box. She seemed not to breathe as she examined it, noticing some lines on the bottom that looked like crudely scratched letters. She opened and smelled it, growing glassy-eyed.

I saw her extract a small folded piece of paper from inside the lid, closing her fingers around it.

"What was that?" I asked.

"What was what?"

"That bit of paper."

"You're seeing things, love," she said, the color rising in her face.

"I'm not!" I cried.

She shook her head dismissively.

"I'd rather have the box than the hair comb," I said, reaching for it.

"No, Clodagh," she said.

"Why not?"

"This is not for a little girl, but for a man."

"It's mine," I said, the thing gleaming in my mother's grasp, the man's penetrating eyes peering up from between her fingers.

"Let's pin this butterfly to your collar, Clodagh. There now, look in the glass."

I stood stiffly before the glass watching my mother's reflection behind me, a new pink in her cheeks as she squeezed the snuffbox in one hand at her side.

I turned away from the mirror in quiet distress.

"You'll take the pin now as your gift," she said, giving it to Mrs. Rafferty to wrap in paper.

I stared at the floor a few feet in front of her and when I looked up I saw her slip the snuffbox to Mrs. Rafferty and whisper for her to wrap it separately. She told me to wait outside but I hid myself behind an old armoire near the door.

"Is this from himself, Mrs. Rafferty?" she asked the shopkeeper in a covert voice.

"Yes, Mrs. Sheehy. The tinker man," the woman said with restraint. "Sold me all those cups and saucers and this little box."

Again there was an expectant quiet between them. "He was on his way to Dublin. Phoenix Park for the fair."

I peered in and saw my mother looking at the crockery, touching the rim of one of the cups.

As we walked back toward the field I asked her why she'd taken the snuffbox from me.

She laughed, a kind of forced laugh, and would not look at me. "It's not a gift for a girl."

"I don't care! I chose it!"

She began navigating her way through the field and I followed close after.

"It's my little box! I don't want the ugly butterfly pin!"

She turned, using her hand as a visor against the sun. "I told you, Clodagh. It's something a man would use, not a girl."

"Well then, why do you have it? You're not a man."

She dropped her hand, the sun bright in her face, a few insects transversing the air around her. She shook her head as if she'd decided not to bother answering, then started off again toward home.

"Can I look at it again?" I asked her, and she stopped.

Her hand tightened around the little package before she unwrapped it, breathing swiftly through her nostrils, a certain humid heat emanating from her.

I searched the thing uneasily. When I'd first seen the man's face it had appeared stern. But under scrutiny it looked sad and reflective. I gave it back to her impatiently and loped ahead across the field.

*　　　*　　　*

She got up in the dark that night when she thought I was asleep and fumbled in her drawer where the box was wrapped in one of her silk slips. She stood there with her head lowered, faintly visible to me in the moonlight, squeezing the box in her hand.

The noise of her breathing was exhilarated, full of uneasy expectation.

The little box enchanted her.

In the morning, feverish about the eyes, she sat in the kitchen waiting for Mrs. O'Dare to arrive.

When there was a knock I opened the door. Mrs. O'Dare had brought one of her nieces to help her carry bottles of milk and a sack of sugar, while she carried bacon and eggs and tea.

After the girl delivered the provisions to the kitchen she returned to the entranceway and looked at me with a coldly inquisitive face. I had seen her before. She was one of the girls who had laughed at my mother the first day of school.

"Hello," I said.

"Hello," she answered, her eyes narrowing.

A cautious silence followed. I kicked the banister softly with the side of my shoe and the girl gave me a disapproving look.

"Your name is Clodagh," she said.

"Yes."

She lifted her head so that her chin pointed at me and said, "I'm Letty Grogan." Mrs. O'Dare had mentioned her niece Letty to me before.

She pondered the stuccowork friezes of swirling leaves on the vestibule walls as if they baffled her.

"Look at this," I said, opening the dummy closet door. She gasped and stepped back. I felt a little thrill of advantage over her, though I had not predicted it or sought it. "This is a real door, though," I said by way of reassuring her and I swung open the other closet, showed her and closed it again.

She followed me into the parlor and stood stiffly looking around, then up at the shadows of the beech trees filtering the sunlight, moving slowly over the high wall.

"Would you like to see a great blue room?"

"Yes," she said, and I took her to the big room at the back of the house, opening the door and entering as if I were mistress of the place. She remained at the threshold while I sallied forth, feeling my figure ignite as it passed into great uneven sprays of sunlight swirling with particles of dust.

I knew she was watching me though I could not see her. I waved my arms and turned on my heel. The buckles of my shoes glinted like they were on fire, throwing sparks with every noisy step.

"Come into the light!" I cried.

But she did not move so I stepped back into the shadows and pointed out the stucco herons near the ceiling. She stared at them inscrutably, then all around the room. We strolled back out quietly and I understood from the manner and rhythm of her breathing behind me that she was unused to such echoes and such cold, expansive rooms.

I learned from her that she was ten years old, one year ahead of me at Immaculate Conception. She would be coming every weekend and sometimes after school to help her aunt, whose arthritis was giving her trouble.

Mrs. O'Dare and my mother stood outside on the porch talking when we came back to the vestibule.

"Can you stay with Clodagh a day or two, Missus?" my mother asked in a low voice.

Mrs. O'Dare shook her head resolutely. "No, Agatha."

"Then I'll have to take her with me."

She spotted Letty and me inside and lowered her voice. "Ye should not do that, Agatha. Come, Letty," she called out to the girl. Before Letty left she opened the dummy door again, pressing her hand to the dead-ended wall, examining the texture of the stone.

"What manner of madness is this?" she asked in a whisper to the air then walked off after Mrs. O'Dare without saying good-bye to me.

"Or just until tomorrow evening, Missus," my mother called after the old woman.

"I'm sorry, love. But I'll not do it."

When they left, my mother went into her china cabinet taking out favorite pieces and setting them all about her on the floor, forgetting to give me dinner. I ate cold custard that had been left from the previous evening's meal.

All night my mother haunted the foyer, opening and closing the cabinets, wrapping and unwrapping different pieces of china, loading them into a box.

In the morning she woke me early and we ran across the field and along the old Dublin Road to get the northbound train. We got off in downtown Dublin at a station near a cathedral blackened by exhaust fumes. The air was damp, oppressive, pervaded by a scorched smell that she told me was the smoke from grain cooking in the Guinness factory.

We walked awhile up a crowded street until the space opened up and we reached a spread of land, well camped by caravans and ramshackle linoleum and tar-paper houses, figures huddled around little fires that sent up smoke into the gray air. Dogs barked and the voices of children and women called out to each other. A group of horses stood together at the far end of the encampments where some traveler caravans were parked. Now and then a breeze sent the odor of manure in our direction.

"Phoenix Park," my mother said, stopping a few yards short of the first encampment. It was the horses that she focused on first before she raked the rows of caravans with her eyes. The harder she searched the more dismayed her expression grew. She placed her hand over her heart as if to still it, her face unevenly flushed.

I squeezed the hem of her jacket in my fist and she waved her arm at me as one might dismiss a pesky dog. We proceeded to walk through the fair, searching every booth. Finally she stopped and murmured to the air, "Too late. Too late."

I touched her arm. "Mother."

Without looking at me she blinked her eyes, a vaguely cross expression wrinkling her brow. She walked toward the nearest caravan, where a table was set up with hats and scarves at its back doorway. She stopped there, examining a green hat with a limp brim.

In the shadow of the caravan's interior a small child, a girl, sat on a mat. She had a smudged, serious face. One of her legs lay out before her like something dead, and she wheezed as she drew breath and released it with a sound not unlike the bleat of a weakling lamb.

My mother, holding the green hat in both hands, stopped at the sound. The girl drew air and wheezed again. My mother's eyes flashed a moment on the child then moved back to the hat, which she now stared at with a vacant expression.

"Do ye like it, Missus?" the woman asked.

My mother pulled herself out of her stillness, making an effort to focus on the crushed green brim.

"Do ye like it?"

"Aye, I do," my mother answered, picking up the pitch of the woman's voice and her intonation.

The child in the caravan drew in a hoarse breath and the noise began again. I gazed at her and she back at me before she picked her leg up like a bundle of clothes, then pulled herself along on her hip into the deeper shadows.

"Fifty pence, please. I can give it ye for fifty pence."

My mother did not acknowledge the woman, but seemed to be fighting a stillness that was taking her. Her eyes dampened. I touched her arm but she withdrew it. The child's uneasy breathing had misplaced the present with the past.

"Thirty p. then."

My mother opened her bag and pulled out fifty pence, exchanging it for the hat. We wandered aimlessly away and farther in among the caravans, her eyes scanning the grounds. She stopped for a few moments then turned to me and said, "Wait here."

She went back to the caravan where she'd bought the hat and

spoke to the woman. They leaned into each other as if sharing confidences, my mother showing the woman something in her hand. It flashed faintly in the daylight and I recognized the snuffbox. The woman shook her head and touched my mother's arm sympathetically.

When she came back, she stared ahead, leading me past the tables of tinware and crockery, and out of Phoenix Park.

We walked through traffic and went into a tea shop at the station where we waited for the train back to Bray. It began to rain. My mother drank her tea, gazing at a high window of grayed opaque glass, watching the rain run in rivulets. She held the carefully wrapped parcel in her lap, a strand of her white-blond hair stuck in a piece of tape in the wrapping.

I watched the rain on the window, too, thinking that my mother should not have gone back to the woman at the caravan. We had left, I thought, without stopping to see the crockery or to show our own, because of the disconsolate noise of the girl's breathing.

For days she was strange, looking at herself in the full-length mirror.

Once I came into the kitchen and found her, face rapt, mouth moving vaguely as if she were engaged in a conversation. She flushed and got angry when she saw me watching her.

A few days later a box arrived filled with crockery, each piece wrapped in sponge, heavy white paper and more sponge. They were endless, and various.

"Jelly molds," she'd said, trembling.

"Who are they from?"

She hesitated and said, "I ordered them myself."

But later that night I overheard her say to Mrs. O'Dare, "They were a gift, Missus."

Mrs. O'Dare remained silent as if she did not need to ask who the giver was.

"Nineteenth century, the note says, porcelain," my mother told her. Many of them were cracked, discolored, and each was decoratively impressed with the forms of sea creatures, like crabs and starfish and herring. Deep and open as dishes, some fluted or rilled along the edges, odd uneven rounds and elongated ovals.

They were more like seashells than crockery; white and cream colored, opaque but almost transparent with the light behind them, tinged beige or pink like they had once been the living cases of mollusk-like creatures, now perished or evacuated. I imagined the naked inhabitants come loose of their shells, freefalling along the water curtain.

My mother was overcome by this gift, and after Mrs. O'Dare left that night she held one shaped like a scallop shell in both hands and kissed it; then pressed its cool edge to the hot pink of her cheek.

· I O ·

I WOKE ONE NIGHT NEAR THE END OF SUMMER WITH MY MOTHER missing from bed. We'd fallen asleep earlier with the window open and now a breeze blew the curtain forward into the room. I saw the flash of a lamp in the field that led to the sea. I stared out until the light moved and washed up over my mother's figure.

The walls and boards of the upper house shifted and there was a muted thud of footsteps. Outside my mother moved toward the sea, the light from her lamp partly hidden by her body, except for once when it swept across the horizon like a diluted searchlight. The noises increased in the upper house, then stopped abruptly. Looking out the window I saw a figure emerge from the shadows and run across the field toward the sea, but because it had no lamp, I could not see its true form. I waited awhile but could see nothing else. I opened the curtains all the way and sat down on the bed.

It must have been hours before I heard her tread softly into the room, my heart writhing with anger and relief, her hair and nightgown bright with the moonlight through the open curtain. She stopped moving, spotting me sitting up on the bed watching her. The silence deepened, and as if my gaze alone sustained her there she seemed unable to move.

A moment passed and she came farther into the room, holding her forearm over her face, uncomfortable with the incandescence from the moon. She circled around the foot of the bed to close the curtain.

When she got into bed beside me she brought with her the night air and the smell of the tide. Heated and disheveled and full of secrets, she stirred a moment under the blanket then grew still.

I wondered over the footsteps, the heaviness of the ghost; how he'd made the house creak. How he existed so solidly in this world while Mare was invisible, no longer engaged in matter. But the curtain between the two worlds was flimsy, transparent. Ancient and as easily broken as old lace. Didn't the air that blew the curtains of the rooms shift and whisper with the susurrations of the dead?

"I saw you with a lamp outside," I said. "I saw someone follow you."

"Nightmare, Clodagh. Just a nightmare," she said, turning under the blanket, issuing the smell of horses and fire.

My heart raced with awe and fury. Alone in the dark, I had been practicing asking the question: *What does it mean, Mother, to consort with the dead?* But now that she was back, I was afraid of turning her against me. I left the words to burn in my throat.

I fell asleep soon after with the word "nightmare" on my lips, thinking of horses; thinking of my sister; of things half there and half not.

Two nights later I stood at the window of the piano room watching my mother moving afield in the rain looking toward the lights of Bray. She was grasping a pewter heart that hung at her breast on a chain, something I'd never seen before.

The door creaked open and Letty Grogan, who'd been helping Mrs. O'Dare wax the floors in the foyer and the parlor, came in.

"Look," she said. "You can see the fires the tinkers have built in the fields near the town." Little tufts of smoke hung heavily on the air.

"Your mother is a right odd one," Letty said.

"What do you mean?" I asked cautiously.

"Wearin' those long, lacy dresses. Walking the old Dublin Road with a twinkle in her eye."

I peered out at my mother's white-clad figure navigating the field in the direction of the smoke, her hem dragging after her on the sodden grass.

"How did your father die?" Letty asked suddenly.

It took me a while to answer her. My father had always been dead. It was, to me, his nature to be dead. "His heart," I said.

She nodded her head. "He probably died planting the seed of you and your sister," she whispered. "Your father had to be an insatiable man to beget two children at once. It must have killed him." She peered into my face, her large eyes watching mine closely.

"In-satia-bull . . ."

"You *do* know the things a man does to his wife in order to make her beget a child inside her, don't you?"

"No."

"I have read in my older sister's catechism that when a man marries he must plow his wife like a field, working her like earth to plant her with children." She spoke in a low, covert voice though Mrs. O'Dare could not have possibly heard us from the distant kitchen. "First he takes off all of her clothes, then he examines her relentlessly, then rolls over her and climbs on her and does all manner of alarming things to her. And then he puts the thing he pisses with between her legs and pumps her full of white milky seeds, which are the beginnings of children."

I tried to imagine my mother undergoing such an ordeal. If my father had planted two at once he had to have been a man that had known no moderation. My father had died with the great effort, and Mare had remained unfinished.

I thought of what I had witnessed between my mother and the ghost of my father, but so much sadness had there been in the struggle between them, I was certain that this was not what Letty was describing.

I felt a twinge of anger at her and had the urge to frighten her. "My dead father has visited this house," I said.

"Really?" Her eyes widened for a moment and she seemed to lose her composure.

"Is he here now?"

I hesitated. "No. But he could appear."

"Really?"

"Yes."

"Does he come and go?"

"Yes," I said.

"That dead father of yours has got to be what's wrong with your house."

"What's wrong with it?"

"So creepy and full of echoes. These big old rooms . . ." She looked up at the stucco infants frozen in the ivy, the blue light of evening gathering in the room. "He must haunt this place out of anger at your mother."

"What do you mean?"

"Because of the tinker man, of course."

"What tinker man?"

"Everyone's seen your mother with the tall tinker man. Where do you think she's off to now? He's in the fields somewhere and she knows it. He leaves little presents and messages for her at Mrs. Rafferty's." Letty Grogan walked into the shadows toward the cold fireplace and ran her fingers along the marble rim of the mantel.

I remembered Mrs. Rafferty mentioning a tinker, but she often dealt with the tinkers who brought her interesting pieces from estate sales in Antrim and Drogheda. And hadn't my mother been looking for someone particular at Phoenix Park?

I looked out the window and watched my mother slowly making her way across the distant field.

"I've heard she's besotted with him. Let's pray none of it's true. I've heard that tinkers do it in open daylight like rams and ewes." She pinched the extended foot of a cherub.

"Do what?"

"The strenuous thing I told you about. The body plowing and planting of seeds."

"My mother would never do such a thing." I felt agitated and ashamed. "My mother goes to the tinkers to buy from them."

She approached me again, standing at my shoulder and looking out the window at my mother. "Your mother's a pretty woman and a tinker man's not above plowing a good field and then bolting. Tinkers don't wait around to see what they've planted."

I shot her a furious look, then looked at my mother, who had stopped in the middle of the distant field, her head thrown back in the rain.

Letty Grogan laughed. "Look at her. She's sniffin' after it."

"Whisht your talk, Letty Grogan!" I cried. "It's you who's nasty and sniffin' after it!"

"Don't get angry, Clodagh! I'm only telling you what I heard."

"Why are you saying these things to me?"

"The girls at school don't like you because your mother consorts with tinkers even as she puts on airs with her hats and jewels, parading around like she's the Queen of England, above everyone else."

I stood stiffly at the window pressing at the casements with my knuckles, my heart in my throat. I wanted to cry. I wanted my mother near me and Letty Grogan gone. "Go away! Get out of my house," I said.

But Letty Grogan did not go. She stood quietly behind me and a few minutes passed in silence.

Something occurred to me suddenly regarding what she'd said about my father. "You're probably as wrong about my mother as you were when you called my father insatiable. He didn't beget two children at once. My sister and I were identical twins. That means we were only one baby split into two."

"That's worse. That's the work of the devil or a mistake of nature. A mother can never love both of them at once."

I held my breath. I wondered if everyone could see this so clearly.

She walked out of the room, the sound of her heels shuddering behind her.

That night I went into the parlor and switched on the overhead lamps. I opened my mother's forbidden drawers and started taking things out. Tangled necklaces, beaded gloves, earrings and pins. Folded pound notes and fifty-pence pieces. I found an angel shell that I held up in the light. It glowed like a bright edge of moon. Once, earlier in the spring, my mother had sat at the foot of the bed holding it to her ear, eyes closed, head tilted. She seemed to be listening to the voice of the creature that had once lived within. I wondered how such an eyeless, mouthless creature, a slug or a mollusk or a scallop, breathed, being composed only of salt and mineral and muscle. It must have made an awkward, stifled noise, like the breathing of my sister when she was in pain. The memory made me feel wild and insufficient in myself. Mare was a part of me like my fingers, my teeth.

I found the little watch with the garnet above the twelve that our mother had shown us one day not long before Mare had died. I squeezed it hard until I felt the thin metal bend. I let go of it, moving my hand carelessly through the mess of things, unraveling a small framed photograph from a scarf. It was of my father standing with my mother. He was frail, leaning on a cane, only as tall as she was. Letty Grogan was right. It had to have been the tinker man I'd seen my mother with years before in the kitchen. The tinker man was the barge of shadow that came and went at night. The one who brought in the night air, that left his smell of dark earth and horses on my mother's skin.

I remembered the little portrait of my father's face that I had studied so carefully after Mare died. I had sensed even then that he hadn't left a ghost. Not one that I could feel.

I sat outside in the damp grass that night, watching the fires in the tinker camps and waiting for my mother to come home. I wanted her to find the mess I had left; all the forbidden drawers ransacked on the bed and the floor.

From where I sat I could faintly make out silhouettes of figures passing back and forth in front of the flames and I wondered if my mother was among them, or if she was hidden in darkness, lying on the damp grass somewhere with the tinker man.

But she did not come home until the next day, and by that time Mrs. O'Dare had straightened up the mess I'd created.

LETTY GROGAN BECAME A FIXTURE AROUND OUR HOUSE ON weekends and summer afternoons. Mrs. O'Dare set her to various tasks and while she was doing them she sighed and whispered complaints. I hated her.

When she'd been cruel to me she had most likely not counted on being thrown so often into my company. Or maybe she had been fooled by my quiet demeanor and had not counted on the steadfastness of my anger. She watched me uneasily from across a room as she swept a floor or dusted a lamp.

One morning while I sat in the kitchen finishing my breakfast I heard Mrs. O'Dare in the hallway instructing Letty to collect and wash the breakfast dishes. Letty walked in slowly with her head held high, trying to hide her dismay at finding me there.

"Here," I said coldly, thrusting my oatmeal bowl toward her. She stared at it and didn't breathe. She turned to leave the room, probably to ask her aunt if she might give her a different task, but stopped suddenly before a crumbled bit of stuccowork design: an isolated cherubic face, oddly placed there on the middle of one kitchen wall. Morning light hit it through the small window, making it appear vexed. Inset directly beneath the cherub was a thick niche of glass, like a dark, distorted window. Letty put her face to it, squinting and peering as if she might see something behind it. She stood back, shaking her head with disapproval and looked again at the face.

"What an ugly, uninvited thing," she said in a soft, passionate hiss.

"You're the ugly, uninvited thing!" I cried out loud.

"Close your bloody trap!" she yelled.

Mrs. O'Dare rushed into the room. "Such language, Letty!" she cried, grabbing her niece by the shoulder. "What happened here?"

"I just said that this was ugly," Letty said, pointing to the cherub.

"It isn't just that. It's what you said before," I said.

"What did you say before?" Mrs. O'Dare insisted.

Letty breathed hard, avoiding her aunt's eyes.

"She said terrible things about my mother and my father, and she said that twins like Mare and me were the work of the devil."

Mrs. O'Dare squeezed Letty's shoulder. "You'll beg Clodagh's forgiveness."

I was surprised to see the power Mrs. O'Dare had over her. Her mouth trembled and her eyes filled.

"'Tis a terrible thing to tattle on a soul," Letty said to me in a wan voice.

"'Tis a worse thing to be a cruel liar!" Mrs. O'Dare cried. "Apologize!"

I was relieved to hear that Mrs. O'Dare thought it was a lie, and that such a thing about twins was not generally considered to be fact. It amazed me that Letty might concoct it simply to hurt me.

She turned to me with an anguished face. "I'm sorry if I was cruel."

But I made a show of not forgiving, keeping my jaw set against her and fixing her with a cold eye. Later that same day I walked through a pile of dust as she was attempting to sweep it up.

About a week after Mrs. O'Dare had admonished her, she approached me in the parlor and said nervously, "I want to ask you about something frightful in your kitchen."

I hesitated.

"It's that little door I found there while scrubbing the grime from one of the ovens."

I got up and followed her through the hallway into the kitchen and she pointed it out.

"There," she said. I had never noticed it before: a square about three feet high and wide, but camouflaged by the heavy cast-iron range that was never used.

She reached back and pulled at a small indentation on the side and the door gave way with a huff, and a cold dank smell rose up into the air around us.

"Where does it go?" she asked me.

I paused, not wanting her to know that I had always been unaware of it.

"I've heard that some big houses have these tunnels that lead to stairs to the upper floors," she said. "The gentry didn't like to see the faces of the servants in the old days if they could help it."

We looked at each other cautiously.

The oven had been set in front of the door and the two of us with great effort moved it enough that I could fit inside. With the bit of light that followed me in from the kitchen, I could see boxes and a few pieces of dilapidated furniture.

"Give me the box of matches on the stove," I said.

She handed them in to me and I crept all the way in and lit one, the walls issuing a black-smelling cold. Before me was an alcove where I saw the old makeshift bed I hadn't seen since I was much smaller; the one that my mother had set up that night for her and the tinker man. A storm lantern hung on a nail above it, and the alcove turned into a kind of passageway.

I went around two corners, lighting and relighting matches before I came upon a kind of window of thick warped glass through which I could see the kitchen and the wall I had come through, and Letty's back as she squatted at the entrance near the oven and began to crawl into the darkness after me. It had to be, I figured, the square of glass under the stuccowork face that I was looking through. It struck me as awful that someone hidden within the walls could see into the kitchen through that glass.

I heard Letty moving toward me in the dark, drawn to my lit match. She followed me into a final passage where we came upon a flight of stairs lit by a spray of daylight filtered dim and greenish by the upstairs walls. She followed me up the creaking stairs and we stood tremulously on the landing looking down a hallway. The air was cold and rang with a blurred, high-pitched echo.

"It's like the bleedin' walls are crying!" Letty gasped, grabbing one of my hands in hers. "Let's go back down!"

"All right," I said calmly. "But you'll have to let go of my hand so that I can light the matches." She clutched the sleeve of my cardigan.

I stopped a moment before the doorway to that upstairs hall. It was flanked by the heads and trunks of two armless stucco women, each about eighteen inches high. Like the figureheads of ships they emerged from the plaster itself, their hips, thighs, and legs stuck within the wall.

The figures thrilled me with their smooth, snow-white curves and their lovely breasts. Each one's eyes were half closed and her head tilted. Each wore an expression that could have been rapture or suffering.

I shivered with illicit joy as we made our way back down in the blackness and followed the dim shaft of light to the doorway behind the oven.

When we emerged we pressed the door closed and moved the oven in front of it.

"Our secret," I said to her.

"Yes," she whispered, trembling.

I looked for Letty in the rooms at the back of the house and spotted her in the music room, humming some nondescript melody, moving lackadaisically as she dragged a dusting cloth over the piano.

She saw me in the doorway and stiffened.

I smiled at her and she smiled back uncertainly.

"I want to ask you a question," I said.

"Yes . . ." she said.

"You say you've seen my mother with the tinker man."

She paused. "Yes."

"What does he look like?"

"He's big," she said. "In old clothes."

"What color is his hair?"

She blinked her eyes and looked away from me and for a moment I mistrusted that she'd ever seen him. "Dark," she said.

"Have you really seen him?" I asked.

"Yes!" she cried.

"Where?"

"On the Dublin Road. Talking to your mother . . ."

"How do you know that he's the one she loves?"

"It was the way she was with him," she said quietly and my heart began to drum. "She touched his arm in a certain way." Letty touched her own arm and tilted her head.

"His arm?" I asked doubtfully.

"And I saw her kiss him!" she said.

"On the Dublin Road?"

"Don't get angry at me for saying so, but if tinkers do the other thing in the bright of daylight, they're not above kissing for the whole world to see!"

Tension shivered in the air between us.

"Will you point him out to me?" I asked.

"If I see him. Yes."

We walked into Bray that afternoon to an area at the end of Carroll Street, not far from Mrs. Rafferty's, where tinkers went to sell their wares. A few caravans were parked at the roadside and Letty eyed the men. None was tall and dark haired.

"I don't see him now," she said. "Maybe another day." She shrugged and started back to the house on her own. We hadn't told Mrs. O'Dare that we were leaving and Letty was feeling a bit nervous over it.

A caravan rounded onto Carroll Street pulled by a big yellow horse with a dirty white mane and tail. The driver, a large man with a grizzled brown beard, parked it and got out, carrying a box into Mrs. Rafferty's shop. I wandered into the shop after him, feigning interest in a Waterford vase displayed among other crystal glassware.

"Mrs. Rafferty," the big man said warmly in a voice that matched the timbre and quality of the voice I'd heard with my mother in the dark, "here is a service out of the Coughlan estate in Antrim. The plates are almost perfect, only one chipped. And that's the lady herself,

Hibernia, in the center among the shamrocks." He smiled at her, holding one hand open in presentation.

I watched obliquely while Mrs. Rafferty put on her glasses and examined the plates and cups. The man shifted his weight to one leg and put a hand on his waist.

"These are fine, Mr. Connelly," she said, squinting, holding a platter at an angle in the daylight. It gleamed, the color of cream, a frail burnish of gold along its edges. From where I stood I could just make out the central dark-haired figure sitting with her harp. "Isn't she lovely?"

"She is at that, Mrs. Rafferty," the big man said reverently. He showed her a few other pieces he had with him, including a jelly mold the shape of a slipper shell, one I had not seen in my mother's collection.

My heart raced. This was him, I thought.

They bargained until they came upon a suitable price and the big man took his pound notes, folding and pocketing them as he passed me, and went out the door.

A man outside yelled after him, "What did ye get from her, William?"

Connelly smiled and shrugged in a gesture that seemed to suggest that it was innappropriate to yell such information across a busy road.

As he stood talking to his friend, I ran after Letty, screaming to her to come back.

"I think it's him, Letty!" I cried. We ran back onto the tarmac road. "That's him there, is it not, Letty?" I asked, breathless.

"Yes," she said, struggling to catch her breath. "That's the one, all right." She headed back into the field.

William Connelly climbed onto his caravan, his weight causing the hinges to squeak and the whole carriage to wobble. He reigned the horse out, slapping it lightly on the backside with the straps, and it clopped off noisily around the turn in the road.

He was the barge of shadow. The gentle giant in the dark with my mother. The one who'd left a secret message in the snuffbox.

"Yes," I thought, vacillating between pleasure at liking him and fury with my mother's secrecy and withholding. "William Connelly."

A few hours later, a lone fire burned in the north field and the smell of it set my mother on edge. I knew she was restless for night to come. I waited for her to leave the kitchen that I might attempt to go through the hidden door. I wasn't sure that I could move the oven on my own but I was anxious to attempt it.

But my mother would not budge from the kitchen table where she sat with the jelly molds set out all around her. She flushed when I came in and I felt her wishing me away.

A flux of anger filled my chest. "Mother, what goes on between a man and a woman?"

She stiffened and her face grew red.

"Is it something horrible?"

"Whisht your talk!" She looked at me warningly.

"Do you miss my father, and the things that go on in bed between men and women?"

"Such filth," she whispered, her eyes narrowing upon me.

I picked up one of the jelly molds, a deep one impressed with a decorative scaled herring. It was as if the fish had molded itself in silt and then departed, leaving a perfect impression. I held it up to the window and it appeared pinkish.

"Who gave these to you, Mother?" I asked her. "Was it William Connelly?"

She stood and began gathering the molds, her hand shaking as she wrapped each one in white paper and began to return them to their box.

"Who, Mother?" I asked. "Was William Connelly the man who used to come in the dark of night?"

"It was the ghost of your father, Clodagh," she said.

"No, Mother."

She looked at me steadily. "How do you know that, Clodagh?"

"I've seen my father's picture. He was only as tall as you are. The man I saw was tall. He was William Connelly."

She approached me suddenly and tried to take the jelly mold but I grasped it to my chest, confronting her with my eyes. "Please tell me!"

She stood before me, her lips pressed gravely together. I wrapped my arms tightly around the mold and felt my heart beating against it.

"Give that to me!" She pulled it away and the thing flew from her hand and crashed to the floor.

For a moment she didn't react. Then she squatted down over the shatters, touching them gently with her fingertips.

A jolt of agonized guilt shot up from the base of my spine. I knelt down to help her gather the pieces.

"Don't touch them! They're mine," she cried, lifting her arm threateningly.

That night in bed she lay on her side, curled away from me. My heart was swollen in my chest, pulsing so hard I could feel the blood at my eardrums like waves rushing the sides of cliffs. When I heard her long, extended breaths and knew that she was asleep, my heart slowed.

I woke later and found that she was not in bed. From the window I watched the field and the sea. There was no wind and the sea breathed like it was sleeping.

The next day when Mrs. O'Dare came with Letty Grogan, I told them that my mother was gone. Mrs. O'Dare stared past me as if she was not surprised. "Well, now," she said. "Have you had anything to eat?"

I did not sleep that night, waiting vigil at the window and listening to the upper house, but there was only a sweeping feeling of vacancy. I thought of trying to move the oven to go upstairs but I was aching too much with guilt. Trespassing into my mother's secrets cost too much.

Mrs. O'Dare woke me in the morning when it was still dark and insisted I give myself a wash over a basin of hot, soapy water, using towels she'd warmed before the turf fire in the kitchen hearth.

She set the table with my mother's white enamel dishes, the bowls filled with porridge, the pitcher with milk, and we said the Hail Mary to the white steam of tea and butter and oats.

"When the hound is hungry she forgets her whelp," she said under her breath, shaking her head, staring at the limited view of sky through the window. She made the sign of the cross. "Praise be to the Mother of God."

That afternoon when I arrived home from school, Mrs. O'Dare was waiting at the door. "Ah, Clodagh!" she cried out as if she hadn't seen me in weeks.

"I'll stay with you until your mother comes home," she said. She wore a red scarf around her hair, her face shiny with sweat. A veritable great-ship of sheets and tablecloths and nightgowns blew on a makeshift clothesline that came out the parlor window and wound itself around two beech trees.

She had put bulbs in all the lamps and fixtures and as the afternoon darkened, the house was so bright it seemed to float.

We sat down together in the parlor and she kept her legs up. "One must pay old age its tithes," she said with a sigh.

The room smelled of pine cleanser and polish. Everything shined. My mother's clothes were folded in neat piles on the bed.

"Maybe she'll not be back," I said.

"She will be," the old woman said with a single nod of the head.

"How do you know?"

"She's tied to this place, Clodagh. She's still stunned by her luck. Your father marrying her, saving her from the wind and the rain and the empty stomach. She'll not soon go back to such a hard life."

"Did she love my father?"

"She did, Clodagh, and she's still in wonder over his love for her."

"And what about her own mother, Missus? Why was she alone on the crags in the west?"

"You know I don't know the answer to that, love."

"But you do know about the tinker man," I said.

She fixed me with her eyes. How could she have expected me not to find out? As Letty Grogan had said, everyone knew. She reached into her apron pocket for a cigarette and lit it. She smoked quietly, looking at the window.

"Does she love the tinker man?"

"I don't know, lass."

"You do know, Missus."

Her forehead grew fraught. "I don't know much about what's between them, love." Her eyes moved unseeing about the room.

"His name is William Connelly, am I right?"

"I don't know, lass."

"You hold out on me just like she does," I said.

She looked hurt, tightening her lips together and shaking her head faintly trying to think of something to say.

"She's with him now, is she not, Missus?"

She shook her head again.

"She misses the west."

The old woman reached for me, her eyes wide and damp. "She'll not leave you, love," she said with too much effort at reassurance in her voice.

Her pity bothered me. "I don't care if she does."

"Clodagh!"

"I don't bloody care," I said.

It was a smell that woke me. An animal smell, but not the smell of horses. An animal of the sea, a faint stink of kelp. I opened my eyes but did not move. It was my mother, I was sure. She was looking for something on the other side of the room but couldn't find it. I remembered that Mrs. O'Dare had rearranged everything in the room when she'd cleaned. I heard my mother make a barely audible noise of exasperation.

She came toward the bed, the smell deepening. I'd smelled it before, I thought. She passed through a slice of moonlight coming through the edge of the curtain and I was stunned to see the garment she wore. A dress of animal skin, silvery, speckled in places, fitted to her body. The hem was fraught with something that looked like fishing net, but thicker, like dark macramé riddled with small shells, which I could hear clicking against each other.

My heart clamored at the strangeness of it. She squatted down right near the bed and was trying to open her chest of keepsakes without making any noise. On the floor behind her, the skirt of the dress lay in a clump away from her body. I reached down and touched it. Heavy silky fur so rich it left oil on my fingers.

She struggled with the key. It glinted in the bit of moonlight as she turned it this way and that. I don't know if she retrieved what she'd come for. I was lying there trying to decide if I should confront her, when she got up and rushed from the room.

I waited a while before I got up and moved toward the kitchen following the smell of the dress. I heard sounds of shifting and creaking. My heart beat reckless and loud as I realized my mother and the tinker man were in the passage behind the kitchen wall. I pressed my ear to it, their voices all pitch and timbre, his the more driven of the two.

It was the desperate breathing between them, the sorrowful mystery I'd witnessed as a small child.

"Christ Almighty," I heard him say. "Oh, Christ . . ." like a man who had been wounded. She made a low, keening noise broken by intakes of air that made me want to cry. I hated her in that moment. Resented her secrecy. The man, who I now felt sure was William Connelly, seemed overcome, at the end of himself. There was a soft bumping noise against the wall. She made the keening sound and gasped while he cried out to God. "He is the more human of the two of them," I thought.

She began to hum, to say "Oh, oh, oh . . ." I couldn't stand to listen to her. I couldn't stand the residue the dress had left on my fingers. I ran back to my bed.

I thought of how the selkie had been drawn to shore by the human man, lowing like a bull seal from his boat.

When I got up in the morning my mother was with Mrs. O'Dare in the kitchen. I stood dead still in the hall and listened.

"He wants what he always wants, but I'll not go off in a bloody caravan and freeze and get ill."

"No, of course you should not. I'm glad he's gone, love."

"All the baubles and crockery I've collected couldn't fit in a caravan. He tries to draw me away from the things I own."

"And from your daughter . . ."

There was silence and my heart beat frantically. I waited for Mrs. O'Dare to leave the kitchen before I went in.

My mother had a penitent look in her eye and she smiled at me as if she was sorry over what had last occurred between us. I moved cautiously, cutting a hunk of bread, looking for the marmalade. We sat together at the table and she watched me thoughtfully.

Her eyes warned me not to be angry with her. I looked at my bread.

"Clodagh," she whispered. "Come here to me."

She held me and my heart drummed so hard I could feel it in my head. I wanted to scream at her, to beat my fists against her, but I held everything in, hunching in her embrace.

Two days after she'd reappeared I woke at night to find that my mother was not in bed. I walked quietly through the dark rooms and, hearing the bathwater softly sloshing, stopped outside the lavatory. The door had been left ajar, and a candle burned on the toilet. My mother's head rested on the rim of the tub. Her eyes were half open and she gazed at it. I could see the locket hanging between her bare breasts. One hand was in the water between her legs, moving almost imperceptibly. Her knees were bent, her thighs open, each resting on the opposite side of the tub. She hummed as she had done with the tinker man. The water stirred faintly with the movement of her hand, the candlelight floating on its surface. The water sloshed as she arched her head back, letting out anxious breaths.

Her eyes opened and her face was damp with tears. She put a hand to her head as if to stifle the weeping.

Suddenly she was dead still as if listening hard. She sat up craning her head, her mouth tightened. I moved away quickly into the dark.

The next day she told Mrs. O'Dare that in my quiet look she recognized a bold and obstinate nature.

"Not at all, Agatha," Mrs. O'Dare had said.

"I swear she knows my thoughts, the little intruder."

"You're dreaming it out of your own guilty conscience."

"No, Missus. It's no dream. The girl's eyes are full of blame."

"It's sadness I see there," Mrs. O'Dare said.

"What's she got to be sad about?" my mother snapped at her.

The old woman did not answer.

There was a pause before my mother said, "The mothers of Ireland can't always take care o' their children, Missus."

My throat tightened.

"What are you saying, Agatha?"

"I can't take care o' her, Missus."

"Ah! I'll not listen to that. In a few days you'll be yourself again and all will be fine between you."

"No, Missus. Things are hard between me and that one."

"Why, Agatha?" Mrs. O'Dare asked in a soft, pleading voice.

"She tries to get into my skin with me and I can't bear it."

"Tsk. Agatha, she's a child. Your own child."

I woke again to find her gone. I crept from bed and, seeing candlelight through the lavatory door, moved down the hall toward it.

She lay in the bath in the same position she'd been in the night before. Her head was turned away so that I could not see her face. She traced a rose on the wallpaper with her finger.

The floor creaked faintly under my feet and she jumped out of the bath and rushed to the door. She stood before me dripping wet, the locket swinging between her breasts. Her arm flew out suddenly and I felt her hand burn the side of my face.

For a long moment she seemed to fade and I could see through her body. She was like a smear on the air, and through the insubstantial smoke of her, I could see the bathtub with the water still sloshing from side to side, and the white oak cabinet under the sink. I heard myself thinking, "I can see the end of her. There is the place in her that is nothing."

She leaned close to me, yelling, but I couldn't hear what she was saying. My face must have been filled with awe, maybe terror, as I peered at her, waiting for her to fade again like a ghost.

But she didn't. The burn of her slap spread across my cheek, over my ear, and up the side of my head.

"Why can't you leave me to myself? You're like a bloody ghost following me!" She looked down at herself, crossing her arms over her breasts, then went back into the lavatory and wrapped herself in a towel.

"Go to bed!" she cried, slamming the lavatory door. I heard her moving about inside, opening and closing the cabinet. She came out a few minutes later in her nightgown holding a comb. I waited, making sure that I could not see through her anymore. She was fully incarnate.

"I told you to go to bed! What do you want from me, for the love o' God?" She waved her arm at me with irritation and stomped off to bed.

I did not go back to bed. I went to the vast blue room at the back of the house and sat huddled at the window looking toward the streetlights that remained on in the distant town. I had seen the end of her. I could not quite explain it to myself any better. My cheek and ear burned. I grew hot like a flame shaking on a candle. I imagined her blowing me out and something black and darkly mineral-smelling wriggling away onto air.

I cried into the sleeve of my nightgown. A frail vein of light connected my mother's heart to mine. In the dimness of the moonlight with the world in the pall of sleep, I was certain that my mother was a selkie. I had seen her in her animal skin. I resented her for having come up from the sea with her incomplete humanity, her lack of repentance over the derangement of our births: Mare's insufficient respiratory system, and my heart, knotted with cords that betrothed me to her in a terrible way.

I wished now that she would hurry and go with the tinker man or back to the sea; hurry and finish herself. I wondered what would become of me if she did. Would Mrs. O'Dare take care of me or would I be shipped off to an orphanage?

I curled up on the sill. The window was cold and as I pressed the slapped side of my face against it, I closed my eyes and heard phrases of the "Sea Turns," soothing in their insistence and in their symmetry. The melody varied itself, deepening into something euphoric, rendering me, for a few minutes, bodiless.

I DID NOT SEE THE FUR DRESS AGAIN UNTIL A MIDSUMMER NIGHT when I was twelve years old. I followed my mother at a careful distance as she crossed a neglected field toward the Wicklow Mountains, the inland sky clear and brilliant with stars. Bonfires illuminated the hillside and a brisk wind rushed the grass. In the moments when the wind died, faint reveling voices rose from the tinker camp.

She stopped suddenly midfield and dropped the bag she carried under her arm. With graceful vigor she lifted the white dress she wore over her head and threw it to the windy grass where it stirred, then she took another out of her bag and put it on. Even in the dimness I recognized the silvery form of it, the pale shells at the hem catching starlight.

For days I thought I'd smelled it on the air of the house as if it were a living thing that had wandered in out of the weather and hidden itself somewhere. Its proximity had made me anxious, sick to my stomach. She rolled the other dress up and slipped it into the bag then sallied up the hill.

When she disappeared behind one of the fires I felt the familiar ache of resentment. But something was different in the feeling: a jealousy of what she was doing; for what she was about to enjoy with the tinker man.

She climbed gingerly into bed beside me in the early light of dawn, controlling her breathing so as not to awaken me. Soon she was asleep.

I got up and looked for the dress but couldn't find it. I stood before the big mirror, pulling my nightgown tight at my waist and belly wanting to feel it strain at my hips, thinking of the slopes of my mother's body in the fur dress.

At school the nuns had grown vigilant over our collective puberty; the air frenetic with confusion and excitability. They wore dismayed faces, found themselves driven to go on and on about the sins of the flesh and the role of the young Catholic woman to be guardian over her maidenhead. We sang the "Hymn of the Virgin" at the opening and close of every school day.

The day we'd received the lectures about reproduction it was in the convent all-purpose room where a large wood carving of the Pietà presided, the brokenhearted Mary holding the body of her dead son across her lap.

A nun called Sister David showed us graphs of the female reproductive system: the uterus, fallopian tubes, and ovaries depicted bright yellow and glowing like some elaborate light fixture in a dim purple sea.

Hazy, poorly photographed slides were shown of a luminous egg being rushed by sperm, or "frog spawn," as Letty Grogan would later say. One slide showed a sperm having broken into the egg, decapitating itself in the process. The next two or three slides showed the egg in various stages of bubbly mytosis.

This, we were told, was what sex was all about. This was all we really needed to know.

The following weekend when Letty Grogan had stood scrubbing the frying pan in sudsy water I'd approached her, dying to talk to someone about the slides and the lecture.

"Did you notice," I asked her, "that Sister David has a little mustache?"

As if her own mind was occupied with the same things, she'd turned to me without a beat and asked, "Did you see how it twitched when she talked about the sperm?"

"Yes!" I cried.

"It was obscene the way she pointed that pencil at the cervix. 'This is the course that the sper-sper-sperm takes!'"

I burst into shrill laughter and she went into an energetic tirade about the red-faced nuns who had attended, flustered and sweating.

"Another minute and they'd all have to have been carted off to the hospital for palpitations!"

Talking about it made me lightheaded. I helped her with the washing up, my hands shaking as I handed her each sudsy cup or utensil. We whispered covertly about things the nuns had not shown us or told us. She had a reliable source who told her that the first time a man puts his thing in a girl it hurts something terrible and that when they're going at it there's a great deal of moaning and crying out to the Holy Family in Heaven.

We made an agreement to try to find out other things about sex that we had not known so that we could share the information every time she came over to help her aunt. Letty came through far more often than I did, having more resources in cousins and friends. I was forced to look in encyclopedias at school and once came upon a picture of a fetus. It shocked me with its overblown head and praying hands, suspended like a sea creature in water.

Over the years Letty and I had grown easier in each other's company. Once when we were eleven, we'd walked together on the beach and had thrown stones and shells into the waves. After that I looked forward to her coming and helped her with her chores.

She'd often stay for tea and sometimes spend the night. My mother bent her head and put her hands over her ears as we shrieked over our shared confidences. Mrs. O'Dare would set up mattresses for us in the far room with the blue walls. When we were certain that my mother was asleep we'd share a cigarette, blowing the smoke out the casement window.

I'd seen the way Letty tormented her own mother, sneaking into her things, using her lipstick and powder and scent. Letty reveled in the animosity between them. Once she'd taken me in her mother's room and showed me a garter belt with a frill of lace along the elastic. "Can you believe the fat cow wears this thing?"

There was something in the battle between Letty and her mother that made me envious. Their animosity was full of recognition. They gave each other cautious, serious attention. They occupied each other's thoughts. I longed to elicit such a battle between my mother and me.

I looked for ways to incite her impatience and irritation, even while I suffered a fascination with her secrets. And now with the boldness of adolescence upon me, I emulated Letty, talking back to my mother, saying "bloody" this and "bloody" that. Calling her a cow half under my breath, looking for a fight.

I went into her drawers, borrowing her jewelry, or came home wearing Letty's mother's lipstick and nail polish. I felt a pleasurable sensation if she yelled or went into a huff. I laughed quietly with satisfaction even as my eyes filled with tears.

As I stood that dawn before the mirror with my mother so heavily asleep I could have thrown her soup tureen through the window and she'd not have stirred, I took off my nightgown and stared at my body. The tuft of hair between my legs was ginger colored like my mother's eyebrows and eyelashes, like the hair in her armpits. I was restless, standing outside the mysteries of sex but so close, the promise of it swimming in me.

Impatience caught in my chest each time I breathed. I wanted a man to be overcome with me as the tinker man was with my mother. "Oh, Christ," I remembered him saying as if my mother's beauty had brought him to the end of himself.

"Oh, Christ."

I had grown, over the last year, expert at watching her and remaining undetected. Even listening from another room I knew what she was doing. It was the temper and odor with which she infused the air; a faint heat or coolness. Or certain sounds she made: sighs, whispers, the hesitation of her footsteps. The springs in the bed when she sat on it or rose from it. The cough of the brush in her hair. And when she was changing I even knew which dress she was putting on by the sound it made as she pulled it over her head. Wool and crinoline and cotton each produced distinctive sloughing noises against her body.

*   *   *

At night when my mother'd sleep, I'd touch myself the way I had seen her do in the bath. The first few times I did it, it felt as if my heart had sunken down between my legs and was pressing hard against my pelvic bone. I imagined myself a tinker, and as if that gave me ease to be wild in my thoughts, the uneasy, fidgeting pleasure intensified.

The sensation made me malleable, and I attributed the sudden and swift changes in my body, my elongating waist and the swelling of my hips, to the heat that burned between my legs. I practiced it more and more and it transformed me like a glassblower's fire. One afternoon, touching myself under the covers, the pleasure built until it was excruciating and the muscles pulsed of their own volition. I knew that I had unwittingly come into one of my mother's secrets; something outside of language. I had opened an archaic door where an old fire was kept alive.

Early one morning I trespassed into the upper house, my purpose making me strong enough to move the cast-iron range alone. I moved slowly through the second-floor hallway, overwhelmed by the profusion of stuccowork bodies: naked white nymphs emerging from decorative waves, some with arms, some without. Sunlight filled the rooms and the white of the stucco made me snowblind. Flecks of electric dust swam and shimmered on the air. The floors creaked. The farther I went into the hall, the more the nymphs stretched and arched away from the walls that held them. Spines twisted. Rib cages lifted into the air, arms reached to one side or the other. There was a series of girls who held their hands delicately around their faces as if to present them in their rapturous states. Each was different. While one cocked her head, another touched a round shoulder to her cheek. Each appeared intoxicated, lost in the langorous condition of her own beauty. Parted lips, tongues stirring faintly in the shadows of white mouths. One with half-open eyes softly clenched her teeth.

Clusters of girls were decoratively interrupted by the bodiless heads of Bacchanalian boys garlanded in grapes, wickedly smiling. Not like the despondent, isolated soul downstairs in the kitchen above the glass niche. A few stuck out little pointed tongues. One was depicted smiling with tears running down his cheeks.

I sensed Mare watching me from the foot of the bed as I touched myself. What I was doing made her lonely. It was inscrutable to her. I felt ashamed and the sadness between us interrupted the pleasure.

"I'm sorry," I whispered, wishing her to disappear.

I was moving steadily farther and farther away from her; the child I'd once been breaking at the seams like an old dress.

On my thirteenth birthday I walked south of the convent school to a rock beach where I saw a group of seals lying on a large stone. Their barks made my eyes dampen; a fierce chorus more forlorn than the keening of gannets or petrels riding the swells. I was captivated by the way they slept on each other's bodies, restless sleeps from which they constantly disturbed each other, barking, snipping, small heads resting on glossy backs as if their necks were broken.

The selkie story lurked always in the back of my thoughts, though it no longer threatened me. It was less immediate, less real than it had been to me when I was small, yet it pulled at me, an invitation to mystery.

That night I looked everywhere for the fur dress, which I was certain was sealskin. I associated its brackish, unsettling odor with sex, at once repulsed and drawn, reaching into dark places, almost afraid to feel its glossiness against my fingertips and palms. I imagined being insulated in its warmth.

My mother had passed no secrets of womanhood to me as Letty Grogan's mother had to her. It had been Mrs. O'Dare I'd gone to when I'd gotten my first period. It had been Mrs. O'Dare who had straightened out the cockeyed information Letty had given me about reproduction.

My mother'd not speak of sex, like she'd not speak of her past. She pretended to be shocked at the mention of it. But she lived it. She reeked of it, preserving her secrets like jewels.

Finding the dress seemed a necessary aggression against her.

What she withheld I felt driven to take. It was my rightful legacy, I told myself. With it I might, like the selkie, hear the lowing of the bull seal rocking in his boat over the bedroom in the night sea.

It was in the spring that same year, a month or two after my thirteenth birthday, that my mother and I saw a tinker woman moving in our direction as we crossed the field past the train tracks. Mrs. O'Dare was in Dublin visiting her sister and we were on our way into Bray to buy food.

A few feet from us the woman stopped and held my mother's eyes with her own, which squinted and glittered in her leathery face. Neither moved. Time stopped without breath or heartbeat.

"Who is that?" I asked my mother.

A breeze came up and lifted a frazzled tuft of the woman's hair. She took a step toward us.

"Hello, love," she said to my mother. "A fine lady like yerself . . . must have a few pence for a poor unfortunate soul like me."

My mother drew in a shaking breath. The woman came slowly closer, looking me over once as she approached.

"A few pounds, love," the woman said.

My mother handed her the purse she carried and the woman looked impatiently through its contents, taking out the notes and coins and throwing the empty bag on the grass. She started away and my mother followed her, calling out softly, "Wait. Wait."

"Ye ought to be on your way now, love," the woman called out.

Still my mother followed, not taking her eyes off the woman.

"Off with ye now," the woman cried, fixing her with a cruel, rheumy eye.

My mother stopped short and drew air as if out of breath.

"Come," I said, but she waited until the woman disappeared past the train yard.

As we walked back to the house I asked again, "Who was that woman?"

She stared blindly ahead, pausing before she answered in a thin, high-pitched voice, "Me own mother."

*　　*　　*

The next morning she filled a pillowcase with baubles and keepsakes from her little chest and walked to the field where we'd seen the woman. She stood in the same place until evening. She did the same thing the next day and the next. On the evening of the third day I watched her standing in the field, her chest caved. She saw me but looked away. It didn't seem to matter that I was watching her; it only mattered that I was not the one she was looking for.

She had a mother. Any trace of belief left in me that she was a selkie was utterly gone now. Without that mystery it hurt me to look at her, the wind playing randomly at her hair like it might play at the mane of a horse.

She was waiting for something that would not happen; for that uncanny vagabond of a woman to return and accept her gift of little porcelain curiosities. When the sky began to darken she left the full pillowcase in a clump of grass and walked home slowly through the fields, her face reddened by the wind, tear streaked.

The next morning she did not get out of bed. I brought her a plate of eggs, which she left to dry. "Why don't you get up?" I asked impatiently, careful not to let any softer feelings register in my voice. She stared at me as if she could not quite take in my question. I made a frustrated noise and she looked pained by her own bewilderment.

That afternoon she came out to me where I sat on the porch and looked toward the sea with her arms crossed, distracted by the passage of clouds, the sudden inland noise of the surf.

Later I found her in the kitchen standing near the oven. The kettle was boiling so hard it seemed to be trying to inch its way off the flame. But she would not turn it off. She seemed fascinated by the sputter and panic of the thing.

"Turn it off!" I said from the doorway and she looked at me as if what I said made no sense to her.

I pushed past her and turned it off. She withdrew, ashamed, the steam having made her face damp.

*　　*　　*

The next morning I walked into the kitchen and found it dark. A tea towel had been tacked over the one small window and smoke from a turf fire clouded the air. I could hear my mother breathing in her sleep, long drawn exhalations trailed by faint sighs.

"What are you doing in here?" I cried, but she did not stir.

A stench of urine suffused the air and I thought of the old woman, her own mother, that she'd given the money to. For a moment I wondered if she were here in the dark with my mother. I tore the tea towel from the window and saw my mother lying naked on a pile of clothes, curled into herself.

I telephoned Mrs. O'Dare, who had just returned from Dublin the night before. She came and washed my mother and put her to bed in the parlor. After she cleaned the kitchen, she said, "It was like the buried bedroom again."

I told her about the old tinker woman, my mother's mother, and Mrs. O'Dare made the sign of the cross. "Jesus, Mary and Joseph," she whispered, shaking her head.

My mother slept for two days and on the third morning Mrs. O'Dare said to her, "Let's go to Rafferty's today and get you some new baubles."

"We'll go one day, Missus, but not today," my mother said.

For the next month or two, she spent the days gazing toward the sea wearing an almost imperceptible smile. In the evenings when the sun was going down, the riotous noise of the gulls made her eyes fill.

On an afternoon near the end of May I saw her playing a game with the high tide, letting it knock her on her hip again and again. Each time she struggled to her feet she'd laugh slowly and look at the sky, then rush forth into the violence of it again.

"Stop it!" I cried, running out to her across the field. "Stop it!"

She walked toward me soaked and dreamy faced, then followed me up to the field like an admonished child.

"Are ye my lamb, lass?" she called to me over the noise of the surf. I quickened my pace in front of her but did not respond.

"Are ye my lamb, Clodagh?" she called out after me, this time with a trace of penitence in her voice.

But still I would not answer.

After she hung her wet clothes in the lavatory and towel dried her hair she put on a nightgown and sat in the parlor, one shoulder pressed to the window watching the moving clouds in the darkening sky. Oblivious to me in the doorway, she laughed and hid her face in her hands.

She forgot the tinker man. I knew by her complacency, the weight her body seemed to be to her.

She was having a cigarette in the parlor, and through the smoke, which shifted and rose, hanging on the angled light like moving veils, she looked at me like she'd never seen me before. As if she was trying to surrender to the idea of me for the first time. As if I had been until now only a planet orbiting her.

Her eyes were shiny and amazed. A vertigo took me and I could not tell where I ended and the air began. I moved out of her field of vision, rushing from the room and pacing in the dimness of the passage to the kitchen. Through the wet of my eyes I saw the vestibule window dislodge from its frame and float upward to the ceiling.

I wished that she might ask me again if I was her lamb. I felt a terrible regret that I had not answered before; that she might not be so strange now if I'd only answered; if I'd told her that I was.

Two days later the air was pregnant with the coming summer. The tides were high, full of unexpected turns, roaring as they moved inland. An uncharacteristic warmth came in over the water and gathered in the rooms of the house.

I could not find my mother. A jelly mold sat on the kitchen table emitting its own milky light. A gust of air coming through the little window smelled of loam and cool grass, and a cowbell rang out from some distant field.

The shadows on the stuccowork face made it appear distressed so

I turned on the overhead light and watched it calm. I saw my mother's heart-shaped locket and chain hidden within the jelly mold on the table.

The house was still and conscious, a disorienting atmosphere I attributed to the advent of early summer winds. Reaching into the jelly mold I took the locket in my hand; its warmth surprised me. I studied it with fascination, running my fingertip round its shape, excited, slightly ashamed, as if I were touching something sexual and forbidden.

I heard a creak in the wall and understood all at once. The range was moved slightly forward at an angle. My mother was watching me from behind the wall, beneath the stuccowork face. For a moment I did not breathe, wondering if in the artificial light she was able to see the flush on my skin. I took great care that she not detect in any twitch of muscle that I knew she was there.

I tried to open the locket but it was stuck. I fingered the latch, picking at it, but it would not give. I went to the drawer and got a vegetable knife, pried it sharply, angrily, bending a flap of metal, disengaging a small screw, until the two hemispheres separated.

Inside I found nothing but a piece of broken seashell lodged into half of the heart.

With the thing dismantled in front of me I felt the irreparableness of my act. I played with the hinge of the locket. It would not close. I surveyed the damage a moment, the dent and the scratches, put it on the table and left the room.

I was supposed to meet Letty Grogan at the halfway point between our houses, on one of the dirt roads that led into Bray. She had heard that a boy she had a crush on was going to the cinema. She wanted me with her so that we might sit near him as if by coincidence. As I walked along the old Dublin Road the wind came up forcefully against me. It blew my dress up and threw me into disarray. Deciding it was too difficult to manage, I walked back to Mercymount Strand, pushed along by the force of it.

As I approached the house I saw my mother moving toward the sea. When she reached the sand dune, she took off her shoes and put them in the grass, then stood poised to play her dangerous game with the surf.

But everything seemed to distract her: the light changing suddenly; a man's voice calling a name, "Ellen! Ellen Colgan!" and a woman's voice answering and fading into distance.

She picked up something: a shell or stone or some garbage from the sea, then dropped it. For a minute she stood still with her head lowered as if thinking, then touched the spot on her chest where the locket used to hang. She looked toward the house and saw me there in the distance. Neither of us moved for a few moments, the wind wild in our hair and clothes.

She lifted her dress off over her head, billowing and twisting. It was carried off high on the wind. She had nothing on and, hit by the cold spray of the sea, doubled slightly into herself then moved toward the inland-rushing tide, which knocked her on her hip. She got up and followed the outward-moving water until she was waist deep.

I squeezed my fists and started to cry. "Go! Go!" I chanted.

Three times the water took her then dropped her. But she pursued it until she found herself carried along seaward. A wave lifted her dramatically, catching her off guard as if a man had lifted her suddenly into the air.

She turned and looked at me sadly, relaxing as it pulled her under.

For a long time I did not move from the place where I stood, watching the sea crest and move.

As dusk deepened the moon pierced the clouds and the sea grew calm and shimmered.

I listened, hardly breathing, for the distant bark of seals.

I went inside and sat down on my bed watching dusk subsume the room.

*   *   *

The ringing telephone startled me from sleep. I got up with a pounding heart then navigated through the darkness until I found it and picked up the receiver.

It was Letty Grogan.

"Are you asleep, Clodagh? It's not even eight o'clock, you fool!"

"Oh. Is it only . . . ?"

"What's wrong with you?"

"Nothing."

"Why didn't you meet me today? I couldn't go alone to the cinema! You botched things up for me with Finian."

"I'm sorry."

"Well, make up for it by meeting me tomorrow at half two on Carroll Street."

"All right."

"You better be there! Even if there's a bloody hurricane."

When I met Letty the next day I struggled to behave as if nothing had happened. And later at home when Mrs. O'Dare asked me where my mother was I told her she'd gone after the tinkers.

For days I thought of telling her the truth. But something made me hoard the memory. Every time I closed my eyes I felt myself rocked and lifted by the sea. Once while she prepared a meal I walked up behind her and touched her shoulder.

"What is it, Clodagh?"

But I was not able to tell her.

"You're so strange about the eyes," she said.

I wanted the words to come but I could not give up the mute closeness I shared now with my mother; the terrible secret no one owned but us.

"What is it, lass?" the old woman asked again.

But I just looked into her face. My head felt like it was glowing. I was an oracle that could not open its mouth.

Four days after my mother had gone into the sea the tinkers were in Killiney and men were sent there looking for her. That night from the north window of the blue room I saw a bonfire in the field along the Dublin Road, a figure crossing now and then in front of the flames.

Three lakes were dragged north of Killiney before I unclenched my fists and told Mrs. O'Dare what I'd seen. I woke one night to the distant shouts and the lights of the men patrolling Mercymount Strand looking for my mother's remains.

My aunts came from the west. A decision had to be made about me. They stayed with me and I felt it was a kind of testing, a trial period to see if they wanted to bring me back to Dunshee, to see if they wanted to alter their lives that profoundly.

They sat me down to tea to try me at conversing and they drilled me with questions of manners and decorum. I gave the correct answers but without heart. They tried to teach me to play card games. They were overly attentive, nervous, and sat up talking together late into the night. In a few days they wearied and when I woke one morning they were gone, having left me and the house in Mrs. O'Dare's care.

And so things were meant to go on, it was decided, until I finished at Immaculate Conception. In the fall when I was ready to go away to convent school the house might again become uninhabited or Mrs. O'Dare might go on with its upkeep and perhaps my aunts would find tenants.

Mrs. O'Dare's sister, Sister Veronica, the nun who had helped deliver Mare and me, arranged for a service to be said for my mother. It took place in the nun's chapel known as the Sepulchre of the Little Virgins, a chapel offshooting a long stone hallway connecting the convent with the school. The passage echoed with footsteps of students and nuns and the soft booms of numerous doors. The air was cold and smelled of sacramental oil.

At the altar hung a life-size crucified Christ; not an Irish-looking Christ, but dark skinned, blood spattered, with deep shadows between his narrowed eyes. His head strained forward from the cross as if to get a closer look at me, his piercing eyes full of mercy and immeasurable sadness.

A nun moved through the chapel offering us each the slip of a card with my mother's name on it and the words *In Memoriam*. The prayer inscribed beneath ended: "And I will dwell in the house of the Lord forever."

I looked up from the words to the statue of the Blessed Mother near the altar standing at a pinnacle of ascending votive candles, her arms open, one knee slightly forward under the hard drapery of her gown. Her face struck me as remote, while the many little flames surrounding her leaned and trembled with desperate zeal.

The priest appeared on the altar and offered the Mass for the Dead, calling my mother a victim of drowning.

The wind blew hard that night. Mrs. O'Dare had neglected to bring in the washing, and through the parlor window I saw the empty effigies of my mother's nightgowns waving on the clothesline.

I felt afraid that the curtain between worlds was not sufficient. Air blew things in and away and water exiled its creatures onto dry land and rushed away from them. It seemed to be the nature of water and air, to be random, heartless.

· 14 ·

LIGHT INFILTRATED EVERYTHING THE SUMMER THAT FOLLOWED my mother's death, washing and warming the damp old stone of houses and buildings and causing the wildflowers to come up in profusion.

I took to watching the tinkers; walking along the outskirts of their camps, looking at their wares. William Connelly was not among them and I was certain that it was because of my mother's death. I felt a pang for him, little blooms of affection when I remembered the gentleness of his manner.

Letty Grogan spent much of her time at the house, sometimes helping her aunt, but mostly spending time with me. The door to the upper house was unlocked and the rooms swept. The noise of doors whining and slamming in the drafts from open windows frightened me and I walked the corridors looking for my mother, wondering if something of her remained. But never had the house seemed less haunted than that summer after my mother died.

Slowly, and finally, Mrs. O'Dare, Letty and I aquainted ourselves with the upper house. The stucco nymphs looked giddy, too bright to look at, bleached as they were by sunlight. Cracked paint hung in big peeling flakes from the ceilings, pieces floating down on us now and again.

The third floor was badly in need of repair: the wallpaper decrepit, stained and bubbled, pipes broken within the walls. There was a fetid smell like dead mice. One day, Mrs. O'Dare, Letty and I discovered a large bedroom on the third floor with a single wall crowded from top to bottom with nymphs. These all had legs and arms and many were twisting at the waist, displaying their buttocks. In the center was a satyr with an erect phallus. Mrs. O'Dare made the sign of the cross and insisted we go back downstairs, closing the door behind us.

At tea after a long silence she told us that there was a similar wall in an upstairs room in Drumcoyne House and that the aunts kept vast tapestries hanging over the figures. She told us that some perverse ancestor of mine, a famous Dublin stuccodore, was responsible for the designs.

Mrs. O'Dare took the parlor for her room and helped me set up a bedroom for myself in a corner of the blue room. With the distance from the parlor, Letty and I, when she spent the night, were free to stay up late, smoke the cigarettes that she'd brought and drink an occasional bottle of smuggled stout.

She had already been a year at convent school, St. Brendan's, fifteen miles to the east, where I would be going in September. She'd boarded there during the week and had taken the bus home on the weekends. She had attended one of the summer dances held at St. Malachy's, the boys' school, where she'd danced with Finian Bourke, the boy she'd wanted to see at the cinema the day my mother had died. He was the newsagent's son, a tall, sandy-haired boy who we'd both seen in his father's shop and in town all our lives. They'd necked in the back of his father's car.

Finian was the focal point of our conversations. Letty talked about him and I sighed and exclaimed with peripheral passion. "Perhaps you'll marry him," I said to her, to please her; to keep the conversation kindling. What I did not tell her was that I too felt powerfully for Finian.

One rainy dismal day a few weeks after my mother had died I had gone with Mrs. O'Dare to the newsagent's and had seen him working there. He had grown suddenly larger than I'd remembered him being the month or two before, and his voice had deepened but was strained with the old higher pitch. He'd said, "Good morning, Mrs. O'Dare," and when he'd said "Dare" his voice had broken. He blushed and his eyes flashed to me and away again. A moment later two women walked into the shop. One of them made the sign of the cross when she saw me and whispered to her friend, "Agatha Sheehy's girl."

I turned away, feeling my face heat. I stood beside Mrs. O'Dare, who handed Finian money for the *Irish Press*, while the women went to the back of the shop muttering to each other. I met Finian's eyes and read in them that he had heard it, too, his own shame over his voice still pink on his skin. He extended his hand to me, offering me a piece of chocolate, which I accepted.

I recorded his breaking voice in my memory and would hear it in my thoughts as the petrels cried in the background, Mrs. O'Dare and I walking home across the field. I dwelled on his kindness and fed myself with the memory of his own transparency; those private exposed moments between us.

I thought constantly of Finian after that day. The summer air grew warmer, more lucent, and I shivered with the exhilaration of the world. I felt light, buoyant; in love with the new potential of my body, feeling as if I were about to discover that I possessed gills or wings.

Every Saturday Letty and I went into town and walked past the newsagent's window to look in at him.

Finian brought a date to the next dance Letty went to and she'd come over the next day crushed. He'd nodded to her but had danced each dance with the red-haired girl whose name, Letty found out, was Mary Morrissey.

We wrote a nasty charm against the girl: "Mary Morrissey, Mary Morrissey! Legions of the damned, take Mary Morrissey!"

The next week Letty obtained a school photograph of the girl, and we burned holes in it with a cigarette. We wandered all the way up to the third floor, thinking that we might find a frightening place to put the defaced photograph. We threw it into a rusted lavatory basin and ran in circles singing "Legions of the damned, take Mary Morrissey!"

"Let's sing the song in front of that devil in that room," Letty said, referring to the satyr.

We went to the obscene room, uneasily approaching the mythic tableau, the satyr's graphically depicted organ rising from a bed of thick curls that covered his legs down to his cloven hooves like a pair of woolly pants. He wore an evil-looking smile and out of his head rose a pair of spiraling horns, elaborate as the headgear of a ram. The two nymphs flanking the creature seemed to be trying to rush away, as if flustered by his presence. One had a hand on her forehead, the other on her heart, yet they both wore little smiles.

"Jayzus," said Letty, gazing at the central figure.

On the other wall of that same room hung a massive mirror in a gilt frame, the reflection interrupted in places by dark flecks. Through them, we watched ourselves gravely exit the room.

One day not long after, she came over bursting to talk to me, driving me almost backward into the parlor and away from Mrs. O'Dare.

"Last night I went to the dance and he asked me to dance three times, and then we went out to his car. He was hard the whole time, Clodagh! I could feel it pressing up to me."

"Holy God!" I cried, imitating her inflection.

"He put his tongue in my mouth. Jayzus Christ, I thought he'd choke me with it, Clodagh. It was so lovely. What a way to go! Chokin' on Finian Bourke's tongue. And listen to this!" She bowed her head so that her chin touched her chest and put her hands over her eyes. "He asked me if I would take off my blouse and show him my breasts."

"Holy Mother o' God!" I cried. The revelation caused me pain and I felt my face go hot. But I was hungry for details.

"I wanted to, of course, but I didn't," she said. "And I was torn about it, so later when we got out of the car I deliberately rubbed my breast against his arm so he'd feel it."

She said she was desperate for a cigarette, but we heard Mrs. O'Dare's footsteps moving all about the house. "I know a certain room she'll never go into," Letty said. We snuck quietly up to the third floor where we sat before the massive mirror watching ourselves smoke, the mythic tableau reflected behind us.

When we finished the cigarette she got up and put it out in a dark crevice in the window casement, rubbed the ashes until they looked like smudges of dust, then hid the cigarette butt in her pocket. She looked at herself in the mirror and pulled her blouse off over her head, posturing and posing. I pretended to be Finian, crying out, "Lovely! Lovely!" until we both doubled over with laughter.

"Holy God, Clodagh. Last night was bloody brilliant," she cried. We shared a second cigarette, red in our faces and damp-eyed with the exertion of our joy.

"Now it's your turn," she said.

"For what?"

"To show Finian your breasts."

I lifted my blouse self-consciously, feeling her eyes examine me. I looked at the floor and held my breath, my face and the edges of my ears burning.

She turned from me suddenly then fussed with her hair in the mirror. "Let's go see what's in the kitchen," she said. "I could eat the head off a bloody horse."

It was dizzying, my closeness to Letty. When we stood side by side at the window of the blue room blowing smoke through the screen, I found myself remembering the comforting heat of Mare's breath on my temple and the smell of her hair like dry shoregrass. I restrained an impulse to smell Letty's hair. Sometimes I stopped listening to her words, letting myself dwell in the hum of her voice. I wondered what she would do if I embraced her.

One afternoon we sat on the porch with little to talk about. Letty had not managed to steal any cigarettes from her mother. "Bloody cow hid them in a new place," she said.

It struck me that I might teach her the "Sea Turns." "Come with me," I said, leading her into the house to the piano room. "I'm going to teach you to play the piano."

She laughed and said, "Oh! That'll be great crack!"

She sat to my left and I struggled to teach her my old part on the low keys. She had little patience with herself but I was insistent and praised her each time she got something right. I was surprised at how effortlessly I remembered the notes, and even more surprised to find that I knew Mare's part, which I had never played before.

Synchronizing things with Letty was exhausting. She hadn't a musical bone in her body. "Bollocks!" she kept shrieking, banging the keys in frustration. "I can't bloody do this!" But I stayed on her and we managed our way through the piece, me squeezing her right hand with my left. The second time we managed through I leaned toward her and pressed the side of my face to hers. She started slightly but stayed where she was.

"Idiot!" she said softly.

After that day, Letty'd not play "Sea Turns" with me again, telling me that frustration was not her idea of fun. But I found myself driven to the piano again when I was alone, playing both parts of the "Sea Turns," amazed at my instinct to lead; my right hand, my melody hand, as anxious as Mare's. The flush of warm excitement I felt when I touched the keys overpowered any residual fear or uneasiness I had of the instrument. It seemed to respond so immediately to me as if it had been waiting for me.

I lost myself in the rush and ebb, the music quickening my heart and warming my skin. I let all the longing and exhilaration of that summer flood the music and ignite the walls of the room.

A few days after I'd started playing the piano again, I turned once and saw Mrs. O'Dare standing in the doorway with her arms crossed, listening.

"It's so lovely, Clodagh," she said, and wiped a tear with the back of her hand. She went out to the shops and when she returned she had a pile of old sheet music, mostly complex classical arrangements and a few Irish folk songs that she'd picked up for me at Mrs. Rafferty's.

I leafed through the crinkled pages, studying the barred lines and symbols. "But, Missus," I said. "I don't know how to read music."

"Oh," the old woman said. "Of course, love. Should I return these?"

"No," I said, taking the pile in my arms.

Among the pages was the music to "Clair de Lune," the melody which the old woman had taught Mare and me. I enlisted her help in deciphering the notations. She had some very basic knowledge that she struggled to remember and to impart to me. By playing the melody and studying the notations, I began to unravel the codes. Lines and flecks and ovals carefully charted. Maps to mysterious territories of feeling.

Letty telephoned me on a Saturday morning. Mrs. O'Dare was going to drive her to the Dublin bus in a few minutes. She wanted me to meet them and to take the bus into Dublin with her. She was bursting to talk but she didn't sound happy. Something about Finian. "We could talk all the way there, Clodagh," she said. "I'll burst if I can't tell you. Then you can take the bus back on your own."

And so I met them. It had been raining since the previous night and the sheep in the fields were sodden. Dirt roadways rushed with water.

We had taken seats farthest in the back, isolated from the other passengers, and when the bus was moving at a steady pace she began anxiously telling her tale.

"Well, you know how he locks his father's shop up at eight o'clock on Friday evenings . . . so I got there just at that time. It smelled of rain but I left my umbrella home deliberately. He was lockin' up just as I got there and I said innocently, 'But I've got to get the *Irish Times* for me old da.' So he opened up again and I got the *Times*. Some of his friends came and we all walked off together up Carroll Road and he started up with showin' off in front of his friends, smiling at me like a rogue, giving me a bit o' the blarney, tellin' me I had a lovely face on me, the two boys listenin' and laughin' and he was givin' me a kiss when the rain came peltin' out of the heavens and soaked us to the skin. The lads left and we ran off back to the shop holding hands."

She paused, pressing her lips together.

"What happened then, Letty?"

"And then we see this figure under an umbrella comin' up the road. Of all souls, Clodagh, who do you think it is but that ma-faced bitch Mary Morrissey. And of all things what does Finian do but wrestle his hand loose o' mine. Well, I didn't let him. I grabbed it, squeezin' the bloody life out of it, makin' sure that witch saw."

She sighed. "He said a quick good-bye, jerkin' his hand free. Off he went, Clodagh, huddled under the umbrella with his arms all around her. I walked home alone and got drenched entirely."

"That bastard," I said.

I put my arm around her. She told the story again and again in relentless detail, tears streaming down her face, and we resolved that we'd work another charm against the red-haired girl.

I got out at the station with her in Dublin where we had chocolate biscuits and tea in a shop, then walked a little while on O'Connell Street looking in shops and at posters in front of a cinema. Letty's aunt and cousin picked us up in front of the General Post Office then drove me back to the station where I got on a southbound bus. The trip back would take longer by half an hour, this time the bus driving through some of the narrower village roads. The rain had stopped and the air was saturated and overcast, yet there was a clarity to everything: the grass, the trees, the sheep emitted an odd incandescence as if from within.

The bus moved along, rocking slightly to the side as we reached the narrow, winding hill roads near Howth. I saw a tinker man coming toward the bus wearing an oil-cloth tarp, followed by a gray woolly animal that I thought was a small horse, then recognized to be a wolfhound. A caravan attached to a big brown-and-white horse facing north, which I took to belong to the man, was stuck in the muddy ruts on the roadside.

The bus driver stopped the bus and opened the door. The tall, broad-shouldered tinker man stepped on and stood at the front. He looked suspiciously at the passengers then turned to look out the window. The driver was of a friendly disposition and engaged the tinker man in talk as he drove, asking about the conditions of certains fields and roads.

"The roads further south are all mud from the deluge." The tinker man's voice, though reticent, was deep, resounding through the bus, causing a shiver at the base of my spine. He pronounced "roads" *roods* and he drew out the *u* in "deluge." His consonants rolled at the back of his throat. He ran one hand repeatedly along one side of his head as if to smooth the long damp waves of his hair, the gesture striking me as nervous. Two or three times he shot uncomfortable looks at the passengers closest to him, but quickly averted his eyes, leaning his body away and facing out the front window.

He emitted a dark grace: his whole figure projecting a fierceness. Now and then he'd turn to the side window to spot the wolfhound who was running along the side of the bus. The man was a giant of deep grace and feeling like my mother's William Connelly, but with a dark edge to him and younger, I thought, though I could not tell what age he was.

I stared at his profile; his prominent jaw stippled with two or three days of growth; his skin red and weather bronzed. Once he turned suddenly, his blue eyes sweeping the bus and stopping a moment on me, and I saw in the directness of his look an earnestness. I warmed to the roots of my hair, but the driver asked him something about the roads just in that moment and he turned quickly to answer, something about flooded fields in Delgany. He pronounced the place-name musically, holding the first syllable and saying the second two quickly.

I found myself thinking of my mother. All summer I'd managed to let her memory retreat, but the man's strange beauty aroused in me an uneasy, palpitating grief. I was intent on him, hardly breathing, my stomach pressing against my heart. He lowered the hood of his tarp and water dripped slowly from one long curl of hair hanging over his collar. I was certain it was from him that a smell of burned, wet trees traveling through the bus issued.

At Killiney a group of people boarded and the tinker man got off. He reunited with his dog, patting the beast on its side. In the daylight his hair had a coppery gleam. As I watched him walking down the road, I suppressed an urge to go after him. Wild unsettled feelings were aroused in me. I attributed to him a natural connection to me; I imagined that if I could be in his company, he'd recognize something essential about who I was and that I might see it reflected back at me in his burning eyes.

I could not catch my breath as the bus drove on, gaining speed along a smooth tarred road. When I lost sight of the tinker man I closed my eyes, and realized that my skin was drenched cold with perspiration. I heard a loud noise and felt a shooting pain on one side of my head. Voices called out around me but I could not understand what was being said.

I felt the motion of the bus stop.

"She must have fainted," I heard the woman in the seat behind me say.

"Are you all right, dear?" a man asked. I opened my eyes and found myself lying on the seat, my head pressed to the metal wall under the window.

"Clodagh! Clodagh, is it?" sounded a familiar male voice.

It took me a moment or two before I recognized Finian, who had probably gotten on in Killiney.

"I know her. She lives in Bray near me. I'll see her home."

He sat down next to me and the bus proceeded.

By this time I was able to sit up.

"Are you all right, Clodagh?" he asked me.

I nodded faintly, confused, holding my hand to my head. But as the bus moved, Finian's arm and shoulder pressing into mine, a strange calmness came over me. I looked at him closely, his eyes, his lips. His skin was pale, vaguely freckled, his eyes gray-blue. He was nothing like the wild copper-haired tinker who had aroused such a reckless yearning in me. I breathed him in, the warm easiness of him, his smell vaguely sweet like dry oats.

"Are you all right now?"

"Yes."

"What was wrong?"

I didn't know what to say. "I couldn't breathe."

"Did you eat today?"

"No," I lied.

"That's it, then."

We got off the bus in a village just north of Bray and went for a sandwich in a shop. After eating we walked along the beach toward Mercymount Strand where from a low cliff we could see a small herd of seal cows on the rocks below. We sat down in the mild sunlight, the grass beneath us still a bit damp, and Finian talked about his father's business and how it would one day be his. He spoke with a practiced formality that made me want to laugh at him, but made me pity him as well. He was more interesting to me when he was blushing, at a loss for words, or roguish as Letty Grogan had reported him to be.

The shore was raucous with the barking of the cows and the noise of the petrels riding in over each heavy swell.

A bull seal had come up onto the stones, his deep, rakish bark causing my insides to soften. Finian stopped midsentence and we both watched the massive creature roll onto its side. It was awful, I thought, how heavy and amorphous the bull was, how crippled on land. The cows dove into the water in a flurry and swam away, all but one, her sleek head breaking the skin of the water as she regarded him.

The bull's sex emerged suddenly from under his fur. Long and pointed like a horn and bright red as something bleeding. Finian let out an embarrassed laugh and looked at me to see my reaction. "Late in the year for seals to be mating," he said.

But I could not take my eyes from the bull. It slid on its side into the sea, skimming the surface after the cow. They flew together in the water, two graceful weightless shadows, twisting.

The cow threw herself up onto the rocks and he hoisted himself up after her, imposing his great weight upon her. She shifted and tried to turn, armless, wiggling, her head arching away from her body. Her resistance seemed to increase his resolve and I remembered my mother's soft protestations against her tinker man.

In a moment they were in the water again, all dark grace under the surface, the surf in their wake lapping and foaming at the rocks.

When I turned toward him, Finian's face was flushed and uneasy.

He pushed me back onto the damp grass, his mouth coming down on mine, one hand rushing up under my blouse to cup my breast. Once it was there he seemed not to know what to do, startled that I did not fight him.

From below us came the bull's wet, aching bark. I slid my tongue into Finian's mouth and he froze.

He jumped to his feet, offering me his hand and pulling me up. We walked together to Mercymount Strand, his cool, damp fingers nervously clutching mine.

At home I sat before the piano playing "Clair de Lune," my fingers moving carefully over the keys. The breeze shifted in the curtain and I thought of Finian, trying to imagine the act itself; restless, ponderous to discover it. But I was haunted by the handsome, uneasy face of the copper-haired man from the bus. The mustache around his lips had made me think of the hair around my sex. Each note I played of the melody felt like an exhilarated cry.

I practiced for hours that afternoon until I could play the piece in its entirety.

In July Finian went for a month to see cousins on the Isle of Wight. During those days a strange gravity came over me and Letty. We both grew sad, nostalgic, as if we had lost something. Late in the afternoons I met her in the top of the house and we'd sit in the deep-shelved sill of the long window, the sea air coming in at us through the screen, the sun some evenings angling, changing the color of her face, causing her to squint, her worn shoes on the floor, her bare legs pulled up to her body, her arms embracing them as she told me about Finian. Before he'd left she'd had another half-drunken encounter with him in his father's car.

She went on about his wet kisses and his probing tongue and how he'd tried to grab her breast suddenly as if it were a defensive move. He'd pressed himself against her and she'd felt it there, swollen hard, straining insistently at the soft corduroy of his pants. I felt jealous. Her readiness to fight him had aroused him more than my willingness to comply.

"It seems to have a life of its own. And the size of it, Clodagh! I've heard tales of boy's things and this one breaks all the records for size. And they say that once the thing has broken into you, torn away the little tissue, that it hurts no more and that such a size increases the pleasure, touching every cell of you."

Letty talked and sighed and grew dreamy eyed and I listened, my body stirring like something being pulled this way and that by the tides. And I'd close my eyes and wish that she'd leave just at that moment, that I might lay down in the last long square of daylight, my arms around myself, rocking to-and-fro.

"The only problem with giving in, Clodagh," she said with a sigh in which I sensed relief, "is that that would leave a woman with nothing to hold over a man's head; nothing to bribe him with."

I wondered at Letty's codes and rules; her ability to manipulate a situation. I had no use for such things. Perhaps it was missing in me, perhaps because of the animal nature I'd inherited from my mother.

We stood side by side before the massive mirror on the third floor and she unbuttoned her blouse.

"Well, go on," she chided. "Your turn."

I undid my buttons slowly, an uneasy seriousness in the air between us.

On the last afternoon of summer Letty and I met as usual to smoke in the upstairs room with the mirror. I sat on the floor facing the window, gazing after a passing cloud.

She stood in front of the mirror unbuttoning her blouse, examining her breasts. I knew she was waiting for me, but I stayed where I was.

A minute or two passed before she sat down next to me, breathing unevenly. "I wonder what it feels like to have your nipples sucked," she said.

A bird crossed the sky.

"Clodagh."

"What?"

"Would you?"

"What?"

"Would you . . . suck them?"

The shock of her words floated on the air above us, and then began to fade. She lay down on the floor beside me, her blouse open, her breasts pointing away from each other at gentle angles. She blinked and I heard her swallow. She fixed her eyes on the clouds.

The light crept over her skin, which appeared to wear a subtle powdery fur. I leaned over and took one of her nipples in my mouth.

I sucked gently, chastely, a calm, almost sought-after sadness taking me. A cloud passed over the sun and the room went dark. A warmth spread at the back of my head as if someone were holding it in place, though Letty's arms were lying on the floor at her sides.

The tides on Mercymount Strand rushed upward in peaks, calling out in whispered choruses. My eyes dampened, waiting out each inward-coming rush.

I looked up at her. Her face was turned away from mine, her eyes and lips tightly closed, her hands in fists. Dismayed, I hovered over her in the near darkness. I touched the side of her face with my fingertips and she jumped up, buttoning her blouse as she walked out of the room and through the dark hall and down the stairs.

After that evening she would not look me in the eye again.

15

A FEW DAYS LATER I WAS AT ST. BRENDAN'S FOLLOWING A NUN through a narrow, forbidding hallway. In a long dormitory room, my bed was one among many facing a wall of windows and the last gray light of afternoon.

Girls stood solemnly at their appointed beds unpacking their things and placing them in the small cabinet that stood at each iron footboard. Sister Vincent, a tall, pleasant-faced nun with a low-pitched, mild-sounding voice, told me to be in the chapel for Vespers in half an hour and then to proceed to the dining hall.

The chapel was dark and the Virgin's cheeks streaming with glass tears. I knew which girls were new because they stood, like me, looking around. My attention was drawn by the wistful isolation of a small, dark-haired girl gazing at the altar. She seemed to be listening closely to the chanting that descended upon us from the dim choir loft at the back of the chapel.

In the dining hall I lost sight of the girl, but saw Letty Grogan, who flushed scarlet when she found me staring at her.

I turned away and closed my eyes. Her face blurred a moment with Mare's and then with my mother's.

Filing back to the rooms I saw her turn into another dormitory room and overheard a girl telling another that the hall I was in was for the first-year girls. I understood then the melancholy air of that room.

The small, dark-haired girl had a cot right next to mine. She undressed, hiding under the tent of her nightdress, maneuvering her clothes off onto the floor. A nun standing in the doorway commended her and told us that this was the modest and proper way for a young lady to dress and undress, and that it was convent rule that we hide under a nightshift whenever we changed. Most of the girls were quite adept at the practice.

I was the last to finish, stumbling my way through the process, all eyes on me. I kept my face down, burning to the roots of my hair as the nun led us in prayers. When she turned the light out we climbed under the dank blankets. My pillowcase was frayed at the edge and smelled of vinegar. I remembered Letty Grogan complaining to me once that the domestic nuns, the uneducated ones who did all the cleaning and cooking, washed the linens in white vinegar. They did this, she said, so that we'd fall asleep remembering that Christ had been given vinegar to drink before he was crucified.

I was tired but the muffled sound of the dark-haired girl's weeping kept me awhile from sleep.

I woke deep in the night. It was raining hard and the shadowy figures of two nuns had come in to place buckets under various leaks. When they left I got up and walked about in the corridor, which was dimly lit by weak bulbs in wall sconces. To the left, the hallway continued, but was blocked by a door constructed of iron bars, above which hung a sign: NO ADMITTANCE. The rain tapered off and I heard the faint sound of a woman singing from some far corridor behind the iron bars. I wondered if I was imagining it, so faint was the sound. But it swelled suddenly, melodious and distinctive in pitch. I thought it odd, knowing that the nuns' cloister was in the other direction.

The eeriness of it sent me back to my bed. Somewhere in the darkness of the room another girl was crying softly. Listening to the rain hit the windows, I imagined Finian in the dormitory of his own school, sound asleep, oblivious to the weather. I imagined the copper-haired man, wherever he was, unable to sleep, lying on his back in the dark listening to the rain. I wondered if he was cold with only the walls of the caravan to protect him.

My third day at St. Brendan's, I wandered the maze of hallways past the dining area, and through a narrow window saw a piano in a small room. I tried the door but it was locked. I went to the principal and asked if I might play it and she sent for a nun named Sister Bernetta who gave piano lessons.

When I played "Clair de Lune" for Sister Bernetta she complained about my posture before the instrument and my hand positioning. When I explained that I could not read music she said we would have to begin with a primer. She showed me how to practice the scales, then gave me a little metal key to the practice room, which I strung around a shoelace and wore around my neck under my clothes.

The following afternoon, after a long day of instruction, I walked into a garden on the grounds outside the nuns' cloisters. Two girls that I'd seen Letty eating her afternoon meal with huddled under a walnut tree sharing a cigarette.

A group of wild geese flew across the sky and I pointed them out to the girls, who looked at me, then consulted each other in a whisper before one of them said, "There are nits and creepy crawlies in the first-year mattresses."

I forced a laugh and one of the girls said, "But you ought to feel right at home among the nits since your mother was a tinker."

My heart sank and as they stifled laughter I left the garden, walking along a pathway around to the front of the school, where, from a certain angle, the setting sun caused the windows to glow like sheets of fire. Through one I caught Letty Grogan watching me. When our eyes met she turned immediately away.

I'd believed something might soften again between Letty and me. But it sank in now that she despised me; that she resorted to saying the worst things possible about me. And it was on those September days that I felt myself falling, getting lost. I tortured myself over Mare, remembering how I'd abandoned her the night before she'd died, to look at the little glass dog with my mother. I was overcome by the pain that must have caused her, and the loss of her opened in me like a fresh wound.

I learned to read music quickly, almost eerily, I thought, the way the "Sea Turns" had come to me through Mare. Eager to share my excitement with someone, I telephoned Mrs. O'Dare and told her how well I was doing and she reminded me how much I'd struggled with it on my own in the summer. "You're smart as a whip, Clodagh," she said. "I'm not surprised you're doing well."

When I arrived at the threshold of the practice room for my next lesson the door was ajar. Unaware of my presence, Sister Bernetta played a soft piece of music, a melody resonant with both brightness and grief. I stood without breathing, the notes growing in volume, making small, passionate ascents. The little practice room seemed filled with an underwater light, the nun bowing over the keys, her copious sleeves undulating as she played.

I felt Mare pulsing in me, euphoric; wild in love with the melody that shifted, heightened into something searching, before the notes softened again and ebbed into silence. When it was over the nun sat quietly as if waiting for all traces of sound to disappear. She turned, sensing me there, now. I took a few steps toward her and looked at the sheet music: Maurice Ravel, "Pavane pour une infante défunte."

"I would like to learn this, Sister," I said softly.

"First the simple Bach pieces, Clodagh," she said. Her voice had an echo to it in the sudden quiet; her words short and staccato sounding.

"Sister," I whispered. "What does this mean . . . this title, in English?"

"Pavane for a dead princess," she said.

"What is a pavane?" I asked.

She considered and said, "Music for a dance. A sort of stately dance."

I played my faster-tempoed Bach piece poorly that day, haunted by the excruciating enchantments of the "Pavane for a Dead Princess."

One Saturday afternoon I walked into the reception hall just as a postulant was receiving a plant from a postman. She thanked him officiously, placing it on the ground, then securing and locking the door as he left.

"What a lovely plant," I said.

"A maidenhair fern," she said proudly. This particular postulant, Philomena Leahy, was thin and odd-looking, with a long, heavily freckled face. I'd overheard girls jeering her as being wandering a bit in the mind. She'd been reprimanded once for attending Mass in only black stockings with no shoes and had once been seen near the incinerator in the yard behind the kitchens dancing in circles.

"A maidenhair fern?" I asked.

"Oh, yes. These grow rampant on the western isles where no trees grow at all. Every few months a particular nun here receives one through the post." She lowered her voice covertly. "A particular nun who is from Inisheer in the western sea. She misses the rocky west something desperate, poor creature."

"She gets one every few months?"

"They keep dying," the postulant said.

"Why?"

"Out of their element here, I'd say," and she whispered again, "just like the poor nun herself."

"Which nun is it?" I asked.

The postulant's eyes opened wide and she peered at me as if she were of a mind to share a confidence, but then pressed her lips tightly closed as if to tease me.

She puffed up proudly. "There are secrets among the nuns, my girl, which I am not at an advantage to share with you." And she was off to deliver the plant.

I followed at a distance and saw her unlock and go through the iron door from behind which I'd heard the melodious singing.

One early October evening I had to wait for the practice room. The other two girls who took lessons practiced one right after the other. I was anxious to get in, Sister Bernetta having given me a little Bach fugue to play. When I finally got in, I hadn't been there fifteen minutes when the bell rang for evening prayer.

In the middle of the night I snuck through the hallways to the piano, determined to practice. I wasn't working on the fugue more than ten minutes when Sister Vincent appeared at the door, reprimanding me and taking the key. She restricted my practice hours to one a day, instructing me to go the next day to the domestic nuns for a baking timer that would go off like a bell at the end of an hour.

Walking back to the dormitory that night I imagined I saw Mare's shadow moving beside my own on the dark tiles of the hallway floor. I felt her sadness infiltrating my thoughts the way the damp cold of the evening infiltrated me and the voices and words of the girls.

When I was very tired she was the stronger part of me. As Sister Amelia taught the square roots of numbers it was all I could do to resist the urge to kick the desk in front of me or to throw my pencil or to scream an obscenity onto the air. Instead I chewed my fingernails, or twisted knots into the ends of my hair. Sometimes I would laugh quietly into my hands, hardly aware that I was doing it until I got a disapproving look from another girl or saw a few girls whispering, looking at me.

One day in Religion we read the Parable of the Lost Sheep: *"How think ye? If a man have an hundred sheep, and one of them be gone astray, doth he not leave the ninety and nine, and goeth into the mountains, and seeketh that which is gone astray? And if so be that he find it, verily I say unto you, he rejoiceth more of that sheep, than of the ninety and nine which went not astray."*

Sister Fatima progressed to the story of the Laborers in the Vineyard, but I read and reread the words of the Parable of the Lost Sheep, feeling moved by it, gooseflesh rising on my neck and arms, uncertain if it was Mare or myself I imagined as the lost sheep. Who, I wondered, would be the one to find me; the one who would rejoiceth of me? I could think of no one, and grew impatient with the hope the parable inspired in me, a little flare of anger beginning in my stomach. I tore the tissue-thin page from the Gospel, then quietly ripped it into dozens of tiny pieces. When the door was opened suddenly from outside by a girl who'd gone to the lavatory, the pieces lifted onto the air and fluttered over my head like ashes. If it had not been gentle Sister Fatima presiding I would not have gotten off with only a reprimand as

I did, but would have been sent to Sister Vincent and possibly expelled.

After that incident girls whispered "Heretic" as they passed me in the hallways. And one day a girl whispered "Daughter of the damned." I wanted to vanish off the face of the earth. My life had become unbearable.

At night when all the girls were settled into their cots, I imagined the copper-haired man holding me naked against him, making the soft uneasy sounds my mother's lover, William Connelly, had made with her. He would love my desire for him, I told myself. He would not be afraid of it like Finian was. Pleasure had a calming effect. Impure thought, word and deed. The things we were constantly warned against were the things that helped me go on.

It was at this difficult time while I kept myself in the throes of sexual dreaming that I discovered among Sister Bernetta's sheet music Debussy's "Reverie." A tender, glorious piece. Sensual and romantic.

The two final classes of each day, Arithmetic and Religion, were painful to me, my allotted practice hour following immediately after. While Sister Amelia moved in great sweeps and arcs along the blackboard, littering it with numbers and symbols, chalk dust flying, staining her hands and veil, I heard the "Reverie" in my thoughts, my heart beating high in my chest. I could hardly wait to feel the keys under my fingers; to feel the music enfold me and alter the climate of the air.

In Religion class Sister Fatima said in her soft, reticent voice, "What is natural is weak and unformed. Adam's recognition of his nakedness in the Garden of Eden is a moment of humiliation. The right instinct is to cover one's self. To be human is not to be naked but to be clothed. We are not born complete. We must put on God. We must have something added to us in order to be ourselves. 'Put on the Lord Jesus Christ,' Paul says, 'and make no provisions for the lusts of the flesh.' "

I'd walk quickly from Religion class to the piano room. The first moments before I touched the keys, all the heat inside me rushed to my hands. The keys warmed to my fingers, the music all tension and response. When I'd captured a cohesiveness in the piece, it built and ignited to a delicate crescendo and fell again with a sigh, so I could not stop playing it. Each time I played I conjured the copper-haired man more fully, my body thrumming as his mouth touched my temples, my eyes, my lips, until the end of the hour when the timer went off and my heart sank, finding myself in the bright, cold cubicle, smelling the cooking from the dining hall. As I got up and closed the piano, I steadied my breathing, afraid the damp between my legs had soaked through the heavy wool of my uniform skirt.

One night I heard the small dark-haired girl whose cot was next to mine crying. "Eileen," I whispered across the darkness, "what's wrong?" She told me that she'd received a letter that day from her mother that her dog had died. His name had been Murphy and he was sixteen years old. "Older than me," she said.

"I'm sorry for your loss," I whispered, and we sat up in the dark on the edge of our beds facing each other.

"He was a lovely, sweet dog. I had hoped that he'd never die."

"That's sad."

"It sounds funny, but I can feel him here right now."

"I can, too," I said. Her eyes fixed mine with the bit of starlight through the windows and she reached over and took my hand.

"Can you really?" Her voice was warm and full of yearning.

"Yes."

"How is it where you are, poor old Murphy?" she asked the air above us. "Is it so terrible to be invisible?" The sloughing noise of a girl stirring in her bed startled Eileen. She started to cry again, and neither of us spoke for a while before she whispered, "He was ill. He suffered in the end."

Like me, Eileen was often alone in the dining hall or when other girls gathered in groups. She seemed baffled by the other girls, afraid of their brusqueness. She was truly an innocent, pious, chaste by nature. I could not imagine her thinking an impure thought, and that drew me to her; that and her genuineness.

I was moved by an urge to comfort her. "He's out of his misery," I said. "It's better to be dead than to be suffering. He's at peace. I feel it."

"Ah, but Clodagh, we're talking silly. It can't be, can it?"

"Why not, Eileen? His soul is free now," I said.

"Maybe the soul of a dog is as real a thing as a human soul," she whispered, squeezing my hand. She was so strangely forthcoming, so pure in her grief. I felt my own heart burn with love for her.

After that night if I woke uneasy I'd feel her there across the darkness. I worked to discern her breathing from the sounds of all the others and it was the steady purifying melancholy of that breathing that I took with me into sleep.

I'd sit with her at meals and she would tell me about Murphy and about her father and mother and brother. And I was so grateful for the noise of her voice and for her crinkly black hair in its permanent state of disarray, numerous pins trying to tame it, and her wan figure and chapped lips, her naked, uncomplicated heart floating between us.

Eileen wanted to be a nun. We walked together in the garden, which was now dead in the early November cold. We sat on a stone wall and she told me how she'd received her vocation.

"I was planting flowers in my mother's garden when I was seven years old. I saw the little statue of Christ move, the one my mother kept in a grotto to oversee the garden. He showed me his wounded palm, and that's when I knew," she said.

"That's amazing," I said.

She told me that she longed to one day make the pilgrimage to the convent in Lisieux where Saint Thérèse, the Little Flower of Jesus, had lived in silence and isolation. "You're like me, somehow, Clodagh. I think you have Christ in your heart," she said. "You remind me of Saint Thérèse of Lisieux."

"You can't think I'm like Saint Thérèse!" I cried, surprised.

"Therese had many imperfections, Clodagh. She was full of pride and selfish at times. She even told lies. But she still overcame her littleness and became a great saint. You have a greatness of heart in you, too."

I smiled inside, moved by her innocence, her readiness to see me in such a misguided way.

"The ideal marriage is the marriage to Christ. Don't you think so, Clodagh?" She looked so earnestly at me that I could not disappoint her.

"Yes, Eileen," I said. "It is the ideal marriage."

I was stunned one day to receive a letter from Finian asking me to meet him during the Christmas holiday. He promised to call for me at Mercymount Strand. The letter was filled with small talk about his school, which I supposed he thought was obligatory. I skipped over that and read again and again his request to see me. I folded and unfolded it so many times that the paper began to soften and fray with the moisture of my fingers.

I showed the letter to Eileen, unable to contain my exhilaration and impatience.

"Are you in love with him?" she asked me.

"No!" I cried.

"You seem so anxious over him."

"I'm not," I said.

She asked me if I really believed that the ideal marriage was a marriage to Christ.

I said yes, but she felt the falseness of my answer, and her look of disapproval weighed heavily in my body.

At the evening meal she was distant. Nervous of losing her, I tried to engage her, asking her to tell me more about the sins and vocation of Thérèse of Lisieux. But she was distracted and after the meal parted with me in the gallery, saying that she needed to pray.

16

Much to my despair I had to stay at St. Brendan's for the Christmas holiday, Mrs. O'Dare having gone to her sister in Dublin. I was certain that ordinarily I would have been invited but I knew that Letty Grogan had had a hand in my being left out. Mrs. O'Dare sent me chocolates, a box of new stockings and knickers, and a new pair of shoes. In her letter she apologized and promised that she would telephone soon and we would make arrangements for me to visit Mercymount Strand for a weekend soon. But I felt furious and abandoned.

I wrote to Finian in care of his father's shop and asked him to come to me at St. Brendan's. I did not have a pound left to my name so I could not take a bus or a train anywhere, and the nuns would not have let me go if I had. I surmised that Mrs. O'Dare had sent me no money because she thought it safer that I be trapped in the convent than have means to go off somewhere. This thought doubled my fury and frustration.

The weather was disastrous, freezing rain and dismal skies. The great empty rooms of St. Brendan's were full of echoes and the walls issued odors of mildew. For days I waited for word, practicing the piano, struggling with a Bach Invention that Sister Bernetta had given me to challenge and occupy me over the lonely holiday. I found the sheet music to "Pavane for a Dead Princess," but was afraid to try it, afraid to even remember the exquisite pain it aroused.

When I wasn't at the piano I was lying on my cot in the empty dormitory watching the rain beat at the window, or in the vacant classrooms watching the bit of road I could see through the trees below, praying that any distant male figure was Finian's.

Two days before Christmas I despaired of hearing from him. Sister Vincent gave me permission to telephone my aunts in the west to ask if I might visit. The request took Aunt Lily very much off guard. She said she'd speak to Aunt Kitty, who had not been well, and that she'd telephone Sister Vincent with an answer.

On Christmas Eve an area of sky brightened strangely and the nuns gathered on the stone steps in front of the school looking expectantly into the light as if they were about to witness some proof of their faith. When that area of sky closed, their dark figures drifted off in different directions.

My heart stopped when I saw a wolfhound sniffing the dead grass outside the iron gate. I pressed my hands and face to the creaky glass of the window, fogging it so I had to move to see. There on the road, under the dead and dripping trees, one of the old domestic nuns, Sister Mary, stood talking to the copper-haired man. The caravan, on the roadside behind him, wobbled on its hinges as the horse shifted its haunches. The man was wearing a pale leather coat worn at the seams and faded blue jeans. A wind came up and his disheveled hair blew all about his face. Sister Mary drew her heavy black cardigan close around herself.

The man handed her a large tin pot, which she examined while he spoke emphatically to her, pointing at its various features, then running her hand over it. She set it down and reached deeply into the pocket of her apron, drawing out a few coins that she counted before giving them to him.

I rushed down the staircase and out the front door. She was locking the gate in the cold wind, robes and veil flying, the tin pot on the ground near her feet.

"Sister, can you open the gate, please?" I asked her. I could see the back of the caravan moving up the road and hear the horse's feet clopping on the tarmac. I had no idea what I might say to the man, yet I felt desperate to go after him.

"You need Sister Vincent's permission," she said, startled by my urgency. "Do you have Sister Vincent's permission to go out?" she asked.

My mistake was that I hesitated before saying yes, and she refused to unlock the gate for me.

"Let's just go speak to Sister Vincent," she said.

"Please, Sister!" I cried.

"I'll be happy to open the gate for you, dear, once we've spoken to Sister Vincent."

I rushed into the school ahead of her looking for Sister Vincent, up and down the corridors, breathless. "She allows me to go out," I screeched, angry tears in my voice. "She allows me to browse in shops!"

I intruded into the nuns' quarters, throwing doors open onto private cells; each one a sparse little room with only a cot and a crucifix. Sister Mary could not keep up and had stopped running after me, remaining at the foot of the hall.

Through a window at the end of the corridor I could see the brown-and-white horse pulling the man's caravan at a steady jog along the two-way northbound road, cars racing past.

Sister Vincent appeared but I had stopped now, already despairing. I did not know what I would have said to the man, yet I imagined that such a chance might never come again.

From where I was panting at the window, I could discern their whispers through my panting.

"She's all alone this Christmas. . . . She's waiting on a telephone call from her aunts."

I heard the firm, clunking echoes of Sister Vincent's nailed shoes as she approached me. "Clodagh, I have not yet heard from your aunts. Shall we ring them again this evening?"

"No," I said. "Don't ring them."

I walked with her slowly out of the nuns' quarters. Sister Mary, clutching the copper-haired man's pot, gave me a pitying smile.

In the middle of the night I fled from the dormitory to the kitchens of the domestic nuns, who were awake at all hours baking. I wanted to be near Sister Mary, who had touched the copper-haired man's hand. I wanted to hold the pot she had bought from him. Since the incident in the afternoon, Sister Mary had grown important in my thoughts because of her contact with the tinker man. Through a maze of forbidden corridors I followed the smell of stale cake and baking flour and the faint noises of faucets running and spoons hitting against metal bowls.

She was there, looking at me with dismay at first and I knew by the way that she gestured to the other nun and pointed at me that they were keeping a vow of silence while they worked.

Sister Mary pointed at a chair and I sat with them. Under her silent instructions I placed cakes of yeast in tepid water and helped to knead dough. In the course of hours, lumps of dough rose in bowls under damp towels and were formed into loaves, then placed on pallets in a great system of ovens that looked like a blackened dresser of drawers.

All the time I watched her and saw her softening toward me; curiosity and pity in her face.

On the wall across from the ovens, enclosed in a wooden frame, was a picture of the Annunciation, bubbled and curled from years of oven heat and humidity. The glass of the frame was cloudy as if faintly layered with grease. The Virgin knelt at a podium turning away from an open book, hands and forearms lifted with surprise as she regarded the Holy Ghost at her shoulder, a white dove with a golden halo.

While the nuns cut flour or swept it from boards or scrubbed bowls, or read their novenas, waiting for the baking bread, keeping the silence until 5 A.M. Mass, I contemplated the picture.

If I moved my head at a certain angle, the bright overhead light pooled on the glass, obscuring the image from my view. I remembered Sister Fatima's words about the Annunciation: "The Holy Ghost, in the form of the dove, impregnated the Virgin by entering through the ear. Thus she conceived of the Lord, remaining Virgo Purissima. Uncontaminated."

I tried to sleep in the chair, my head on my arm on the table. My eyes were almost closed so all I saw were the shadows of the nuns moving on the dull shine of the tiled floor. As I began to drift to sleep I saw, as if in a dream, the dove entering through the Virgin's ear with a rustling of wings and a terrible struggle. The Virgin's face grew ago-nized and a stream of blood fell from her ear.

I sat up panting, feeling afraid for Mare; afraid of invisible things that drifted on air. The nuns stopped their cleaning up when they saw me crying. Sister Mary sat down with me and held my hand. There was no point, I thought, in trying to explain my tears. I leaned my head against her shoulder. Her habit smelled of cut pine, like it had been stored in a new cabinet.

I followed her to Christmas Mass at 5 A.M. The chapel was lit only by the votives at the feet of the Virgin, and by the two heavy white altar candles on gold stands at either side of the Eucharist. A postulant swung the censer and the incense made my tired eyes tear. I copied Sister Mary's gestures, beating my heart softly with my fist.

As Sister Bernetta began to play the organ, a small nun was wheeled forward out of the shadows. From where I sat I couldn't see her clearly, only that she was small and misshapen. Her voice was exquisite in the acoustics of the chapel: like one angelic voice with three dimmer replicas following after it. It was the voice I'd heard from behind the iron gate. It moved in registers with the fluidity of water, each wave of the vibrato almost languid. In the lower registers it was dark, dramatic; at moments almost guttural in its conviction. I closed my eyes, struggling to translate the Latin words, but understood only one full phrase: *"Ad te omnis caro veniet."* "All flesh shall come to Thee."

I knew what animated this voice. I understood in my body that the small crippled figure was singing out of her own incompleteness.

In early light, mist hung over the dead grass in the courtyard and I ascended the stairs to the dormitory where I fell into an exhausted sleep.

The next day I saw two caravans of tinkers pass in the rain. It was with a mysterious nostalgia, as if I had once lived their life, that I gazed at the men driving with lowered heads, the fierce patient faces of the women. I envied the young girls with their wet, tangled hair and mud-spattered dresses weathering the rain with the resignation of horses.

Sister Mary came suddenly into the room to tell me that Sister Vincent had spoken to Lily Sheehy, who apologized, saying that her sister Kitty was too ill right now.

I looked away from her and back at the tinkers passing up the road. "There's a lot of tinkers around these past few days," I said.

"They gather here this time of year," she said, "to sell their things."

"I'd like to go to them. To see what they have."

"In this miserable weather?"

"Please, Sister. Will you take me?"

In the light from the window, downy white hair showed on her cheeks and on the soft folds of her chin. Cataracts made her eyes a dark, cloudy color, and I felt as if her focus was just past my shoulder.

"All right, then," she said. "Go get your boots and coat and we'll walk into town."

When we reached the gathering of caravans the rain had stopped. I saw him immediately under a makeshift awning that extended from his caravan, shielding his wares from the weather. He stood with his back against his caravan, his arms crossed at his chest, watching the passing people with a still face that expressed both disdain and resignation. Sister Mary did not notice him. She was drawn to a woman's display of holy medals taped to a sheet of cardboard.

"I'll just look around a little," I said, and she nodded. I moved slowly in the direction of the copper-haired man's display where a man and woman were examining a tin pot with a decorative metal coil soldered to its rim.

"Where'd you get this?" the dark-haired man asked. He was clearly a city man, well groomed, the collar of a gray tweed jacket showing from under his overcoat. The woman with him wore a smart-looking hat with a blue feather on it and a tailored raincoat.

"I made that," the tinker man's voice came from the shadow under the tarp.

"This looks old," the well-groomed man said. "Iron Age. Like it was dug out of a bog."

"I made that," the tinker man said again.

As the couple swept past me I heard the man say under his breath, "He seems a relic of the Iron Age himself." The woman's red lips puckered, suppressing a laugh.

Sensing their condescension, the copper-haired man also said something under his breath. I moved slowly to his table and stopped before it, my heart wild, and stared at the pieces on display: beaten tinware and a few pieces of crockery. The rain began again softly.

I felt the man's eyes on me but couldn't bring myself to look at him. I kept my head lowered, watching drips fall from the ends of my hair. Someone approached, picked up one of the pots on the table and asked for a price. I moved woodenly away and back to Sister Mary's side. When I'd regained my composure I turned toward him and met his eyes. There was no disdain in them now, but a thoughtfulness as if he sensed the hammering in my heart; as if he sensed how at sea I was in the world.

"Sister," I asked as we walked back to St. Brendan's, "do you think Sister Bernetta has any sheet music from the Iron Age?"

The old nun laughed. "Ah, Clodagh, that's precious."

"When was the Iron Age?" I asked awkwardly.

"Ancient times, Clodagh. I can't even say myself. Ancient times." And she laughed again and peered at me and through me with her cloudy eyes until I felt Mare twitching in my side.

I returned to the fair the next two days, but the tinker man was gone.

17

In early January, the noisy tyranny of the returning girls sharing the events of their holiday with one another, showing off new sweaters or ribbons or books, was a relief to me.

When I told Eileen that Mrs. O'Dare had not come for me, she asked, "So you did not see the boy?"

"No," I answered.

"That was the Holy Mother intervening in a dangerous situation. Don't you see how she preserved you?"

She told me excitedly that her brother and his girlfriend had announced their engagement and they'd had a party with a lot of friends and relations. And on Christmas morning there had been a brief snow flurry that was miraculous proof, she said, of God's love. Her parents had given her a copy of *The Story of a Soul,* Thérèse of Lisieux's autobiography.

"I've read it cover to cover," she said. "And now I'm giving it to you to read, Clodagh."

I studied the sepia image of the sweet-faced Thérèse in her nun's layers on the book's cover. I leafed through and read randomly. I found passages marked and my name written near them in Eileen's hand in the margins.

One such passage read: "I feel that if, supposing the impossible, you could find a soul more weak than mine, you would delight in lavishing upon it far more graces still, so long as it abandoned itself with boundless confidence to your infinite mercy."

I was moved that Eileen's thoughts were so much with me but I felt far away from the words of the saint.

I kept the book on top of the cupboard at the foot of my bed, but weeks passed and I did not touch it. She asked me repeatedly if I'd read the book and I grew tired of the deception.

"Eileen," I said one afternoon as we sat on our beds facing each other, "I don't really think about being a nun."

She gazed at me, distressed.

"I'm not good, Eileen. Not in the way that you are." I said it pleadingly, wanting her to accept the truth of me. "I did want to be with that boy."

"Clodagh, Thérèse talks in this book about her own sinful, stubborn nature and all she had to overcome for Christ. It makes you no less beloved of God."

"I'm not beloved of God . . ." I said, letting out a little laugh at her innocence.

"Oh, Clodagh! It can happen in an instant. Jesus can flood the darkness of your soul with torrents of light. You are His precious daughter," she said, and touched my face.

"No, Eileen. I want to be your friend but I don't want to talk about Thérèse of Lisieux or Jesus flooding my soul with light," I said, watching her face darken.

Over the next weeks we grew more separate. I was granted more hours at the piano and while I spent most of my time in the practice room, Eileen was in the chapel. The nuns awakened her at four-thirty for nuns' Mass. She offered little mortifications of the flesh, skipping meals, lying prone on the cold chapel floor for hours at a time.

Still, we ate our meals together and sometimes walked on the grounds. One day when the weather was wet, we sat on the vestibule steps talking. "The day I am married to Christ, the world will look different to me, Clodagh," she said. "He gives me little glimpses. . . ."

"Christ does?" I asked.

"Yes." She leaned in close to me and shivered as she said, "Last night I woke up and saw the Holy Ghost suspended above my bed."

"Are you afraid?" I asked.

"All brides are nervous," she said.

Moved, I squeezed her hand.

That same day as we sat together she told me that many of the mortifications she endured she did in my name, to bring me closer to God.

I felt nervous that when she saw her prayers coming to nothing, she'd stop confiding in me and eventually even stop sitting with me at meals.

One uncharacteristically sunny day in March I skipped the afternoon meal and went to the piano. Among the sheet music I found a Mozart piano concerto: the Andante from *Elvira Madigan*. As I struggled to play it, the sun came through the small window, lighting my hands, warming the keys to my touch. I lost track of the time, breathless over the beauty of the phrases.

When I left the piano my Arithmetic class was half over, so I went to the sunlit dormitory. The cleaning nun had been in and the air smelled of pine and the windows were open.

Hearing the Mozart within me, I lay on my bed with my blouse unbuttoned, caressing my breasts with the palms of my hands. I heard a voice across the room cry out, "Disgusting." I had not noticed another girl lying ill in her bed at the far end of the dormitory.

I pulled my blouse closed. She got up. "You ought to be afraid for your mortal soul, you filthy girl!" and she rushed off. I dressed myself, burning with shame. If I turned right at the dormitory door, I'd surely run into the nuns, so I went left toward the forbidden corridor and through the iron gate, which though normally locked was now ajar. I assumed that the cleaning nun had gone in and left it open.

As soon as I was through the gate and safely out of sight, I heard nailed shoes distant, behind me. I walked faster deeper into the corridor until I came upon an open door and saw the back of the small nun hunched in her wheelchair. The air was thick and humid and smelled of eucalyptus, and something else, like rotting leaves, and little fumes of alcohol. At a table to her right a little tray of bottles and elixirs was set on a lace doily. She stiffened, sensing my presence, then turned, raising an arm to shield a crooked, deformed face, and I saw that her fingers were webbed.

I stood very still and slowly she lowered her arm. Our eyes met. Hers were wet and I wondered if she'd been crying or if this was their usual condition. For a long moment neither of us breathed. I could hear someone moving about in the connecting room.

"You have a beautiful voice," I said. She watched me with a cautious silence.

"I'm like you," I said.

"We're both musical," she said. "You're the girl who practices the piano. I've heard you as I passed that hall."

"Yes," I paused. "But I'm like you."

"Are you?" she asked softly. Her wet eyes glinted so much I wanted to look away, but didn't.

"Yes."

A gentle smile altered her crooked face, causing one of her eyes to close partway and overflow.

"Would you one day like to sing a cantata while I play?"

Her smile faded and I had difficulty reading her expression.

"Would you?" I asked again.

Her eyes pierced mine and she was on the verge of answering when Philomena Leahy appeared holding a rumpled sheet.

"Get out of here! You're not allowed here."

She threw the sheet to the floor and took me by the arm. As she dragged me out to Sister Vincent, I remembered my mother holding a misshapen plate. "The imperfections in the firing reveal the soul of the thing," she had said.

When Sister Vincent asked me if the girl's charges were true I thought of lying or somehow softening the truth, but I hadn't the energy. I sighed and said, "Yes."

She winced. "What about modesty and decorum? What about chastity? And if you've so little shame for your sin, why did you run into the private corridor? Another disobedient act."

"I'm not without shame, Sister" was all I could think to say.

As a punishment my piano lessons were suspended.

Rumors quickly circulated. Girls deliberately bumped into me, then made the sign of the cross.

*   *   *

That night, hungry for company, I sat down next to Eileen at dinner.

"God forgive you," she whispered, not looking up at me.

"Eileen," I said, touching her hand.

She stiffened. "You're a girl full of secrets, Clodagh. Sometimes I watch you in class or in chapel and I see that you're always thinking, but you never share your thoughts."

I gazed at her thin face, the shadows beneath her eyes. A metal crucifix like the ones the nuns wore at their waists hung from a chain around her neck.

"I'm sorry, Eileen. I've always liked to be in your company and it doesn't matter to me so much if we talk."

She looked at me. "It matters to me."

I felt heavy in my chair. "I told you I wasn't good."

A distressed quiet passed between us. She raked her peas absently with her fork.

"You really did do the awful things they say you did?"

"Yes."

"You're not supposed to ever be naked. Even when you're having a wash. But the other thing . . ."

For a moment I almost laughed at her, so ridiculous did it all seem. But in the silence now between us I sensed that she was giving up on me. I looked into her face and saw the fragility of her own piousness. I had crossed a line. Her association with me threatened the softness of the little system she was maintaining. I felt a twinge of affection and pity for her.

I excused myself, leaving my peas and meat untouched, neglecting to return and stack the plate and cutlery. As I moved toward the door, the dining hall grew quiet, and I felt the eyes of the girls upon me.

The next evening the nuns gathered us in the chapel for Vespers. From the choir behind us we heard a pitch pipe tune the air. A choral of voices chanting in Latin floated down over us. As they faded, the voice of the misshapen nun pierced the air.

"*Ad te omnis caro veniet,*" she sang. "All flesh shall come to Thee."

Her voice rose wildly up and down the scales. *"Ad te omnis caro veniet,"* she sang, the volume and vibrato barely containing her energy.

Girls looked up at the choir trying to see which nun was singing but it was impossibly dim.

A tear ran down my lowered face as I touched the back of the pew before me. A Latin phrase I'd been struggling to translate since I'd first heard the song suddenly became clear to me. *"Fac eis Domine; de morte transire ad vitam . . ."* "And let them, O Lord, Pass from death to life."

We both longed for other worlds. She was a refugee waiting to pass through a curtain into death where she imagined her true life awaited her.

Her voice transported her so she could nearly touch her longed-for place. I shivered, feeling for her a kind of phantom pain as if she were as much a part of me as Mare or my mother.

Mrs. O'Dare had written me several letters that I had not answered, and had even telephoned once, though I refused to take the call in spite of Sister Vincent's admonitions. She retrieved me from St. Brendan's in May, and as she drove me back to Bray tried to engage me in conversation, giving me news of her sister, and chattering on about the people in Bray. I remained quiet. Once she touched my arm but I stiffened, pulling it away.

Rolled into a tube, secured with rubber bands and hidden among my clothes, was the "Pavane for a Dead Princess" that Sister Bernetta had allowed me to borrow from her collection. Half an hour into the ride I told Mrs. O'Dare I wanted piano lessons. Could she help me to find someone to teach me?

"Of course, love. I think there's a woman a few doors down from Mrs. Rafferty's shop who gives lessons. I'll arrange it for you." She shook her head. "Yes," she kept saying, "I'll arrange it," anxious over an opportunity to do something for me.

I was sure Sister Vincent had told her about my transgression but the old woman did not bring it up, walking on eggshells as she was, as if she was afraid I might explode.

Mrs. O'Dare took a nervous breath and said, "Clodagh, love. It was wrong of me to leave you at St. Brendan's over Christmas. I'm sorry."

She waited for a response but I looked away from her, out the window, watching the passing trees in the wind.

A few minutes later I glanced at her, the wind through the car window runneling through her disheveled gray hair as if it were dry grass. Her eyes were damp behind her glasses as she gazed at the road, her mouth pursed with regret.

"It was because of Letty," I said. "Wasn't it?"

Her silence answered my question.

"That bloody little bitch," I said calmly.

"Clodagh!" the old woman gasped. Her shocked expression made me burst into laughter. I kept laughing and her confusion made me laugh more. Soon I forgot why I was laughing. It was the relief; the freeing sense of relief that she felt pain for me, that she was steady and unchanging, that made me laugh. That there was history that lived between us.

When I got back to Mercymount Strand I was so grateful to be free I was ready to burst. I walked long miles along the coast, mad for the new warm breezes and the noise of the sea, hoping for an early arrival of the tinkers to the north field.

The first evening back at the house I sat with Mrs. O'Dare in the kitchen drinking tea and eating a bit of cold roast beef. "There's a nun at St. Brendan's who's all misshapen," I told her.

"Bless the poor creature," the old woman said, stopping her fork.

"She's short and hunched and has webbed fingers."

"God give her peace."

The beef on the plate was a bit too red and I pushed it to the side, then tore at a piece of bread. Mrs. O'Dare left a respectful pause before she cut her meat and quietly chewed.

"Why was she born that way?" I asked her.

She shook her head and stared at the steam rising from her teacup.

Birth, I thought, was as dangerous a crossing place as death. "Abandoned by God," I said, watching her eyes.

"Don't breathe such words," she whispered, as if there were someone nearby who may have heard. Her face shook faintly as she looked at me.

"You believe it, too," I said. "You're just not as honest as I am."

"God is merciful, Clodagh. It's not for us to understand such things."

"But why do such things happen? If God is so very *merciful*?"

She stiffened at my tone, her eyes darting back and forth as if it were incumbent upon her to defend God. "It's the parents. Often such children are born to parents who are cousins one to the other, or other times, God forgive them," she made the sign of the cross, "to even closer unions. Bloodlines too close."

"That's no answer," I said, pushing my chair noisily from the table and getting up, leaving my dishes for her to clear.

That night I woke and for a moment could not figure out where I was. The blue room was vast and shadowy. Amid my own thoughts I heard the nun's voice, quavering with isolation.

I rushed out through the dark hallways and into the parlor. The moon through the open curtain cast a whitish aura over the edges of things. As I climbed into bed beside her Mrs. O'Dare woke with a start.

"Agatha!" she gasped.

"It's Clodagh," I said.

"Oh." She put her hand to her heart, then lowered her face. "You remind me of your mother, coming to me like this." The moonlight lit a tear beginning in her eye. "You're like her in this light."

"Am I?" I asked.

"You could almost be her, love." She put her arm around me and pressed my face into the humid warmth of her neck. Her heart beat hard with the shock.

"I'm like her," I thought. "In the moonlight I'm like her."

I had a terrific urge to hunt for the sealskin dress. How many days would it be before tinkers arrived in the north field? What if I found the dress, put it on and walked into William Connelly's camp one night? Would he think in the moonlight that I was her?

When Mrs. O'Dare fell asleep I crept from her bed and stood outside on the dark porch. The sea rushing inland and retreating seemed to repeat: "Aga-thaaa. Aga-thaaa."

I asked Mrs. O'Dare if she'd found a dress of fur anywhere and she made a face. "Heavens, no. I'd certainly remember such a thing."

I took a flashlight with me into the space behind the kitchen wall, determined to find it.

I broke the tape on a box of my mother's things and went carefully through it. I found the little snuffbox with the painting of the man's face on it. Inside there were a few coins of foreign currency. It no longer smelled of oak but of metal and dust. Under it was a man's beaten, pigskin billfold with cigarette papers and a pound note in it. William Connelly's things.

In the same box I found a little cream pitcher with an etching in green of a woman drinking out of an urn. On the bottom were written the words: "Artemesia drinking her husband's ashes."

I took the cream pitcher, the snuffbox and the billfold with me and put everything else away.

I began piano lessons with Miss Flint, who lived two doors down from Mrs. Rafferty's shop. She was a gray mouse of a woman who admitted me each time with reservation. The walls and curtains of her sitting room, which faced the main street, reeked of decades of cooked mutton.

I knew by the way she grabbed the three pound notes from me after each lesson why she had agreed to teach me at all. But her criticisms, while given in a spirit of condescension, were helpful, and I took in everything she said, determined that she'd not be able to repeat a criticism. I channeled my dislike of her into my playing and loved to hear her reluctant approvals.

One June morning after a lesson I visited Mrs. Rafferty's store, remembering that Mrs. O'Dare had sold some of my mother's things back to the antique store.

I asked Mrs. Rafferty about the dress. "It was strange," I told her. "Made out of a kind of fur. Sealskin, I think."

"No. I saw nothing like that," she said.

"So she didn't buy that from you to begin with?"

"I sell antique dresses. I've sold coats made of fur, but never a dress. That I'm certain about, dear," she said.

She invited me to look at the beautiful things, addressing me as "Miss Sheehy." She showed me a delicate mahogany trinket box, watching me expectantly as if I might be interested in purchasing it. I pulled open one of the tiny drawers and the thing exhaled a dusty rose-smelling air. I closed it and put it down on a table. "It's nice," I said, nodding to her and touching things appreciatively as I moved toward the door. She watched wistfully as I left, clearly disappointed that I did not have my mother's passion for inanimate things.

A piano tuner came to adjust the instrument at Mercymount Strand. After he left I had to get used to the new sound of it, feeling nostalgic for the old dissonance. I practiced fiercely most of the daylight hours, a bright, vigorous Mozart sonata and the gentle Andante from *Elvira Madigan*. But in the evenings my thoughts shifted. I stood on the old Dublin Road praying for tinker caravans to appear on the horizon. I was starved for communion with someone. Some engagement. I had thought I'd find relief in being away from the silences of St. Brendan's, but the same isolation filled me here.

Mrs. O'Dare was my only real companion, and her permanent state of penitence and pity for me incited my impatience.

One day, three weeks after I'd arrived back for the summer, I cooked a pan of eggs and left them sitting awhile on the stove. When I came back into the kitchen to eat them, Mrs. O'Dare had dumped them out and was frying slices of black pudding in the same pan.

"Where are my eggs?" I cried.

"They were dry, love," she said with surprise. "I thought you cooked them last night and forgot them."

"You're lying, damn it!" I screamed. "They were my eggs and you dumped them on purpose!"

"Clodagh!" she gasped.

I picked up a glass from the table and smashed it, hard and deliberate, on the floor between us.

She peered into my eyes with confusion. "Lass . . . ," she said, as I stormed out.

I ran to my room and cried. I beat the mattress with my fists, screamed into the pillow. Lying on my side, I saw myself in the standing mirror a few feet away. My face looked different, I thought. Different muscles had come into play about the mouth and eyes. I got up and went to the mirror. The closer I looked the more I shuddered. My eyes caught the light deeply and under their surface glimmer they were cold, without memory, the eyes of a dead girl. I longed for Mare's company, remembering the way we'd drifted together over the shore and the Wicklow hills after she'd died.

I went to the piano and, shaking, attempted the "Pavane for a Dead Princess." The melody came fumblingly at first, but after a few hours of concentrated work I played it almost seamlessly, music resonant with pain and enchantment.

Mare inhabited me, her grief to know the world swelling up in my muscles. I felt her wishing that the flesh might find again the impulse that had once divided us into two selves; that we would not have to go to a mirror to find the other, but that we could hold each other's hand or sleep in each other's arms or, at last, cleave away and move off in different directions.

After the fifth or sixth time through, I felt Mare growing weaker, dimming like a bulb. The music receded on its own, fading into silence. Slowly I removed my hands from the keys and sat a long time without moving.

The gray day had darkened outside.

Walking on Mercymount Strand the next morning, I saw Finian coming toward me out of the distance. "Clodagh!" he called, waving.

I waved back, my heart galloping with calm fury and exhilaration.

He was taller, wider in the shoulders. His skin fair and scrubbed.

"Do you like St. Brendan's?" he asked, his mouth tensing around a smile.

"No," I said, my cheeks going warm. "It's hell on earth."

"You'll come to a dance this summer at Findlay Hall, Clodagh. They're brilliant."

We walked a little and it started to rain. I said that he could come to my house for tea and we ran across the field with the rain coming down on us. When we got inside he followed me into the kitchen where I put on the kettle. My damp blouse clung to my skin causing me to shiver, and the rain ran from my hem in cold rivulets over my calves.

I gave Finian his tea and sat across the table from him watching his eyes. He seemed curious, uncertain of himself. His hand shook slightly as he reached for his cup, as if he sensed a certain determination in me. When we finished our tea I took him for a tour of the house. He was attentive, but mostly quiet. As he followed me through the lower house, I could hear him breathing behind me the way Letty Grogan had when she'd followed me through the house that first day.

The rain on the windows of the empty second-floor rooms cast moving shadows over Finian's white face as he gazed at the parade of nymphs.

Two steps above him on the next flight I turned and told him that the third floor was more decrepit.

"I don't mind," he said, his eyes wide.

The rain came down hard now, battering the roof and the windows. The dim bulbs I switched on did little to cut through the shadows so I lit an oil lamp and carried it to the room with the satyr and nymphs. Lightning made the walls shimmer and dim. I stood in the doorway holding the lamp as he went in, his footsteps creaking as he crossed the bare floor.

"Jesus Christ," I heard him mutter. "Bring the light over here," he said, standing before the satyr. I hesitated, then walked over, my heart thumping against the wall of my chest.

"Holy Christ," he said softly. The lamplight cast dark shadows around and between the figures, accentuating their contours. He seemed uneasy as he had when we'd watched the seals mating.

While his back was to me I unbuttoned my blouse before the massive mirror. In the reflection I saw him turn. I reached around and undid my bra, then faced him, leaning my back against the cold mirror, the shadows of the rain moving over my skin.

He stood almost gravely still, one half of him visible in the afternoon light, the other half of him in shadow. I took off the rest of my clothes and lay down on the bare floor. The fear went out of his face and when it did I felt a thrill lift my stomach.

He unzipped his pants and was on top of me, struggling to enter me. I pushed against the pain until he was in me, rocking me under his weight, holding me to the floor.

"Kiss me, Finian," I said, holding his head in my hands.

But he kept his face turned from mine as he thrust into me. His energy terrible and frenetic.

Any feeling of certainty left to me was gone.

I disconnected from what was happening, wincing against the force of him, waiting for it to end. I thought of the snuffbox, the little pitcher, the image of Artemesia drinking her husband's ashes, as he squeezed my hips, holding me tightly in place, sweat gathering where his skin slammed against mine. His forehead grew fraught as if he were in pain, his teeth showing, the corners of his mouth tensing.

All at once he pulled out of me and was up on his knees with his sex pulsing in his hands, an arc of milky spray hitting the mirror, the rest caught in his palm, some spilling from between his fingers.

As he recovered himself I closed my eyes again and thought about the misshapen nun hidden in the far corridor. Hot tears mixed with the sweat on my face. I did not watch him as he dressed himself quietly and left in near darkness, the way Letty Grogan had almost a year before.

The first month of summer was gone.

A week passed and I had not seen Finian.

It was the time of the evening when the red light of dusk was streaking the western sky and thin clouds streamed after the sun, dark, but ignited along the edges.

I lay on my bed looking up at the stucco herons when I smelled the first summer fires through the open window and knew that tinkers had arrived in the northwest fields.

I prayed that the copper-haired man was among them. And if he wasn't, maybe William Connelly would be. I would go to him and tell him who I was. Perhaps he'd think of me as a daughter.

I ran outside into the chill of the air, the cold grass grazing my bare ankles and calves, walking to the edge of the field where I saw a fire. One figure, a man's, stood facing the flames, all his weight on one leg, his arms folded, the red glow of a cigarette deepening and dimming at his mouth.

A gust of wind caused the fire to swell and in the sudden yellow light I recognized the copper-haired man. He turned and saw me, watching without moving as if I were a shy animal that might scare.

I don't know how long we stood that way. The flames went down a bit and something crashed and fell away from the fire and he had to knock it back in. That's when I left, running across the pitch-black fields, stumbling in the uneven grass, the small dips and ascents, back to the silence of the house and the blue room.

In the morning I went farther, crossing the fields and walking into the camp. A girl was squatting in some grass at the side of a caravan, doing her water. When she saw me she jumped to her feet, hastily adjusting her clothing. "My mother has tinware, Miss, if you're looking for it." I nodded and followed her into the circle of caravans.

A woman bent into a washtub, the shadows of her breasts visible through the scooping neckline of her blouse. She stood up as she saw me, squeezing out the dress she was washing, holding the damp thing by the shoulders on the air before her, the sun shining through the bright yellow seams.

"Is it tinware you're after?" she asked.

"Yes."

She led me to the back entrance of her caravan where she opened a curtain. A kettle and three tin cooking pots sat on a square of muslin. In the shadows within, the supine figure of a black-haired man stirred vaguely in the light.

"A pot," I said.

"Fifty pence," she said, and I handed her the coins.

The caravans were spread out over a shallow slope and I scanned them, but could not see any of the inhabitants.

Near an isolated caravan at the bottom of the hill I saw a wolfhound lying on the ground. It wagged its tail easily without rising as I approached, and the horse, grazing nearby, raised its head from the grass and looked at me.

The copper-haired man sat smoking under the shade of a makeshift awning, facing away from the camp toward the Wicklow Mountains, his tinware and a few pieces of crockery set out on boards. I could hardly breathe, my heart crowding my throat.

"This is a lovely thing," I said, touching a gilt-edged saucer with a painting of a cluster of grapes at its center. A film of dust remained on my fingertips.

"You've a good eye." His voice resonated from under the awning. "It's an Irish piece from one of the old estate houses in Antrim."

"It's lovely," I said, my own voice quavering.

"Such an object gives great pleasure." While the crockery and the table and everything else glinted in the sun, the man remained dim. "If I were not a traveler, Miss, I'd keep the thing as my own, but such a creature needs a settled place to stand, not a household rocking back and forth in the wind."

The horse had come up behind me, pressing the length of its face between my shoulder blades and pushing me forward into the boards that held the crockery, upsetting things but not breaking any.

"Declan!" the man cried to the horse, leaning his head out into the sunlight, his hair glinting brightly. "Move off! He'll not hurt you, Miss. He's looking for a kiss," he said, and stood up. He pushed on the horse's side and it lifted its head crankily at him, curling its lips.

"Ah, ye big bastard," he said, laughing. The wind blew his worn cotton shirt against him, revealing the power of his upper body. "I want to show you a piece, Miss." As he came near me he brought with him a smell of dead fires and cold air, and something else; something like sheep.

"Look at this one." He picked up a sugar bowl and I recognized it as the sister piece to my small broken pitcher, etched with the same image of Artemnesia drinking her husband's ashes.

"I've seen this image before," I said.

"Have you? Well, there are some pieces circulating."

The piece was missing its handles, and there was a crack in the side that must have, I thought, made the thing difficult to sell.

"The crack and the broken handles don't make such a thing worthless," he said, as if reading my mind. "The thing is precious as Greek sculpture. Missing her forearms, Venus becomes something more." The comparison struck me as sweet, and a little sad.

"The imperfections are how you see the soul of a thing," I said without looking up at him.

I felt his focus on me deepen and he paused before he said in a soft, composed voice that implied an intimacy between us: "Such pieces mean something more to me with their little histories of trouble." He waited again and then said, "I've seen you before."

"In the field, the night before," I said. "You were building a fire."

'Was that yourself standing there?"

"Yes."

He shook his head. "Before that."

"I saw you once on a bus," I said, "and once at a fair in Kildare."

"Yes," he said, nodding, looking thoughtfully at me.

"Do you live near here?"

"Yes."

"Ah, well, I've been back and forth to these parts all my life. Surely I've seen you many times in town or on the roads."

He smiled and my blood rushed. His face was handsome, at once rough and finely chiseled, weathered and ageless. The prominent bones of his cheeks cast shadows through a few days' growth of whiskers.

I looked away, unable to keep meeting his look. "How much do you ask for this?"

"Two pounds," he said.

"If I had the money for this bowl I'd buy it from you. But I'm given an allowance and I've spent the lot of it already this week. Will you be here in another week?" I held the bowl up in the sunlight.

Without answering, he took it from me gently and wrapped it in heavy white paper, the kind my mother had used, tied it in coarse string and gave it to me.

"I'd hate to deprive you of the pleasure of this," I said.

"I keep it in here," he said, pointing to his temple, "and in here." He pointed with one finger to his heart, his fingernail outlined black with grime. I smiled up at him, holding one hand as a visor to the sun. I felt him watching me as I moved away. When I was out of the range of his vision I turned and saw a placard leaning against the back of his caravan. It said: ANGUS KILHEEN: CROCKERY, TINWARE.

As I was crossing the field I saw Finian standing in front of the house.

"Clodagh," he called out, spotting me, squinting and smiling in the sun.

The tide rushed inland and the petrels screeched in the sky.

"What have you there?" he asked, gesturing with his head at my parcel.

I ignored his question, my face burning.

"I've come to see you before I go off to the Isle of Wight for July. I've family there and . . ."

"Good-bye," I said, pushing past him.

"Clodagh, I'm sorry. I shouldn't have left that day the way I did. Come walk on the beach," he said.

"I'll not go with you," I said, holding my white package carefully in both hands, realizing that I'd left my tinware pot among Angus Kilheen's crockery. Finian followed as I moved resolutely toward the house.

"Clodagh, wait. Don't go," he said.

"It's a fine day," he said. "Please. I just want to talk to you a bit. Please."

I stopped in my tracks. The air blew the folds of my summer skirt fanning it out wide, then convoluting and twisting it around my legs. The air was full of light, the water glittering.

"Such a sweet, gentle girl you are," he said, coming up behind me.

He touched my hair and it caused me to shiver. I pulled away and looked at him archly.

His skin was so clean, so lightly freckled. He emitted a fragrance of white starch and civilization. There was no filth lining his finger-nails.

"What do you want?"

"To say I'm sorry. I was a bastard last week."

"Yes, you were."

"I've come to say I'm sorry for that. You took me so off guard."

"That's no excuse."

"You're right. And I want to say good-bye, too. I'm off tomorrow for the Isle of Wight for a month."

"Good-bye," I said.

"Where's Mrs. O'Dare?" he asked, his eyes flashing away from mine.

"In town. But I'll never do that again with you." I moved off ahead of him. I was thinking about Angus Kilheen, remembering the wisps of his mustache curling into his upper lip. I touched the coarse string that bound the package.

Finian came up behind me carefully putting his arms around me, leaning his face down into my neck. "A sweet, gentle girl," he whispered into my hair, and a chill rose over my skin.

I pulled loose of him. "Go away, Finian!"

He followed me to the door and I slammed it shut. A lightness filled me as I walked back to the blue room, thinking of the expression of dismay on his face as the door closed before it.

I sat on my bed carefully unwrapping the package, and finding a strand of copper-colored hair stuck in the knot of the string, I ran it along my lips and closed my eyes, remembering the man's smell of wind and dead fires.

I WENT THROUGH THE DREGS OF MY MOTHER'S OLD CHINA AND found a discolored teapot painted with violets, the inside surface etched with hairline cracks. I wrapped it in the paper that Angus Kilheen had wrapped my sugar bowl in and went to the traveler camp to find him.

The early afternoon sky was overcast as I crossed the fields, a smell of rain on the wind. The camp was quiet except for an old woman sitting on a rock near a dead fire, banging with a hammer on a piece of tin. The rhythm of her hammer slowed as she watched me walk to Angus Kilheen's caravan at the bottom of the hill. The wind shuddered in the flap of black vinyl that served as his window shade. The horse, disengaged from its harness, stood in a clump of grass, switching its ears and tail at me.

I knocked on the caravan door three times and when there was no answer, I opened it. Standing at the threshold looking at the interior, the wind rushed after me, blowing the black shade open and closed on the small unfastened window. Against the farthest wall a bed on a scaffold of boards was covered with a blanket; something Arabian-looking: a fraught pattern of dark reds and black. A dull fleece lay rolled up at the bottom of the bed.

On a wall above the bed hung a holy card depicting the Virgin of the Sea, meek, Spanish-looking, in a crown and a great dress, suspended over the tides. With every gust through the window the picture twisted on its nail and fluttered against the dry wood where it was posted. On a small shelf rigged to the same wall stood a plastic statue of the Virgin Mary missing one of her praying hands, a votive candle in a dark red glass, and a framed black-and-white photograph of a nun with glasses and a wide crooked smile. The presence of all the religious images confused me, not fitting with the man I had imagined.

I looked on the shelves where his things were arranged: an open carton of milk sitting in a bowl of water, a bit of carton with two eggs in it, boxes of matches and tea, a vial of paraffin. On another sat a box full of contraptions and tools, tin bowls and pots, some half made, some dismantled.

The wind blew in intermittent gusts, rocking the caravan on its hinges. Except for the sound of an occasional car on the distant road everything was quiet. My nerves fine-tuned themselves to the place. This far inland I barely heard the sea. I leaned back against an area of wall and watched the horse grazing in the high grass. After an hour of waiting, a light rain began. The horse whinnied and I reached my hand out the door to him. He came up close, pushing his great, sweet head against my chest and stomach. I stroked him awhile and he moved away, looking out into the empty field, resigning himself to the rain. Having slept little the night before, I lay down under the roughly lined sheepskin. The bed had a beautiful, familiar smell of wet earth and fire.

On a bit of a shelf nailed into the wall within arm's reach of the bed, lay a deeply worn paperback, *The Collected Poems of W. B. Yeats.* I opened randomly and read:

> *"All dreams of the soul*
> *End in a beautiful man's or woman's body"*

When I woke my heart was racing. I sat up, flustered, rearranging my skirt over my knees. The copper-haired man sat on a wooden chair at the foot of the bed, his long legs stretched out, his feet almost touching the opposite wall. A lamp lit the space behind him. He looked at me intently, almost sadly. There was a great calm to him. I wondered how long he'd been sitting there looking at me.

"You're the girl who has the sugar bowl," he said.

"I'm sorry," I said, swinging my legs around so my feet were on the floor. "I was waiting for you a long time and fell asleep."

"What's your name, lass?"

I almost told him the truth but hesitated, feeling suddenly wary about conjuring my mother between us. He may have known her, or at least known of her. I felt a fierce urge not to include her. To claim him for myself.

"My name is Mare," I said.

"Mare?"

"Yes. Mare Grogan. I'm here to thank you for the sugar bowl. I've brought you something." I pointed to the package on the table.

"What's Mare short for? Mary, is it?"

"No. It's just Mare."

"Like the female horse?"

"Yes," I said with conviction.

He smiled at my seriousness and I pointed again to the package on the table.

He glanced at it, then back at me. "Where do you live?" he asked.

"To the south. On the Greystones Road," I said, describing the area where Letty Grogan lived.

"How old a girl are you, Mare?"

"Nineteen," I said.

"Are ye now?" he asked, winking at me. "You don't look it."

"Look at the present," I said.

He unwrapped it, his weathered hands turning it gently in the lamplight. "Isn't this a fine creature?" he whispered.

"Look inside it," I said.

"Ah. Little maps of sorrow lining its insides." His low-pitched voice resonated in the soft of my stomach.

He held it again in the lamplight. "Look here," he said, and I approached, bending over him, the ends of my hair grazing his face. The light deepened the breaks, casting hundreds of little shadows.

"So many little breaks," I said quietly, the magnetism between us exerting a pressure on the air. Neither of us moved until he got up suddenly, brushing past me, and set the teapot on a shelf. Little pulses throughout my body beat like drums.

I stared after him but he faced away from me with a serious, thoughtful expression. He gathered some things and went out to build a fire.

The wind made a tentative howl reminiscent of a human voice. It stopped and started, whipping at the linoleum shade and dropping it suddenly. "A south wind," he said. "They say a south wind fills people with exhilaration, Mare."

I felt a twinge in my gut when he called me Mare.

"We'll see if I can get a fire up in this fickle wind." He squatted down, raking the old ash bed and replacing the coals. I stayed inside, standing at the open caravan door. I caught my reflection in a piece of sheet metal and though it was faintly distorted I saw that I wore the expression I associated with Mare; the mouth slightly tense at the corners.

He turned to me from his place before the coals. "Will you have a cup of tea?" he asked.

I answered overreadily that I would, a high dissonant pitch to my voice that made me cringe. He kept his eyes on me a moment and smiled faintly. He knew the power he had and it seemed to amuse him. His restraint mesmerized me.

He told me to come down and join him on one of the rocks near the fire. The wind rose as I did and the new flames leaned and crackled.

I faced him in the firelight.

"You look at me like you know me," he said.

Once in the throes of love for Finian, Letty Grogan had said that their destinies tied them together. I had liked the sound of that and sitting there, not knowing what to say to him, I said, "I think you and I are tied together by destiny."

He seemed surprised. He gazed a few moments at the fire before he smiled and let go a soft laugh. "And what makes you think such a thing?" he asked. I felt ridiculous and looked away into the field. Declan was coming toward me, his head raised, his nostrils searching the air. When he reached me he nuzzled me with his head.

"This creature's mad for you," Angus said. "It must be because your name is Mare. Get out o' here, Declan!"

The horse whinnied at him and Angus bent into himself with laughter. "You're more human than horse, aren't you, ye bastard?" He stood up and gave the creature a pat on the backside, laughing as the horse turned and almost knocked him down. He took the creature's head in his arms and kissed it. The sweetness of the man sent a thrill through me.

The sun was going down while we drank our tea, and he said, "This is my favorite time of the day. Light and dark touch for a few moments."

A few red clouds streamed westward.

"I used to wish dusk would last longer, but its quickness seems to add to making it special," he said.

"Special things shouldn't be brief," I said.

"Ah, but that's not the nature of the world now, is it, Mare?" There was, in the easy tone of his voice, that same assumption of intimacy I'd heard the day before.

"There's an island north of Donegal where, if you stand on a cliff at the north point you can see glaciers in the distance. One afternoon, deep in the winter there, I saw the red ball of the sun seeming to float on the surface of the sea. I waited and waited for it to go down, but it didn't."

"Is it like that there every night?"

"No. It has to do with the position of the earth. It happens for only a few nights every winter."

"Do you travel to that place often?"

"Oh no," he said, taken a bit off guard by the question. "I was in Holy Ghost Orphanage not far from that place I described to you. On an island. Did you see the photograph of the nun inside?"

"Yes."

"That's Sister Margaret Mooney, the nun who ran the orphanage."

"She must have been kind to you . . . that you keep her picture."

"Sister Margaret Mooney is my mother in this world."

I thought of asking what had happened to his own mother, but he'd grown a bit far away at the mention of the nun, gazing at the light

in the western sky. "Is that place in Donegal your favorite place in Ireland?"

"No," he said softly and emphatically. "Have you ever been to the
west, Mare? To Galway and Clare? And to Kerry?"

"No."

"The coasts there are the edge of the world. The cliffs fall sheer
hundreds of feet to the sea."

Voices rose up from the camp behind us. A baby cried sporadi-
cally.

It grew dark as he told me about the Aran Islands, and the Isles of
the Dead, which appeared and mysteriously disappeared on the horizon west of Dunshee Beach. Dunshee, he said, the place he traveled
to most springs and autumns, was a crossover place between worlds.
Right near Kinvarra on the coast of the western sea, and not far from
a grouping of megalithic stones believed to be the prehistoric tombs
marking the graves of the Irish chieftains.

"I've heard of Dunshee Beach," I said.

He gave me the fervent eyes and asked, "From whom?"

I paused. "A friend's mother lived there once," I said.

He was quiet and I thought he was about to ask a question.
Instead he looked into the fire.

Sitting near Angus Kilheen with the firelight in my face, the world
felt exciting and undiscovered. "I have a desire to travel," I said.
Sparks rose before me into a black column of air and the fire popped
and huffed. "I want to move through strange landscapes. I'm sick to
death of places too familiar."

"You see the beauty in a place if you can leave and then return to
it," he said softly.

He went inside a moment and brought out a picture of some western cliffs torn from a magazine.

"Lovely," I said, surprised by the jagged height of the cliffs in comparison to a tiny boat in the water near them. "They almost don't look
real."

"Oh, they're real! They're more real than most things in this world!" He switched on a radio that sat on the makeshift table where he had displayed his crockery the day before, fiddling with the reception until he got an air of fiddles with a staticky, crackling background.

He sat down on a stone closer to me and went thoughtful with the music. Though I kept my eyes on the picture of the cliffs that I held on my lap, I felt him looking at me.

"Why do you park your caravan at a distance from the others and facing away?"

"I like a measure of privacy," he said. "I travel alone most of the time, but among other travelers for the fairs."

When the music waned I heard sheep bleating in the distance somewhere, and the voices of men and women from the darkening camp, Angus's caravan like a luminous shell on the field.

The static from the radio broke and a lone uilleann pipe began to plead with the air. The music built in pitch: long, climbing notes. I felt his warm hand on my hair, his fingers sweeping strands back from my face. Tingles of electricity ran over my skin, a soft nervous thrill thrumming through my body.

"Why did you come to me?" he asked. He had gathered my loosened hair in one hand.

"To give you the gift," I said wanly.

"Why do you say we're tied together by destiny?"

I looked into his face, longing to feel the weight of him on top of me. Hardly breathing, we held each other's eyes.

The pipe stopped almost suddenly and a lamb bleated from the fields. Angus dropped my hair softly and looked into the fire. His restraint cast its shadow between us again. In spite of the fear I now felt hurt, desolate at what felt like a broken promise. I wanted to tell him that I was not a virgin. That I could bring myself to rapture again and again.

I squeezed my mouth tight, then looked at the fire.

"What's causing you to fret?" he asked.

The question angered me because I knew he knew the answer.

I threw the picture from the magazine into the flames. Startled, Angus tried to read my eyes, but as the page became no more than a smear of red glitter and smoke, he shook his head, smiled and let out a little laugh. I looked away from him, listening to the soft noise of the fire.

"You have a lad, Mare. I'm sure of it. A boy who loves you."

"Yes," I said. I held his eyes. "One day I took all my clothes off and gave myself to him," I said.

He smiled distantly. "The lucky little bastard."

I felt suddenly ashamed and he seemed to sense my discomfort.

Summer lightning began in the distance, followed by muted thunder.

"Haven't you a mother waiting on you, lass?"

"Of course I have a mother. But she's in Dublin tonight."

"And your father?" he asked. "Where is he?"

"Dead," I said.

"It'll be teeming rain before long. You ought to get home to your warm bed," he said. He stood, taking my hand and bringing me to my feet.

"Off ye go now," he said.

But I stayed where I was, swaying in the night air like a reed. "I don't want to go," I said in spite of myself. He smiled. I imagined he pitied me for my transparency and that caused an ache of fury to rise up in me.

"Take this lamp," he said.

"No. I don't need it to find my way."

"Ah, you're a little spirit of the night, are you, Mare? I'll send you home to your bed now, lass. Take this." He stepped back from me, holding out the lamp.

"I'll not take it," I cried, and ran from him into the black fields.

The next day I returned to the camp. Staring men and women went quiet as I passed. I was stunned to find Angus Kilheen's caravan gone.

In its wake was only dead grass, scorched stones and ashes from his fire. I climbed the hill again looking for Declan, hoping that the caravan had only been moved.

The mother and daughter from whom I'd bought the tin pot were sitting before their fire eating bread smeared with margarine. As I looked around, I noticed the woman eyeing me.

"Angus Kilheen has gone to the west," she said.

"To the west?"

"Yes."

"He didn't tell me. . . ."

"Why would he? A young settled girl like you should stay away from a man like him." The thin-faced, dark-haired man I'd seen sleeping inside her caravan the day before stood in its threshold looking at me with his arms crossed.

"Why doesn't your mother have her eye on you?" the woman asked.

I turned away from her, my eyes raking the land as far as they could see.

"Landed girls shouldn't mix with travelers, Miss."

The little girl stared at me, gnawing on a hunk of bread.

"He's a friend is all. He tells me about his traveling."

"You're after a stud ram, Miss," she said, standing up, wiping her hands on her skirt. "I have two eyes and they see clearly enough. If you're looking for a stud ram, find one that's kept in a barn, for he'll make a better husband to a settled girl than a traveler man will."

A few men and women had come out of their caravans to listen.

I turned and walked off across the field, the woman shouting after me: "I hope you didn't take down your knickers for him. He'll not be near these Wicklow Mountains till three seasons have come and passed."

There was a scattering of laughter. I felt my eyes tearing up. A surge of hurt and disappointment drove me to run, and I thought, "They'd not be so cruel to me if they knew I was one of them."

*   *   *

I wrote to my aunts in the west and asked if I could come and visit, and Aunt Lily wrote back saying that it was not a good time. Aunt Kitty's nerves were worse than ever. She asked if we could try for Christmas again this year. She was hopeful that by then Kitty would be better. She told me to telephone her before my winter break at St. Brendan's and we could plan it.

But I didn't wait, telephoning a few days after I received her note.

"Oh, please, Aunt Lily, please. I'll not disturb Aunt Kitty. I'm dreadfully bored here," I said to her. The plea made her coldly quiet and she ended the conversation by saying, "Write to me in December. Perhaps then." But I doubted that Angus Kilheen would be there in December since he'd told me that the autumn and spring were the times he'd spend there.

When I wasn't practicing the piano, I walked restlessly in the Wicklow Mountains, my eyes raking the landscape, as if he might reappear magically.

The woman's chiding had made me shy of the tinkers and I did not visit the hillside where they'd camped until they were gone. I took off my shoes and walked in the ruts left by Angus Kilheen's caravan wheels. I built a little monument of stones around the site of our fire. It rained one day and left a pool in the caved-in bed of ash. I stared at my face in the reflection. The westward-moving clouds in the blue sky behind me were much clearer than the shadows of my face. It was Mare I saw there. Quiet. Inconsolable. I reached into the pool and stirred the soft, silty earth.

I visited the library and read about the islands to the north where Angus had seen the red sun. I looked for maps and photographs of Galway in the west of Ireland where Dunshee was located. I found pictures of the Aran Islands and the Bens in Connemara, and the Cliffs of Moher in County Clare.

When Finian was back he called on me a few times but I didn't answer the door, watching from the third-floor window while he waited around in front of the house or stood out on the beach.

*   *   *

Anger and frustration fueled my progress at the piano, and Miss Flint was often left dumbfounded by my determination. She made what I'm sure she came to feel was a mistake, by giving me, at my second-to-the-last lesson before summer's end, a certain furious Beethoven piece.

I practiced it strenuously all week and when, at my final lesson, I played it for her, I did so without inhibition, hopping from the bench with the raging leaps and plunges of the music; jerking my head and gritting my teeth as I pounded the keys.

When it was over she was dead still, leaning back in her chair as if she'd been slapped. I put the three pound notes on the hot piano keys, and left that mutton-smelling room forever.

I ran back across the field to Mercymount Strand, laughing until my eyes were damp. When I got home I still felt wild, defiant. I openly lit one of Mrs. O'Dare's cigarettes in the kitchen.

"I'll not have a fifteen-year-old girl smoking!" she cried.

I took the whole package and threw it into the dishwater.

"Christ give me patience," she said. "You're like your own wild mother!"

"Well then," I said, "you won't be shocked to learn that I plan to travel with the tinkers one day to see Ireland."

"Clodagh!" she cried. "There are better ways to see Ireland than with the tinkers. They're a *destitute* people, love," she said pleadingly.

"And so am I," I said.

"I'll not have ye mixed up with tinkers!" she cried out, flecks of moisture appearing on her red face. "It's a heartbreaking life, Clodagh, and you have the chance for other things."

I glared at her defiantly, and thought I might laugh. I understood the urge my mother had felt to taunt her.

"Don't break my old heart!"

All that evening she was distracted. "I'm going to speak to Letty," she said to me at tea. "I'll tell her that she must come and the two of you must get over this row with one another. God knows a girl your age should be doing things other than daydreaming in empty rooms and running around in the fields."

"What bloody difference does it make? The summer's over now."

Deep in the night I woke, dreading going back to St. Brendan's. I felt a pang of guilt for the way I'd treated Mrs. O'Dare, remembering the brokenhearted look on her face when I'd yelled at her. I went to her, standing at her bedside in the parlor. "I'm sorry," I whispered.

"Agatha!" she gasped as she had before, her head lifting from the pillow. When she realized it was me she lay back, whispering, "Saints preserve us!" I got into bed with her, huddling into the warmth of her body, her worn white nightgown damp with perspiration.

"Promise me ye'll not go off with the tinkers, love," she whispered.

I said nothing and she pleaded with me again. "Promise me!"

I wanted to tell her about Angus Kilheen, and about the tinker woman's cruel words to me, but there'd have been no comfort in it. "I can't promise, Missus. I can't."

She sighed so I felt her breath in my hair. "God save you, lass. God save you."

On the last day of summer I walked outside in the field, the tradewinds wild in my hair and skirts, the sand stinging my calves. Finian, coming along the beach in the distance, started running and waving when he saw me.

We walked for a while along the coast to the north and he told me about his time spent on the Isle of Wight. "Where's Mrs. O'Dare?" he asked. "She's at the house," I told him, lying. But he was not discouraged, taking me to a sheltered area, a kind of cove under some overreaching dunes. I did not submit to him only out of an urge to be touched but out of some wish to go blank; to hear obliteration in the noise of the sea.

I found myself desolate the entire time he was inside me; desolate because I missed Angus Kilheen; because I wondered if I'd ever see him again. I could not, no matter how I tried, pretend that Finian was the other man.

Finian seemed oblivious to my sadness. The sea rushed closer and closer to us. "I'll not get you with child," he panted, then pulled out, spraying the sand before the edge of the tide rushed in and washed us cold.

IN THE CONVENING YEARS I GAVE MYSELF FULLY TO THE PIANO. I met Angus Kilheen on the shores of Debussy's "Reverie" and the walls of St. Brendan's dissolved around me. In the music I smelled coal fire, the mineral and iodine of waves. I felt wind on my skin.

But always, in the end, the quiet of the room came back, and it was Angus Kilheen's absence that remained; that followed me, so I fell in love with the steadfastness of that absence. Somewhere in Ireland, he existed in his hard, palpable separateness; not the ghost I conjured out of my own heat. But mysterious. Unknown to me.

I watched the travelers from a distance, still wounded by the chiding of the tinker woman. She had been cruel, but she'd been right when she'd said that she saw things clearly. It had been thoughtless of me to try to move so carelessly into their world.

And one temperate evening, home for the summer at Mercymount Strand, I saw a single fire burning in the field where I had first seen Angus. I went outside, with a feeling of presentiment that it was him, the winds gusting from the sea. I could not bring myself to go closer, to find out if it was him. It was his absence I trusted. His absence I had grown to sustain myself upon.

My third and fourth years at St. Brendan's I played at every Sunday service and for Christmas and Easter recitals. A calm fierceness had come into my demeanor. I no longer cared what the other girls thought of me. They left me alone. I did not often meet their eyes and when I did, it surprised me to recognize looks of awe, or even of approbation. And the nuns left me alone if I practiced in the middle of the night.

I rarely heard the misshapen nun singing; only a faint strain now and then from past the forbidden iron doors.

And I no longer heard from Finian. I overheard Letty telling another girl at school that he was serious now with Mary Morrissey and that she kept her eye on him.

It was in my last year at St. Brendan's that Sister Bernetta told me that she could no longer teach me; that I'd surpassed her. Two afternoons a week I took a bus east to St. Mathilde's, a high-class women's college with a strong focus on music, to study with an old Spanish nun named Sister Seraphina.

I fell in love with St. Mathilde's. It could be seen in the distance from the Kildare Road, white and palatial with columns, like a modern-day Parthenon. It seemed to have been constructed for a sunnier, warmer clime with open-air walkways and arcades that led from classrooms and study halls and studios.

The nuns wore white wimples and veils and layered crimson habits with little ceramic crucifixes on cloth ribbon around their necks.

On mild days I'd wait for Sister Seraphina on a bench outside the music room, watching the nuns moving in silence along the arcades, robes and veils luffing in the breeze. I was on fire with the idea of going to college there, though places were difficult to obtain. I procured application papers, working and reworking my answers before writing them carefully on the forms.

The first weeks with Sister Seraphina I struggled with a Chopin Nocturne. She smiled and nodded as I played. Softly, dramatically, she'd whisper in her strong Spanish accent, "Pianissimo!" her raised hand cupping the air.

She pronounced the first syllable of my name with the long *u* sound. "Good, *Clu*-dah!" she cried after some of my attempts. But I felt her holding back, reserving comment. She made me play certain pieces over and over, squinting her eyes at the ceiling as she listened.

At our fifth or sixth lesson, she asked me to play one of my favorites. I played the "Reverie," giving myself fully to it, feeling Angus Kilheen's breath on my neck. I returned from the piece breathing hard, hair in my eyes.

"Cludagh," she said. "Control! You go through the music like you go through a door. Stay in the music!" She squeezed my forearm, iron and certainty in her hand.

I felt ashamed, exposed. I wondered if she knew what the music aroused in me.

"What makes you say I go through it like a door?"

"The music changes when you disappear. Reverberations. Notes mixing with notes. Give me clarity!"

She made me play it again. "Don't go through the door!" she cried once, sensing my temptation. She smiled at me with little glimmering eyes, pulling me toward exactitude. I resisted the music's invitation to delirium, and that resistance infused the sound with a peculiar tension.

"Nice!" she cried.

I was stunned to find myself in her intuitive, demanding hands.

I left that day, challenged, exhausted, but with sparks in my blood.

One afternoon as I worked on a new Chopin Nocturne, she stood suddenly. "Come with me," she said, and I followed her through the library, the high white walls resounding with thoughtful silence. Heavy mahogany shelving issued a clean odor of trees.

"This is your library now. You will be in school here next year. I've seen to it," she said.

She opened a heavy door and we entered the empty chapel, flooded with gold and green light from the high, leaded windows. She walked imperiously up the aisle to the harpsichord and sat down before it.

"Sit!" she cried, pointing to a pew near her.

She pulled her elaborate sleeves to the elbow and raised her hands in the air above the keys where they hovered a moment before she flew into a Bach Trio Sonata with a wild agility, rocking slightly side to side with the quick lightness of the notes, a concentrated smile on her mouth. Gooseflesh rose on my body, tears wetting my lashes at the force that drove the music. There was something at once wise and childlike about her; at once intimidating and funny.

I was trembling when she finished and turned to me.

"You will study harpsichord, Cludagh!"

"Why?" I asked.

"More formal. You can't disappear so easy."

I did not like the idea of dividing my time between the piano and a new instrument. There was a certain agony involved in submitting to this sweet, ferocious little nun.

"Restraint!" she'd cry at every lesson.

Once as she interrupted me with this cry, I asked her with irritation if this was her philosophy about music; if she demanded such restraint from all her pupils.

"Oh no!" she cried, eyebrows raised in surprise. "I demand more emotion from them. Restraint from you only!"

"All of them?" I asked.

"All of them," she said, and nodded her head once for emphasis.

A second of quiet passed and she said again, "Restraint from you!"

A week before the graduation ceremonies were to take place at St. Brendan's, we were awakened at 5 A.M., confused by the tolling of the church bell. It was a Thursday and not a holy day. We were summoned in our nightgowns into the gallery where a solemn Sister Vincent informed us that there had been a death among the nuns and that classes were canceled for the next two days. We were sent without breakfast to prepare ourselves for an early Mass.

I walked slowly past a small group of girls who were whispering in the hallway, trying to guess which nun it could be and what might have happened to her.

"Perhaps one of the old nuns. Sister Rosalita."

"Or the one with the cane," whispered another.

After a long Mass in which we were given no clue as to who had died, Sister Vincent led us into one of the study halls. She folded her hands over her heart and looked at us gravely. "There was a young nun who lived here whom none of you met. She lived in the north wing to which none of you had admittance. Sister Clarissa, who suffered from terrible afflictions of the body." She could not stifle her tears, and having no handkerchief, wiped them on her sleeve. "It was her memorable voice that you heard at Vespers sometimes."

The hall was filled with reticent silence.

"What did Sister Clarissa suffer from?" one of the girls gently inquired.

"Deformities, and many maladies of the heart and lungs that come to the misshapen. It astounded us that she could sing at all, but so gloriously . . ." She wept again. "So dear is such a misshapen creature to God."

"Sister, why is a misshapen creature dear to God?" I asked, wanting to understand.

"All unfortunates are special to God," she said. One of the girls handed her a handkerchief and she pressed it to her eyes. "All who suffer in this world are closer to God."

For the rest of the day, in an atmosphere of melancholy reflection that prevailed among even the fiercest girls, I pondered Sister Vincent's words.

At Vespers we were each given a holy card with an image of a lovely, sad-faced Virgin on it, two fingers pointing to her small ignited heart. On the back it read: "Sister Clarissa: Daughter and Beloved Wife of Our Lord."

Phrases from Sister Vincent's reading from Isaiah caught in my memory: *The Lord called me from the womb . . . from the body of my mother He said my name.*

She was leaving her misbegotten body; leaving what did not fit her or serve her. Sister Vincent spoke about suffering and redemption; that at the end of darkness there is light.

As we filed into the dining hall for the evening meal, the sky, unnaturally dark for the hour, broke into intermittent rumbling.

That night it rained a deluge, and there weren't enough buckets to catch all the leaks. Girls were forced to camp out in the chapel on the pews. No one slept, while the nuns prayed in Latin all night in Sister Clarissa's name.

The next morning we discovered that the classrooms were flooded. We walked around in coats and mufflers with dripping noses and terrible bronchial coughs. The nuns wore softly agonized faces, sloshing through the rooms, dragging their heavy skirts, seeming to sleepwalk. Some gathered wistfully at the windows, trembling with the cold, watching the rain spatter the puddles. Sister Vincent sat among us in the dining hall. No evening meal had been prepared. Packages of white sliced bread and plates of oily, slightly rancid-smelling butter were set out on one of the tables. We ate the bread and drank numerous cups of tepid tea. I remember little else being eaten those three or four days except a meal of boiled cabbage and bacon that was brought in by an aunt of Sister Clarissa's, who, after an interview with Sister Vincent, made herself scarce.

"When Sister Clarissa resurrects, will her earthly body be returned to her?" asked one of the girls.

"Yes," Sister Vincent said, "but without its imperfections. She'll go to Christ in great beauty."

Late at night while the nuns were engaged in soft, sustained chanting at the front of the chapel, many of us lay wrapped in blankets on the back pews. The girls guessed at Sister Clarissa's deformities. "Perhaps she had no hands. I knew a girl who had a sister with no hands. But I was never allowed to see her."

"Maybe she had a head too big for her body," said another. Others chimed in, sharing stories of unfortunates with maladies that they'd seen and had been haunted by.

"It's wrong to be unkind to such people," someone said, and there were murmurs of assent.

A girl who'd been very quiet said she saw Sister Clarissa once, but she could not see her face because she was hunched in her chair looking down and to the side. "She had . . . strange fingers."

"What do you mean 'strange'?" one of them asked.

"Webbed," the girl said.

"Like a mermaid!" someone cried.

"How terrible," another girl moaned, gazing up at the dark vaults of the ceiling. "But now she walks bedecked in lilies."

At the funeral service, the flames of the two altar candles pulsed, long spirals of smoke rising from them, dispersing above on the chapel air. A dizzying lightness flooded the chapel; weirdly spirited air left in the wake of Sister Clarissa's ascension.

She had drifted to heaven like a kite cut loose of its string. She'd reached her longed-for place. Through one small, clear pane in the stained glass I could see a bit of blue sky. I whispered her name, "Sister Clarissa," and felt stratosphere between us.

Why couldn't Mare leave so cleanly? Whose inconsolability kept her here so close to the ground; deepening and fading? And deepening again. Whose inconsolability? Mine or hers?

When I closed my eyes I saw the white arcades of St. Mathilde's, and heard the "Pavane for a Dead Princess."

PART II

Angus

THE WEST OF IRELAND
1980–81

I saw the danger, yet I walked along the enchanted way,
And I said "Let grief be a fallen leaf" at the dawning
of the day.

—Patrick Kavanaugh

I HAD BEEN ATTENDING COLLEGE AT ST. MATHILDE'S A YEAR AND a half when the Reverend Mother presented me with a notification that upon Sister Seraphina's recommendation, I had won an apprenticeship. Only one girl was given the honor each year out of the two hundred who attended the school, to be groomed for recitals and concerts in Dublin and in London.

It was mid-February. So far I had been matriculating three days a week from Mercymount Strand, but because of the rigorous work ahead of me, the Reverend Mother suggested that I move into a dormitory room in September when the apprenticeship was set to begin.

I walked about the campus looking for Sister Seraphina. When I found her in the chapel she took me in her arms. "Are you happy about this, Cludagh?" she asked.

"I am, Sister. I am. Thank you," I said.

"I think you should perform, Cludagh! We must make use of all that passion!"

I was surprised by her words and the intensity in her eyes. "What about 'restraint'?" I asked.

"One day your technique will be strong enough to carry all that emotion. And I'll never say that word to you again!"

I smiled at her, moved.

"We will work hard together, Cludagh!" she said.

"Yes, Sister," I said.

I rode the bus back to Mercymount Strand in a daze. My future suddenly had shape.

I dreamt that night that I was searching for the sealskin dress in the upper house, in a spot where the wall had caved in. I dug uneasily in softened plaster and dirt until I found it and put it on. In the next moment I was in the sea swimming, tossed about in the cold boil, certain some moments that I'd drown, other moments that I could not get enough of the spinning and turning. I had a desperate wish to go deeper. I pulled myself down until I could feel the floor of the sea with my fingers.

I woke with my heart pounding and sat up in the dark, certain that I smelled the smoke of a tinker fire. I went outside in the frigid blackness, the inland skies over the fields pocked with stars. There were no fires.

The salty iodine odor of the sea was strong and in the bit of starlight I could see a great heap of kelp rotting in the sand. I shivered violently but did not want to go back inside. I had a terrible urge to run in my nightgown, barefoot as I was, through the frosty grass to the place on the hill where I'd seen the tinker fire that could have been Angus Kilheen's.

When I did at last go back inside I did not go to bed, but to the piano room. I tried to play but felt too restless and stood at the window staring out, pressing my forehead to the icy glass, remembering the time I saw Agatha putting the sealskin dress on in the field before she'd gone to the tinker camp. The animal smell of it conjured itself on the air around me and I felt afraid.

I telephoned Aunt Lily that morning. We'd grown cordial over the years. Occasionally people from Dublin had come to look at the house, but their terms were not satisfactory to her. The search for tenants had gone on for years, but that was not uncommon with these old estate houses, Aunt Lily had told me once.

"Aunt, I've been awarded an apprenticeship at St. Mathilde's College," I said. "They want to prepare me to play recitals in Dublin. And maybe even in London."

"Clodagh!" she said, her voice pitched brighter than I'd ever heard it. "Well, I'm . . . I'm so pleased. That's wonderful!"

"Thank you, Aunt," I said.

She let go a flustered breath. "Your father would be so proud of you for this, Clodagh." For the first time I felt her claim me.

*   *   *

The third week of April I received a telephone call from Aunt Lily, inviting me to come for a visit.

"Clodagh, Kitty's feeling so well! She's up and around now for three days. . . . If you could, this would be a wonderful time to come. Her mood has been so consistently good. Anyhow, I know you have school, but I told her your great news and she said she'd love to see you."

I went to Sister Seraphina and asked if I might take a fortnight off from school, explaining the situation to her. She went to my other teachers, who were happy for an opportunity to accommodate me. I had applied myself academically with diligence at St. Mathilde's, and Sister Seraphina said that I could tie up the loose ends of the term on an individual basis with my teachers whenever I returned from the west, even if that wasn't until some time in the summer.

In the last week of April, I left for the west.

Aunt Lily picked me up at the train station in Galway. She seemed thinner and less formal than I remembered her. We drove uphill along rocky dirt roads, with little green anywhere around, and I remembered Mrs. O'Dare describing Galway as "a rough and unearthly place."

As we approached Drumcoyne House we entered an indigenous oak wood, "A rare occurrence," Aunt Lily explained, "this close to the force of Atlantic winds." She said it had to do with the shape of the cliffs fronting the woods, serving the land like rocky battlements, preserving the acres from the gales.

I could see the porticoes of the house and the front foyer window lit up with lamps, bright yellow light cutting the dense shadows of oak trees, bramble and holly. Black mulch rotting under leaves made the earth around the house spongy.

Aunt Lily led me into the front room where Aunt Kitty sat by the fire, peering at me over her shoulder, wide eyed and reticent across a great expanse of polished, firelit floor. She clutched her teacup in both hands.

I went in and greeted her but she did not respond except to look at me with damp, surprised eyes.

Aunt Lily led me along uneven floors, through vast, high-ceilinged rooms painted aqua and cream. Ornate stucco crustaceans intertwined with foliage of the sea. She pointed things out that I might get my bearings for the evening. I had an eerie feeling that I knew this place, it seemed so truly a sister house to the one on Mercymount Strand. But Drumcoyne House was larger, and well furnished, the floors covered with great faded rugs, threadworn and dulled by light.

The guest room where I was to stay had deep green walls and a lumpy bed under a white crocheted coverlet. A painting of a stern-faced girl in a pink bonnet standing before a dark backdrop hung above the bed. Winged stuccowork angel heads festooned in leaves and acorns enhanced the wainscoting.

From the small garret window I could see the horizon in uneven washes of light, a vague delineation between sea and sky. But it began to rain and that separation dissolved and the horizon became all mist and amorphous distance. "The edge of the world," as Angus Kilheen had told me.

Early the next morning I stood on a cliff looking down at the Atlantic Ocean pounding the high rocks near Dunshee Beach, spume whisking inland from the breakers.

On a long stretch of shore, herons alighted and rose again with effortless grace, their legs trailing after them on the airstream.

The sky was broken in margins of overcast light, the wind whistling in the cliff rock. I stared out into the tumultuousness of the sea, thinking of my mother, the air cold and biting, causing me to shiver, to pull my jacket tightly around myself.

My eyes raked the shores for seals. Down on the rock beach I saw an old woman in a wind-battered skirt and a red coat, moving through clotted kelp caught in the boulders. She bent forward, pulling something loose of the kelp, cleaning it off. From the distance it looked like a small shoe. After examining it she threw it aside, then tied her skirt in a clump at her hip, navigating the rocks toward the land, bare-legged, the water eddying in.

A slew of gulls rode in on an air swell, screeching as the incoming tide broke, splashing and filling the spaces between the rocks, rushing the woman's legs so she swayed, struggling to keep her balance. The sea must have been freezing and I wondered how she stood it.

She waited for it to retreat, then clambered from the rocks onto the sand and stood squeezing out her dress.

A weatherhead moved inland and the sky rumbled as the woman walked south on the beach, disappearing behind a cliff.

I sat with both my aunts at the fire drinking tea.

"Isn't Clodagh like her mother?" Aunt Lily asked Aunt Kitty.

Aunt Kitty looked at me wanly and did not answer.

"About the eyes, the bones of the face," Aunt Lily said again.

"Yes," the other answered and turned away, her face shaking. "She is a bit like Agatha. But her hair isn't as white."

"No, you're right, Kitty. It is darker and there is a bit more curl in it. Agatha's hair was so long and straight and white blond."

"Yes, it was."

Kitty frowned and stared at the fire.

Lily watched Kitty, though she addressed her question to me. "How do you like St. Mathilde's, Clodagh?"

"It's very nice."

Lily nodded her head.

"I like it very much," I said.

"And do you have many friends?" Aunt Kitty asked suddenly, turning to me.

"Yes."

"That's good," Kitty said.

"Yes," I said.

"And it's wonderful about your apprenticeship."

"Thank you."

"Clodagh's promised to play the piano for us later, Kitty."

I reached for a biscuit and bit it carefully. The clock ticked and I felt Aunt Lily searching for something to ask, but the silence went on.

"This is a lovely tea service," I said.

"Spode Copelandware," Lily said. "Very fine collector's set. Very old."

"Agatha stole a butter dish," Kitty said crankily, narrowing her eyes at me.

"I'm sure that she didn't, Kitty," Lily said.

"I'm sure that she did," mumbled the other.

"How is Mrs. O'Dare?" Lily asked.

Before I could answer, Aunt Kitty clutched a little bell hanging around the arm of her wheelchair and rang it furtively. The serving woman came in from the kitchen and wheeled her around to the conservatory window. "Give me the beads," she snapped. "All of them!" The woman gave her three sets of rosary beads and Kitty poured them on her lap then waved the woman away. I looked at Lily but she shook her head as if to say that this behavior had no explanation.

"I'm sure you want to spend more time outside. The rain should stop tomorrow," Lily said, rising.

"How do you know?"

"I can feel it. The mood of the air is changing."

"I'm glad."

"It will still be cold, mind you." She coughed and the tiny beads on her bosom trembled.

The sound of the rain stopped and the room was suddenly lit with the sun. She stood and went to the window, peering up at an area of sky above the oak trees. "This time of year the skies change so violently in the course of an afternoon."

The serving woman, Mrs. Dowling, adjusted the screens around the fireplace, the turf embers deepening as her skirt whooshed the air around them.

As I moved past Kitty to go upstairs she stirred through the beads with her hands, whispering to herself. I saw that her eyes were full of tears.

*   *   *

I ventured out into the damp sun. I reached the cliffs, transported by the vast unearthliness of the place.

When I'd walked about a half mile south along the headland the sky went dark again and I was caught in a rainstorm. I found shelter at a little isolated hotel called the Hibernian. The restaurant inside had massive windows overlooking the sea. In a connected pub, local men drank and played darts.

The rain went on a long time and I ate a smoked mackerel salad and looked out the window. Only one other customer sat in the restaurant, in a shadowy corner booth. A thin, fair-haired young man poring over a heavy volume. He looked up and gave me a smile, which I returned. He blushed faintly then looked back at his book.

The waitress, an older woman with dark hair piled up on her head, came to give me a fresh pot of tea. "Awful weather to be wandering out in," she said.

"Yes. This is a nice place, though. I'm glad for the rain or I might not have come in."

She smiled then went to the young man in the corner.

"Finished your food, love?" she asked him, turning to me as she collected his plate. "Denis's father owns this hotel, Miss. Denis is going to begin at Trinity College, Dublin, in September. To study literature."

His mouth tensed into a crooked smile.

"Yes," the waitress said. "He'll be a poet himself one day, or a teller of tales. He's full o' the blarney, Miss, so be careful of him."

"Please, Mrs. Shea. I can speak for myself," he said.

"Well, why don't you then?" she asked. She gave him a haughty look and disappeared into the kitchen.

"What's your name, Miss?" he asked.

"Clodagh."

"I'm Denis," he said.

"What are you reading?" I asked.

He closed the book and I read the words engraved in gold on the jacket: *War and Peace.*

"I've not read Tolstoy," I said.

"Are you in school, Clodagh?" he asked.

"I study music at St. Mathilde's," I said.

His eyes brightened. "Music? What do you play?"

"Piano. And harpsichord," I said.

"Harpsichord! Do you know Bach's Trio Sonatas?"

"Yes, of course! I play them!"

"Is that right? I heard them performed at the Royal Dublin Society by a woman named Hilda Fitzgibbon. Have you heard her?"

"Only on a recording. She's wonderful."

He stood, smiling widely at me, extending his hand toward a chair at his table, inviting me to join him.

"Are you from Wicklow then, Miss?"

"From Bray. Just south of Dublin. I'm here visiting relatives. The Sheehys."

"Lily and Kitty Sheehy?" he asked.

"Yes."

"The Sheehys know my family, the Lanagans, well." He looked at me thoughtfully, trying to figure out who I might be to them.

"A cousin or some such, are you?" he asked. It was striking that if his family knew my aunts well, that he did not immediately know who I was. Clearly, my aunts did not speak of me or of my dead sister and mother. Having banished us to Mercymount Strand, they'd almost succeeded in erasing us.

A feeling of shame stopped me from telling him the truth. "Yes," I said. "Distant cousins."

"How is Miss Kitty Sheehy feeling these days?"

"Not well."

"Ah. I'm sorry to hear it." He paused.

"Yes . . . ," I said.

"St. Mathilde's. That's not at all far from Dublin," he said.

"No. A twenty-minute bus ride."

"I am really looking forward to school in Dublin, Clodagh. I saw *The Plough and the Stars* at the Abbey Theatre the last time I was there. I have the list of plays for the fall." He fumbled through some papers in a notebook, but gave up looking for it all at once, looked up at me with his face a bit flushed and said, "You should come to Dublin for recitals."

"There are buses that girls can take in from St. Mathilde's for particular events," I said. "I've never gone to any, though. You see, I've been matriculating. But starting in September I'll be living on campus."

"Well, you'll have to come to Dublin for plays and recitals. The Royal Dublin Society often presents symphonic music."

"Brilliant," I said, smiling at him. It would be nice, I thought, to meet him in Dublin; to be ushered about in his enthusiasm.

"Everything's there, Clodagh. You can see the hall that houses the Book of Kells from the dormitory I'll be in. There are Rodins in the National Gallery. Do you like sculpture?"

"I know very little about it."

"Well, in Dublin you can learn. I'll be happy to show you around."

"Thank you."

He gave me a flushed, captivating smile. "You have to forgive me. I've never met anyone who can play Bach's Trio Sonatas on harpsichord."

"Lily Sheehy has a piano that she just had tuned for me. Maybe one day soon you can call around and I'll play for you."

"Grand," he said.

When the sky cleared we went outside and walked a ways down the cliffs. The rain had left its fragrance in the rocks and a silvery light in the sky.

"Have you lived here all your life?" I asked.

"Yes, right in the hotel."

"Is Dunshee really the edge of the world?"

"Yes, 'tis. A beach where the two worlds meet."

"Which worlds?"

He looked out over the pewter-colored waves. "Do you know the story of the selkie?"

"Yes," I said.

"Of course you would," he smiled. "You're a Sheehy."

"What does that have to do with it?"

"Well, there was talk that Frank Sheehy married a selkie. He died not long after and she went back to the sea."

"Really?" I felt myself clench at his words.

"This is the beach of the selkies, Clodagh. When I was a little boy I saw a selkie, myself. I used to watch the shores from that window with the red curtain," he said, pointing back at the hotel.

I looked up and saw the red curtain moving with the breeze.

"One morning," he said, the tone of his voice growing dramatic, "I saw something moving in the kelp. It took her near an hour to unwind herself. By the time she was loose of the green, she'd already come partway out of her sealskin. When finally she was free she stood on the stones. A woman more lovely than any under summer stars and I was besotted with love even at my tender age."

The descending sun penetrated the mist at the horizon. I tried to read his eyes. I felt flooded with the old uneasiness the story inspired in me.

"For near a fortnight I'd not let my own mother near me for want of the selkie. Isn't that funny? I wanted the selkie to be my mother. And if my old mother had not been a strong-as-iron Irish woman I might have broken her heart." In these words I heard a ghost of resentment. He looked out over the water.

"Is it true, then?" I smiled skeptically at him.

"I'm telling you what I saw with my own eyes, Clodagh."

"Your voice is different when you tell the story."

"I've told it many times in my life. But 'tis true."

It got dark almost suddenly, the bright head of the moon appearing, clouds passing it swiftly, insubstantial as smoke.

"I don't believe it," I said. "What you told me about Frank Sheehy's wife."

"Some do, some don't."

"I don't think Lily and Kitty believe it."

As he walked me north to Drumcoyne House along the headland, the sky cleared and stars became visible. He pointed out the floating red lights of the night fishermen moving on the water far below.

"They say all fishermen in their heart's heart are longing to come across a selkie. For don't we all really have it in us to go to the devil?"

"Why do you compare selkies with devils?" I asked, unnerved.

"A man never heals from contact with one. Men drown or go to the drink if she gets away from him with her sealskin after they've been intimate. It's like they've been burned or branded. A man who takes her must hide her skin. Some men forge the skin into a dress."

"A dress?"

"Some men make the dress, thinking it might domesticate her. It's justified as an attempt to balance the animal with the human. But with the skin shaped for a human body she'll never get her seal shape back. The man destroys that possibility. It's the more desperate man that makes the dress, mutilating the skin into human form. It's like trying to reforge her nature. The thing the man loves is the thing he is most afraid of. It's an agonizing thing to love a selkie."

I walked uncertainly on the rocky path, a temperate wind blowing up from the sea.

He must have seen distress in my face because he asked, "Are you all right, Clodagh?"

"I'm cold," I said.

He took my hand as we walked. "Are you? Your hand is so warm."

"I'm all right, Denis," I said.

"Clodagh, I'm going to Galway for a few days and then I'm coming back with my cousin and her lad. The May fires will be lit in the fields north of the Hibernian for the next week. Will you come with us one night to see them?"

"Yes," I said, and smiled at him.

"I'll telephone you when I get back," he said.

We said good-bye at the gate of Drumcoyne House. As soon as I could no longer see his figure descending the hill, backlit by the sea, I walked down again a little way and sat on a rocky ledge.

The water came in and went out slowly, the last of the western light beginning to die.

In the parlor at Drumcoyne House hung a great painting of my father. He was drawn, not handsome. His expression remote.

I asked Lily if she'd show me the rooms where my father had lived and she led me to a back staircase and up a narrow flight.

On the landing she took my wrist and peered into my eyes. "Everything is as your father left it. Please don't touch any of the curtains or any of his clothing. Time has made them fragile."

I emulated her grave, silent walk.

A series of starched infant dresses preserved in glass boxes lined the walls, along with photographs of a baby in a ruffled bonnet and gown gazing irritably into the camera. And several photographs of a brooding boy at different ages, dark haired with shadows about the eyes. And a photograph in which he stood on a chair, wearing a little suit and a confrontational expression, flanked by two teenage girls.

"Your father was fifteen years younger than Kitty, and twelve years younger than myself. Our mother died when Frank was very small and Kitty and I raised him with the help of servants and little help from our father, who traveled a great deal and eventually moved to Dublin. Our father died around the time your father married your mother."

In my father's bathroom, a pipe from a water heater fed into an eerie copper tub. A massive china cabinet was lined with medicines and tinctures that had separated, the dark concentrated at the bottom of the bottles. All with little Latin names printed on strips of paper around them.

She did not let me stay long in the rooms, but I returned later when she said she was going to have a rest. Somehow she'd heard my footsteps though her room was across the house, and she appeared in the doorway as I stood in my father's office looking at the open book on his desk.

"I'm sorry," I said.

"It's all right, Clodagh," she said. "You're his daughter. You should look." But she appeared fretful, protective.

She took a breath, struggling to relax. "Come here," she said, taking me to a room with an iron bed and a large armoire. "This is the room your mother lived in with him. You stay and look. Some of her things are still in this closet. Look." She opened it with a creak and a rush of cold air. "These linen maternity dresses I had made for her. She didn't know that she was expecting a child until a week after he'd died." Most of the dresses were black or dark floral prints.

She held one of the black dresses up to me in front of a vaguely warped mirror in a long frame. "They would fit you well, I think. Though most are black, and of course the midriffs are extra spacious . . ."

"Did she wear these?" I asked.

"Yes, she did. I just ask that you leave his things. You see, I've pressed the clothes and they're in a certain order." She fidgeted a moment then moved to the door. "I'll leave you to look."

"Please, Aunt," I said, and she turned.

"Yes?"

"Did my mother really live in the cliffs before she came to this house?"

"I know only that she was a traveler girl. That she was on her own. She'd tell us nothing else and Frank'd not let us press her."

"Denis Lanaghan thinks she was a selkie," I said.

She let out a little snort. "Clodagh, there are people in Dunshee who believe that fairies put coins in their pockets."

"What can you tell me about my mother, Aunt?"

She looked at me thoughtfully. "She was smart," Lily said, the color coming up in her face. "Frank thought she was an innocent but she was a bit wily." She gazed at me, the muscles around her mouth tightening.

"You never liked her," I said before I could stop myself.

"I just meant that she knew where things came from," Lily said. She sighed. "I'm sorry, Clodagh. It was hard for us. She followed neither codes nor decorum. She had her ways about her and it was hard."

I sat down on the edge of the bed and ran my finger along a swirl of raised threads on the embroidered bedspread. I felt angry and didn't want to look at her. I tried to remind myself how difficult my mother could be. How she had sometimes driven Mrs. O'Dare to the end of herself.

"I understand, Aunt," I said, but did not look up from the bedspread.

She hesitated a moment in the doorway. When she was gone I opened my father's drawer looking for clues to who he was. Everything was neatly arranged: some papers about geological findings, sentences underlined, passages starred in the margins, but all in scientific language, inscrutable to me; a pipe so clean it could never have been smoked; a shoe brush and blacking. I got little sense of him from these things.

I closed the drawer and sat on the bed with my head in my hands. A part of me wished I had never seen the weatherbeaten woman who'd taken my mother's purse; the woman she'd said was her own mother. I wished I could believe that she had been a selkie; that the story of my father finding my mother driving cattle was just a cover for the truth: that he had made love to her on the rocks and had cut the heavy sealskin and formed it to fit her human body; sewn it with coarse thread and decorated the hems with fishing net and seashells. And that it had been the call of destiny that had drawn her back to the sea.

I yearned to feel the heavy satin fur of the sealskin dress. The story of the selkie had a terrible draw for me, but nowhere in myself did I believe any longer that my mother had been a seal that turned into a woman and back into a seal. If such a thing were possible at all, it had not been my mother's truth.

I got up and moved about the little museum of a room. The air seemed to remember a blighted girl; a girl who had come into this house having hired herself out to farmers to drive cattle. A girl with filthy feet who'd slept in a cave in cliff rock. If she was like an animal it was in the way a girl raised outside of houses was like an animal: more intimate with the elements than with the stillness of rooms. Startled, in love with the luxury of decoration. But not inhuman. Not magical.

Early the next morning when I smelled smoke coming from the indigenous wood, the racing of my heart told me it was a tinker fire. I went outside and walked swiftly through the oak trees where I saw the brown-and-white horse standing unharnessed, looking at me from the edge of the clearing.

Angus Kilheen sat on a rock tending a fire, his head turned, looking toward the trees out of which I issued. He seemed afraid to breathe, and what must've been in his mind moved into mine as well: the sense that I was not altogether real. I touched the slim trunk of a tree to steady myself.

An insect moved past my face and I recoiled, waving it away. With that, Angus's face softened. I stayed where I was at the edge of the clearing and the silence went on between us awhile.

"You don't remember me," I said.

"I do remember you, of course. A man doesn't soon forget a lovely, clean-skinned girl waiting for him in his bed." He adjusted a kettle in the fire, the morning light so bright I could barely discern the flames. "You took me aback, love. I thought you were a phantom."

I kept my place in the trees until he said, "Come here to me now, Mare. I'll give you a cup of tea."

I felt a shock at the sound of my sister's name.

He squinted in the sunlight watching me approach.

"Sit down," he said, gesturing to a rock. As I sat, he rinsed two cups distractedly in a pail of water and set them on a flagstone. "You're a lovely sight to see, all grown up as you are now. Are you staying in that fine house in the oaks?" he asked.

I wondered how he knew. I would tell him, I decided. I would tell him who I was and ask him if he'd ever met my mother. But the steadiness of his look made my blood rush, and like the time I'd awakened in his caravan, the thought of conjuring my mother between us made me wary. A darkness filled the soft of my stomach. I looked at the ground. "Yes. My friend from Bray has relatives there."

"And what is your friend's name?" he asked.

"Her name is . . . Clodagh."

"And is Clodagh there in the house in the oaks?"

"No. She's in Bray. She was here but she left."

"And so you're staying with her relatives?"

"Yes, I'm staying on to visit the west." I paused. "Do you remember that time on the Wicklow field . . . you asked me if I'd been west and told me it was the best place on earth?"

"I've thought of you often since that night in Wicklow."

He held my eyes and a breeze blew the smell of him to me, something like wet ground, arable and warm; weather-softened. A smell that excited me.

"Why did you go the next day?" I asked.

"You were too young a girl for what I found myself wanting from you."

His words made me feel the heat and definition of my body.

"I went to Wicklow the last few summers looking for you."

"You did?"

I remembered the fires in the field. "Why are you always alone?" I asked him.

"I'm not alone. My ghosts keep me company, lass," he said.

My heart quickened. I felt envious of his ghosts.

"I have ghosts, too," I said, and regretted the childlike defiance in my voice. I looked away from him. The noise of the sea grew louder from the beach below us. A petrel reeled in the air, its shadow breaking the sunlight between us.

When I looked at him again, he was smiling a little; his face full of expectation. It struck me that he had looked different five years before in the evening light in Wicklow. The naked light of morning illuminated every nuance of his face now. It was not less beautiful, but sadder than I remembered it. He was an older man than I'd thought him to be. He changed his mind about the kettle and took it from the fire before the water was halfway heated, settling it in a bed of earth and ash.

"I lit fires on the edge of the field where we'd met. When you didn't come I camped on the Greystones Road where you said you lived."

"I thought of you too, Angus," I said, and laughed faintly at the inadequacy of the words.

"Do you know the story, Mare, of Finvarra, the Fairy King of Ulster?"

"No," I said.

"He carried off a beautiful human woman to live with him in the Land of the Dead. That was what I dreamt of after that night on the Wicklow field. Of carrying you off."

It was almost uncomfortable, the quickness with which my blood rose to him, my body so ready to betray me. He touched my cheek and I closed my eyes, pressing the side of my face to his palm.

"We live in two different worlds, don't we, Mare? This is the second time you've crossed into mine," he said, intent on me. I tried to control my breaths but they were audible and uneven. "You came to me and waited in my bed when there weren't a dozen words between us. And here it is now, love. Beltaine." He laughed softly and shook his head. "You walk into my camp on the eve of May. The day fire and light enter the blood. Every Irish soul is pagan on this day."

The sea air blew my hair against the side of his face and lifted the hem of my dress, exposing one of my knees.

I shivered, knowing something irreparable was going to happen.

He leaned in and his mouth touched mine softly again and again. When his tongue parted my lips an alarm of pleasure fountained up inside me, followed by waves of warmth.

We stood and he drew me toward the caravan but we did not go inside.

"I study music," I uttered strangely, as if to remind myself who I was.

He sat on the steps and faced me, kissing my skin as he unbuttoned my dress. I could not keep my mouth still with the trembling and the pleasure. He pulled the dress down over my shoulders and I felt the rough of his palms on my breasts. He drew me closer and took a nipple in his mouth, pulling and tightening with the soft heat of his suck. I looked up at the sky and watched the clouds rush toward the sea as the dress slid off, his breathing at my neck amplified over the noise of the surf. A sweat came up on my temples, under my arms, a slickness between my legs; my body a languid weight I could not hold alone.

He tried to make me look at him but I kept turning away, closing my eyes. "Mare?" he kept asking. "Mare?" as if it were a question. I hid my face against his neck and he lifted me onto his lap. There on the caravan steps, in the bright of morning with the sea roaring below us, he guided me onto him. I cried like I'd never been entered before, like what I'd done those few times with Finian counted for little now.

I lost my face in his hair, holding tightly to his neck and shoulders, clutching his thighs tensely between mine. He hardly moved his hips beneath me and I found myself driving against him breathlessly, the pleasure building and breaking until I was all salted air and the screeching of gulls; the bounding rush of water. I felt the burn of my mother's slap on my cheek; saw her standing damp and naked before me, her skin red from the heat of the bath, the pewter heart swinging between her breasts.

I wept, my hair wet, stuck in my mouth, my thighs aching. I lifted myself off him and crouched down on the ground gathering my things. In a moment he was with me on the limestone earth, his mouth on mine. What had been held for so long in abeyance drove us now and we grew defenseless in the heat of it.

When it was over, we lay entwined listening to the crash of the sea, waiting for the clamor of our pulses to quiet. He winced as he disengaged, as if my body had burned him, then reached out and grabbed my dress from where the wind had blown it, caught in the wheel of the caravan.

I took it from him and put it on. "They'll be waiting on me for the meal," I said. "I told them I was just going for a walk."

He stood and buttoned the top button of my dress.

"Can I come back to you tonight, Angus?" I asked.

He took my face in his hands and kissed me. "Yes, lass," he whispered.

"When the ladies in the house are asleep," I said.

I ate the meal with my aunts in half a trance, my body surging; little clocks beating in all the soft junctures of my muscles. I wanted to cry, like I'd survived something dangerous and mysterious. Like I'd gotten somehow lost, ravished by elements; left sore and dreaming and without breath.

I went upstairs and drew a bath, but hesitated before it and did not get in. In my room, I lay naked on my bed and touched the dampness between my legs. Like silt, I thought, from the floor of the sea. A sweat broke on my upper lip, under my breasts. How would I wait out the hours, remembering what he felt like inside me?

Tears fell down over my temples and hair and onto the pillow beneath me.

That night at eleven o'clock the house was quiet. I crept down the stairs and quietly out through the door. I found my way through the pitch darkness, the night air rich with the odor of bracken and the residual smoke from Angus's fire.

He was standing, having heard me coming through the trees, his fire down to red embers. He was already beside himself for me when I rushed into his embrace, and that night on his caravan bed in the dim light of a votive candle set before the Blessed Mother with the broken hand, we lost ourselves in each other.

Walking back to Drumcoyne House through the trees before dawn, I remembered my mother returning quietly from her trysts, hardly breathing, heat and ocean smells issuing from her as she got into bed beside me.

The next afternoon I met Angus at his camp and rode with him in the caravan to a fair at Ailwee Head. I helped him set up and watched him sell his tinware and crockery, make trades with other travelers.

We were there a few hours, the fair growing progressively more and more crowded, when I took a walk among the makeshift booths, looking at displays of such disparate things as kippered fish and rotting fruit, heath brooms and old rope, and found myself lost.

Against a fence a group of traveler girls turned on their heels, smiling and ranting at three boys from town who were dressed in clean pressed trousers and shirts. Two of the girls circled the handsomest boy, asking him if he wanted a look at their knickers. An old woman on the sidelines cried out to them that they were a pair of whores.

The handsome boy stood against the fence with his arms crossed, giving the girls a negligent smile. There was such a lot of screeching and laughter from the girls that I found myself mesmerized by the little scene, watching it unabashedly.

The handsome boy noticed me and said, "And who is this girl? I've not seen her before." He gave me a winning smile.

In that moment I felt a hand grip my arm. "There you are. Come on, now," Angus said, a sternness in his voice that startled me.

"Her bleedin' father's a bit too protective," one of the boys said.

With Angus's turn they all fell quiet.

But on our way from the fairground two of the local boys threw rotten fruit at the caravan. An apple hit Declan and he bridled and screeched, pulling the caravan off the road and down a slope into the field. When Angus had reined him still he jumped from the caravan, racing after the boys who ran for their lives into the field.

"Fuckin' tinkers!" one of them cried out.

"Lunatics!"

"Children of the dead!"

Time passed and I could see none of them. I stood holding Declan's reins, waiting anxiously. Angus came back ferocious, out of breath. The boys had gotten away unscathed. As we headed back to the woods at Dunshee he said, "That's the stinkin' truth between tinkers and landed people. We're belittled and laughed at like we're bloody idiots. We're animals in your eyes."

"Not in mine!" I cried, but he didn't bother to answer.

*   *   *

It was almost evening when we arrived back at his camp in the oak woods. He started a fire and we sat on the stones waiting for the kettle to boil. He had not recovered from the incident. The impotence of his rage ate at him.

After tea he sighed, looking up from his cup. "You don't belong with the likes of me," he said.

"What do you mean, Angus?"

He shook his head, looking into the fire. "Settled girl, clean as rain."

"That doesn't matter."

"It's wrong what we've been doing together."

"No, it isn't."

He hesitated then said, "You haven't asked me my age, have you, Mare?"

"No."

"Why not?"

"You're ageless, Angus," I said. "You haven't an age." I approached him, touching the side of his face with my palm, and he stiffened.

"I'm thirty-nine, Mare. I'll be forty on the first of November."

"You're a young man, Angus."

"I'm a tinker and you're not," he said harshly.

"I wish I were a tinker."

He sneered at me. "You think it's romantic to bloody live this way. You're young, and protected as you are, you only see the surface of things."

A little storm of anger started in my chest. "You don't know that. How can you say that?"

"Go back to the rich house, lass," he said harshly.

I shook my head in disbelief.

"You're just angry now. You wouldn't send me away . . ." My voice softened as I said, "Not after what we've done together."

His eyes drifted to mine. "What did you think would happen between us, Mare?"

"I want to be with you," I pleaded.

"What do I have to offer you?"

"Things, objects, don't matter to me."

"They'd matter to you soon enough."

"No, Angus," I said, but as I reached to touch him he stiffened and averted his face.

"It's better that we put a stop to this now. If I have a conscience in me that's what I'll do."

I stood, waiting for some change in him, afraid to move.

"I'm a traveler. I'll be gone from this place in a few days' time." He looked up at me plainly. "Don't come back to me here again, lass."

I stumbled back through the woods and saw a little black car parked in front of Drumcoyne House. I smoothed my hair and wiped away the residue of tears from my face.

Aunt Lily greeted me at the door in a stiff purple dress with a gold and garnet brooch at her throat.

"Father Galley is here," she said. "Giving Kitty Extreme Unction." She grasped my wrist, squeezing tight, her distress making her unusually forthcoming.

"Oh, Aunt," I said, shivering.

"I think she might leave us, Clodagh." I took both of her hands in mine. "Father Galley is alone with her now."

We ascended the stairs together to wait in a study near the room where the priest was with Kitty.

Lily went abstractedly to the window, the fingers of her right hand moving over the brooch at her throat. I wanted to touch her, to reassure her somehow, as if I might find reassurance for my own pain by offering her the same.

"I'm sorry I went into my father's rooms without asking" was all that I could think to say.

"You never knew your father. You have a right to your curiosity. I never knew my own father either, Clodagh. He never had a word for me or for any of us."

"I'm sorry to know that, Aunt," I whispered. She looked at me with thoughtful curiosity and gave me a small, halfhearted smile.

"Of course if Frank were alive he'd be a wonderful father to you!"

"Would he?" I asked in earnest.

"Oh yes." She looked at me uneasily. "Are you cold, dear?"

I had not stopped shaking. "Yes, a little."

"Sit near the fire," she said, pointing to a little range in the corner of the room. I nodded but stayed where I was.

"I've always loved this window. You can see above the forest and far inland." But when she looked out it was at a great drift of shadow in the sky moving in from the east. "Watch and you'll see the shadows of day change right before your eyes."

She looked at the door to the room where Kitty was. "There's a terrible momentum to the days lately," she said. "Like the course of everything is set, impatient to find its finish."

"I feel that, too, " I said, moved that we shared the same perception. I felt a powerful wish in that moment that she should love me. I renounced Angus Kilheen in my thoughts. I had an urge to confess what I had done, to get some kind of absolution from her. But I knew what a mistake that would be.

The floor creaked near the window and she turned toward it with wide eyes, hand on her bosom.

She seemed so startled that I asked, "Are you all right?"

She shook her head. "I've lived here all my life and I'm afraid here."

"Of what?"

"The strangeness of the light in a room sometimes."

"Would you ever leave Drumcoyne House?" I asked.

"Oh, no!" she said as if it were unthinkable. "No." She touched the glimmering brooch at her throat. "But I don't want to be alone in this house. I'm glad you're here, Clodagh."

My eyes filled with tears.

"What is it, Clodagh?"

"I . . . just want to do the right thing, Aunt. I want to please you."

"You do please me, dear," she said.

She touched my shoulder. "I want you to think of Drumcoyne House as your home, Clodagh."

As I searched her face I felt her retreating from my intensity, until I detected the faint gleam of mistrust in her eyes.

That night I woke sweating in the dark. I saw Angus Kilheen's horse shifting from leg to leg in my doorway, the light of the hall flooding into the black of the room. I sat up in bed and the vision faded.

In the isolation of that hour I felt dismantled by the lovemaking with Angus, and wished that I had never come to Dunshee.

I could feel him breathing across the darkness of the oak woods.

· 2 3 ·

I DIDN'T SLEEP. THE TASTE OF ANGUS'S SKIN STAYED ON MY tongue. I told myself wanly that I did not want his poverty or his darkness. I relived the words of his rejection, yet my body remained full of erotic volition; my blood clamoring and wild and unafflicted. I wanted him unbearably.

At first light I made myself get up and splash my face with cold water. Wanting to feel a part of Drumcoyne House, I put on a formal dress and went downstairs. Kitty was up and asked me to play the piano.

I attempted a Debussy Prelude, the last piece I had committed to memory for Sister Seraphina, but had difficulty concentrating and asked if I might try it again later.

I took refuge in the kitchen, trying to make myself useful to Mrs. Dowling, helping her make the toast for breakfast.

In the afternoon I walked to the Hibernian to see Denis, to be in his civilized presence. Mrs. Shea told me that he wasn't back yet from Galway.

I sat for nearly three hours waiting for him at a table near the big window that overlooked the strand, trying to hear the Debussy Prelude in my mind. But I was listless, my ears full of echoes.

When they arrived Mrs. Shea met them in the hotel entrance and said something to Denis that made him blush. He came to me looking very fresh faced, his cousin and her friend following.

He introduced me to Joan and Roy. Joan was fair with puckish features like Denis; Roy tall and dark haired, a sharp-featured handsomeness to him.

They seemed pleased that I was there. "Denis mentioned you to us on the drive up here," Joan said.

Certain that his cheeks would be ablaze I spared him by not looking at him.

"Are you looking forward to the Beltaine fires?" Joan asked.

"You're still coming with us, I hope," Denis said.

"Yes," I replied.

"Grand," he said.

"Well," Joan said. "We'll get our rooms arranged, shall we? Are
you staying far, Clodagh?"

"About a twenty-minute walk north," I said.

"Of course. You're a Sheehy. Clodagh should probably get a room
as well, Denis. The fires go very late, Clodagh."

"I don't think I should . . ."

"Of course you should. Ask your mother to telephone Lily Sheehy,
Denis," Joan said.

I followed them into the hotel lobby with its dark wood-paneled
walls and green upholstered furniture, and Denis introduced me to his
mother who stood behind the registration desk; a small nervous
woman with a pair of glasses around her neck that she put on to look
in the reservation book.

"She can take the yellow room. It's number three, just at the top of
the stairs," she said, handing me the key.

"Can you telephone Lily Sheehy and tell her it's all on the up-and-
up?" Denis asked her and she agreed, peering at me over the frames of
her glasses.

As we readied to ascend the stairs I heard Denis's mother going back
and forth with Aunt Lily, insisting there'd be no charge for me to stay.

Joan detained me on the landing.

"Denis is very impressed with you, Clodagh."

I smiled at her.

"It's grand that you'll be in school so near each other."

"Yes, isn't it?" I said, trying to match her cheerful enthusiasm.

"I'm knackered from the drive," she said. "I'll have a lie down for
awhile."

I told her I was going to rest as well and she said she'd knock when it was time to go.

I closed the door on my little room with great relief, lay down on the yellow ruffled bed, and began to cry. I could hear the sea through the open window. When I closed my eyes my pulses thrummed. If I had not met Angus Kilheen in the woods I would have enjoyed the assumption that Denis and I were a couple. But my being here with Denis now was a deceptive act.

Having slept little the night before I fell into a restless sleep full of dreams about playing a broken, dissonant-sounding piano.

We drove to a pub in a nearby village. In the surrounding fields we saw people making piles of wood and paper and broken furniture for bonfires.

The pub was rough, a damp smell of stale lager on the close air; the floor covered with sawdust. Some local young men sitting on kegs nodded at Denis as we entered. He guided us to a table near the bar and bought pints of Guinness for himself and Roy, and half pints for Joan and me. The young men on the kegs were smoking and laughing loudly.

"They're uneasy tonight," Joan said under her breath.

"Why?" I asked.

"No women with them," said Roy.

When I looked confused Joan explained that Beltaine was a time of coupling. That in some isolated places in the west people still took the pagan holidays very seriously.

"Do they celebrate Beltaine in Wicklow, Clodagh?" Joan asked me.

"Travelers light fires. I don't remember any of the people from the village or the town celebrating it," I said,

"Dunshee's one of the places where the old celebrations are always marked," she said. She was a few years older than Denis. I had learned in the car ride over that she and Roy were both Galway University students who studied Irish history and the Irish language.

"It's interesting," Joan said. "There are a few bands of travelers who do keep certain traditions alive that have been lost in many places in Ireland."

"Here's to those travelers!" Denis said, raising his glass.

"To the travelers!" the others laughed.

Through the open door we could see someone lighting a bonfire in the distance.

"Where do the travelers originally come from?" I asked.

"The travelers were created by the famine. Displaced people moving in circles," Denis said.

"Not at all," Joan said. "The travelers were here before the famine. Maybe some are people displaced by the famine. But not most."

"Well, who are they, then?" he asked with a note of irritation in his voice.

"It's uncertain," Roy said. "Some say they're of gypsy stock."

"They're a true relic of ancient Ireland," said Joan. "Some say that they came from the sea."

"Oh," I said with a smile. "Would that make the travelers related to the selkies? Denis and I were talking of selkies the other day."

"Ah, the selkies," Roy said. "Now you've come to bring up the selkies in the right company," he said, pointing to Joan.

"Do you believe in selkies, too?" I asked.

"Yes," she said and smiled. "Don't you, Clodagh? With a story of one in your own family?"

I shook my head.

Joan made a disappointed face and took a sip from her glass before reciting: " 'It was the cries of a fisherman that lured me ashore, lowing like a bull seal, floating in a boat over my bedroom in the night sea.' "

"I remember that part," I said. "We must have heard the same version of the story."

"Selkies are drawn to the erotic desire of the human male, which they can feel across great distances of water and air," Roy said, smiling. "Bull seals just don't do it for them."

He and Denis laughed.

"A selkie is a refined, subtle creature in the ways of pleasure. She can teach a human male to please her better than any oafish bull seal. But only just barely," she added, "for the human male isn't much above oafish."

Denis and Roy moaned.

Two of the young men who'd been on the kegs were standing near our table at the bar, listening and smiling over our conversation. "So they come to shore for sex!" one of them, a dark-haired one, cried out.

"It's the perpetual physical hunger of the human male that draws her," the other one said, winking at Joan.

"The human female being so protective of her charms and so ungenerous," the dark-haired one said.

We laughed with them but left off our conversation for other things until the young men went back to their friends.

"I can't tell if you're serious," I said to Joan as Denis and Roy were talking about something else.

"I know we're laughing, Clodagh, but I believe in everything I'm telling you." She leaned into me and said, "You see, Clodagh, the selkie does not intend to stay. She intends after her trysts to go back to the sea and many of them do, when the man lies exhausted on the rocks beside her. The soul of the man is destroyed because he knows he'll never go on such a wild, arching swim with a mortal woman. Those men are damned. But a virile man'll hold her to him till he exhausts and weakens her. Then he gets her sealskin and hides it and marries her. . . ."

The pub had grown crowded, full of smoke and noise. The three of them were downing their drinks and ordering more. Soon glasses of Guinness were lined up on the table and I could not keep up.

"We ought to go out now. It's near dark," Joan said.

When we went outside, the hill was brilliant with bonfires. We walked a bit then stopped on the outskirts of a roadside fire. We all went quiet, staring into the flames, the air around us rippling with heat. A chair stood on a heap of wood in the center of the blaze, shaking, its edges smoldering, dissolving in red glitter.

I felt Denis move closer to me, and a shiver of revulsion tightened in my stomach. I turned from the fire and looked toward the sea, remembering the heat of Angus Kilheen's body. I moved a few yards out of the fire's range where the air was cold. A purple mist still stirred vaguely at the horizon over the sea, like a dissolving curtain.

When I turned back to the fire, Roy and Joan were kissing each other. Denis smiled at me and I smiled back. Encouraged, he moved toward me and reached for my hand and I let him hold it for a few moments before taking it back.

When Joan looked in my direction I tried to think of something to say to keep the conversation going. "Why are there no male selkies?"

"The sea is a woman's domain," Roy said and winked.

Denis opened a bottle of Guinness. "Here in this place the stories are only about women." He threw the bottle cap into the blaze.

"Joan, you ought to tell Clodagh your story . . . you know the one . . . ," Roy said.

"Ah, I don't mind telling Clodagh," she said slowly, her gaze returning to the fire. "When I was little my mother saw a group of beautiful women in long dresses standing on the rocks that jutted up through the surf. You'll know the rocks, Clodagh, from the south beach. Pointed, jutting rocks. My father said she was wanderin' in the mind. But she swore she saw them, all lookin' up at her as plain as day, as if they knew her to the heart. Still she was frightened of them. Two days later she was dead, of an aneurysm in the brain."

I looked at her. "Of course her vision of the women was attributed to her illness," she said.

"Who do you think those women were?" I asked.

"Apparitions from archaic Ireland. A woman from Inisheer told me that people near death can see things that elude the rest of us."

"But who were they?"

"We don't really know. Whoever they were, they were kind. My mother said they looked at her with great gentleness in their faces. She felt recognized by them."

The purple mist over the sea had turned into dim streaks. On the inland side of the field the fires breathed and glistened, sending sparks up into the blackness.

Denis moved in circles in the dark field, kicking at the earth.

"Across the western sea lies the Land of the Dead, which was once called the Holy Isles of Women."

"Do you think those women were selkies?" I asked.

"Some guess that in the old days they'd come like guardians to help the selkies ensnared by men," Joan said. "They'd appear sometimes to them in their husband's homes and show them where the sealskin was hidden. They rarely come now. They come for daughters and granddaughters and great-granddaughters of selkies to bring them to their rightful afterlife. Others say they're from pre-Christianity, holy figures like the saints are to us now."

"Like an order o' nuns," Roy said. "A bloody order o' sea nuns."

Joan clucked her tongue at the irreverence of his tone. He shrugged and made a sheepish face and she turned from him with an air of irritated victory. "But they're hardly chaste," Joan said. "They don't involve themselves with men or bull seals. They keep horses and stags as their lovers."

"Surely it's only myth," I said.

"You have to remember that aboriginal Ireland was different from modern Ireland," Joan said. " Shapeshifting was a true thing; a phenomenon. The selkies, and those women, whatever they are, are living relics of an older time. Think of it this way. They're a kind of dinosaur that's survived. Beautiful archaic monsters slippin' through the seams, transcending the centuries."

In that moment I envied her innocence, her patience with the strangeness of the idea and her willingness to suspend disbelief. I had worn those capacities threadbare in myself. I relaxed and let myself feel the drink in my body.

A young man in a group passing the fire recognized Joan and called out to her: "Where are Willie and George?"

"In Ailwee," she answered.

"Who are Willie and George?"

"My brothers."

"Are you close to your brothers?" I asked.

"I am," she said. "The little buggers."

"How old are they?"

"Eighteen now," she said.

"I had a sister," I said.

"Did you?"

"We were twins. She died when we were five."

"Then you have one foot already among the dead," she said. "To have a twin that is dead! You surely must have eyes that penetrate the layers of this world." Though her words made me uneasy, she touched my arm, and I felt in the tenderness of that gesture an implied respect.

I looked into her face. "I'm Agatha and Frank Sheehy's daughter."

"You're Agatha's daughter," she said softly.

"Yes."

"Oh . . ." Her eyes flitted nervously away from mine, all the easiness gone out of her body.

"My mother wasn't a selkie," I said in a tone of appeal.

She hesitated. "She was a figure of local myth, your mother. Many people in Dunshee *do* believe Frank Sheehy had found a selkie. She used to walk in the tide dragging her new brocade skirts after her, frightening the superstitious with her unearthly looks and her white hair, pulling and eating the mussels from the rocks. In Kinvarra the fishermen called her 'the apparition.' My own mother always believed she was a selkie," she said.

A gust of sea air rushed inland, causing the flames to bend. I shivered. The burning chair collapsed and I could no longer distinguish its contours.

"Where is your mother now, Clodagh?"

"Dead," I said.

"How did she die?"

"She drowned," I said.

"Did she now?" Joan asked softly.

My face heated with anger at her assumption. The myth denied my mother's humanity, the difficulty of her circumstances. "You're mad, believing such things," I said.

An uneasy quiet passed between us before she said, "A selkie is not meant to live landed, Clodagh. She wreaks heartbreak on the children she bears."

The wind came up again, blowing Joan's hair into her eyes. Denis and Roy had returned and now Roy claimed Joan for himself, the two wandering off upfield, leaving Denis and me alone. Joan turned, peering after me, her face growing indistinct as she moved farther from the fire.

The flames leaned after them, raveling and unraveling like wind-beaten cloth. Denis pulled up a handful of dry grass and tossed it at the blaze, which sent them back up on the flue, blistering and smoking. He grabbed another bottle of stout and swallowed it down, his silhouette weaving vaguely before the brightness.

"People are all leaving the fires," I said, looking around.

"This is a night meant for romance," he said.

"I'm not feeling well, Denis," I said. I got up and started away from him, heading back to the Hibernian.

"Wait, I'll walk you," he said, coming up next to me in the dark and taking my hand. We walked awhile before he stopped me and tried to kiss me.

"No," I said, pushing him away, rushing toward the Hibernian across a stretch of rocky terrain.

Back at the Hibernian I went directly to my room at the summit of the stairs and secured the door.

Outside the open window the sea crashed and stirred all night in the dark.

The next morning I woke at first light and slipped out of the room, leaving the key at the front desk. I walked north along the strip of beach, remembering all I'd heard the previous evening.

When I neared Drumcoyne House I smelled the fire in the oak woods and moved quietly through the trees. I saw Angus sitting on a rock hammering at a piece of tin. His sadness felt atmospheric, beyond language. I wondered over his life, his isolation, realizing how little I knew about who he was. With his head bent over the tinware he looked like a boy.

He was as surprising as the landscape: its rises and falls; land breaking all at once into precipices; the sea always stirring at its edges, tender and brutal by turns. It had happened suddenly. He'd been mine and then he wasn't. Sparks flew from the tin as he banged at it.

The wolfhound perked up its ears and barked at me and Angus turned and held my eyes a moment before returning his attention to the tinwork. The air was dense now with a promise of rain, the sky steely blue-gray.

I stayed there, sitting on a stone on the outskirts of his camp. The dog came to me and I patted him. An hour must have passed, the sky growing darker. Angus put his things down suddenly and, without looking in my direction, went inside.

I waited a few minutes then went in after him. I found him lying on the bed with one arm over his face, the other hand lying palm down on his chest. He did not stir at the sound of me.

I noticed that he'd taken down the Virgin of the Sea and that the Blessed Mother with the broken hand lay on her side facing the wall. There'd been a fall from grace. I wondered how the Blessed Mother had lost her hand to begin with. In my mind I saw Angus sweeping her to the floor with the side of his fist. There had been falls from grace before. But how long had it gone on, his fury with her, before he'd asked her forgiveness and placed her back on her little altar?

I took a deep breath and approached him. I stood over the bed and unbuttoned the top two buttons of my dress, my pulse running at a loose gallop.

"Angus," I said in a low voice. He did not stir.

"Angus, love," I said.

He made a soft sound. I touched his arm and moved it gently away from his face until he looked up at me. I unbuttoned another button. "Move over and let me lie down with you."

"No, Mare. Leave me to myself now."

My fingers trembled at my buttons. When I did not leave he let out an irritated sigh and turned his face away.

"I want you to know that I'm leaving Dunshee tomorrow, Mare."

My heart surged with pain. I moved away and sat down on the little bench. It occurred to me in the wildness I felt for him that if he wouldn't take me in his arms the world might end. As my eyes filled his form grew indistinct.

What had I expected, I wondered, trying to move into his world? I did not know Angus Kilheen. How could I have expected not to find grief with him; a man who moved alone in poverty?

I asked Angus if I might boil a kettle. He nodded assent and I went out. A few minutes later he came out, picking up the empty cup I'd set out for him on the stone beside my own, and filled it with whiskey. He drank the shot down quickly, closing his eyes. When he opened them his face was flushed and his eyes watery. He sighed and sat down.

"Will you have tea now?" I asked.

"No," he said. He watched me put the tea bags in the metal pot and pour steaming water over them. He took a second shot and as he looked up at the sky after a group of gulls coasting noisily toward the sea, a tightness left his muscles.

We sat in silence. I could smell the coming rain, the cloud cover fraught with dimming light.

After a third drink he said, "There's no such thing as chance, Mare." His face had opened, his eyes bright, the blue of them milky in contrast to the redness. He peered at me, the hint of a smile at the corners of his mouth. He was changed by the drink and I felt mistrustful, and embarrassed by the transformation.

He went inside and brought out a small book bound in dark green cloth called *The Little Book of Trees*. Each plate page shimmered smoothly in the firelight. Under each black-etched tree its name was printed and below that, in smaller slanted letters, was its botanical name. Black Poplar. *Populus nigra.* In the forefront of the picture a close-up of a leaf and a blossom, nut or fruit if the tree produced any.

On a page of coarser grain following each plate was some information about the particular tree and a bit of related folklore.

"Sister Margaret Mooney gave me this book," he said.

"The nun at Holy Ghost Orphanage," I said.

He told me how she used to come to him and hold him when he would cry and tousle his hair and ask him what it was he was crying for. "I never knew how to answer the question so I told her it was because I missed the trees from the mainland, there being none on that rocky island." The day he left the place she gave him *The Little Book of Trees* and touched his face and said to him, "Be good in your life, Little Soul, and if ye ever feel sad for trees again you'll have them at your fingertips." He sighed, shaking his head. "There's no such thing as chance, Mare. It was no chance that I ended up in that place with Sister Margaret Mooney as my mother."

His voice sounded earnest and bumbling. It was as if Angus had gone and left this nostalgic, gently ridiculous creature in his stead.

He looked at me and smiled strangely. "You said once that our destinies tied us together."

"And you laughed at me," I said.

He fumbled with his cup and poured himself another drink, gazing after a dark, seaward-moving cloud. This drink he seemed to take reluctantly, as if he were obliged to take it.

"What happened to your mother, Angus?"

"Died of the typhoid when I was eight months old."

"I'm sorry, Angus. What about your father?"

He stopped breathing, his eyelids lifted in surprise. "My father? Fathers are inconsequential, Mare. They pass in the distance of their children's lives. He took me from Sister Margaret Mooney when I was ten. He wanted me to beg for him, to keep him in the drink. Ol' bastard didn't give a shite if I lived or died. Why should I give a shite about him? It's a mother that matters to a child." He paused, focusing on me.

"Tell me about your own mother, Mare. You've never spoken of her."

"My mother's dead, too," I said.

"When did she die?" he asked.

"Years ago," I said.

"Do you miss her?"

"My mother didn't love me." The words surprised me as they came out.

"How could that be?" he asked.

"She said I tried to get in her skin with her. She didn't like that about me."

"And what of your father?"

I felt uncomfortable with the questions. "You're right about fathers, Angus. They're inseqential."

In his eyes at that moment I saw a trace of the man I desired; but as if to chase the clarity away, he took another drink, wincing as he swallowed.

"Yes, it's the mother that counts," he said hoarsely. I'll never forget Sister Margaret Mooney preparing me for my First Communion. It was thunderin' and the rain was pouring out of the heavens and she leaned in to me with a flushed face and whispered: 'You are about to break bread with God.' The lightning was flashing outside. I'll never forget her, the lovely aul creature, as if she were in a great drama speaking to me in a stage whisper. 'The Eucharist is the medicine of immortality.' " He laughed softly.

We went slowly through *The Little Book of Trees*. He told me that it did not work well as a field guide since the etchings were so ornamental, but that he had memorized some of the folklore, and all the names of the trees. "It's the names I love," he said. "Ash, Cypress, Olive. I used to say them in threes. Sacred Laurel, Sacred Oak, Hazelnut. When I'm feeling anxious I still say them to myself. Silver Elm. Maple. Hawthorn. And then there's the Glastonbury Thorn. That one I always say on its own, but not for comfort. That one I say under my breath as a curse."

I smiled.

"Glastonbury Thorn!" he called out, laughing. "Bloody Glastonbury Thorn!"

Some of the folklore was like poetry. He read: "The cultivated Olive, *Olea europaea,* has an ancient history rooted in the dark beginning of the Wild Olive." And: "Called by the Greeks and Romans 'The Mournful Tree,' the Cypress, *Cupressos sempervirens,* was sacred to the Fates and Furies." And: "The Sacred Oak was known in ancient times as 'The Oracle Tree.'"

The sky had gone darker with the impending rain and the bit of fire had burned itself up. He put the book down carefully on a stone and looked out into the field, raising his hand. "'A sweetheart from another life floats there . . . as though she had been forced to linger . . . from vague distress or arrogant loveliness . . .'" Creases formed at his eyes and I thought he was about to laugh and was startled when he began to cry. "'As though she'd been forced to linger,'" he said.

It was not Sister Margaret Mooney that he was thinking of. I wondered if it was his blood mother, but I felt from his intensity that it was a woman from his past, a sweetheart, as he'd said.

"'Never until this night have I been stirred . . . ,'" he cried, as if someone was in the trees. I stood up, my eyes raking the woods.

The rain began, spattering down in big, warm drops.

I stood forlornly, watching Angus go inside for shelter. "Come," he said. I followed him in. He lay down on the bed with his back to me. The wind stirred the linoleum flap. A bit of tin settled among the tools.

"Angus," I said, touching his shoulder, wanting to ask who it was he'd spoken to in the field.

"When the rain stops you'll go back to the big house, girleen," he said heavily.

The endearment hurt me, touching something old.

"I'm not a child, Angus," I said in a voice that sounded wan.

"You are a child," he said into the pillow. "And so am I."

I fell asleep to the noise of the rain and dreamt I was an infant lying on a white cloth. I heard my mother's voice but could not see her, just a shadow moving past a glare. She said to Mrs. O'Dare, "Put Mary Margaret back inside me, Missus. I want her back in." I was waiting for her to say the same thing about me, waiting, crying. But she didn't and in the dream I was desperate, afraid that she never would.

Half awake, I had difficulty returning from the dream, thinking I was still in the buried bedroom, smelling the air for my mother, my heart quick with anticipation, waiting to feel her hair sweep my skin as she leaned past me to listen to Mare's heart.

Slowly, breathing in the dimness, tracing with my eyes the line of Angus's sleeping form, I came back to where I was. If I'd awaken Angus, it would be Mare's name that he'd call me.

How terrible it was that I had not, five years before, told him another name. Ann or Eileen or Agnes. Jane or Lucy. I said the names into the dark. In the irrationality of half sleep I believed that if I had only given him another name my history might disappear. And that it was the lie I'd told Angus that was to blame for his unhappiness and his distance from me. Even still, I longed for the agony of him whispering my sister's name into my ear.

How far off childhood had drifted, yet I was no different now than I'd been then. To me every dim room on the periphery of sleep was the buried bedroom.

I got up and walked through the rainy woods to the beach, uncertain what would become of me. I gazed into the glittering onrush of the sea. The surf boomed on the rocks and the wind went wild against me, distressing my hair, my clothes.

I approached the tide and it rushed me with an unexpected force, pulling me under, turning me over in the water until my head knocked against a rock. The water retreated and I sat up on the wet sand panting, drops of blood from the ends of my hair smattering my blouse. I touched my temple and my hand was covered with blood.

Disoriented, I did not move quickly enough and the rushing surf took me again. I surprised myself by relaxing as I went under. I thought of my mother giving herself to the sea and I wondered whether the force of it had battered her or broken her bones.

When the tide retreated I got up and ran out of its range, shivering with the cold. Walking to Drumcoyne House my head ached. Still I thrilled as I watched the incoming waves grow progressively more violent.

I startled Aunt Lily, appearing at the door wounded and soaked by the sea.

"You've blood all over you!" she cried.

On my way home I'd pressed my hair into the wound to stop the bleeding. But when I saw myself in the front mirror there were dried drips along the side of my face and down my neck.

Lily and Mrs. Dowling cleaned me up and tended the wound. I went upstairs and took a bath. About to descend the stairs, I stopped on the landing when I heard Aunt Kitty say in a voice still weak with illness: "Just like Agatha."

"Remember, Kitty, she's Frank's daughter, too."

"She's not like Frank," Kitty said slowly. "She's got the vagrant ways of her mother. Going for wild swims on dangerous beaches." She spoke quietly, yet her resolve against me was clear.

I pressed my hand against a bit of light reflected on the cool green wallpaper.

"Yes," I heard Lily assent. I rubbed my finger against the raised, velvety fleur-de-lis design.

"I can't see Frank in her at all," Kitty sighed. There was silence. "Remember how we had to scrub Agatha for a week when she first came here to get all the bugs and muck off of her?"

"Yes," Lily said in a low voice. "She was filthy."

"I'll still never know why Frank wanted her instead of that Dudley woman."

"The Dudley woman only wanted his money, Kitty. You're the one who always told me that," Lily said impatiently.

"She'd have been a better wife to him than that wild little Agatha. This one's brought the smell of her back into this house!"

Lily said nothing. I leaned back against the cool wall looking at the shrine on the landing. The sun through the fanlight window reflected on the votive cups and on the gilded stars around the Virgin's head.

I went to Angus's camp the next day to say good-bye. We went for a walk together along an old cliff road flanked by fuchsia hedges. I was lost in my thoughts, resigned to going back to Wicklow, when the sky opened into deluge and the rain blew over the tops of the hedges. He turned to me and took my hand then pressed me into a bed of earth under the bushes. My heart filled like a pool; the taste of his mouth exquisite, as if tasted for the first time. Tears shot into my eyes as he lifted my skirt and I felt him like a flame inside me.

The rain got in at us through the hedges and pelted at us from the sides, the earth under me turning to mud.

When the rain stopped, we walked, letting the wind dry the mud on our clothes and hair. Everywhere men were plowing the wet clods of their fields.

We wandered along rugged tongues of land reaching into the Atlantic, then climbed up a hilly coastline to a straight fall of hundreds of feet to the sea. Gulls shrieked below us, floating on swells of air.

I pointed at a clump of beach grass and said, "Look! The Sacred Laurel!" and he laughed and tickled me.

It was still damp by afternoon and we shivered, our arms around each other as we walked back to the caravan. I could smell heather and bracken and rushes, the coming summer on the air.

"Come with me south, love. Along the western coast," he said.

I told myself that I had reasons not to go with Angus Kilheen. I had Sister Seraphina at St. Mathilde's to return to. I had Bach cantatas and Chopin pieces to learn. I thought of how proudly Mrs. O'Dare had listened to my clumsy early practicing. At Dunshee I had found affection from Aunt Lily and the possibility of a friendship with her, in spite of what I'd overheard. And there were the carefully preserved relics of a father.

I was driven to my father's rooms that I might try and find something of him left there for me. I touched the edges of his books. Architecture. Botany. *The History of the Holy Roman Empire.* Old books whose pages he'd once touched now smelled of absence and compressed time.

I lifted a blue knit man's cardigan that hung on the back of his desk chair. The shoulders jutted out at two points, the impression a skeleton might have left. He had been a small man. Neat, organized; enabled by his sisters and his wealth in the pursuit of his own hobbies, and in the acquisition of my mother.

I opened the top drawer of the desk and found a black comb with white flecks in its teeth, and two wedding photographs. In one my mother, a girl all in white, looked off to the side, her face blurred, while my father's and my aunts' images were distinct. My father smiled crookedly, leaning onto a cane, his cheeks hollowed, his eyes dark, the fine clothes hanging on him. Kitty and Lily stood a step behind and to either side of them, with poised, self-conscious smiles.

Someone had taken the other photograph from above, perhaps from the steps in front of a house or building. In it my mother and father walked along the road, my mother looking suspiciously into the lens, her lips pursed, the wind blowing a strand of hair across her face. With one arm she linked my father's, while the other hung at her side, the hand in a fist against her thigh.

I sat down in the chair and stared at my mother's expression. She was such a child. If I had not known that she was fifteen at the time I might have thought her thirteen or even twelve. With a jolt of vertigo I understood the alienation she must have felt; the confusion of finding herself with Frank Sheehy and his sisters. And then to find herself sent away across the country with Mrs. O'Dare to give birth to her daughters. And as I gazed at her lost face I thought of her love for the tinker man, William Connelly. Her wild, secret life with him.

The sense of my father, the man I had been struggling to know, shrank away from me into untenable distance. With desperation I moved through the rooms looking for ways to claim him. One of his starched shirts made a soft coughing noise as I shook it. I opened his cabinet of medicines, shaking and opening the bottles, smelling the reeking tinctures, violating Aunt Lily's little mausoleum. The bedroom floor creaked as if he were there watching me through the doorway and I felt across that air, each of us looking in vain to recognize the other.

And then I went back to Angus Kilheen.

The first nights traveling with Angus I didn't sleep at all. Enough moonlight came through the linoleum flap at the window to illuminate him as he slept, his expression elevated, agonized like the face of Saint Francis of Assisi from a painting I had always admired on the wall at St. Brendan's. I was relieved when we lay side by side in the darkness; relieved that his eyes were closed and I could watch him, sensing a man even more fragile than the one I'd imagined.

When in his sleep he'd turn from me onto his side, his body in that bit of moonlight looked like a mass of land, the tall uneven cliffs along the Atlantic. A shoulder, a hip, a leg of earth. As the night progressed and his sleep deepened, he grew solid, still, while I fluctuated in the darkness as if composed of black, always faintly moving water.

I lay trying to read the dim outlines of objects. A fender and iron, perhaps, or a coal scuttle.

Our first day together after leaving Dunshee, we'd stopped at a traveler fair in Ballyvaughan. He'd parked the caravan and set up a table at the back on which he displayed crockery and tin pots. He'd traded four cups and saucers for a hammer and when the man he'd dealt with was gone he whispered and spat over the hammer, then waved the air in front of it with his fingers.

"Saining," he'd called it. "Driving out the demons lurking in an object. Things are full of the secret lives of the people who own them. Flecks of their soul get into the object."

That evening I saw him sain his own blackened skillet before he cooked sausages in it. "The air is full of itinerant souls looking for something to contain them," he'd said. "If something sits too long in darkness, you've got to drive away the legions of the damned." He'd pinked faintly, watching my eyes.

Later when I wanted to revive the fire in the coals I'd asked him if I should sain the flint. "You never sain the flint," he said. "It's the sadness in that object makes the fire come up."

It intrigued me to think that sorrow and memory could be contained in matter; that an object could bear the internal life of a person, as if people could not bear to be the keepers of their own souls. I felt a strange pity for the stillness, the steadfastness of objects.

In the deep shadows of the caravan at night, the coal scuttle appeared to be the armless bust of a very old man, and if I moved my head up in a certain position I could see his haggard profile. Itinerant souls hummed in the tin and metal scraps, echoing in the irons, a homeless shuddering chorus.

Angus and I had contrived a simple plan. I would say good-bye to Lily Sheehy, who Angus thought was only an aquaintance, at the Galway station and get on the Dublin train. Angus would meet me at Athenry, the first stop going east, and we would travel south hugging the western coast.

I had written to Mrs. O'Dare and told her that I'd be staying on a bit longer at Dunshee. I hoped that at least a week or so might pass before she'd speak to my aunt and the two would compare notes. My plan was to write to them both saying that I met a girl I'd known from St. Brendan's on the train who'd invited me to travel with her for the summer. I decided I'd send them cards of all the places I'd visit that summer with my fictional friend.

It was always part of Angus Kilheen's plan that I'd arrive back in Wicklow in enough time to prepare for the fall at St. Mathilde's. But with the passing of each day my previous life felt more remote.

I was an imposter in two worlds.

I asked Angus one night who the woman was that he'd wept over in the woods at Dunshee.

He hesitated before he reminded me that he was thirty-nine and surely I had to understand that there had been women in his past.

"But it's someone you miss," I said.

He thought a moment before he said, "It's no more, lass. 'Twas only the drink getting the better of me."

Those early days together, Angus sensed the anxiousness and uncertainty in me. He was watchful of my moods. He often reached over and squeezed my hand or my forearm as he drove, while I stared off distractedly into the fields. Or he'd pull the reins and the horse would halt. He'd kiss the side of my face. "It's all right now," he'd say, and in the very tenderness of his voice I'd sense his fear that I might bolt.

One night he called out when he was inside me, "Mare! Mare!" as if he were trying to find me through darkness or rain. It hurt that he called me by my sister's name. It felt dangerous. I tried not to hear it; to listen only to the wind stirring the linoleum flap.

I was afraid to open my eyes; afraid I'd find Mare standing at the foot of the bed watching us. I tortured myself, imagining that, like me, she had inherited from our mother a backward nature, wild and wanton. And in some moments when I was farthest from myself, when I hadn't slept or was thinking hard about Sister Seraphina and St. Mathilde's and feeling like I had gotten lost, I was certain that it was Mare that Angus loved. She was the beloved one. She was the one with the soul. And that it was Angus and Mare together traveling the west of Ireland, and that Clodagh had disappeared.

But on bright days with the air full of the promise of summer, Mare's ghost felt faint, easy to dispel. And when I forgot her, she seemed to be nowhere.

We stopped in Doolin, the village just near the Cliffs of Moher in County Clare. While Angus shopped for provisions, I went alone to the post and wrote and posted cards to Sister Seraphina and Mrs. O'Dare.

The messages were identical:

"The cliffs are beautiful. They fall sheer hundreds of feet to the sea. My friend and I are staying at a bed and breakfast in Doolin. In a few days we'll go south to Kerry. I'll write again then. Love, Clodagh."

*   *   *

The farther south we moved, the more the horizon to the east shrank, the clouds touching the edge of the land after a rain. But the west opened into light and I could see no end to things.

On our fourth day together we stopped and camped upfield from a group of squalid travelers in battered, discolored caravans. Children howled and squawked, filthy and half naked in the dampness. Dejected men stood around fires drinking and staring into flames.

Angus had told me that most of the tinkers lived hand-to-mouth. But we always had eggs, a quarter loaf or half a cabbage, and a few rashers. I'd never been hungry before but Angus had when he was small and his father drank. He told me he couldn't bear to look at the poor wastrels with the drunken fathers, knowing they'd go to bed with the pain of the empty gut.

And as if I did not want to think about the sadness I saw in the faces of the children, I thought of the objects they owned, pitying the tea towel tied around a girl's waist. A burlap doll bursting its seams. A dented metal cup sitting on a stone.

From this close the life of the traveler no longer seemed beautiful, yet it pulled at me. If felt closest to the truth of who I was. I found a certain solace in the wind and the dampness; in the ethereal, changing light of the Irish west.

One afternoon while we were camping among the tinkers, Angus went into the little village and I wandered off in the direction of the tinker camp, drawn by the frenetic reel of violins. Two old women sat in beat-up upholstered chairs on the dirt, clapping their hands in time.

Two of the fiddlers were old men. The other was young. He sat on a bench as he played, leaning into the arm of a heavy, cow-eyed old woman.

The bows rose and fell like pistons and a few people danced. My heart pounded, stirred by the wild yearning in the music.

The young fiddler's eyes darted up at me. I smiled and his mouth tensed painfully. He lost time with the music, his face gone red and shiny. He struggled, eyes fluttering, to rejoin the melody.

When the music stopped, the heavyset woman in the upholstered chair nearest me grabbed me by the skirt and said, "I think tha' one fancies ye, Miss." She pointed at the young fiddler, then sucked hard at a cigarette. "Tha' one's a bit touched, though. Soft in the head, though he plays the music with great spirit."

The other seated woman, small and very straight-backed, said, "Ah, sure, his mother there with him, Miss, is a saint on earth. The way she gives her life to that boy."

"She's no saint!" the heavier woman cried as she blew out a lung-ful of smoke. "She's got a stake in keepin' that one to her. Something not right about it." She held the arm of her battered chair as if it were a throne.

"Ye see the dark in all things, Anne," said the other.

"I see the truth. Without him she's a lonely old woman. Keepin' her own demented son with her, so. And the two o' them sleepin' side by side in tha' slim bit of a bed they share."

The small woman clucked her tongue.

I was about to go when the heavier one grabbed my skirt again and pressed a damp, hot twenty-five-pence piece into my palm and said, "Run to the shops and get me ten Silk Cut. And a book o' matches. Will ye, love?"

"I will, of course," I answered, moved by her familiarity.

When I brought them to her the young fiddler watched me with a lowered head, a great oily strand of hair hanging before one eye.

I stayed awhile wandering through the camp, oddly at ease, receiv-ing looks from the different people because I was unfamiliar, but not the mute stares I'd once received as a settled girl.

An old man selling used and battered shoes stopped me and asked, "Do you need shoes, love?"

I picked out a delicate, once pale pink woman's shoe from the bot-tom of the pile, the leather intensely wrinkled at the instep.

"That one has no fellow, Miss," the man said.

I wondered why he kept it if it had no fellow and no one would buy it, unless he understood something good about it. I liked it. The woman who'd worn it had had a very small foot. I was sure it had been a woman and not a girl who had owned it. The foot had been plump, with tapering toes and the sole covered with scuffs as if, while dancing, she'd swept the ball of her foot on the ground over and over.

I stroked it as if it might stir.

"It has no fellow, Miss," the man said again.

"How much is it?"

He paused. "Fifteen p."

I poured the coins into his oily palm and took the shoe with me.

When we left that place I sat with Angus while he drove, Declan clopping along before us, rump swinging between the shafts. Angus told me that when he was a small boy he'd been to Glendad Head in the north of Donegal where he said on a clear day he'd seen the Mull of Kintyre and the Scottish isles, which climbed progressively north into the Arctic Circle. He said he'd always wanted to travel to the Scottish north, the High Hebrides and the Orkneys. He'd heard that the waves of the sea so far north chimed like they were made of glass.

"The northern light inspires fear in the stranger. Like that red sun I told you about, floating all day and night on the horizon. But further north it's constant dark in winter, so you don't know if you're coming or going. Waking or sleeping. But in the summer," he said and looked at me sidelong, "there's no night at all. Imagine the strangeness of it! And the summer fields have a rarefied smell like violets."

I was drawn to the idea of a place so strange; to breakers of indifferent wind. Not a soul to know me but Angus.

"I like the idea of day and night mixing together," I told him.

While Angus went on about a U-shaped valley in Donegal, I thought about how he'd compared himself to Finvarra, the Fairy King of Ulster, and me to the woman he'd kidnapped and brought into the Land of the Dead. I held strangely to that comparison. In Angus's mind I'd leave him in September for St. Mathilde's. But if I gave myself to his world I doubted that I could suddenly leave it to rejoin the other. I had not the evenness of spirit to get up one morning from under

Angus's body, put on my court shoes and go purposefully to the piano to play the Debussy that at this moment was faded in big pieces from my memory. Preludes like torn fabrics. It was as if I had lost a certain kind of concentration; the capacity for applied subtlety and restraint. I felt awe when I remembered the way I'd found seamless connections in the moods of the music.

The road we were on descended into a valley of rocky, neglected fields. Angus was talking about a certain "hanging" lake, catching his breath as he spoke, holding tight to Declan's reigns, trying to keep the horse from going down the hill too quickly. I could not concentrate on what he was saying.

Of course the travelers had recognized me as one of their own, I thought. Being with Angus made me darker, more elemental, like bog-land or arable field. I had stood on the cliffs the previous evening and let the wind torment my hair to a tangled weathered mass. Before bed at night I had stared at the comb among my things but had not picked it up. I'd fingered the knots in my hair and found a dry blade of grass woven through or a bit of woolen fluff from the bedding.

When I'd gone out to squat in the blackness of the field, I'd liked the warm feeling of my own urine on my feet. My dress unwashed carried the odors of Angus's body commingled with my own. My sleeves tasted of salt from sea air and sweat.

Angus stopped the caravan at the bottom of the hill. He'd been talking to me but I hadn't heard him.

"Where are you now?" he asked, cupping my jaw in his hand and bringing me to face him. Even as he did this I strained my face from his and would not meet his eyes, and this unnerved and aroused him.

I jerked my head loose of his hand. I felt my face heat. Gooseflesh rose on the skin over my neck and chest. I bit my lip to hide a smile and he grew boisterous, for he loved to see me try to stifle my reactions to him. I laughed and struggled against his advances but he called me his little colt and said, "You buck and fight, but you'll take the bit in the end."

He drove the caravan onto the open field and brought me inside.

We got quickly out of our clothes and wrestled on the bed. I was a few minutes on my back with him making love to me before he rolled us both over so I was on top. He pushed me gently up to a sitting position while he remained on his back, then held his arms up to me and I used them as leverage to move over him.

"Look at me," he said. But I kept my eyes to the ceiling, my body shaking with exhilaration.

He took my jaw in his hand and tried to make me face him, but I closed my eyes. After a few minutes of rocking at the thigh I relaxed. He'd left the doors open and the daylight came in on us. The clouds had passed and the sun shone brilliantly now. Being so exposed before his eyes made me feel warm and bright, and I thought of a candle I had seen once illuminated by many candles so that the long cord of the wick could be discerned within like a backbone. I was sure that Angus saw every thrill run through my body and that he could hear the galloping of my heart as audibly as if his ear were pressed to my breastbone.

And then the world went slow. We seemed to be swimming, the air around us heavy as water. Now I was looking in his eyes, which were clear and fixed to mine. My hands pressed against his chest; his were on my waist, the touch of them so soft it burned. We moved steadily together, rocking and lifting, riding the water now, the sensation between us building exquisitely. I squeezed my eyes shut. The rapture was drawn out and kept renewing itself like a curtain furling and unfurling and furling again and I heard myself calling out some inarticulate cry that seemed to come from outside on the field. When I opened my eyes I was shivering. The world was blasted with daylight and a sensation of amnesia.

He was anxious, his eyes lit up; and beside himself as he still was with the desire, he did not recognize that I was confused now, overly tender. With resilient strength he lifted me off him and, rolling me onto my stomach, lifted my hips slightly and entered me from behind, something he'd never done before. I remembered Letty Grogan saying that tinkers were filthy and did it like rams and ewes in the light of day.

240 OF REGINA McBRIDE

I felt rushed with shame and cried out for him to stop. As I wrapped myself in a blanket I told him I was not a ewe or a cow. He lay down next to me and said a little defensively, "It's not a position unusual to men and women."

My temples ached. I curled into the blanket, not wanting him to touch me.

"I didn't mean to hurt you, love," he said, touching my face.

"You didn't hurt me!" I cried. "But I'm not an animal."

"I know that well, lass." He stroked my damp hair away from my temples, but as he gazed at me, a little smile grew at the corners of his mouth and it made me hate him.

I pushed his hand away. "I'm not an animal like you," I said.

He stiffened and withdrew his hand, the words passing painfully through him.

I regretted saying it. My heart beat uneasily.

He let out a heavy breath then turned onto his side facing away from me. I lay there waiting for my senses to come back to me, struggling to understand what it was that had just happened.

That afternoon while Angus slept beside me, I heard one of the Debussy Preludes, "Feuilles Mortes," in my head. "Dead Leaves." I sat up and pressed my hands to the blanket, trying to play it, trying to find the emotional restraint the music required, concentrating on the element of stasis in the piece.

I thought of St. Mathilde's. The deep silence of the studio rooms. The discipline required to rein in the heart; to isolate and set it to formal rhythm and intonation.

How could I go back to long hours of striving for control and precision; a little dormitory room with a cold, clean bed and ironed sheets in which I would lie alone at night, remembering the days that Angus and I had moved from one damp embrace to the next? I wanted to tell him that this change was agonizing; that I'd not be able to reverse it.

Under his makeshift bed was my canvas bag that held new clothes I'd bought for that other life. A linen cutwork blouse. A blue serge skirt.

A box of tortoiseshell hair clips and a pin to wear on the lapel of my jacket: a rhinestone dragonfly. I imagined myself dressed in these clothes, walking onto a stage in a crowded concert hall, court shoes clicking on polished wood. I saw myself sit at the piano to play "Dead Leaves," a hush come over the audience. But in the daydream my hands would not move on the keys and mumbled voices rose from the audience.

A phrase of "Dead Leaves" came to me and as I played and replayed it in my memory I realized that I disliked its quiet formality. I wondered if I'd ever liked it. All the pieces of music I'd committed to memory felt suddenly random, impermanent. I could close my eyes and let the winds dilute them; drive the memory of them away like smoke. I sighed at the unexpected relief I felt, even as my eyes dampened with tears.

I looked at Angus Kilheen beside me and my thoughts of music were eclipsed by the memory of the sex; the rapture that had threatened to take me apart. I remembered the weight of his body on my back and felt curious, letting myself imagine what it might be like.

I leaned into him and stroked the hair away from his ear. "I'm sorry, love," I whispered.

Such an act only asked of me a deeper surrender, I told myself. That was all it asked. I'd relax into the confusion. I would learn to go darker, steadier. The overbrightness of the world would hurt me less.

I turned onto my stomach, resting one side of my face on the pillow. "Angus," I whispered again, and he stirred. I felt his breath on my neck, his hand circle my waist.

Angus laughed at me when I showed him the pink shoe I'd bought, but I argued that some of his beloved crockery was also useless.

"It's like sculpture. Something finely handcrafted. Ruined art is still art. But an old battered shoe!"

"You like to drive away other people's spirits from things, but I like the spirit in this shoe. I like imagining the woman who wore it out."

He smiled and said, "Mad as the mist and the snow."

I kept the shoe in my pocket, squeezing it for luck, and when I'd catch him smiling I'd snub my nose at him and his smile would spread, his teeth large and white in his sun-bronzed face.

That's how things went between us. In little ways we grew easy together, foolish and affectionate.

THE EARLY WEEKS OF SUMMER THE WEATHER WAS GLORIOUS strange along the ocean. Thunderheads filled to the skin with light. A shimmer over the sea. Angus laughed at me for walking about without shoes, my feet and shins filthy. At a fair I found a used cotton dress, longish, with tiny yellow and green flowers on a faded black background. It fit my form as if I'd been wearing it for years, snugly at the bodice and waist, the skirts loose and easy. I had taken to wearing it every day, letting the elements blur and soften my edges. I braided my wild, matted hair with dry bits of flower and field grass. Angus left a barrel outside wherever we camped, and we used the rainwater that gathered in it for washing.

We were on our way south to a fair on the Dingle Peninsula near a place called Caherciveen and our plan had been to keep moving slowly south, but in a field near the coast outside the town of Kilkee we forgot the world for a while and stayed. We grew used to the place together. A fat pony behind a fence whinnied at us whenever we went by. I had taken to bringing him the skins of carrots or apples or the tops of turnips left from our meals. Angus called him Phillip Flannery after a boy he knew in Holy Ghost Orphanage.

And every day on the path to the sea we saw the same old dour-faced man who tipped his hat at us, thin as a rake and wearing the same worn plaid shirt. I called him Father Heavey after an old priest from Immaculate Conception in Bray.

"He's come to spy on you in the western fields. A girl from his parish gone to the devil."

We slept on and off, whiling the daylight hours between love and sleep. He was wild for me, as if he wanted to fill me with children; to drive them out of his own body and into mine. As if he could not bear to be the keeper of their blind, amorphous shadows.

Once he laced his fingers through my hair, reciting Yeats: "'I would that we were, my beloved, white birds on the foam of the sea.'" Those days on the field near Kilkee, he quoted Yeats at every turn. In playful, erotic moments he'd tell me half breathless, half laughing that I had "great, shapely knees" or that I was "fit spoil for a centaur."

But it was at night when we had little inclination for sleep that he recited the poems whole as we sat at the fire and I listened with the black of the night all around us, captivated:

> The host is riding from Knocknarea . . .
> And Niamh calling Away, come away . . .

We'd cross the field in the dark into the little village where there were a few flaring gas jets along its main street and geese nesting along the ruin of a castle wall.

"The moment is always departing, Mare," he said to me one night and held my face in his hands in the middle of the vacant street.

I had stopped sending the cards to Sister Seraphina and Mrs. O'Dare. Like the sounds of the Bach and the Chopin, their faces had begun to elude me.

Sometimes we'd listen to the wireless, a station out of Dublin that came in and out on waves of static. I was happy to listen to reels: fiddles and pipes, but a melodious ballad or an occasional tenor in a grief-stricken song made me uneasy. I listened warily as if the sweetness of music threatened to awaken dormant memories. One night no music came in, only voices sputtering, hissing with distance. Angus toyed with wires and makeshift antennae, but could pick up nothing but crackling. "It's dead now," he said. "We have no music."

There was, that particular night, something overcast about his mood. He took out a tin whistle and played a lament, awkwardly, putting me in mind of my early struggles at the piano. I sensed that he wanted to be alone and I wandered off onto the dark field but the tune followed me, taking on a heartbreaking echo the farther I retreated from it.

Angus was a man given to remoteness, and after the four or five days we'd spent blissful in the field at Kilkee, he was driftng from me, his eyes looking through me, fixing themselves to the horizon. I knew it was not the bit of sky or the boreen that drew him. His thoughts were back with his "ghosts," as he'd called them; back where they must have lived before I'd arrived at his camp in the oak trees.

Those days the light and air were permeable, the dark clouds incandescent at the seams. Cold winds brought up mineraled smells from the bogs. He made me a stranger, taken up as he was somewhere else. I was afraid to touch him.

One night he whimpered as he slept.

I woke at first light as he was kissing my neck. "My own love," he whispered as his large, warm hand pressed my thighs open. He pushed himself into me and said breathily, "You're my own love." The anguish and intensity in him was something at a pitch that upset me even as it stirred, bringing me to a fast, unexpected rapture.

I had a distraught feeling as he pulled away that it was not me he'd been making love to.

I watched his graceful figure move through the small activities of a day: the lighting of a fire; his brief wash over the rain barrel; weighting a shirt with rocks and leaving it to the wind to freshen.

Lonely for him I committed to memory everything from *The Little Book of Trees,* and late one afternoon as he lay on his back on the caravan bed staring at the ceiling, I sat down beside him and whispered, "Silver Elm. Maple. Hazelnut."

He looked fully at me, surprised.

"Because of their beauty, hemlocks are often planted as ornamentals," I said.

He smiled.

"Where have you been, Angus?"

He closed his eyes. I was afraid I'd lost him again.

I lay down on the bed next to him and asked him for a tale from the Holy Ghost Orphanage. The request made him thoughtful as he described the crumbled whitewashed walls; the noise of a crazy wind shaking the latches, creaking in the cracks of the door; the constant rain over the little island. He told me of Sister Margaret Mooney administering to a boy with consumption, little drops of blood speckling his collar and his pillow. The memories animated him. He looked into my eyes with an earnest face. "She cared for him selflessly," he said. "That boy died and she suffered the loss of him. She suffered the loss . . ." His voice trailed away.

"That boy, Mare," he said. "I saw him clear as day one morning sitting in his bed. When I remembered that he was dead, he faded."

"Is that boy one of your ghosts, Angus?" I asked.

"He is. The boy's mother had brought him there. Left him. She had too many other children to care for and she said she couldn't care for them all."

"Who is your other ghost, Angus?" I asked.

He stiffened and went quiet. "Tell me something else about Sister Margaret Mooney," I said to bring him back to me.

He told me how once she fried bread and dusted it with sugar meant for the nuns' tea and brought it to the boys in their beds. He spoke slowly, with a soft urgency, his eyes wide as he looked at the caravan ceiling.

He described her eyes, dark blue and flecked with orange, magnified by her glasses; her smell of the kitchen: tea and flour and oats.

That afternoon no wind blew at all. In the dim quiet of the caravan where we lay chastely side by side, I had the sense that his soul was ajar of him, exposed on the air around me; that I could breathe him into my lungs. I whispered, "I love her, Angus. I'm in love with Sister Margaret Mooney."

His face turned toward mine and I felt his breath on my temple. "Lovely girl," he whispered. He leaned into me and kissed my hair. "Lovely, lovely girl."

But minutes later he closed his eyes like a devotee and returned to the sacramental territory where I was not permitted.

*   *   *

I walked into town alone to get food for a meal. I'd left Angus as he was pulling a heavy trunk out from under the boards of the bed. If we were going to make the fair at Caherciveen at all, we'd have to leave soon and travel steadily until we arrived. He needed to go through some of his things, to organize his wares for selling; to make a ledger. We were at the end of our money so something would have to be done.

When I returned I saw Angus out in the field gone after Declan. I went into the caravan and my heart stopped. An animal-skin dress lay on the bed, black and silver point, speckled in places. I told myself it might not have been the thing I immediately took it for, for hadn't I only fleeting memories of my mother in her fur dress? Hadn't I wondered if the thing was real at all, seen only in half or quarter light; illuminated only in sections? Never in its completeness. But it was with the senses that come alive in the dark that I recognized it; its gray-green smell like air before a heavy rain, and its faint animal reek. When I closed my eyes and touched it I knew the heavy, glossy texture warming under my palm.

It kept a semblance of my mother's shape as if she had just taken it off. My eyes filled and the contours of the dress grew less distinct and trembled as if seen through water.

When Angus came in he stopped at the threshold. He saw my hand on the waist seam of the dress, the dampness in my eyes.

"Where did you get this?" I asked.

He paused then let go of a sigh. "It belonged to a woman . . . a woman who is dead now."

"What woman?" I asked.

He said, "That day in the woods in Dunshee you said you had a friend named Clodagh. That her relations owned that big house where you stayed."

"Yes."

"This dress belonged to Clodagh's mother."

"You didn't tell me you knew Clodagh and her mother."

"I knew Agatha, Clodagh's mother."

248 + REGINA McBRIDE

"Why do you have this dress?" I asked him. He sat down on the edge of the bed placing a hand protectively over one of the cuffs.

"She left it with me."

"Why?"

He paused, looking down at the dress, taking the sleeve distractedly in his hand.

"You were friends?" I asked.

"Agatha and I loved each other, lass."

Everything slowed. I stared at the side of his face, his eyes keeping themselves to the dress. For a moment, the familiar curve of his cheekbone seemed foreign to me.

"You asked about a woman out of my past. . . . I've meant to tell you about her, love. Who she was to me. What was between us. You must have known her, your own friend's mother."

"I knew she had a lover. I always thought it was the big dark-haired man, William Connelly, that I saw sometimes at Rafferty's."

He smiled, softly surprised by the revelation. "Not at all, love. Not William Connelly." His face then flushed and grew serious with the idea of it.

"Why did you keep that from me, Angus?" I cried. "When I mentioned Clodagh's name to you in Dunshee . . . you didn't tell me."

"I should have."

"Why didn't you?" I held his eyes trying to read them.

"Because I wanted you . . . ," he said.

I looked again at the dress and ran my hand distractedly through the netted hem, causing the numerous little shells to click together, trying to retrace how I'd come to the certainty that the other man was my mother's lover; at how true it had once felt. I remembered him standing in Mrs. Rafferty's with the slipper shell. A small grief rushed me at the loss of William Connelly and I stirred harder at the threads and shells. Angus looked nervous of the way I touched the dress, as if I might hurt it.

"I've seen this dress before," I said. "I know this dress." Something blighted rose up in a wave from the center of my body, and with it a resentment that he should have the dress. I tensed my mouth, holding back tears. I should have had it, I thought. It was mine more than his. I clutched the net hem in my hand and squeezed it roughly. For a moment I hated him.

He watched me with caution. "Who was she to you, lass?" he whispered.

The air in the caravan filled with a din. I stared at the dress. "She was . . ."

I wanted to say it. To claim the dress. To force him to let go of the sleeve. I stared at his hand, at the strong sinews of his forearm, weather-bronzed, the hair glinting a coppery gold. A slow, velvety darkness filled my chest so I could not feel my heart there. If I told him I would lose him. If I told him, how would we go on together as we had been?

My eyes flashed to his and away again. The question was on his face. The truth he was waiting for me to confirm or dispel.

"She was . . . ," I began and went quiet again. "She was my aunt."

I heard him sigh. From my peripheral vision I saw him lift his arm, run his hand through his hair the way he had that first time I'd seen him on the bus, years back.

"Sweet Christ," he said softly. A long quiet passed between us in which I would not look at him. "Agatha lost contact with her sister ages ago," he said.

My mother once had a sister, I thought. I resented him for knowing things I had never been allowed to know. And the twinge of anger in me compelled me to deepen the lie.

"Yes," I said recklessly. "My own mother was adopted by settled people. As a very small child."

"Why did you tell me once that Clodagh was your friend and not your cousin?"

I felt on the edge of a precipice. Telling him the truth would be like diving into the dark. Even now I knew the revelation that Agatha's blood ran in my veins would change things between us. He would leave me if he knew I was her daughter. My desperation to keep him spurred me on with the deception.

"We knew each other as friends long before we knew we were cousins. We only learned the truth a few years ago."

"You never tell me about your life. About your own mother."

"I've led an uneventful life, Angus," I said, gazing openly into his face. I felt the pressure of lying in my body, the exhaustion of it, something heavy to drag after me. "I lived with my mother in Bray. I went to Immaculate Conception school. . . . There's little more to tell."

I thought he might ask me what Agatha's sister's name was, and then what would I say? But he didn't.

"Why do you have no one in the world to answer to, lass?"

"I do have people to answer to . . . ," I said.

"You haven't much trouble leaving them behind you."

A painful sensation of shame moved through me. I saw Mrs. O'Dare's and Sister Seraphina's faces in my mind.

I said nothing. I thought he'd ask me more questions and I wondered if I'd slip, make a mistake. But he had gone quiet and I sensed that he was reluctant to know anything more.

"You're Agatha's niece," he said softly, as if trying to take in the idea. I felt him studying me the way I had just studied him. I kept my uneasy gaze on the dress.

He moved past me, taking coal from the bin and matches to begin a fire, and went outside.

I studied the stitches, carefully wrought. Who had made this dress? Angus was the craftsman. I'd seen him sew Declan's harness when it was torn. He had a kit of steel needles and coarse leather thread. What did this dress mean between them?

I ran my finger along the perfect scarwork of the seam where the fur was missing and it was only soft black flesh. The man who had constructed this dress knew the slope between my mother's waist and hips. He knew how much room to leave for her breasts.

The dress made me lonely. It was as silent, as unforthcoming as Agatha herself. He had made it, I was certain. She was where his thoughts went when the remoteness came into his eyes. She was who he whispered to that morning of his sad dreaming when he'd made love to me.

I remembered the sounds of them together behind the kitchen wall at Mercymount Strand, her breathy animal cries; him calling out to Christ. I bent into myself, closing my eyes.

That night after the meal, he said, "You're like her, you know."

"Yes," I said faintly.

He shook his head. "I'm a bit amazed at myself."

I could see the flames moving back and forth across his eyes. "Why?" I asked.

"You've always reminded me of her. But I'd never admitted that to myself. But now it's so clear I feel I've been lying to myself."

When our eyes met again I felt we were strangers. His mistrust floated on the air between us like smoke.

"The first time I had you I thought of her. But I told myself then it was because you'd been in that big house where she'd once lived."

He sat awhile with his shoulders hunched, his head down, before he got up and wandered off into the dark field.

I went inside.

I don't know why I put on the dress. Maybe because there were two of us there now. Agatha and me. Maybe because I wanted it just to be one of us. I was afraid of the history between them. But now it infused everything and I had to take the weight of that history onto my own body; to locate it.

When he came in I squinted with the brightness of his lamp. He put it down and stood unmoving before me. The look of me in the dress seemed to cause him pain.

I put my arms around him but he did not move.

"Let's just hold each other tonight, love," he said. But the idea of not having him then was unbearable to me and meant that he belonged to her.

"Angus," I said softly. "Angus." I lay back on the bed holding my arm out to him. He approached and sat down on the bed beside me, his eyes intent on me.

He let go a breath of surrender, his hand shaking as he touched the dress. Intimate with its architecture, he pulled the lacing at the chest. He kissed the sleek, musky seams at the waist and hips and licked the salt from the hems and the coarse threads knotted with shells, then lifted the skirt up around my waist and was inside me in a moment.

"You're the bloody spit o' your aunt," he said, holding me hard beneath him.

That night he fell asleep on top of me, the weight of his body putting pressure on my ribs, pushing my stomach and heart into too close a dialogue. I tried to wake him, tried to make him roll off me, but his repose was terrible and heavy. I tried to adjust to the shallower breathing but still could not sleep, overheated by the sealskin dress and the furnace of Angus's body.

Once I was able to rouse him out of oblivion, but he only rearranged his arms more tightly around me and pressed his face against my neck, making a wet nest of my hair. The noise and rhythm of his breathing did not belong to the graceful man that I knew, but to a more desperate man, each breath trailed by a little windy cry.

All the next day into night, taking the main roadway down from Limerick to Tralee, cars racing past us, we were quiet and serious, Agatha present in the air between us. Riding through a certain valley on the way, littered with the graveyards of the poor, crumbled Irish crosses, the fields dismal with the silence of the perished, I found him staring at me like I was someone else. It was Agatha he was looking for, I told myself. I panicked. Surely, I thought guiltily, he could see that I was her daughter. Had I not been told all my life that I resembled her? If I had always seen Mare when I looked into my mother's face, then surely he saw her when he looked into mine. If he knew the truth it would drive him from me. Being her niece afforded a little distance.

Being her daughter none. How long would it be before I found myself admitting it?

It was the first time since I'd been with him that Angus parked right in the thick of things among other travelers. In the caravan nearest us a man and woman yelled drunkenly back and forth, one to the other.

"I'll tear the face off o' you," the man cried out.

There was a clattering of pans and a stifled yell.

Angus seemed oblivious. He sat with his hand over his brow drawing a ledger for the selling he hoped to do.

I opened the door and looked outside. Three filthy children ran barefoot, squawking as they splashed through muddy ruts full of rainwater.

I lay down on the bed facing the wall. When Angus left the caravan he did not say a word to me.

Angus recognized a woman at one of the fires. I saw him when I came out of the back of our caravan, standing close to her saying something. She laughed and bent her head. She leaned suddenly forward to stir the embers and a little gold crucifix glimmered and swung from a chain around her neck. She sat down on a rock before her fire and the cross lost itself in the dark of her cleavage.

She looked at me with pale, intrigued eyes. There was something ruddy and attractive about her. She was older than him, I imagined, buxom and wide in the hips, and she had thick red hair laced with gray and tiny lines radiating away at the outer corners of her eyes. She beamed at me and I had the feeling there was mockery in her smile.

"Well, introduce me to the girl, you brute!" she cried.

"Mare, this is Nan."

"Sit down at my fire, love." Her purple skirt was patched with dirt, the hem frayed and muddy.

"You're a young lass to be mixed up with himself," she said, jerking her chin at Angus, smiling. Her manner was so outgoing, her voice

254 ＋ REGINA MCBRIDE

so falsely exuberant, that I shrank. She put her arm around me and I smelled spirits on her breath.

"And how do you feel this fine evening, Mare?" Angus stood near Nan, looking down at us where we sat.

"I'm well," I uttered faintly. She dismissed me easily, then went on to Angus about her husband being in the north.

She touched his leg as she spoke and he watched her approvingly, looking at me once with gravity and something deliberate in his eyes, as if he had chosen to put distance between us.

Nan's face was red and heated and I could feel the fire in her body. When a moment of quiet passed between them, she stood up erect and smiled, wiping the ashes from her hands onto her bosoms.

That night Nan poured me and Angus drinks from a bottle of whiskey and we stood among others around a fire. A drunken woman screeched and reeled to music coming from a television set that sat on a rickety chair, the plug rigged up to a box on a cord coming from a caravan door. The figures on the screen were phosphorescent and barely discernible. The dancing woman laughed and tripped over her skirts.

Pretending to listen to the chatter of the men and women, Angus and Nan stood side by side, but it was all heat and exhilaration between them. They behaved as if I were not there, and sometimes she'd lean into him or touch his arm as she spoke. She spilled a cup of liquor and they both knelt down to get the cup, laughing when it kept rolling away from them.

I rushed off, desolate with the whiskey, and went to the caravan to lie down. The voices drifted and the wind came up, breathing a whoosh into the fire.

A bit later when I returned to the site where I'd left them, I found Angus and Nan gone and the dog asleep in front of her caravan. I opened the door a small way and saw them together on the floor, fully clothed. His head lay in her lap and she stroked his hair, her blouse open, pulled over one shoulder.

I ran out into the blackness of the fields weeping and tripping in the grass and the stones. I saw the dim lights from two caravans parked together in a field. As I drew closer I recognized the young fiddler I'd seen playing at a fair a month or so back. His face was streaked with tears. With him were the two old women I'd spoken to that day, and an old man. Only his mother was missing from the group.

A wooden casket sat on a slipshod table between the two caravans.

"Here's to Deirdre McArthy," the old man cried, holding his glass in the air.

"A fine old thing," said one of the old women, "though she had the divil in her."

The others laughed and said, "Aye." But the young, oily-haired fiddler stared at the violin he clutched to his chest. His damp lower lip hung and his shoulders shook with tears.

I stepped on a dry twig and they all looked up into the shadow from which I issued. One of the old women made the sign of the cross.

"I'm sorry to disturb you," I said.

The young fiddler's face tensed and he wiped his chin with the back of one hand.

The small, thin old woman approached me, reaching out her arm. "The old one dies, Jackie Boy, and look what comes in her place. She's tears on her face, as well. Desperate in herself as you are, Jackie."

"Give the girl a glass," cried the heavy woman and the man complied.

"Saints be praised. Is the world not filled with miracles yet? Not a lovelier girl under summer stars."

"Have a reel. Old Bill'll play. Have a reel with the girl, Jackie."

I was swept up, turned in a reel in the young man's wooden arms. His eyes stared intensely at me, watery and flecked with firelight. When we stopped I was breathless, soaked in perspiration.

I sat with the evening air cooling me, drinking the whiskey, beside myself, struggling not to think of Angus.

A gravity had overcome the group; they were discussing something I did not understand, anticipation in the air.

"Before we bury old Deirdre, her son here will eat her sins," the heavy old woman informed me.

"What do you mean?"

"He's a good son and he'll not have her goin' into the gloaming with all the sins that blacken her soul. He'll eat a dish of praities and cabbage from off her chest before she goes into the ground."

The casket was opened and the food ladled into a dish. The putrid odor of the corpse mixed with the steaming cabbage, deepening and dissolving with the wind.

The thin demented man stood there hunched over the casket, huffing, crying, half choking as he ate.

I slept that night with the small old woman who swore in her sleep and kicked at the caravan wall. The heavy woman slept on a pallet on the floor. The old man and the fiddler had disappeared into the darkness to bury the corpse.

Angus found me the next day. It was because the old woman I'd slept with went to the fair and told her wild tale about the young girl who'd appeared out of the dark when Jackie's beloved mother was about to go under. Angus followed her back to camp, the woman wearing a dark face.

"She belongs to this one," she said. "They were after having a row and he wants her back."

The young man gazed desolately at him.

"I'll not go back with him," I said.

"Come here to me, Mare," Angus said impatiently. "Nothing happened between me and Nan."

"I saw you with her and her bosoms sticking out of her dress."

He approached me and clutched my wrist, pulling me after him out of the camp.

The young man bristled but Angus's size must have made him think twice.

"Nothing occurred between us. I had too much of the drink in me."

"So you would have if you could have."

The tinkers were listening. "Leave us some privacy!" Angus cried out.

"There's things need to be settled between us, Mare. It's too lonely a world, love. Too lonely for us that belong to each other to battle. Come on now, lass," he said, and with his arm around me we walked back through the rocky field to the caravan.

· 2 6 ·

BUT WE DID NOT SETTLE THE THINGS ANGUS SAID WE NEEDED
to. We did not talk about the things that had been left unclear. We
kept, instead, a deliberate quiet around them. And even with the
uncertainty and mistrust, the blood wildness between us did not stop.
It was this that kept him quiet, I was sure; as if he were afraid that further revelations might cause that to dissolve.

Sometimes I would find the sealskin dress lying on the bed and I
knew he wanted me to put it on, and when he'd look at me in it the
air around him seemed to take in its breath. He hesitated before he
touched me, and when he did he closed his eyes and I felt him forget me. Afterward he'd turn penitently away and disappear into himself.

It was mid-July when we rode out to the end of the Dingle Peninsula to Slea Head, where Angus said there was an abandoned stone
cottage he wanted me to see and that perhaps we would stay there a
night or two. We stopped on an uphill road overlooking the sea in a
driving wind.

He pointed to the crest of the headland where I could see a bit of
stone wall. A slew of screeching gulls rose up over the cottage, carried
inland by the wind.

"I'll have to find a spot for the caravan out of the way of this wind,"
he said. "There's a break below in the hill."

I got out and wandered onto the headland while he drove the caravan around to settle it. A group of seals rode the rough water below,
looking up at me expectantly with darkly human faces.

"I used to call it 'singing cottage,'" Angus shouted to me across the
noise of wind and sea as he started up the headland on foot. We met
at the back of the cottage, the air full of an undulant high-pitched
whistling.

"It's bits of dead grass or moss caught between the stones causes the whistling in a high wind," he said.

The sky above us was as dark and uneasy as the water below. A difficult coastline jutted out into the sea, descending gradually from the front of the cottage. "We'll hear the water beatin' at the rocks until dawn."

He wandered around the cottage looking at the earth, then squatted down pulling up bits of dry root and rubbing them between his fingers. "If ever I'd have settled, it might've been here," he said. "Many years ago here I planted seed potatoes that I never harvested. Left the little things dead asleep in the earth to rot."

The wooden door creaked open as I pushed it. The stone room inside was cold and full of shadows, purple flowers sprouting from the cracks in the rock under the single window. A blackened pot hung on a chimney crane above a trace of ash in the hearth, and a wicker creel sat on the floor with a few dry ribbons of kelp in it.

"Someone was here not too long ago," I said.

"Me," he replied quietly. "I was here in April before I went north to Dunshee." He'd brought a bag of supplies with him from the caravan and began setting pieces of coal in the ash. A rumbling sounded in the sky and the room went a shade darker. "Light a lamp, Mare. It'll go even darker soon," he said. He went to the door and faced out.

I could find no paraffin for the lamp so I lit a thick candle and placed it in a saucer on the table. I was hungry and began to cut bread and cheese and slice tomatoes for a meal. I set it all out on plates on the stone table and drew two creaking rush chairs from against the back wall.

The gray sky went almost green and the rain deepened to a downpour. "A bloody candle does us little good," he said.

"I couldn't find the oil."

"It's right in front of you, girl," he said, pointing to it among the provisions we'd brought up. I watched his face, hurt by the irritation in his voice. I reached for the lamp but he moved brusquely toward me and grabbed it, filling and lighting it.

I sat down, stung.

Angus kept the door open as the rain came down, letting it pool in the dips in the clay floor at the threshold, shocking me, reminding me of my mother. All the while we were sitting down to eat, the rain dampened the floor. The glass flue of the dry lamp shook in its metal bracelet with the wind, and the flame leaned desperately, fluttering like a flag.

"Why do you leave the door open that way?"

"It's bad luck to close off the weather so completely."

The humid air infiltrated everything, and though it was cool I felt myself sweating, my loose sleeves luffing at my skin. The purple flowers quivered between the stones.

When the meal was over the rain stopped. Angus went outside in front of the cottage while I stayed in the torn rush chair watching him through the open door, a new wind blowing his hair, getting under his loosened shirt.

I turned away from him and focused on the cinders still glowing and crackling under the pot. When I looked up again he was on his way back in, his eyes set on me. He sat down again across from me and said, "Tell me about Clodagh, your cousin. What is she like?"

I stopped breathing. "She's . . . a nice girl," I said.

"I imagine her a quiet girl. Is she?"

"Yes. She is quiet. Why do you ask about Clodagh?"

He turned his eyes to the cinders. "Agatha was the mother of my twin daughters. Mary Margaret who is dead now these many years, and Clodagh. Your friend Clodagh is my daughter."

"No. Agatha was married to Frank Sheehy."

The orange cinders glowed in his eyes. "Yes. But she'd been married to Frank Sheehy for almost a year before I bedded her. She was a virgin. The man was ill, lass."

An awful quiet filled me. Stunned, misty quiet like the air over Dunshee. I tried to concentrate on his words but the meaning of them eluded me.

"Promise me you'll never tell Clodagh this," he said. "When I take you back."

"I promise." My voice floated to me from another corner of the room.

"So you see . . . there was a great deal more between Agatha and me than you knew."

"Yes," I uttered.

We sat quietly for a few minutes, then he left for the caravan to collect the bedding and some more supplies for the night.

I walked outside and stood watching his figure move down the headland in the gray afternoon light, trying to think about his words. He'd said that he was Clodagh's father. For a moment I thought I was not Clodagh and, shivering with the wind, I asked myself the same questions Angus Kilheen had asked. "What is Clodagh like? Is she a quiet girl?"

AFTER ANGUS RETURNED WITH THE SUPPLIES HE TOOK PADDY
the wolfhound and walked down into Ventry, the nearby town. I
found the caravan where he'd parked it below at a break in the hill. I
searched the chest where he kept a few little keepsakes among his
tools. In the main box with the screwdrivers, vials of lighter fluid and
loose coins mixed up with nails and screws, I found an old novena
with finger-worn pages and a man's rough wooden rosary with a
metal cross, and wrapped in a paper bag, a tiny plastic statue of the
Virgin with a magnet at the base. I found what looked at first like a
small metal book. I pressed a catch on the side and it squeaked open,
revealing a double frame attached at the middle. On one side was a
photograph of me and Mare as small girls, Mare looking off to the
side dreamily while I fixed the camera's eye with a serious expression. In the other side was an illustration of the Virgin Mother in a
blue mantle, her palms pressed together. Delicate floral engravings
on the frame enhanced each image. I slipped my fingernail into an
opening behind the photo and pulled it loose. On the back my
mother had written in childlike letters: "Beloved girls—Mary Margaret and Clodagh," the word "beloved" misspelled. Under that
Angus had written it again, spelled correctly.

I held the picture a long time, searching our expressions, then
turned it over to gaze at the letters my mother had penned, trying to
drink in what she'd felt when she'd given him the picture; wondering if
the words were for his benefit or if she'd really thought of me as such.

I scaled the wet hill back to the cottage leaning into the force of a
battering wind. When I reached the summit near the cottage, my eyes
were tearing. I tried to think as I stood, leaning into the wind, looking
out to sea.

A father was of the dead. A father was a shadow, an idea conjured and dispelled, never to be fathomed. But Angus Kilheen was of the flesh; all mouth and skin and anxious heat.

A strange elation bled into my anguish. He belonged even more to me now than he ever had. Silver light, barely contained, showed itself in the edges of the clouds: restrained, as if something were about to break. And while the sea below folded and unfolded, the same silver, almost blinding light appeared and disappeared on the crests of the waves. Anguish and elation overlapping like the tides overlapped and ultimately blended. I could not hold to the gravity of what this revelation meant. I could not hold to that.

The words that I needed to speak to Angus were somewhere on my breath but I didn't know how to say them. I knew that I'd not say them. At least not now. I remembered my mother going into the sea. I had hoarded the knowledge, held to the intimacy it afforded me with her for three or four days before telling Mrs. O'Dare. I'd been an oracle then, as I was an oracle now: my throat, my mouth full of light.

On their way back up from Ventry that night Angus and Paddy wandered along the beach and had a swim. They came back, soaked with the sea. The fire was almost out and I was lying under the fleece in the makeshift bed. When he got in next to me he was penitent for his earlier mood. He leaned close and said, "I'm glad I told you the truth of it. It was eating at me."

I hesitated and said, "It's all right, Angus."

He kissed me, his beard grazing my cheek, hurting faintly, arousing a loneliness in me. I turned away.

"You're angry," he said.

"I'm not," I said and looked earnestly at him. "I'm really not. I'm tired. I just want to sleep."

"You're not tired. I know when you're tired."

"I'm not angry, love. I really am tired."

He gazed into my face, then laughed softly. "You've never said no to me before."

"I love you," I said and touched his face.

Twice beside him that night I reached the edge of sleep but awakened each time feeling afraid, trying to remember what it was that I knew that had caused such agitation in me, but it eluded me like the tail of a dream, and I sought to remember it only halfheartedly.

I looked at him as he slept and a minor convulsion of understanding moved through me. And though the fire was almost out, the room sustained an artificial brightness, the shadows of the flowers throwing configurations on the wall.

The next morning we wandered the headland. The previous day's clouds were long since gone and I found deliverance in the vitality of the elements: the driving wind and blinding sun. In the mad, exhilarated screeching of the puffins and kittiwakes.

Was it not an unspeakable thing? I asked myself. A father and daughter loving each other in this way? In the other world it was. But maybe not here, I told myself. Here the dead were recovered. Or maybe I was newly dead. Coming so far west I'd left one life and had come into another. And now, knowing what I did, I was drawn into a stranger, even more deeply hidden world. An inheritance, I told myself. I'd come into myself. I shuddered and felt within me a great reservoir of emotion, all feelings bleeding into each other: desire into shame into tenderness into loss, and back into desire.

Wanting room for my own reverie, I lingered behind, Angus walking a few yards in front of me. Once, remembering the kiss he'd given me the night before, I lost my footing on the rocks. I wandered off onto the beach, veering away from him. When I closed my eyes a vision of his face was burned there like a light I'd stared too hard into.

Near day's end, we climbed up toward the cottage and sat down on the rim of cliffs. Two herons made slow ascents into the air and re-alighted near the threshold of our cottage. The female walked in through the open door, her faint shadow flashing on the wall. I was certain she was wresting the half loaf of bread from its paper bag. I didn't tell Angus. He was facing out toward the sea and I was worried he'd go in and upset her. The other heron walked nervously back and forth, stopping once and cocking his head, his eye pierced in our direction.

Angus turned, spotting the heron in the cottage, and jumped to his feet. "The trespasser!" he said.

"No, leave her! Leave her, Angus!" I said.

"It'll eat what little we've got left in there," he said.

"I'll go!" I cried, imagining him rushing at her, a panic of wings and the bird panting with an open beak.

I walked slowly toward the house. "Go out, love!" I cried to her. "Go!" But she backed farther inside, knocking the candle off the table. I went in through the threshold and she backed in farther, letting loose an echoing, unearthly shriek.

"No, no, my girl," I said softly. "It's all right."

I stepped to the side and she ran out the door. With a heavy downpushing of wings she ascended on a swell of wind and seemed to lay a moment in suspension over the house, her feet stretched out behind her.

Angus came in and finding me crying hugged me and turned me in a playful circle. "Silly child! Shaken up so by the shyness of a bird!"

In the afternoon I sat for hours inside on the edge of the bed, hardly moving, while outside in front of the cottage Angus worked a piece of tinware. I listened to the exertion of his breathing as he labored; his intakes of air, his exhalations. Every faint sound from him hurt and captivated me.

I asked myself, should there not be in me a reflex against him? I struggled to feel it in the stillness. But it was not there in me.

I went to the doorway and watched as he welded a decorative coil of metal as a design onto the pot in the complicated style that the man in Kildare had said looked "Iron Age," like something "dug from a bog."

He looked up and smiled at me, warmth flooding his expression. A few strands of his hair stuck to the dampness on his forehead and temples. I smiled back and a flame of sadness deepened in my chest.

Soon he would leave the hot metal to set and the sparks to die on the wet ground. If I did not prepare a meal, he would lead me to the bed. I revived the coals on the hearth, peeled a turnip and some potatoes, put them into a pot to boil. Distractedly I set things out. Plates and cups. Butter. I cut bread and made tea.

It was near dark when he came in. I lit the lamp and set it on the table. He held my eyes strangely as he ate, and a panic seized me that he also knew the truth.

I reached across the table and touched his hand. "What's wrong, Angus?"

"It does something to me, this cottage fastened to the earth. The stillness of it under me."

"What does it do to you?"

"I used to think that something tragic awaited me in stillness. I believed that if I could move freely I could avoid it."

"And you don't believe that now?"

"I don't know what I believe now, lass. But the sadness of the world settles in the calm of a house." He paused and said, "Maybe we should leave this place soon."

"No, Angus. I want to stay still for a bit."

With his eyes downcast, he ran a finger along the rough wooden grain of the table and I saw that he wouldn't fight me; that what had drawn him here still held him.

Out of the quiet between us I asked, "Why did you never go to see your daughters?"

He looked at me thoughtfully. "Clodagh believes that Frank Sheehy was her father. And so does everyone else. It's better for her. She stands to inherit things, most likely." He looked down again at the table. A wave of anger moved through me.

"Weren't you ever curious about her?"

"I did see her sometimes . . . and Mary Margaret too, before she died."

"When did you see them?" I asked, surprised.

"When they were infants. Sound asleep they were, in their mother's bed. But I saw Clodagh again after that."

The lamp sputtered, the flame gone low and ambery, before stretching again and brightening the room.

"I used to hide upstairs in that strange old house and Agatha'd come to me in the night. I asked her to show me Clodagh and we walked very quietly into the room and I stood watching her sleep. But I had to rush out because the child stirred as if she could feel me there."

"What was she like?"

"Beautiful shadowy little thing, she was." His eyes shone.

"Didn't you want her with you?"

"What a question you ask," he uttered as if I'd slapped him, and in his pained expression I saw Mare's face pass over his like a shudder in water. I had once moved the rough hairs of his mustache and run my finger along his smooth upper lip, noticing how similar it was to my own in shape and prominence. Like me he always listened with parted lips, and tensed his mouth the way I did to restrain a smile. Like my own, his temples dipped inward slightly between his forehead and his cheekbones. His eyelashes were gold at the roots, like Mare's. I had mused over these likenesses before, never imagining them to be signs of a blood relationship.

"One's child carries on one's heart in this world." He said this not as if it were a sentiment, but a well-known fact.

I remembered the forehead and eyes of the man I'd seen lying in the makeshift bed in the kitchen with my mother when I was five. This was that face. He'd always been there in my life, strange to think. Sleeping many nights of my childhood a few rooms away from me. But hidden from me. Inhabiting another world within the same house.

"You loved Agatha," I said.

His jaw tightened. He ran his finger over the bit of grain he'd been tracing on the table.

"And did Agatha love you as much as you loved her?" I remembered her complaining to Mrs. O'Dare that he wanted her to leave her house and all her keepsakes.

He looked gravely at me. "I'd have laid at her feet but she wouldn't leave the big house."

It struck me then that I now stood at the threshold of my mother's story. But the question floated from my mouth as if it arose only out of curiosity. "Where did Agatha come from . . . before she lived in the cliffs at Dunshee?"

He put his cup down and sighed. The wind outside shrieked softly in the stones. He drew a breath and told me what he knew.

Her mother's name had been Nuala. Before Agatha had been born, Nuala'd had two daughters, both of whom she'd left in an orphanage. One had died there and the other Agatha had never been able to trace.

Nuala was a vagrant who begged on roadsides. For a long time she and Agatha inhabited an empty car on neglected property. When they did join bands of travelers Nuala had difficulty getting on with them because she drank if liquor was available to her and it made her quarrelsome.

When Agatha was five Nuala left her in an orphanage where she stayed for three years. The nuns taught her to read and write and gave her a taste of civilization, but Nuala returned for her, probably, Angus felt, because a woman with a child could beg more money than a woman alone.

When Agatha was thirteen or fourteen, Nuala took up with a man and became pregnant. They were living together near Dunshee in the man's caravan. Some traveler women helped with the birth and delivered a girl with a dark birthmark over one eye and temple. After the women left, Nuala wouldn't hold the child no matter how much it cried. Once while Nuala slept, Agatha gave it her finger to suckle. One night when she thought Agatha was asleep, Nuala took the babe down to the beach, walked thigh deep into the tide and held the creature under until it drowned. Agatha had followed at a distance and had seen. Nuala brought the dead child back to the caravan and in the morning light carried it to the camp of the women who'd delivered it and told them it had stopped breathing in the night.

But one of the women suspected the child had been drowned and the next day Nuala disappeared, leaving Agatha on her own in Dunshee. Agatha lived in coves along the cliffs, begging sometimes, hiring herself out to the locals to drive cattle or to help with planting or harvesting.

It was not long after she'd married Frank Sheehy that Angus first saw her lying on the stones on Dunshee Beach, sunning herself, a herd of seal cows gathered not far away on a jutting rock.

He was eighteen years old and traveling with the same band of tinkers he'd been with when his father had been alive.

Her eyes had been closed and the sea at that hour was crashing so loudly against the rocks she couldn't have heard him in the distance, yet she seemed to sense him there. She lifted her head, meeting his eyes. He did not attempt to approach her but stayed where he was, standing on the foreshore. Sensing that he did not pose a threat to her she lay back again and closed her eyes. The next time she raised her head to look at him he yelled to her over the noise of the ocean, "Are you a selkie?"

She'd smiled and climbed down off the rock, picked up a pair of silvery slippers covered in sand and approached him. The dress she wore was dun colored and silken, finely constructed, the sleeves and hems inlaid with beads and seed pearls. But her fair hair was wild and uneven at the ends, her skin red and freckled with weather, her lips chapped. The long dress dragged heavily, impressing a pathway after her in the sand.

"Maybe I am a selkie," she said, stopping a few feet from him.

"But it isn't sealskin you're wearing, is it?" he asked, dismayed by the opulence of the dress.

She looked down and touched a bit of ruching on her bodice. Her eyes floated up to his and she gave him a little conspiratorial smile, as if the dress were a testament to a certain power she could have over a man.

"It's silk brocade," she said. "Do you like it?"

"I didn't know selkies wore finery," he said, nervous over the anomaly of her.

"You shouldn't presume to know too much about selkies." Her flirtatious smile caused waves of warmth to move through him. He felt for a moment unsteady on his legs.

"Why not?" he asked.

"Selkies are mysterious creatures." She smiled at him again and wandered off, moving north along the beach, her slippers hanging from the fingers of one hand.

He saw her a few more times after that, lying on the rocks or holding her dress in a clump at the thighs, letting the tide rush in over her feet. He didn't approach her but she always spotted him in the distance.

One day he found her sitting in sand with her back to a stone, curled into herself. As he got closer he could see that she was weeping. When she saw him she went into a breathless, brokenhearted tirade about her husband's sister Kitty Sheehy and the stupidity of the servants in the big house. How she was treated worse than an animal might be treated. How she wanted to take something of Kitty's and break it.

He sat next to her, putting his arm around her, and she let go of the anger. After a few minutes of sobbing quietly in his arms, with her face still pressed to his chest, she told him about the birth and death of her infant sister. Angus had a feeling of unreality as she spoke, as if she were relaying a dream. She told him how she'd come to be left alone on Dunshee Beach. How she'd come to be married to Frank Sheehy.

"He's the only kind one in the house," she said.

"Why doesn't he stop them from treating you poorly?" Angus asked.

"He tries," she said, releasing herself from his arms and looking into his face. "But he's unaware of most of it."

They'd looked quietly at each other and she said softly, "It isn't a real marriage."

"What do you mean?"

"He's very ill."

That was the first time he kissed her, her mouth tasting of salt from the tears.

"Now you know all this about me, you'll not think I'm a selkie anymore," she said, with genuine disappointment.

"I'll always think of you as a selkie," he said, moved, and kissed her again.

It was after that day together on the beach that he'd traded for a sealskin, cut it and formed it into a dress for her.

We sat lost in our thoughts a long time before Angus said, "I think she believed that the life of a traveler could never be anything but unendurable."

I was quiet, thinking of my mother with her baubles and tiered dresses and knickknacks.

"Promise me, Mare, never to breathe a word of this to Clodagh."

"Yes."

"She stands to inherit. Isn't it better for her that she believe her father was a rich man?"

"No," I said.

He looked gravely at me. "What have I to give her?"

"Everything," I said.

He shook his head, faintly stunned by my words. He was thoughtful awhile before he said, "The last time I saw Clodagh she wasn't even six years old, in the kitchen at Mercymount Strand. I watched through a kind of distorted window in the wall while she talked to Agatha.

"Tiny, soft-haired little thing. Agatha squatting down holding the little hand in her fingers and the girl's intense face full of the weight of the world. Agatha stood to tend to her cooking and the child gazed up in the direction of that odd distorted window as if she knew I was watching her there, though Agatha had assured me that it couldn't be seen through. The sadness pierced me to go to her, to kiss her wee cheek. That day I almost broke down and went to her."

I listened, hardly breathing. I remembered the moment he was talking about. She'd been cooking bacon and I'd gone in to tell her that the person upstairs was not a ghost and she had crouched down to me and had told me that men were clumsy and that they came and went in death as they did in life.

"Why do you think Clodagh could always feel you there?"

"Because we share the same heart."

"She is your beloved girl."

"Yes," he said and looked at me strangely, a heaviness to him now. He stared at the plate of half-eaten food on the table before him.

"You're a good man, Angus Kilheen," I whispered as the lamp dimmed and the glass discolored with the smoke.

The wick had gone under the oil, but a thread remained afloat and glowing.

"I'll light it again," I said.

"No, lass. I'm tired. I want to sleep."

I lay in the near dark watching him sleep, his head curling toward his chest, breath passing in and out of his nose and mouth. My eyes dampened and the vision of him glimmered and blurred.

He woke, as if the rush of emotion in me had stirred him from sleep.

"Why so sad?" he whispered, his palm to my cheek. I pressed my hand to his and held it there. He looked at me with such affection I felt my heart enlarge, each pulse emitting a small charge of joy. As his face moved closer to mine I drew in breath, remembering my mother drawing in breath for the last time, the wave lifting and holding her aloft. There had been pleasure for her in that surrender.

When his mouth was on mine, a calmness filled me, broken only by a tremble of exhilaration. He folded me in his arms. Hadn't I always looked to him for my origins? He was my history. Before I had a face I was with him, a point of damp light residing in the darkness of him. I was, I told myself, about to recover something impossible to recover.

The rapture came in easy surges and I felt suddenly detached like I was floating, looking down at inlets appearing and disappearing at the hem of the sea. I had the agonized sense that I was watching the receding shore of a beloved place.

When Angus rolled off me I turned from him and wept sound-lessly. How would words ever find themselves now? Why did all unions end with separateness? What had I wanted that I was so grief-stricken now? To sleep inside him? To stop breathing and let him breathe for me?

The thread in the lamp still glowed and the wind screeched faintly in the drystone wall. "Angus," I whispered. He stirred and opened his eyes as if he were looking back from the other world.

"I am your beloved," I whispered. "Tell me."

"You're my beloved."

"I'm your beloved Clodagh," I whispered.

"Aye," he answered faintly, turning onto his side with his back to me. A few moments passed before his body went rigid. I stroked his arm, waiting for him to soften, but he got up suddenly and found his pants and coat and went outside.

I felt strangely at peace and fell into a deep sleep.

He came in at first light shaking with the cold.

"What's your name, lass?"

"Clodagh."

He stared down at me on the pillow a long time with a kind of awe, examining my face as if he were seeing it for the first time. His eyes glowed with tears.

"Didn't you ever think I might be Clodagh?" I asked quietly.

"Yes." There was a long quiet. He struggled with a grimace of grief and anger. "You're so much like Agatha. You've the same sadness in the very skin of you." There was another long quiet before he asked, "Why, love? After ye knew, why didn't you put a stop to it?"

The question confused me and my heart drummed hard. "I need you. I'll not lose you."

"But to know I was your father . . ."

"That was even more to lose, wasn't it?"

I n morning light Angus sat heavily at the table. I went about things, nervous of him, of what he might say now. I boiled a kettle, cooked food. He watched me, his eyes wide open and damp, full of the daylight through the open door. He did not eat what I gave him, holding his fork and staring at it, turning it in the light.

"Christ Almighty," he said softly.

The day was full of the noise of the sea below the cliff. By noon the surf was loud and the gulls keened each time it rode out. Wind filled the cottage through the open door, sending the flowers between the stones of the walls stirring.

I was relieved that he had slept so little the night before and was too exhausted for irreparable decisions. When he went to lie down, I sat on the rush chair watching his face change in sleep, a rapt defenselessness growing in his expression.

For hours I waited for him to awaken. I was standing in the doorway looking out when I knew his eyes were on my back. Though he was still in the bed across the room it felt as if his fingers were traveling down the bones of my vertebrae. I froze, an ache of bright particles between us.

I heard the bed creak as he got out of it. I turned and met his eyes.

"For God's sake, lass," he sighed, shaking his head, disheveled with sleep.

I approached him slowly, holding my hand out to him, but he recoiled, shy of the touch of me.

I looked at him, hurt. "I've always been part of you," I said.

He clenched as if he were feeling physical pain. "We can't stay together," he said sternly.

He moved through the cottage, gathering things together.

"Where are you going?" I cried out.

"I'll stay in the caravan tonight," he said.

"You can't go off!"

"I'll not go off. Not now. We've got to think about this, for God's sake," he said. I watched him walk down the hill in the late afternoon light, then ran back in and searched the room to make sure he was leaving important things behind; things he'd not go away for good without. His oilcloth tarp. His kit of steel needles.

In the dark of night I was awakened by the creak of the door and my heart went wild but soon sank again when I realized that he was searching for something. Feigning sleep, I watched his shadow move through the dark of the room. I heard the creak of a rush chair as he sat down. He whispered something onto the air and I was certain in that moment that my mother was there; that all along the two had been meeting each other secretly in the dark.

As the pain of exclusion burned in my chest, the smell of my mother's skin and hair returned to me.

Angus's whisper grew slightly in volume. "Through my fault, through my fault, through my most grievous fault . . ." He had come for the Blessed Mother with the broken hand. It was her he was speaking to. Slowly, I understood that my mother was not there.

I held my hands to my face and laughed softly until my fingers were wet with tears.

He did not leave that night, but slept on a pile of clothes on the opposite side of the cottage. Smelling him as I could across the darkness, I wept. I could not find repulsion in myself. My desire for him had not disappeared.

I remembered the times in the fields at Kilkee, how he used to reach for me in the dawn, lofting me upon him, groaning through half sleep; how we'd spent our mornings in shivers of bliss and amnesia.

In the morning I gave him a cup of tea. His face had softened to me and he stopped resisting my eyes.

"You can still go to music school, Clodagh," he said.

"I can't remember the Bach pieces or the Preludes," I said.

"You can learn them again."

"No," I said. "No."

"You must be full of regrets," he said.

"No, Angus," I whispered. When I reached across the table he started as if I might hurt him.

"I don't understand how everything can change so suddenly for you."

"Have you no conscience?" he asked, a serious intensity come into his eyes.

"It's missing in me, Angus. Something was missing in my sister's lungs. They were not complete. And something is missing in me, but it's not something of the body."

He looked hard at me, struggling with the idea. Finally he said, "I'm going away for a few days. Alone. To think."

"Don't, Angus," I said. "Please."

A stoniness came into his face that made me suddenly furious. As he moved toward the door I said, "I needed a father when I was little."

He stopped and did not breathe.

"I needed a father."

He stared into the light through the open door, a tiny fleck of his eye brightening painfully, and I felt him imagining me, remembering me when I was little. As if I were not that same girl there with him now.

"When I was afraid of things, I needed a father."

He tensed his mouth. In that moment he looked older than I'd ever seen him look

"Stay," I said. "If only for that."

"You don't need me in that way now. You're not afraid like that now."

"I am. Stay because I'm afraid."

A soft tension transformed his face as he seemed to consider it.

"Stay," I said, putting my hand on his arm.

He withdrew, like I had just gored him, gathered some things and left.

The heron came and stood at the door, looking in. She put one foot in over the threshold and hesitated. I froze where I sat in the rush chair, my heart in my throat, my pulses drumming. She walked in slowly, and stood a few feet away, regarding me.

At the cry of her partner outside she startled, looked a bit around the room and wandered out through the door. I stepped after her, breathless as I watched her take to the air, unable to understand what it was about her that moved me so deeply.

Angus had left only one candle and a stale bit of bread and enough water for a few pots of tea. It was an oversight, I told myself. We'd both stopped paying attention to practical things.

I waited for days, disoriented, worn out by devastation. One afternoon I fell into a slumber, the door held open by a heavy rock, and was awakened at dusk by the tumult of screeching gulls. I dragged myself outside. The border between sea and sky was on fire in the descending sun. The water below the cliff rushed violently inland.

A burned smell was carried on the air, a drift of smoke moving seaward on the wind. I circled to the back of the cottage. In the valley below, a family of tinkers had set camp and built a large fire. A man and a woman in dark clothes sat on rickety chairs while three little girls ran around the flames squealing, throwing fistfuls of dry grass into the fire, which popped or rushed out as sparks, bits of red disintegrating to black.

I smelled food on a gust of air and felt the ache of my empty stomach. As I descended toward them the woman pointed me out and they all stared at me, unmoving. I must have been an unearthly sight in the deepening light, the wind beating my nightgown and matted hair. The smallest girl ran to her father and held on to his legs.

I stopped a yard or so from the fire and addressed the woman. "Please, Missus. Could you give me something to eat?"

She looked desolately at me, as if the sight of me hurt her. The wind blew a gust of dark hair into her eyes, her face, heavily etched with lines. She blinked, then got up and ladled a cupful of beans into a dish and gave me a spoon. I ate eagerly, still standing while they all watched me. The beans tasted of ash.

I asked her if she had something else. She gave me an onion and a potato from a paper bag on the ground and I scaled the hill back to the cottage.

I lit coals in the hearth, heated the potato and ate it, saving a piece of it and the onion for the morning. I went back out and from the summit of the hill watched the girls who had resumed their horseplay around the fire below. The oldest one had tied the sleeve of a battered dress onto the end of a broomstick and lofted it over the flames like a flag. The hems caught suddenly, the dress blowing wildly, issuing a noxious, unsettling smell.

The man roared, "Let go o' the bleedin' thing," and the girl screamed and tossed it onto the blaze.

The next morning I stood cutting the onion when the door opened and the wind came in like a presence. The sun heated my back, my head, part of my face. I stopped my knife midway into the onion, a nausea spreading through me, sweat rising up in tiny points on my temples and neck and under my breasts. I weaved on my feet. The onion glowed wet and translucent and a residue rose up from it like the electricity left on the air after a lightning storm. The emptiness of my belly made me dizzy and I was out the door retching in the grass.

When Angus Kilheen came back to me later that day, I had no inclination in me for anything but water and dry bread and to lie curled into myself before the lit sods of the fire.

He knew what was wrong and said that he remembered that the last time he'd seen a trace of my monthly blood was early in June when we'd been in the fields near Kilkee.

He sat quietly at the table with his head in his hands. "Dear God," he said softly.

He said he would take me to Mrs. O'Dare at Mercymount Strand, that I needed special care now that he could not give me. And we needed to separate for a while, to think about the enormity of things between us.

As we packed everything to return to the caravan I looked for the heron. Once while I was inside gathering the last of our things I heard the unearthly shriek in the sky and ran outside. A heron flew over the north-running cliffs, but too far in the distance for me to discern if it was my heron.

I tore up a quarter loaf of bread and left it scattered on the hill.

Before we left the Dingle Peninsula, Angus drove the caravan off the main road. He got out and stood on the crest looking down at the tide coming in low, uneven turns. I wandered out after him and we walked about on the headland, and down a slope to a barley field we'd seen earlier in the spring newly planted. The barley was full of shadows and so tall now we could have walked within it unseen.

"Soon it'll be time to cut it," Angus said.

The barley stirred and reached with the wind, a dry, sloughing sound like an undercurrent of voices. I felt grief for it, imagining it cut and tied in barrows. The plows rested against the fence like they were dreaming of a day in the field.

"You see the way all moments pass us," he said. He was thinking of the loneliness ahead of him.

"Soon'll be All Souls' Eve and the Advent of Darkness. Sister Margaret Mooney told me I'd been born in November because I was meant to understand the thinness of the world."

"Where will you go, Angus?" I asked.

He shook his head. "I don't know, Clodagh. To the north, I think. I've got to gather a bit of money together."

"You'll write me soon, will you, Angus?"

His eyes shined as he looked at me. "I will, lass," he said. "I'll not abandon you again."

We walked slowly back to the caravan. "How little hold we have on things, Clodagh," he said. "How easily the world leaves us with nothing."

· 3 0 ·

I WOKE FROM EVERY SLEEP WITH MY STOMACH FLOATING NEAR MY throat. I'd make my way outside and retch in the rainy grass at the side of the caravan while Angus cooked sausages or eggs under a tarp. The smell sent me back inside where I buried my face in the pillow.

I lay all day in bed while Angus drove, rain beating the metal on the caravan walls. Near sleep I imagined that the house on Mercymount Strand was flooded to the ceiling and that I was swimming inside it near the vestibule looking down at the tapestry chairs with their collapsed, threadworn seats. The water cast wavering shadows and floating white lights on the walls. I swam along examining the stuccowork swirls as I passed them slowly. I found myself in the parlor high up near the ceiling looking down into the great room, which seemed to float before me and dissolve into the next room: cornices, wainscoting, dead-ended doors, the shapes of things distorted by water.

I had to swim down, down into darkness to find the kitchen, which seemed to have sunk. Two night-fishermen's lamps swayed there slowly back and forth on long cords lighting isolated corners of the wreckage, a dim eerie red as they moved. Things floated in the dark: my mother's music box, her lace scarf, the little glass dog. I dove deeper, feeling the bubbles from my nose running up the length of me. The lamp swayed and lit the water in front of me and there was the stuccowork face from the kitchen wall, free floating.

The rain grew more and more urgent. I woke one night certain that Angus had driven us down to the beach and that it was waves of seawater and not rain hitting the side of the caravan.

There was no place to dry our clothes, everything soaked, and even after Angus was able to repair the caravan roof and walls, the air was so damp inside that nothing would dry. I could not lie on my stomach, so much did my breasts ache. For a week I held down no food and was constantly shivering. One night my teeth stopped chattering and I started to burn up.

For a few hours the rain stopped and Angus opened the door and window. I took off my clothes and lay on the damp fleece like I was about to go up in flames. The oil cooker made my skin glisten a dim orangy color. Moths came in, fluttered around the cooker, and swept past my ears.

I could not bear the rocking of the caravan. Even when Angus wasn't driving, it rocked and creaked in the wind. I cried for Mrs. O'Dare, for someone to take care of me.

The thought of a comfortable bed and an electric fire stayed with me. The moments I actually felt hunger I had a terrific urge for Mrs. O'Dare's steak and kidney pie. I told him I couldn't bear it, squatting in the field to do my water. The dampness never leaving my clothes after a rain. The leaks in the roof. All the things that had never fazed me before.

The pregnancy had brought me back to myself, and though I feared that the child might not be right I felt no panic in my body. Just a wish for comfort. A clean ruffled nightgown. The noise of a ticking clock that chimed the hour.

We rode across Ireland and reached Mercymount Strand in early September. But a strange car was parked outside and all the beech trees were cut down. Unfamiliar curtains luffed at the screens. A serving woman in a white cap walked across the yard when I banged on the gate. I asked for Mrs. O'Dare and she told me she'd moved to Dublin and that the house was now owned by people called the Fitzgeralds from Antrim, who'd moved in the previous month. She had no address in Dublin for Mrs. O'Dare and I thought of going to Letty Grogan for it but could not bear the idea of seeing her as I was.

Angus said we should go to Lily Sheehy in Dunshee and as we left Bray, going westward toward Kildare, I saw the white arcades of St.

Mathilde's College in the distance. I told Angus to stop; that I wanted to see Sister Seraphina and tell her that I was alive. I imagined myself dissolving into tears in her arms, the way my mother had sometimes done with Mrs. O'Dare. He left the caravan on the roadside and we walked the winding road to the gate before being stopped by a groundskeeper.

"Get out o' here, ye tinkers! No begging in this place."

"We're not beggars!" I said. "I've come to see Sister Seraphina. Can you tell her it's Clodagh Sheehy come to see her."

"I'll not. The likes of you'd be after begging from a poor old nun. Now make yourselves scarce."

Angus clenched his jaw. "This girl here has won an award at this school, you bastard."

The man looked me up and down, filthy as I was with my disheveled dress and knotted hair. "And pigs fly. Now get your filthy arses out o' here or I'll beat ye both senseless."

Angus spit at the ground near his feet. "If you weren't hiding behind that rake I'd have you callin' for your patron saint."

As we drove off, Angus red-faced, holding in his rage, I heard a distant bell and saw the arcades swarm with students moving between classes. I gazed after the distant figure of a girl who could have been me, moving there along a walkway with an armful of books.

We rode along the dark wooded passes of central Wicklow, around Glencree and the Sally Gap, along austere mountaintops into the valley of Glendalough, lush and quiet, heavy with ancient monastic ruins. As much as I wanted a bath and a clean bed, I kept making Angus stop, unable to bear things swinging and creaking in irregular rhythms; a tin and metal cacophony. We'd set camp in various places, once in a gutted church surrounded by heather.

The September weather was temperate, even cool, but I felt hot and would get up at dawn to walk barefoot in the early frost.

That month, ailing as I was, Angus cared for me as if I were a sick child. I begged him to tell me about the bird sanctuaries on the Donegal isles in the north where he'd seen boats propelled by polar winds.

I longed for unfamiliar landscapes, a place with no trace of my own history, and I told him that we had to leave Ireland and go into the white face of the north, far into the Scottish Hebrides.

For a while he laughed at me for the notion. "Such a place is annihilating in winter, lass."

But in my mind's eye I saw a sun like a great star of Bethlehem blinding me as I crossed a remote field. I'd fall asleep imagining the sea frozen and composed at my feet and dream of my mother's jelly molds, her cups and saucers set upon it as if upon a gleaming table.

The queasiness in my belly lasted all day and all night. I'd call out to Angus where he slept on the floor at the foot of the caravan, crying about the heat, begging him to take me from Ireland, telling him it was a godforsaken country and I could no longer bear the place.

"Clodagh," he'd say, cooling my temples with a damp cloth. "You don't want to get out of Ireland. You want to get away from yourself and from what's inside you."

But his words made me angry and we'd fight; him admonishing the idea, insisting that I stop; me going on that if I could ride in a sled and feel the sting of snow on my cheeks I'd be all right.

I indulged the irrationality of the notion because of the way it perplexed him, imagining that this was the way a daughter might torment her own father. I told him about a picture I had seen as a child in a book of Russian fairytales, of a girl wrapped in furs in a sled the shape of a swan. A picture full of peace and remoteness. This is what I needed, I told him. The cold and the white. The sled drawn smoothly along on the ice. He owed me this, for the love of God. After all that had happened between us. And though my words pained him he often laughed and shook his head at me. I was secretly pleased with his tender incredulity. Grateful to excite it in him, and pleased.

One morning the sun was bright and I came out wrapped in a blanket and sat with him near the fire drinking a cup of tea.

"You must miss your music," he said.

"Sometimes I hear strains of the Debussy," I confessed.

"Is Debussy your favorite?"

"Yes," I said. "He was one of my favorites."

After tea, he took the radio apart attempting to fix it. "I know there's a classical station comes out of Dublin. This close we should be able to receive it."

I watched him set the pieces about him. His hair had grown very long over the summer and a curtain of wavy strands hung before one eye as he unscrewed a cluster of wiring from a little metal plate.

"Angus, I don't really need to hear music," I said to him, nervous of what it might stir in me.

He looked up, half hearing, disregarding. I went back inside and lay on the caravan bed, vague transmissions coming and going as he worked, voices and cries and breaking music. He came in to me later and said he was taking the radio into town to have it fixed.

"Angus," I said. "I don't like the radio. The noise and the voices."

"You're missing your music school because of me. You'll not be cut off from music," he said. "A sin to waste a gift. My daughter has a musical talent. God knows I've enough to feel guilty about over you, love."

But when he came back he had a small used record player with two plastic speakers, and a new record wrapped in cellophane. "The only Debussy I could find," he said. It was an orchestral symphony, *La Mer.* "I could not find any Debussy for the piano."

"I'm glad," I said. "I don't think I could bear to hear a solo piano."

He rigged the phonograph up somehow to the battery of a car and the turntable began to rotate.

He put the needle on the record and moody orchestral impressions rose around us like attenuated veils. There were vigorous, emotional exchanges between strings and air. Graceful tidal waves of sound. As we listened, I caught him watching my face with crushed regard.

We played it again and again. He'd bring the little phonograph outside sometimes and we'd sit on the rocks at the fire and listen, or walk about the outskirts of the camp, the music sweetening the wind.

"Wasn't this a good thing I did? Buying this?" he asked me more than once. He seemed pleased with himself, surprised. The music restored a dreaminess to the air between us; an innocence.

A hope rose in Angus. He had not tried again to begin the trip to Dunshee and I'd said nothing about it, both of us holding our breath at the way things were with us.

He built a separate bed for himself, narrower, fashioned of boards, and placed it at the foot of the caravan. He came back from every fair and every excursion into town with a gift for me: a rose-pink coverlet for my bed; a crucifix made of quartz crystal on a metal chain. A sea horse pin for my coat. Things a father might buy a daughter. He looked at my court shoes one day for size, and came back with a pair of heavy boots. "For the rough weather ahead of us," he said.

At the end of September, the nausea and the heat were gone. I was famished. First it was for custard with lashes of cream. Then cake loaded with currants, and chocolate biscuits with jam inside. Angus called it "children's food" and bought a mutton chop and cooked it in the skillet and I ate it with my hands, sucking the marrow out of the bone.

He laughed at me. "You've a fiery look in your eye for that chop, lass."

The October fires were already burning in the fields and the trees dropped their fruit on the roadsides. I gathered apples and pears, eating them as I walked, tossing the cores into the overgrowth.

When I looked in the mirror my face was bright; my eyes vivid, a flush to my cheeks. Angus watched me in the firelight. He was no longer easy going to his bed when I went to mine. He sat very late at the fire, breaking up the banked coals, stirring bright sparks under soft ash.

I awoke in the dark one night, my bones knocking together with the cold. I remembered the chill nights earlier in the spring when I'd slept warm against the furnace of Angus's body. I crept from bed with all my blankets, got in with him, and curled into his sleeping back.

*   *   *

At first light I opened my eyes. Angus had turned toward me and was watching me, his face close to mine on the pillow. In that half-state between dream and awareness, a burn of anticipation moved like liquid under my skin. When his lips brushed mine I touched them with my tongue.

For moments we were suspended in the half-light of the kiss, a sensation of unreality between us. When the caravan moved suddenly in the wind, Angus broke the kiss and looked gravely at me, his eyes wet, unnaturally intense.

He got up abruptly, put on his pants and jacket, and went out, slamming the caravan door closed so hard it flew back open with the impact. Tears shot into my eyes. I lay there breathing hard, staring at the ceiling. If he had not torn himself away, I knew I'd not have stopped it. There must have been something monstrous in me, I thought, my body still pulsing from the touch of him.

He'd been protecting me and caring for me. We had been managing as father and daughter. Grief filled me at how easily that was lost now.

That day as he was driving west toward Dunshee, Declan scaling the narrow passes, the occasional car maneuvering around us, I reminded Angus that I had no claims to Lily Sheehy since she was not really my aunt, and he told me that she didn't know that and that I had to think of what was good for me and the child.

"She may not take me in," I said.

"I'll wait in the woods a few hours. In case she won't."

"I'll miss you too much," I said.

"We can't make the rules ourselves," he said sternly.

"I'll go mad if you disappear from my life, Angus."

"I won't," he said in an admonishing tone.

"You'll come if I want you, Angus! Won't you?"

"I will, though the devil may take us both."

"The devil'll not take us," I said softly.

"Lily Sheehy has a piano, does she not, Clodagh?"

"Yes."

"Another thing I could never give you," he said.

"Stop, Angus."

"You'll have Lily Sheehy and the vast rooms and chandeliers of her house."

"I have no use for chandeliers. It isn't Agatha you're talking to," I said. A detectable tremor passed through him at the words.

But as the caravan rocked along in the October air, I was mostly quiet, struggling to set my mind to seeing Lily Sheehy; wondering what I might say to her. Thinking of it made me tired and I found myself remembering the comfort of the green bedroom and the fireplace with the screens and the great porcelain bath with the colored bottles of Lily Sheehy's ablutions.

We reached Drumcoyne House by dark, the bracken and trees dimly lit, moths fluttering in the porchlight. We stood together outside the gate saying nothing.

"You'll write to me soon, Angus. Promise."

"Promise," he said. He lifted his hand to my face, hesitating before he touched my cheek.

I bowed my head and pressed it to his chest, feeling the force of his heart at my forehead. I turned from him suddenly and walked through the gate.

Lily Sheehy did not recognize me immediately there in the porchlight with moths fluttering above my head. But then her eyes went wide and she recoiled.

"Holy Mother in Heaven," she said. "Is it Clodagh?"

"Yes, Aunt."

She opened the door for me and I stepped into the brightly lit vestibule. I saw someone move from the corner of my eye. It took me a moment to understand that it was my own reflection in the mirror, my hair matted with leaves and bits of wool from Angus's fleece.

She closed the door and we stood where we were.

"Did someone hurt you, Clodagh?"

"No, Aunt. Not in the way you mean. I went willingly where I went."

Across her mouth flashed the same look of disapproval I'd seen when I was small and had asked her to tell me about my mother's past.

"We were all desperate over you." She sat down on a chair in the vestibule, her face blanched.

On a little table surrounded by votive candles stood a framed photograph of me taken earlier in the spring in front of the house.

"Who were you with, Clodagh?" she asked.

"A man." She turned her face from me and looked down. "I wouldn't impose myself so upon you or ask your forgiveness if I were not carrying a child."

She made the sign of the cross and there was a terrible silence. The floor creaked under my feet. I had forgotten how such small sounds were amplified by the enclosure of solid walls. The silence had a smell of furniture oil and boiled potatoes. All odors complacent with no gust of air diluting them.

"Kitty's seriously ill," she said with accusation.

"I'm sorry to hear that, Aunt," I said.

She looked at me as if she hated me. "We thought you were dead. We suffered and grieved as if you were dead. Mrs. O'Dare was devastated."

"I'm so sorry," I said.

"The police were out searching for you in the ditches and fields of Ireland."

My throat constricted with guilt. What I had done seemed unforgivable. "Are you going to turn me out?"

"You're Frank's child." She lowered her head, tightening and untightening her lips. "Go upstairs now and have a wash," she whispered heavily.

On my way up I stopped on the landing to look at a memorial card set on a little table, a school photograph of me from St. Brendan's, wreathed in lilies. Under the picture the words "Beloved daughter of Frank Sheehy" were engraved.

I heard Lily's footsteps below. "They've given your apprenticeship to another girl, of course."

My heart fell, but what had I expected? I walked heavily up the rest of the stairs.

I took a hot bath, washed and rinsed my hair, and broke the teeth of a comb trying to get it through.

I stared at myself in the mirror. I had changed over the summer. In the artificial light my eyes were like broken gem beds, brilliant and unearthly, my skin the color of sand and freckled at the nose and cheeks. The bones of my face cast soft shadows and my neck looked longer and more graceful. I watched my chest rise and fall as I breathed.

Mrs. Dowling put me into Kitty's old room; the room she'd occupied years back before she'd been confined to a wheelchair. "It's larger and airier than your old room. And two sets of stairs may get to be an indisposition for you," Lily said with a dour mouth. "And there is a nursery across the hall. The one that your mother had prepared for you and your sister."

The bed was comfortable but dipped in the center where Kitty had once slept. The curtains as I drew them smelled of faded hyacinths and the bedstead of the shellac she had once used on her pincurls. I remembered at Mercymount Strand when I was small, one of her stiff pincurls grazing my cheek when she'd kissed me.

On the dresser arranged around a framed photograph of Kitty as a young woman, a romantic enthusiasm in her posture and bright eyes, were cards and devotions that had been distributed at Masses said for me. Some were from the nuns at St. Mathilde's, sentiments and prayers for a dead girl.

Mrs. Dowling turned on the radiator, which banged and whistled and emitted a comforting warmth. I lay back in the bed and let out a deep sigh. Pressing my cheek to the flowery starched sheet, I cried myself to sleep, thinking of the nuns passing up and down the white arcade at St. Mathilde's, their crimson skirts and veils blowing behind them. I saw Sister Seraphina's old hands crawling sideways on the black and white keys, joy flickering across her face. I slept fitfully, the words from the parable streaming in and out of my dreams. ". . . doth he not leave the ninety and nine to go into the mountains to seeketh that which is gone astray?" I woke at odd hours uncertain of the time. A little clock on the nightstand read always a quarter past two, though sometimes I thought I heard it ticking.

In daylight with the curtains open, dark clouds moving swiftly toward the sea sent distended shadows across the foot of my bed, and I had the eerie sense, as I had had before at Dunshee, of the hours passing too quickly, the course of my life already set, swept seaward. At odds with the clouds, shadows of birds moving east streaked across the afternoon light on the wall.

My body in its stillness felt intensely active. On the edge of sleep I heard water rushing and swelling at the center of me. I relinquished myself to the powerful volition of my cells, dividing, emitting light. I dreamt of strange multifaceted flowers, geometrical things duplicating and enlarging, out of control. Terrible dreams about the dummy doors at Mercymount Strand; a dummy child; an idiot child. A misshapen child. A girl with her head in a vige.

Inside things were the secret beginnings of other things. The determination of the child in me made me sad. I wondered if it was human-looking yet. I remembered the picture I'd seen of a child in its mother's womb with a large head and praying hands, and the thought of it gave me a chill. Still there was something about the child inside me that set me oddly at ease. I felt, in my repose, its quiet urgency for the world.

Once I awakened with the sense that Lily Sheehy was standing in the doorway regarding me. I lifted my head and, for a split moment of vertigo, thought that I saw Mare. But the woman there did not look like us. She had long dark hair and I thought she was naked until I saw that she wore a thin pale pink dress that could have been a nightgown. She looked at me with a tilted head and a sad concerned expression.

I tried to sit up but felt heavy and slow and by the time I did, the woman was gone.

Later when I asked Lily who the woman was who'd come to my room, she seemed surprised.

"No one is here but you, Kitty and me. Mrs. Dowling isn't even here today."

"I saw a woman in a thin dress looking at me like she was worried."

Lily's face darkened. "It's the light. Keep the curtains open during the day, and a lamp on at night."

A week passed of baths and sleep and plentiful, delicious food. I went one day to Frank Sheehy's library looking for something to preoccupy me, and found a heavy book about trees indigenous to Ireland, full of photographs. I sat in a velvet armchair and tried to read, but felt disturbed by a din on the air, emitted, it seemed, by the heirlooms and objects around me: a collection of old military medals displayed on wine-colored velvet; butterflies encased in glass boxes; a stuffed barn owl with polished eyes and beak.

I left that room carrying the book with me through the halls, marble busts of unidentified gentlemen issuing imploded silence. The air throughout the house was heavy, unvigorous, given to exaggerated echo, so that my own footsteps seemed to follow me up the stairs.

Approaching my room I noticed the door ajar to the old nursery room across from mine. It had been Frank Sheehy's sickroom before he died, and afterward, when my mother revealed that she was pregnant, it had been converted into a nursery. I thought it strange that it was preserved this way; another relic of Frank Sheehy's life. A room prepared over twenty years ago before the aunts had changed their minds and sent my mother and Mrs. O'Dare to the other side of Ireland. I went in.

An antique crib stood in the corner, the edges of the ruffles on the bedding slightly yellowed. On the wall over the crib hung a framed illustration of a lamb wearing a ribbon around its neck, the image artificially washed with pinks and pale greens, and covered by a thick oval protrusion of glass.

It was an oddly shaped, sparsely furnished room that smelled, in spite of the recent cleaning, of dust and dead flowers and time. One wall protruded out in a square with a door on it, giving the appearance of a closet. I opened the door, shocked to find that it was a dummy. A thin space descended and I could see the black of the inner house below, a draft rising and exhaling into the room. On a shelf of splintered wood before the window, a large conch shell sat arranged among many smaller shells of all kinds. Lily Sheehy had told me once that my mother had spent many hours walking along the sea after my father had died, collecting shells. I was certain as I stood there that these were my mother's shells.

I touched the yellow ivory inset of one of the crib bars. I thought of Mare in her little box of polished wood and felt a throbbing in my temples. I rubbed my eyes, afraid for the creature inside me, and thought of the terrible story of my mother's infant sister and all the sadness that could befall a child. I swayed on my feet, grasping the bars of the crib. The air was stale with the feeling of things perished, of expectations left unfulfilled.

*　　　*　　　*

To get out of the house I took to walking on the windy beach or sitting on the rocks close to the water, the rocks where Angus had first seen my mother. Deafened by the power of the waves, I watched them batter themselves against the cliff walls. I was biding my time, waiting for a letter from Angus.

I wrote to Mrs. O'Dare, begging her to forgive me. I was sure that Lily Sheehy had relayed the information, so I did not mention my pregnancy; only that I missed her and had dreams about her steak and kidney pie.

I heard back from her within a week and was relieved and a bit surprised that she did not admonish me. She said she was grateful to God that I was alive; that she had, in the depths of her heart, known it. She was living with her sister and her husband in Dublin since Mercymount Strand had been sold, but it was a small flat and an uncomfortable situation. She was hopeful about a kitchen position in Drogheda, where she would have her own room.

I felt sad when I finished the letter. She was old now, past seventy. When I'd left Bray in the spring, her arthritis had been plaguing her. I wondered if anyone would really employ her. Things at her sister's flat had to be desperate that she was looking for a new serving position.

I mentioned this to Lily Sheehy, wondering if she needed someone. She looked at me as if I had a lot of nerve for even suggesting it. "Mrs. Dowling's been with me many years, Clodagh," she said.

"I wasn't suggesting that you sack her," I said.

"I only need Mrs. Dowling," she said.

Some days Kitty didn't wake up. When she did I visited her, sitting on her bed, holding her icy hand in mine as she gazed with a vacant face toward the window. In the evenings she'd weep bitterly for hours before she'd fall again into unmitigated slumber.

The priest, Father Galley, came every week to try and administer Communion to her. And every week if she could not be awakened when he came, he gave her the last rites, and Lily waited outside the room.

I had been there a little more than a month when one day, Father Galley waited in the living room to hear my confession. "He'll administer the Host to you after you give him your confession," Lily had said before he'd come. I knew that what was expected of me was contrition for sins of the flesh.

I gazed past him at an oil painting, a dim still life of fruit. "I am sorry for having hurt other people," I said, and went quiet.

His eyes widened, rimmed with pink. "You should make a formal confession."

He waited expectantly, his mouth tense and disapproving. "Well?" he said. "Make the sign of the cross."

But I refused, vacillating between anger and shame. I stared at the chalice that held the Blessed Sacrament. *"Libera, Domine,"* I said finally, at a loss.

He mumbled that someone was a child of Satan, and I didn't know if it was me he meant or the child inside me.

I climbed the stairs while Lily went in to him and closed the door. I put my fingers in the soil of the geranium on the windowsill at the landing and leaned my face into the leaves, which felt like chilled skin.

I heard them talking below but couldn't tell what they were saying. There was an angry and halting rhythm to the priest's words and what sounded like single syllables of assent from Lily.

Breathing the smell of the geranium earth I closed my eyes and whispered to Angus, "Come take me from this place, for the love of God."

When the priest was gone I went downstairs. Lily stood as if frozen in the vestibule, her head lowered. The floor creaked under my feet and she gasped as she turned.

"Aunt," I said.

Her jaw stiffened and a tear moved down her cheek. "I've asked Father Galley to keep our secret," she said.

"Secret . . . ?"

"Yes! Secret!" she cried impatiently.

I said nothing.

"I want this kept secret!" She assumed an imperious stance, her mouth tightening. "I don't want you to tell anyone."

"Who are you afraid of me telling?" I asked.

"I saw Joan, Denis Lanagan's cousin, in Dunshee yesterday. Someone told her they saw you walking on the beach. I told her there had been a mistake, that you had written more letters in the summer that never reached me. I told her you were well but she wanted to know why you weren't at St. Mathilde's. I told her your apprenticeship had been postponed." She fumbled with an ornate citrine pin at her throat. "I'm upset that I was driven to that lie so I confessed it to Father Galley."

"And now he's going to go along with the lie, too?"

She went rigid. "When your condition begins to show you can't go outside anymore."

"I'll not stay inside, Aunt," I said quietly.

"You will."

"I don't care if people know."

"I care! I care, Clodagh! Did you think of that? Clearly not. No. You're the only one that matters!"

"No," I uttered. "No."

A fraught silence held the air between us.

"You're half Sheehy, Clodagh," she said, I was sure, to remind herself.

"Aunt," I said, wishing I could tell her the truth. I peered into her face and saw her eyes retreat from mine. "I'm . . . more tinker than you know."

The quiet in the room rang in my ears and I felt on it Lily's devotion to Frank. What would she do if I revealed such deception against his memory? Her face strained and her eyes darted. She was tied to him in ways that I did not understand. I often heard her haunting his rooms. She had to have suspected my mother but she did not want to know. I sighed, exhausted by the convolutions of the lie.

"I'm sorry," I said, "for all the pain I cause you." I felt an intense ache for Angus. "Wouldn't you be relieved, Aunt, if you did not have me in this house?"

She looked accusingly at me. "You'd like to go again, wouldn't you?"

I was surprised by her reaction, wondering why my leaving might cause her pain. It seemed impossible to me that she might genuinely care for me. It had to be only because she believed I was Frank's daughter.

"You aren't sorry for your predicament. You aren't changed by your troubles," she said, struggling to contain her fury, and left the room.

I did not come down for dinner that evening. When I rang, Mrs. Dowling brought a tray to my room.

That night in my dream I found myself in bed with Angus. I heard someone else in the room, looked up and saw a separate Angus, a replica of the one in my arms. The standing one was weeping. "My father," I kept thinking. "My father." I felt that he should not have been witnessing what I was doing. He should not have been seeing me that way. The sexual feelings dissolved in the face of the pervasive agony I felt over the father. I disentangled myself from the lover, pushing him away.

I woke up panting and full of dread, longing for Angus the father. He'd been so clear in the dream, so separate from the lover.

I sat up in bed, looking around me. A dull light issued from the gilt fixture on the wall. Beneath it a porcelain figure of an angel stared at nothing. I had a piercing, almost panicked feeling in that moment that, again in my life, I was in the wrong place. I belonged with my father. Not breathing the dormant air of this mausoleum of a house. This place I had no claim to.

A few days later I received a letter from Angus.

"Are you all right? Are they caring for you? You're in my every thought." I read and reread it, trembling. He'd sent a Donegal address where I could write him for the next three weeks.

I wrote immediately. "Angus, I'm desperately unhappy here. Please come. I need to talk to you. Your daughter, Clodagh."

I honored Lily's wish that I not go outside. I took up a needle and thread, remembering how my mother had done chaotic little embroideries to fill long hours. Dragging thread through cloth, I stitched long chains of color around the sleeves of an old blouse, finishing one strand of thread and beginning another immediately after, my fingers aching, little smears of blood on the fabric from the pokes of my misdirected needle.

The baby kicked me gently and tears came to my eyes.

I bowed over the blouse, piercing the cloth again and again.

In December, long curtains of rain fell over the sea. When the skies cleared a soft incandescence bled from the clouds. My heart quickened when I heard the floor creak in the hallway outside my room. I rushed out with the wild notion that Angus had slipped secretly into the house.

But no one was there and the disappointment caused me to sway.

I opened the door to the nursery. The dark glow from the Atlantic cast shadows from the crib and a small table, throwing the things into radiant relief. There was a din on the air, a kind of memory of noise like the sea recorded in the contours of a shell. I hardly breathed, feeling a presence; my eyes raked the light, certain that the apparition I'd once seen in my room was about to emerge from it. I caught a hint of movement from the corner of my eye in the alcove where my mother's seashells were arranged. The fear flooded me. A rictus of six or seven long hairs glowed and trembled among the shells. I took a step closer to make sure I really saw them. Blond hairs. White blond. They must have always been there but the light had not come in on them in the way it came in at that moment. The room felt airless and cold and it hurt to breathe.

These are the things my mother's left me, I thought: her hair caught in these shells. This nursery.

Mrs. Dowling awakened me one morning.

"A man is here to see you, Miss," she said with a clipped formality. "He's waiting in the red drawing room."

I dressed myself breathlessly, shivering as I splashed my face with water from the ewer on the dressing table.

When I appeared at the drawing room door he startled and stood. In spite of his efforts at presentation, a dark blue shirt and tweedy-looking jacket, his hair cut and combed and his beard shaven, he looked like a strong but terrified animal, wildly out of place.

I closed the door and faced him. He winced as he gazed at my swollen belly. His eyes squeezed shut as if of their own volition. He lowered his face and stood there shaking with silent tears.

"Angus," I said, going to him.

He covered his face with his hands, convulsing like the weeping father in my dream.

"Christ on earth. What have I done to you?" he cried.

"Sit down, sit down," I said, taking his arm and guiding him to the sofa where I sat beside him. But his grief was pervasive and I was at a loss as to what to do.

"I'm all right, Angus," I kept whispering. "I'm all right."

There was a knock at the door. He quieted but did not raise his head or open his eyes. Mrs. Dowling swept in with a silver tea service, her eyes flashing expressionlessly to Angus and then to me. She put the tray on a side table, left and closed the door.

We sat awhile, his tears stopped, his breathing broken now and again by faint tremors. When he opened his eyes he gazed at the riches around us. The heavy crimson curtains were closed and the ambery light of India lamps made all the gilded fixtures and statuary glow. Some Sheehy ancestress in a yellow dress watched us from her dark oil portrait on the wall.

"Look at all of this," he said.

"I hate it," I said.

"You don't."

"I bloody well do."

"You're well cared for," he said, nodding once, but not fully looking at me.

"I'm oppressed by this place. It's full of death . . . and I'm constantly reminded what a cross I am to bear."

He remained motionless, staring down at the pattern of crowns and Celtic motifs on the carpet. A painful quiet held the air between us. "I have something to give you," he said slowly, without looking up. He waited before reaching into his jacket and taking out a piece of paper folded several times. It looked frayed, old. He handed it to me and I opened it. Written in his slanted, looping penmanship were two lines of poetry.

> *O may she live like some green laurel*
> *Rooted in one dear perpetual place.*
> —Yeats

I gazed at the familiar spindly letters of my name printed in a different hand in faded pencil at the top of the paper, and my heart quickened.

"That's your mother's printing," he said.

I stopped breathing a moment and looked warily at him.

"The last time I saw Agatha, a few days before she died, she told me I'd read her a poem once. A poem from a father to a daughter. I knew the one. Yeats' 'A Prayer for My Daughter.' She asked me to write down these lines; she wanted to give them to you."

He stared down at the carpet again, bemused. I read the words over, trying to understand.

"But she never took it with her. She left it inside the book where I found it months later. I thought she had it with her when I watched her walk across the field back to the big house that night." He paused. "There were signs of it in her that night, what she was planning for herself. She told me she'd seen her own mother. That she had looked for her again and had not been able to find her. She talked about the dead infant sister drowned in the sea and said that the child hadn't suffered. That water was easy and carried you if you let it. There was a feverishness about her face. She moved awkwardly, whispering and laughing to herself, then looking at me, suppressing a smile as if I'd caught her at something. She mentioned you . . . several times. Saying she needed to give you the lines of poetry."

"But she forgot them, didn't she?"

"She wanted you to live settled."

"She didn't want anything for me."

"She did, love."

"Then why didn't she give it to me?"

"I don't know."

"Maybe she really meant for you to read the lines of the poem," I said.

"What do you mean?"

"To remind you . . . because she knew you wanted to be with your daughter. So she could always deprive us of each other. . . ." My voice was strained with resentment.

"She thought she was doing the right thing, Clodagh."

"Why are you defending her?"

"I must have also believed it was right that you live settled and have money or I would have claimed you."

I squeezed my fists in my lap and looked away from him.

"She thought living settled was the right way to live. She was not really comfortable settled but she thought that was her own failing. She moved between worlds, no home in either. In the way that you've been doing yourself. But now you must make a home in the world of houses."

"Why? Because that's what she wanted?"

"Do that much for yourself, love."

"I can't stay here!"

"You'll have a doctor to deliver the child here. I can't give you that."

"We can find midwives."

"There's more dangers that way."

"I'm young and strong."

He looked straight into my eyes. "The child may need special care, Clodagh," he said.

My heart stopped a moment. "You'll not leave me here, Angus," I said.

He sighed. "This is for you," he said, handing me an envelope with money in it.

A storm of panic and fury broke in my body and the baby started kicking me. "I don't want this!" I cried, throwing it to the floor, three ten-pound notes slipping loose. Angus bent down and gathered them again, then slid the envelope between the cushions of the sofa. "It's here if you want it," he said. "I'm going back to Donegal. Sister Margaret Mooney is ill."

"I want to meet her," I said.

He let his eyes settle fully on me and they began to glow again with tears. In a quiet, clear voice, he said, "No, lass."

A heavy, helpless feeling bled into my anger, overtaking it. I felt as if I were floating.

"We were both looking for Agatha in each other, were we not, love?"

"What?" I cried.

"Like magnets we were because of it."

"No," I said, the words threatening to dismantle everything between us. "It isn't because of her. What's between us has never been because of her."

"It always has, Clodagh. We're a trinity."

"She kept you from me and now she's taking you from me again!"

"No, lass."

"I want my father. I deserve to live with my own father."

"Daughters leave their fathers at the age you are now."

"There's no danger of the other . . . what was between us before . . ."

"Clodagh, we could never get by what was between us before. It eclipses everything else. . . ."

I said nothing, things floating in the light of my tears. I could not see him clearly. I remembered the heat of him, suddenly, reluctantly, the taste of his mouth.

After a silence he stood. "Are you playing the piano again?"

I shook my head. "No. I don't even hear the music anymore. I'll not touch the piano again," I said. "Never again." I sat stiffly with my head turned away from him, pressed to one shoulder. He was a shadow, a dark presence cutting the unnatural light of the India lamps.

"You will," he whispered. "A time will come when things settle and you'll hunger again for the music."

"No. I'll not."

For a long time he stood before me, waiting for me to look at him, but I wouldn't. Finally he said, "I'll write to you. I'm sorry, love. I'm sorry," and moved from the room, a smear of dark. A sound of footsteps.

When I woke at twilight there was a spatter of blood on my sleeve. My throat ached and my head pounded. I remembered Mrs. Dowling and Lily Sheehy bringing me to my room. I remembered screaming, spitting up. I remembered hitting Lily with the back of my hand. Mrs. Dowling had restrained me but I had no sense of how long it had gone on and no idea what I was yelling at them.

I had a vague feeling of presentiment as I stood, weaving my way to the window and opening it. When I smelled the smoke of a campfire in the oak trees, my heart began to clamor. He had not been able to leave me after all, I thought. I put some things into a bag and went down the stairs. I retrieved the envelope of money Angus had left between the cushions and went outside into the oaks, stopping every few yards to brace myself against a tree.

Not Declan, but a gray-and-white horse stood in the clearing and an old woman in a red coat sat before the fire. The woman I'd seen my first day in Dunshee, who'd been gathering on the rock beach, searching among the garbage of the sea.

I brought the heels of my fists to my face and began to cry.

The old woman stood up and reached for me. "Come here to me, love," she said. "What is it?"

"Where's Angus Kilheen?"

"I'm all that's here," she said.

"Do you know him, Missus?"

"I don't," she said apologetically. "Come to the fire and have a cup of tea." She reached her hand to me carefully as if she were attempting to lure a deer.

"No. I can't. I've got to find him. He's got to be here."

"You need something to eat and a rest," she said.

"Are there any travelers camping north of here, Missus?"

"Maybe on the road to Clarinbridge . . ."

I handed her one of the ten-pound notes. "Will you take me there, please?"

She would not take the money, but she packed up her things and we moved slowly north in near darkness. When we arrived I walked through the settlement with a lamp, touching the muzzles of the horses, looking for Declan. A few men sat drinking around a dying fire. They said they knew Angus, that he'd left earlier in the day for Donegal on his way to the shores of Lough Swilly, and unless he'd stopped he was surely in Castlebar by now.

At first light we started back to the oak woods near Dunshee. I lay on her bed inside while she drove, the caravan lit up with lamps. In baskets on the floor were spools of thread, lace trims and packets of needles, the things she sold to earn her bread.

When she asked me, I would not tell her where I'd come from, only that I had no place on earth to go.

· 3 2 ·

I've been more than a month camping with Mrs. Cleary when I wake her early one morning. My water has broken and has soaked the muslin nightgown she's given me to wear. She tells me to be calm, it will be a while yet. She rubs my shoulders.

It is the feast day of Saint Brigid, she tells me. The lactation time of the ewes. The beginning of light in the Irish year. If she had not told me this I would not know that it is the morning of my twenty-first birthday.

Between the pains, I'm praying. It is the Angelus mostly that comes to me. *Be it done unto me according to Thy word.* And sometimes words from the Act of Contrition: *Through my fault, through my fault. Through my most grievous fault,* my lips moving silently to the prayers in my thoughts. I hear Mare's voice saying the words and sometimes Mrs. O'Dare's.

The prayers are second nature to me. I never knew, though I must have said them in my life thousands of times, I said them most often without zeal or intent. At the end of me there they are, streaming up to the surface like something held for years under a stone at the bottom of the sea.

Air rushing toward air.

Another pain rips me apart and she gives me a tea towel to bite. I tear it to shreds.

When the pain subsides she asks, "Do you have a jacket or garment belonging to the baby's father to wear while you lie in?"

"Why?" I ask.

"So he can bear some of the pain, the brute."

"No," I say, panting. "I should have gotten my mother's dress from him."

"What, love? Your mother's dress?"

"Yes. He belonged to my mother first. He still belongs first to her."

"*He* did?"

"Yes."

"And where is your mother now, lass?"

"Dead. In the sea."

"And who is this man to you?" she asks softly.

"He's my own father."

She keeps her eyes to mine and makes the sign of the cross.

"Inne an vain, a chroi istig," she says softly, but I cannot see her. My head is back. I am soaked and shivering.

I hear the wild falsetto shriek of the baby. The old woman stands, cleaning the blood from it. "Bless us, Holy Mother in Heaven, he's a perfect fat thing." She places the infant on my damp chest.

His hair looks fair though it's wet and burnished with blood. His eyes are open and he's struggling with the light.

The first week my heart races at every noise. Each time the wind creaks in the hinges I startle and my milk stops and the wee boy at my breast writhes and whines.

"Angus," I call out.

The old woman tells me to calm down, it's only the wind. But I keep clenching and straining to hear footsteps in the trees.

"Ah, lass," she says. "Let go, now. Let go. However high the tide, it ebbs away."

And I settle back again soft with disappointment, the tears running down my face, dropping on the infant's velvety head like rain.

"Such golden hair the child has, " Mrs. Cleary marvels. "Like the King of Fairies."

"Finvarra," I say, thinking of Angus. "Yes, that suits him. After the Fairy King of Ulster."

When I call him by the name the child looks at me as if with curiosity.

"He looks at me, Missus Cleary, as if he knows me."

"Of course he knows you, lass. A child gets its heart from its mother."

Maybe it's these words that help me stop the waiting and wishing for Angus. Or maybe its whispering the name Finvarra to the child and seeing his eyes intent on my face.

There is a wonderful relief telling Mrs. Cleary about my childhood, about my mother's death and about Angus Kilheen.

"Maybe my mother really was a selkie," I say, watching her eyes. "Maybe Angus lied."

"Ah, love. You don't believe such stories."

"A part of me wishes to believe it."

"They're stories is all, lass. You know it as well as I. People make such magical stories to soften the hardness of the world."

Her words cause my eyes to fill. "How do you explain all that's happened? Wouldn't you call it unearthly?"

She looks into my face with earnestness and pity. "It's none of it outside the realm of human beings, Clodagh," she says and grasps my hand.

Mrs. Cleary sends me off for fresh air, tells me to take a walk along the strand. But I stay on the headland, sitting on a promontory looking to the west. The sea below makes me uneasy; its ancient filmy skirts bouldering forth then flattening and retreating.

I feel raw to the world. Even the daylight hurts my eyes. But I breathe it in. Not another soul in sight. Maybe a fishing boat far out in the distance. The movement of the seals in the sea.

When the milk soaks my dress I know Finvarra is crying for me and I am drawn irrevocably back. If he sleeps too long my breasts ache. There's relief in the fierceness of his suck. I tell Mrs. Cleary that my breasts have ears.

In the quiet hours that I hold him, joy simmers in my chest. Even with all the loss. All the uncertainty. My hair grazes his brow and I whisper, "My lamb. My lamb."

*   *   *

One day we hear funeral bells from the Star of the Sea Chapel.

"I wonder who it is that's died," I say, thinking of Kitty Sheehy.

Mrs. Cleary goes off into Dunshee to sell some needles and threads and when she comes back in the evening she makes a fire and while the infant sleeps we sit together near the flames and have a cup of tea.

She seems pensive and keeps refilling my cup; I feel her hesitating, holding something back. "Keep that wee one suckling a long time and you'll not soon get coltish."

"I know, Missus," I say. I can hear a guilty timbre in her voice and I realize when she cannot hold my eyes that she is trying to make advice a parting gift to me. She plans to be off somewhere.

'What will I do if you go, Missus?" I ask.

She laughs. "You see clearly enough, don't ye, Clodagh? The bells were for Kitty Sheehy."

"Oh," I say. "Well, it's been a long time coming."

"I spoke to Lily Sheehy, Clodagh. I said to her, 'I can take Clodagh and the wee boy with me, Miss Sheehy. But it's a harder life they'd both have ahead of them. And yourself all alone in a great house.'"

My jaw tightens and I look away from her.

"I asked her couldn't she find in her heart a place for the two of you. 'Clodagh made a mistake and isn't it like the young to do so, for isn't it how they learn to live in the world, Miss Sheehy?' I asked her. 'And Clodagh's beside herself over the loss of you.'"

"How could you, Mrs. Cleary?" I ask.

"Stop it now. You can't afford to be proud. You've got Finvarra to think about and it's a shakier life circling the roads and byways of Ireland when he could live in a great plush castle and eat all the trifle and cream he can fill his gullet with. She's afraid to be alone. It's written on her face."

"I'm not really related to her," I say.

"She knows you're not Frank's child."

"How?"

"She's always suspected it. But you confirmed it yourself, that last day you were there."

I said nothing.

"She knows everything, Clodagh. Still she wants you there. Her brother loved your mother. You're the closest thing left to a relative in this world for her."

"How can I face her, Missus?"

"*Buadhann an thoighde ar an gcinneamhain,*" the old woman says softly.

"What does it mean?"

"Patience conquers destiny, my girl."

The last evening with Mrs. Cleary, I hear seals barking out on the cliffs. I watch them sun themselves in last light and think of Angus forging a sealskin into a dress.

I remember the weighty silk of it and its unsettling fragrance. I imagine throwing it into the sea, watching it catch in the rocks, twisting back and forth with the rushing of water before a tide washes over and lifts it. I imagine it riding out, water filling its contours, arms opening wide as it descends.

There is nothing mysterious about the dress now. It's a relic of Agatha and Angus, of their private story. The selkie had grown tired of being human and dreamed of a second chance at grace; "pushing at the seam between worlds, looking for the dark glimmer of an underwater room."

After everything, it is not my story. I will go to Lily Sheehy, following my child back to the realm of air and civilization, "the sun igniting everything" in our path.

It is difficult at first, going back to Drumcoyne House with Lily knowing I am no one to her; with all her fears and suspicions justified about my mother's nature and mine.

She has brought out a cradle with a lace skirt around it and has placed it thoughtfully next to the chair where I am to sit down to tea.

"That was Frank's bed," she says, looking at Finvarra as if it is him she has addressed.

She avoids my eyes as she passes me the cream. I lift the cup: green and pink filigree and delicate as eggshell. I take a sip. Lily's mistrust colors the air of the room like fog.

I am given the last room I had in this house, across the hall from the nursery. But I keep Finvarra in bed with me.

Most of the night I do not sleep but listen to his breathing. He smells buttery and clean. When he wakes he presses a tiny hand to my face. He bleats at me like a lamb until I draw him to my breast.

When Lily holds Finvarra in the air before her, her eyes are strange and bright. Her voice climbs an octave, all inhibition gone from it. She speaks to him in a private language, bits of Irish strewn with English babble. "Wee babeen! My puck o' the rushes! *I smilis an rud an t-anam*," she says. And I have the sense that I don't know her at all, the older, stiffer woman melted down to a girlish, animated creature.

One afternoon with Finvarra asleep in her arms she tells me that he brings Frank back to her. That Frank was like her own child when she was a girl of twelve. "And even though Kitty was fifteen and it would seem that she'd have been the one to mother him, it wasn't that way. It was always me. I was his little mother and he was my beloved boy.

"I've loved no one else in my life as I've loved Frank, Clodagh," she admits, and her face and the tops of her ears go pink. Lifting her free hand, she fingers the cluster of diamonds at her collar.

"They're all gone now," she says.

Finvarra stirs against her and opens his eyes. The pain goes out of Lily's face and it floats as she looks at him.

It occurs to me that she thinks I might leave him with her; that I might be eager to be off again after Angus Kilheen, and the thought makes my muscles clench. I move between anger and pity that she could think such a thing. But why shouldn't she think it? Like my mother I've been frightened by permanence.

She has no idea now that Finvarra is the very quick of me.

I remind Lily that Mrs. O'Dare knew Frank; that she'd been very fond of him. They'd be able to reminisce over him and wouldn't that be a comfort to her?

"She's old and hasn't much money. She sleeps in the kitchen of her sister's flat. Couldn't she come here, Aunt?"

She agrees and telephones the old woman in Dublin and invites her to come to us.

What I marvel at when I think of my father is his capacity for adoration. His fidelity to my mother; to Sister Margaret Mooney. I remember the boyishness of his posture when he knelt before the Blessed Mother with the broken hand and made the sign of the cross.

I wonder over the way we lose each other; how a new love only blurs the face of the first love; how in each other's faces we look for our origins.

He recedes from me. On the verge of sleep my body remembers him as he originally was: the barge of shadow, smelling of horses and fire and night air.

For days I have found myself standing in the doorway of the parlor, looking at the piano. When Lily is out and Finvarra fast asleep, I go to it and slide my finger along middle C. The note plays faintly.

My hand runs up and down the keys. The piano is out of tune. It is true how quickly sea air seeps through wood, warps the tension in the hammers and strings. I look through a pile of sheet music I left in the piano bench, the more complex pieces I used to play, inscrutable to me now. I try a simple Bach exercise, but am immediately disturbed by the sadness the dissonance produces.

When she thought I was dead Lily bought a record of the piece I played for her and Kitty. I turn on the phonograph, place the needle on the turning record, and hear it crackle before the Debussy Prelude begins. Listening, I try to remember the girl, Clodagh, who had once come into that territory of herself.

Finvarra awakens, cooing upstairs. I go up to him and see a woman standing over his cradle looking at him. It is, I think wildly, my mother. And then for the flash of a moment, my sister. But she is both of them. And neither. She is the sadness of the nursery room. As I come in closer, my heart pounding, she withdraws, leaving a greenish, ill-smelling light on the air after her.

I ask Lily Sheehy and Mrs. Dowling to make up another room for me; that I don't like the feeling of that nursery room across the hall. They put me in another wing in a large room that gets a lot of afternoon light. I think of asking Mrs. Dowling for heavy curtains to make it dimmer, but I resist. It feels like an impulse to close out the world.

Rocking Finvarra's cradle with my foot, I fall asleep and dream of a damp dress trailing from the door. I startle. I hear the creak of a floorboard, see a smear of light. My pulses riot. I blame myself for the ghost, believing it to be something wayward in me that draws her.

Afraid that I won't be able to protect him, I feel my mother's ache and panic of the world; of corridors and rooms unlived in. I want to keep Finvarra to me as my mother kept Mare to her. How desperate she must have been those early months, with two of us to care for, and one so sickly. My fierceness for her must have frightened and diminished her; I close my eyes and feel the loss of her like an excruciating emptiness in my chest. The tears run down my face. And isn't it the turf fire from the buried bedroom that I smell, the reddish light twitching on the lids of my eyes, remembering itself in the heat and blur of all my gestures?

If the apparition comes again I'll look into its face. I'll breathe its ill-smelling aura. I will have to learn to soften to it, to live with it at my shoulder.

Finvarra stirs. His hands ball into fists and he kicks at the air. He screeches for me and I am breathless, taking him in my arms.

His eyes search the contours of the room, fix themselves to the headboard of the bed, the embroidery on the curtain. He struggles to make objects into landmarks.

But he tires of that and shifts his eyes to mine. I bow my head over him and together we hear the pulsing of my heart, something that keeps the time between us; a steady drum in water.

When he sucks, he dribbles pearls.

About the Author

REGINA McBRIDE's poetry book *Yarrow Field* won an American Book Series Award. She is the recipient of fellowships from the National Endowment for the Arts and the New York Foundation for the Arts. Her poems have been widely published in literary journals and magazines. She lives with her husband and daughter in New York City where she teaches creative writing at Hunter College and at the Writer's Voice.

This is her first novel.

© Teri Bloom

The Nature of Water and Air

Discussion Points

1. McBride paints vivid portraits of two very different Irelands: one of mansions peopled by the privileged upper class, and another of roads and fields traveled by itinerant tinkers, people with no roots who are "suspicious of houses." Discuss McBride's evocation of both the tinker and "settled" lifestyles and how they relate to the themes of permanence and impermanence in the book.

2. Objects are imbued with symbolic meaning throughout the book. Why is Agatha so enamored of knickknacks, trinkets, and jewelry? What do her collections represent, and why is she so fiercely protective and possessive of them? Does Clodagh share her mother's intrigue with the aura of special objects?

3. Clodagh is loyal to her mother despite Agatha's often rough, dismissive treatment. Why is Agatha so critical and reproachful toward Clodagh? Why is Clodagh needy for Agatha's attention, and fascinated by what she perceives as her mother's "secret life"? In what ways are Clodagh and Agatha most similar? In what important ways are they different? Is their troubled relationship caused more by their similarities or their differences?

4. Angus says to Clodagh: "Fathers are inconsequential. . . . It's a mother that matters to a child. . . . it's the mother that counts." Do the events and relationships depicted in the book support or refute this statement? What does the book suggest about the importance of mothers? Recall Angus's adoration for Sister Margaret Mooney and Mrs. O'Dare's protectiveness toward Clodagh and discuss the role of these "surrogate" mothers in the novel.

5. Should Clodagh have been told the truth about her real father? Do all children deserve to know their own histories? How damaging can family secrets be? When is it more harmful to withhold information than to divulge it? How likely is it that Clodagh will tell her own son the truth about his father? Do you think she should?

6. Recall how the mystery of Agatha's past fueled her daughter's curiosity and how uneasy it made Clodagh feel that her mother "seemed to have come from nowhere." What does the book suggest about the

importance of origins? Why do we have an instinctual need to know where we come from and where our parents come from?

7. Clodagh's childhood is literally haunted: by secrets, ghosts, illness, death; by "things half there and half not." Recall the visceral way in which Clodagh is often inhabited or visited by Mare and Agatha after their deaths. How else do the dead and the living commingle and interact throughout the book? Discuss McBride's treatment of the spirit world and its relationship to childhood and imagination.

8. How does McBride personify the estate house on Mercymount Strand where Clodagh spends her girlhood? Recall, for instance, the stucco nymphs and satyrs in the hidden room Clodagh discovers with Letty and the secret passageways and hideaways where Agatha carries on her affair with Angus. How do the house's own secrets heighten Agatha's mysterious nature? And how does the room with the nymphs serve as a backdrop for Clodagh's childish innocence and emerging womanhood?

9. Compare Clodagh's early friendship with Letty Grogan to her later friendship with Eileen at St. Brendan's. What does Clodagh seek in each girl? What needs do each fill in her life? How does each girl contribute to Clodagh's maturation, sexual development, and view of her place in the world? Why does each friendship come to an end?

10. Why is Clodagh so drawn to Sister Clarissa, the disfigured nun at St. Brendan's? What does she mean when she says to the nun "I'm like you"?

11. Recall the pleasure Clodagh derives from her mastery of the piano. How would you describe the role of music in Clodagh's life? In what way does Clodagh's piano-playing coincide with and contribute to her sexual awakening? Discuss the novel's exploration of the interplay between music and sensuality.

12. The myth of the selkie captures Clodagh's imagination as a young girl and resonates throughout the story. Recall Clodagh's alternating fear and hope that her mother is a selkie. How does Agatha's life story both debunk and exemplify this myth? Why is Ireland a place known for myth-making? What role do mythology and folklore play in the book? Mrs. Cleary, the tinker woman who helps Clodagh give birth, says: "People make such magical stories to soften the hardness of the world." Do myths make life's truths and tragedies easier to bear? If so, how?

13. Should Angus have tried to contact Clodagh after Agatha's suicide? When he learns of Clodagh's pregnancy, is Angus right to encourage his daughter to "live settled" and offer her baby a comfortable life? Is it wise or cruel of him to distance himself from her? Would it have been possible for them to establish a normal father-daughter relationship considering the tragic outcome of their ill-fated affair?

14. At the end of the novel, Clodagh finds herself back in Drumcoyne House, nurturing her son in the same nursery where her mother was pregnant with her. How do Clodagh and Agatha's lives mirror each other up to this point? How has Clodagh matured over the course of the book? How does becoming a mother change her? Will she be a better mother than Agatha? How do you believe their fates will differ?

How I Came to Write *The Nature of Water and Air*

I began this novel as a poem in which I intended to explore the mysterious history and internal life of a mother who chooses suicide. The selkie myth, which has always resonated powerfully for me, suggests a metaphor for suicide because it is about a mother who is drawn to a more aboriginal world, the darker world of the dead, over the world of the living that she shares with her daughter.

In the same way that the selkie is fated to leave her life on shore, the inevitability of Agatha's departure enshrouds Clodagh. Even when she outgrows her literal belief that her mother is a selkie, Clodagh doesn't entirely dismiss the lore as holding some key to her mother's mystery. Agatha, embraced the story and ultimately, she slips herself into it, "returning," like the selkie, to the sea.

I love the way myths suggest that in an act of desperation there might be a concealed harmony with nature. In the same way that her mother has been pulled back to her "origins," Clodagh is intensely compelled to find her own. Without realizing the extent to which she does so, she chases the truth about who she is until she finds herself at its very heart.

Browse our complete list of guides
and download them for free at
www.SimonSays.com/reading_guides.html